BENDY™

CRACK-UP COMICS COLLECTION

BENDY™

CRACK-UP COMICS COLLECTION

Scholastic Inc.

All rights reserved. Published by Scholastic Inc., *Publishers since 1920.* SCHOLASTIC
and associated logos are trademarks and/or registered trademarks of Scholastic Inc.

ISBN 978-1-338-65206-2

10 9 8 7 6 5 4 3 2 1   20 21 22 23 24

Printed in the U.S.A.   40

First printing 2020

Cover illustration by Mady Giuliani

Syndicated Comics illustrated by Mady Giuliani

Dime-Store Comics and Promotional Comics illustrated by Ciro

Tones by Mady Giuliani

Additional Artwork by TimetheHobo

Letters by Taylor Esposito

Edited by Michael Petranek

Book design by Betsy Peterschmidt

TABLE OF

CONTENTS

INTRODUCTION BY

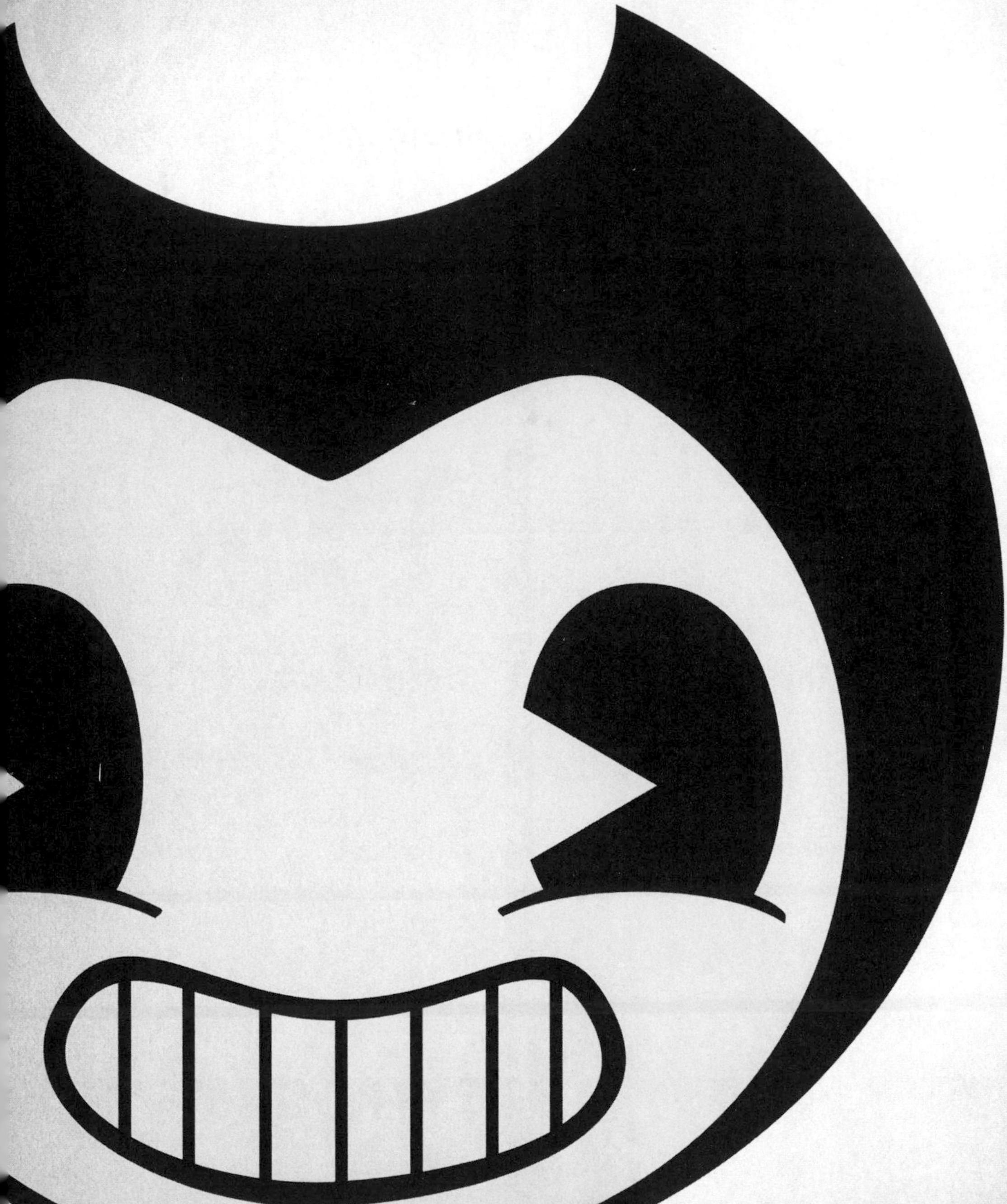

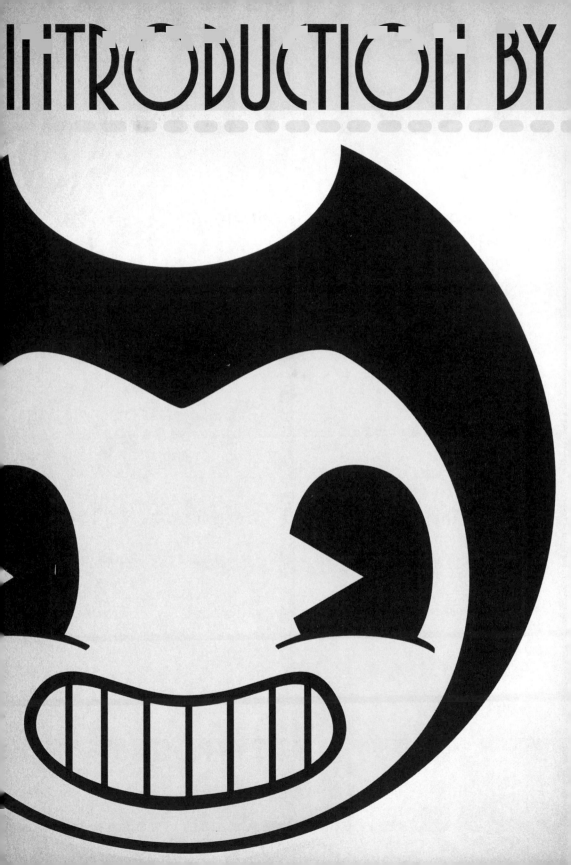

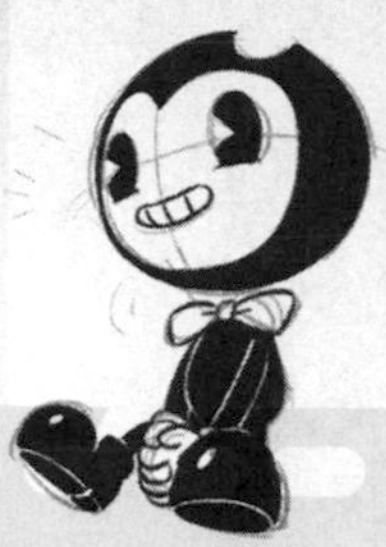

NATHAN ARCH

CEO of Archgate Films

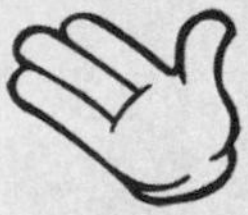

When I bought the Bendy library from the estate of my longtime friend Joey Drew, the world was a bit surprised. Why would I, a so-called business tycoon, buy the life's work of a man whose company made silly cartoons? To that I say, "why not?" I've always envied those whose occupation was in producing entertainment for the enjoyment of all mankind. Oil, steel, and industry are lucrative but ultimately heartless. Bendy is all heart, perpetuated through the decades by Joey's heartfelt creativity and endless positivity.

Bendy was dancing in theaters all over the world but was a late introduction to the newspaper comic pages in 1931. By then the papers were filled to the brim with space men, detectives, crazy cats, dreaming boys, and sailor men. There just wasn't room for Bendy. But during Joey Drew's childhood, newspaper comic strips were the most respected cartoons in the world. For that reason, Mr. Drew saw getting Bendy into newspapers as one of his highest achievements. According

to his employees, Joey would keep the latest funny paper on his office desk and show it to any visitor. "Now this," he would say, "this is my finest work yet." He'd then point to a half-drawn page on the drawing board and say, "That'll be my finest work yet . . . TOMORROW!"

We know now that Drew did not, in fact, draw any of the Bendy comics. At first most were drawn by miscellaneous employees in the art department waiting for an assignment. But as the frenzy for Bendy cartoon animation grew, it appears art duties shifted to a couple main collaborators whose names appear lost to time, but whose creativity is presented here for all to enjoy.

What we do know is that these strips took on a life of their own. Bendy and Boris were drawn as down-and-out vaudeville actors, performing in rural America during the height of the Great Depression. As the United States began to come out of the Depression, though, audiences no longer wished to be reminded of their past destitution. The strip was cancelled in 1935.

The writer/artist team moved on to a far more lucrative medium where Bendy truly thrived: comic books. A brand-new, truly American art form, comic books were selling like gangbusters, and Mr. Drew's great business sense put him at the head of the wave. Bendy, Boris, and Alice became much more versatile as characters. In this collection you can see them in dime-store science fiction adventures, Gold Rush escapades, and superheroic stories. These issues sold in the millions, which is astronomical compared to today's sales figures.

Joey Drew Studios had never been short on ink, but when the United States joined the war, ink and paper was needed for all manner of purposes. The last handful of issues pushed for war bonds, almost as a last-ditch effort to save the series from supply shortages. The once-great comic book division of Joey Drew Studios was shuttered in 1942. Most of the large presses in the basement were scrapped and their metal repurposed.

One press did remain in operation until 1946. Joey Drew used this last remaining machine to create promotional pamphlets for his cartoon visions, trying to drum up money from investors and excite interest in Hollywood. These efforts did not succeed, and most of the remaining pamphlets were lost in an accident involving a burst ink pipe.

What you hold in your hands is the work of careful archiving by the dedicated Bendy fans here at Archgate Films. I'm proud to bring these comics to a new generation who've likely never even heard of Bendy before.

Stay smiling, dear reader, and remember that dreams DO come to life.

Nathan Arch

CEO of Archgate Films, 1972

SYNDICATED

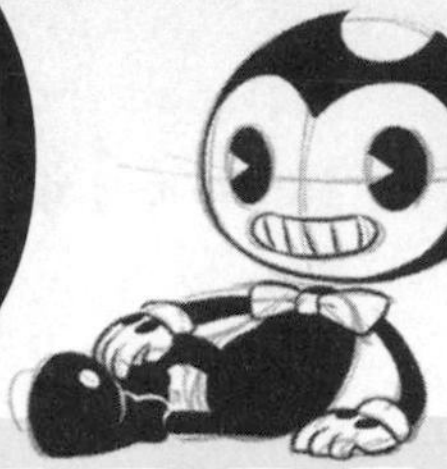

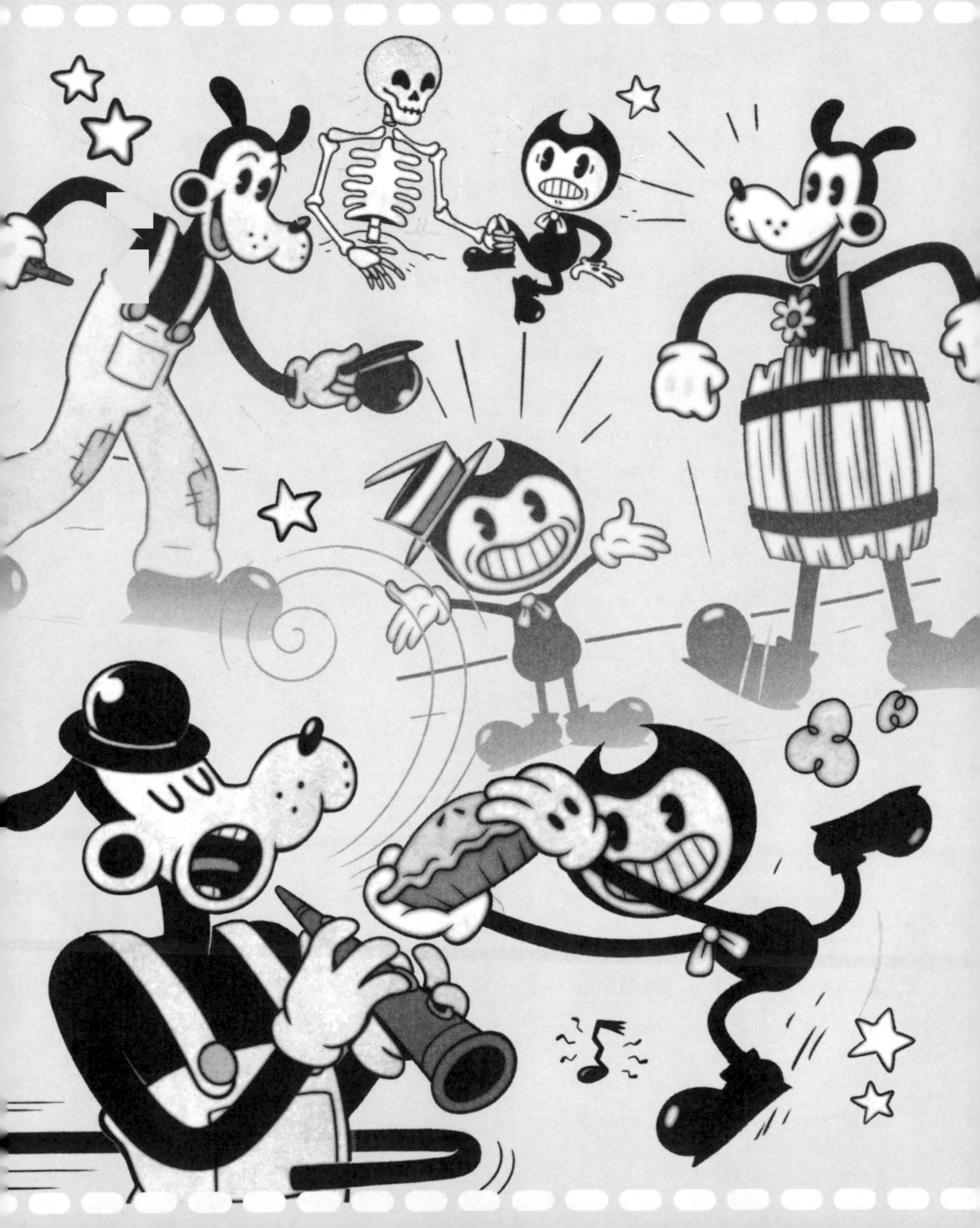

COMIC STRIPS

1931–1935

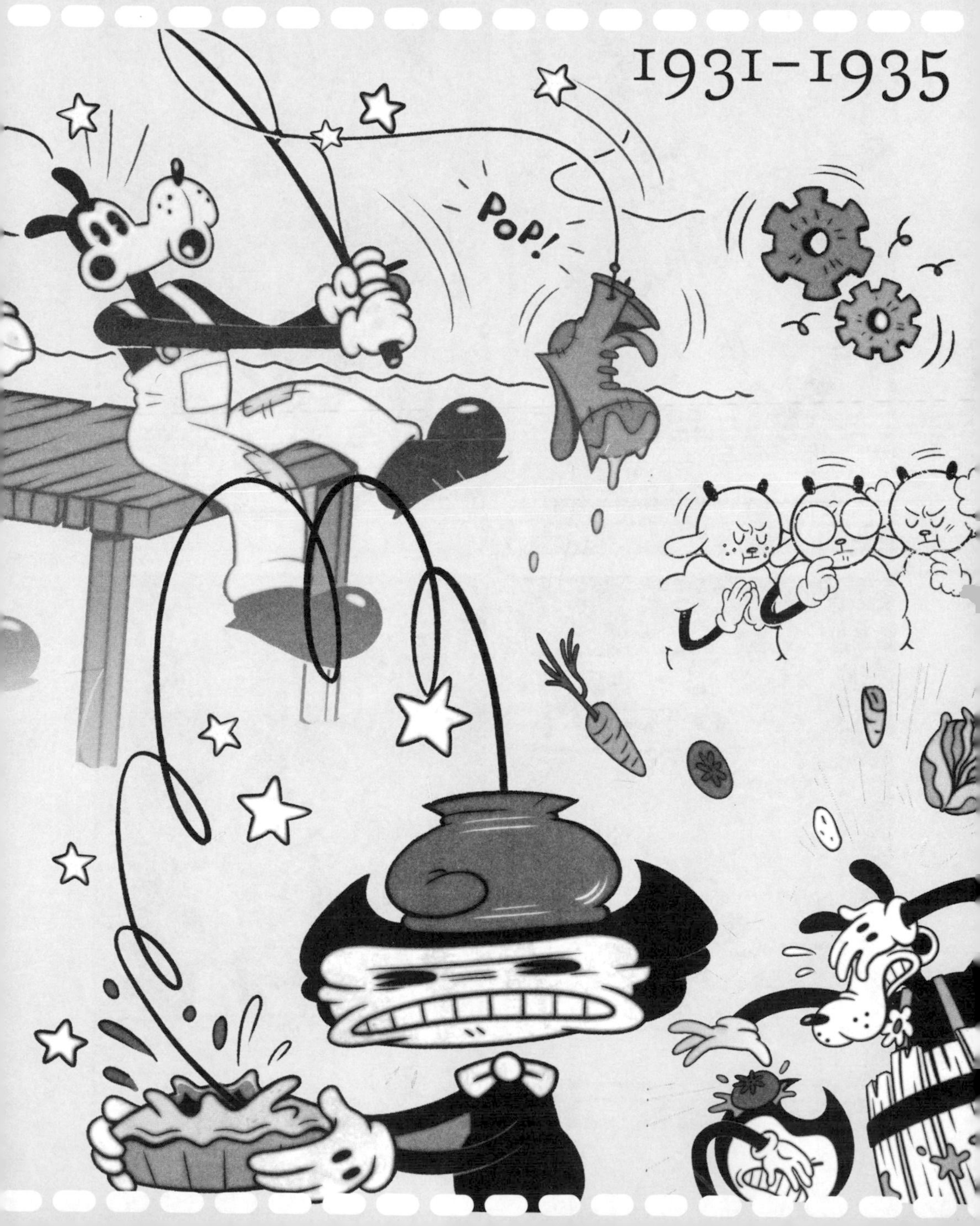
POP!

Barnyard Opry • November 3, 1931

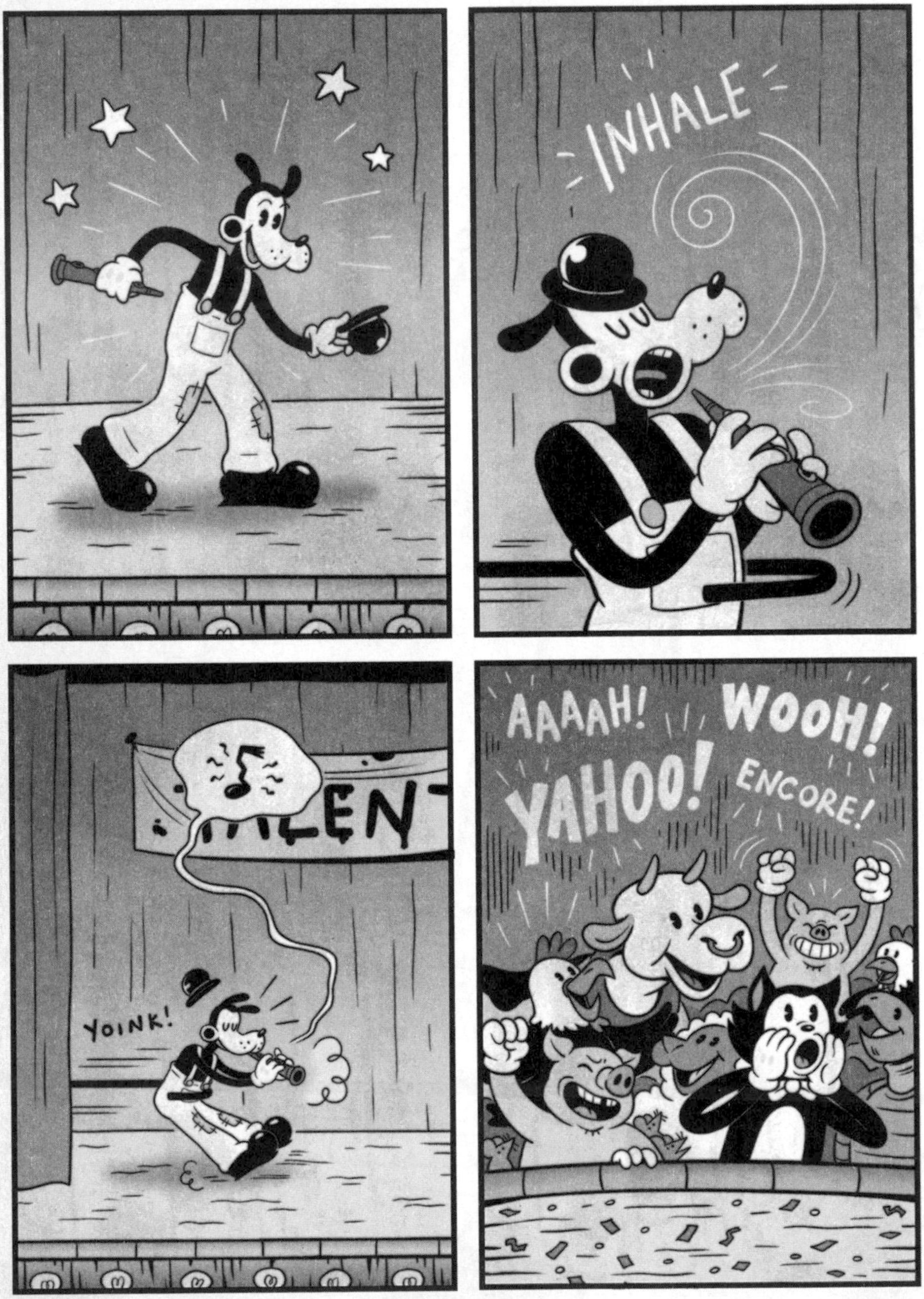
INHALE
YOINK!
AAAAH!
WOOH!
YAHOO!
ENCORE!

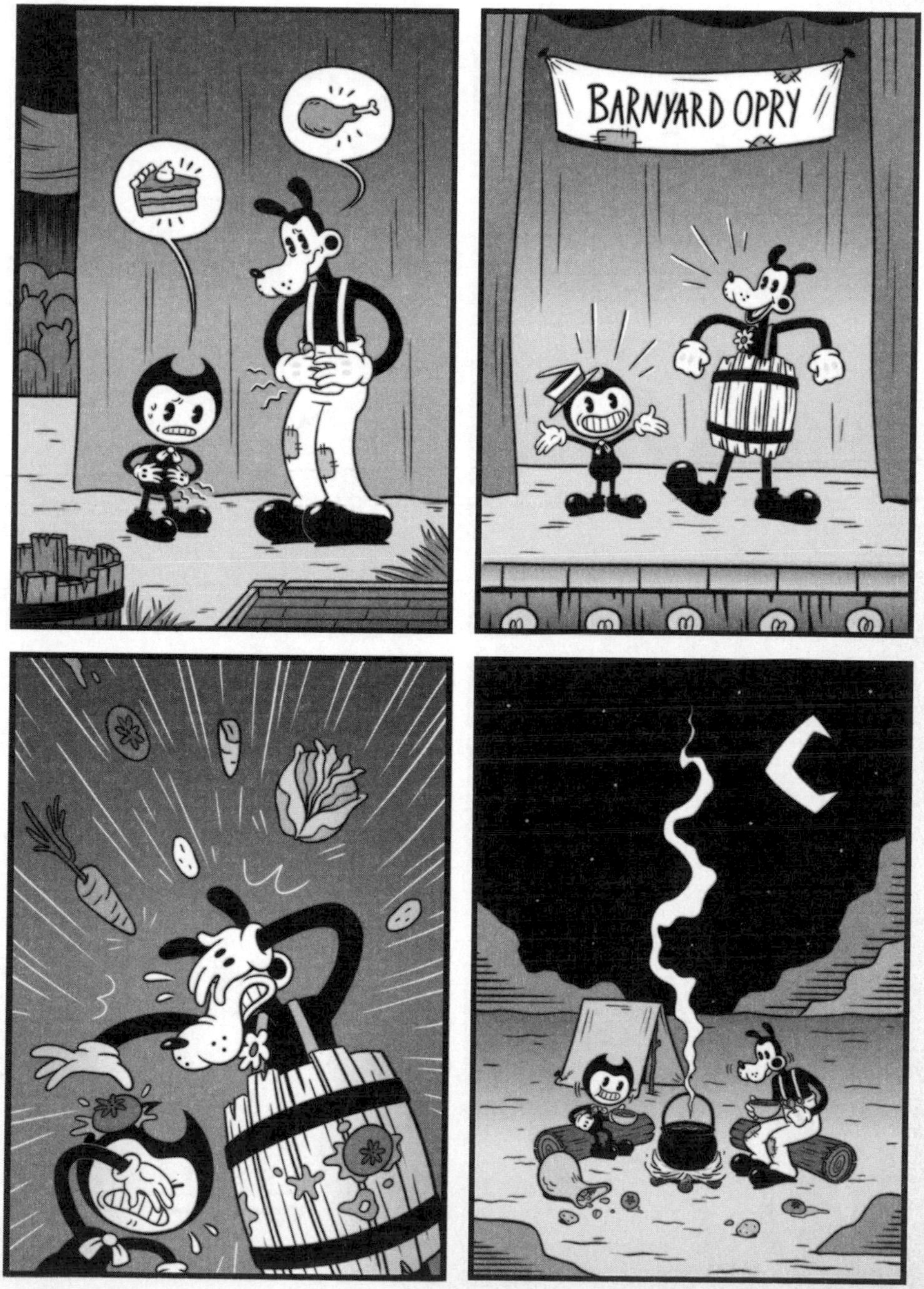
BARNYARD OPRY

Sole for Supper • December 4, 1931

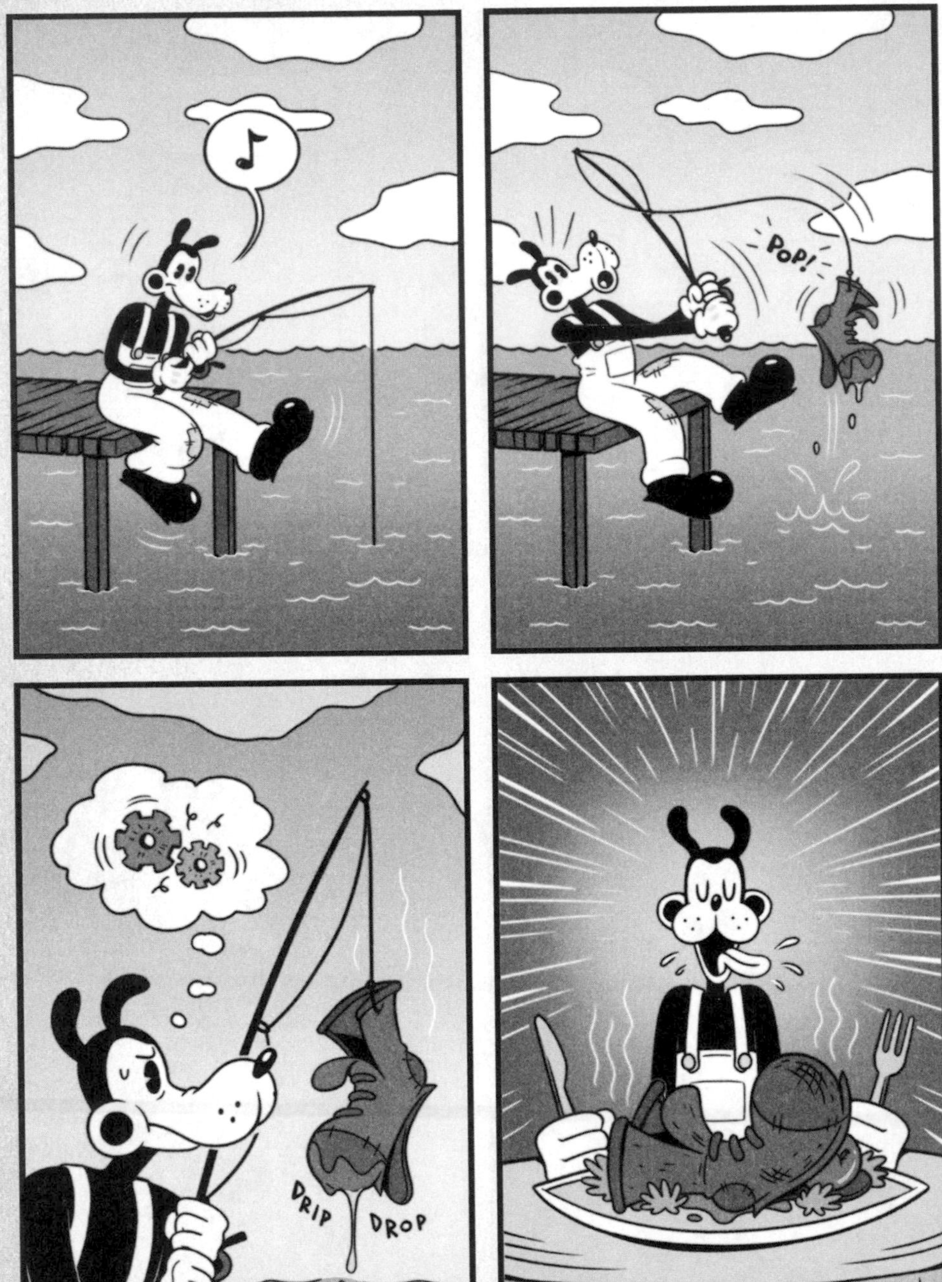
POP!
DRIP
DROP

Pie and Pop · December 18, 1931

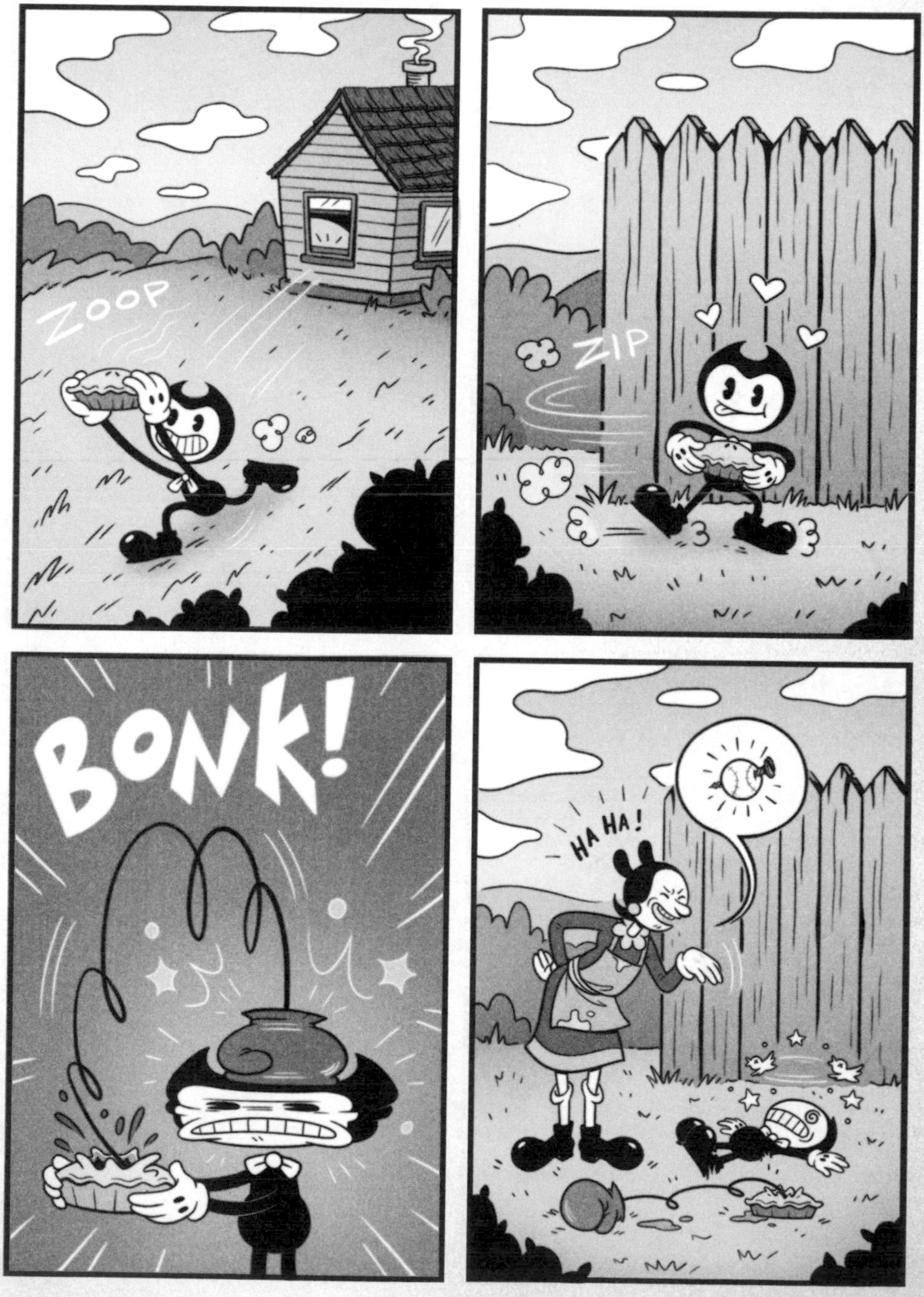
ZOOP
ZIP
BONK!
HA HA!

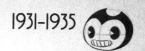

Up in flames • January 13, 1932

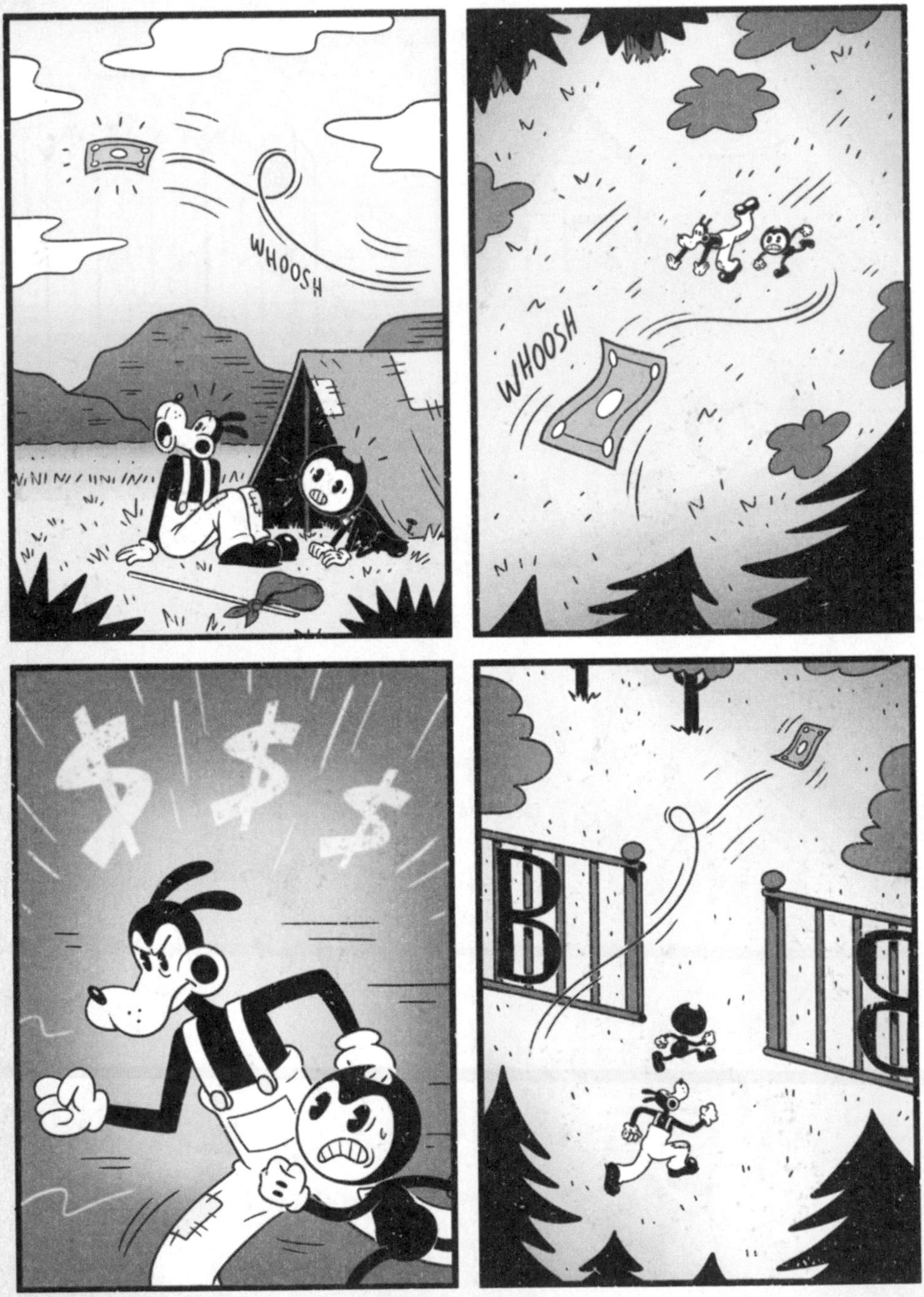
WHOOSH
WHOOSH

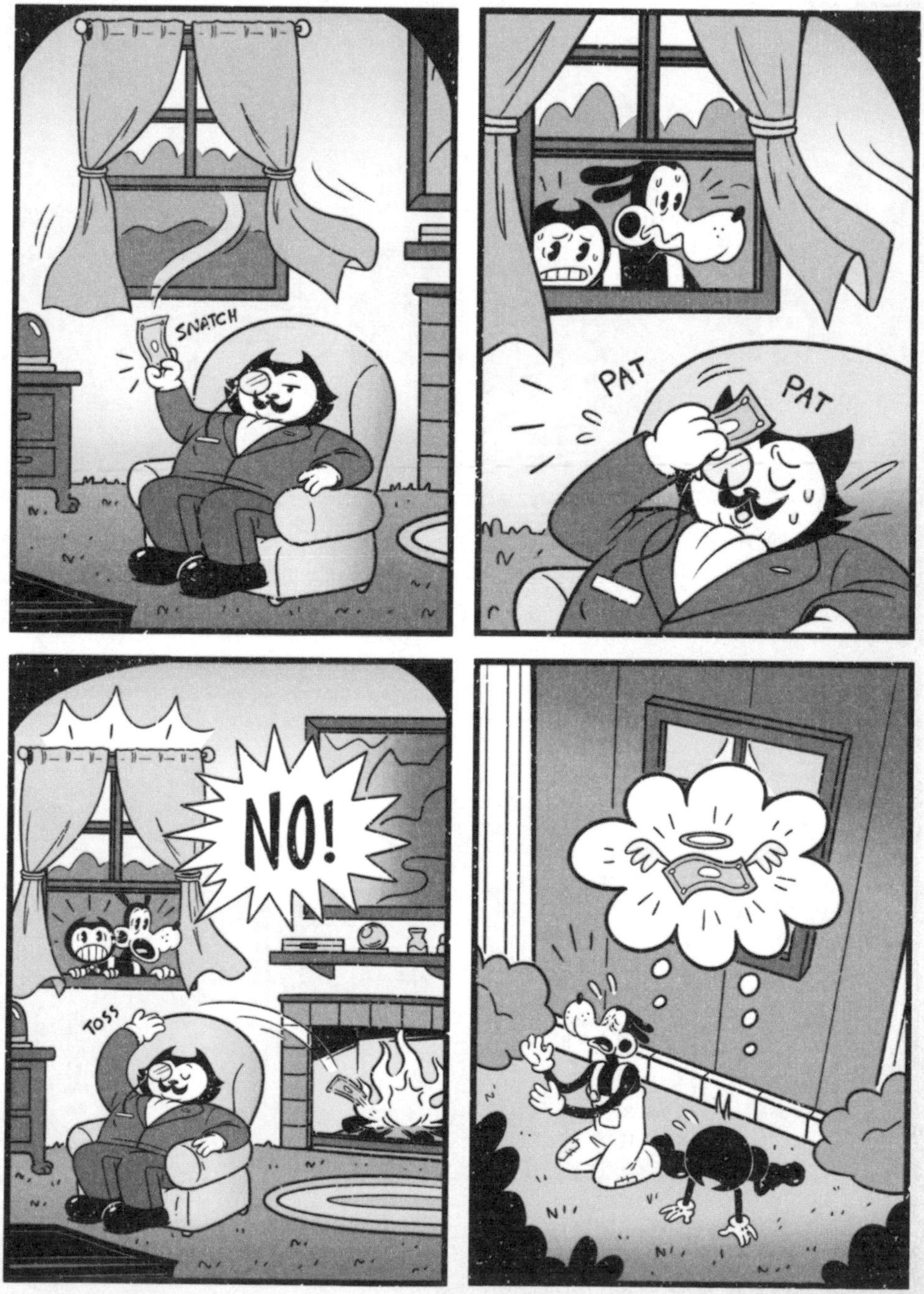
SNATCH
PAT
PAT
NO!
TOSS

What Crumbs Around, Goes Around • March 2, 1932

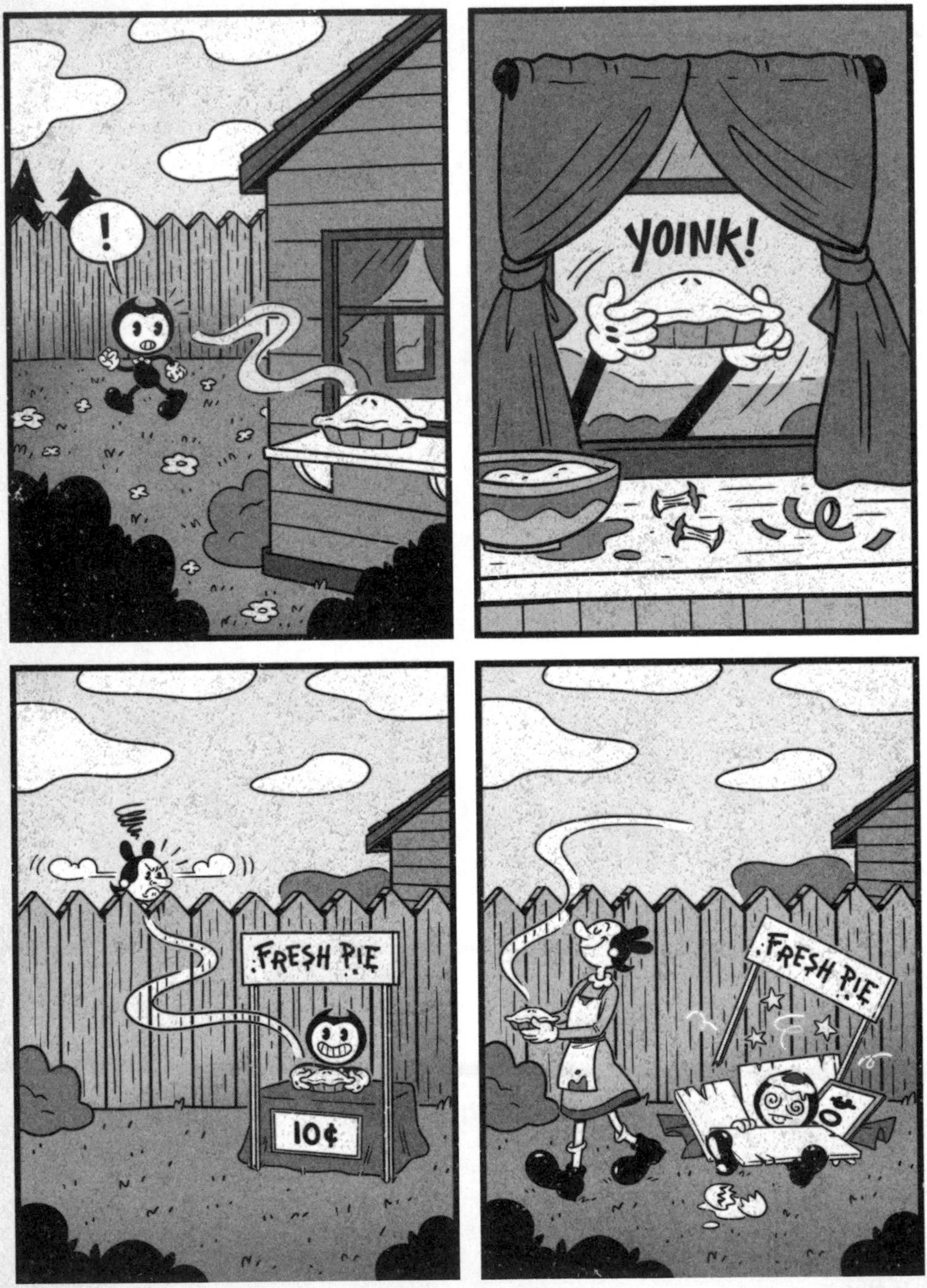
!
YOINK!
FRESH PIE
10¢
FRESH PIE
10¢

The Artist • March 17, 1932

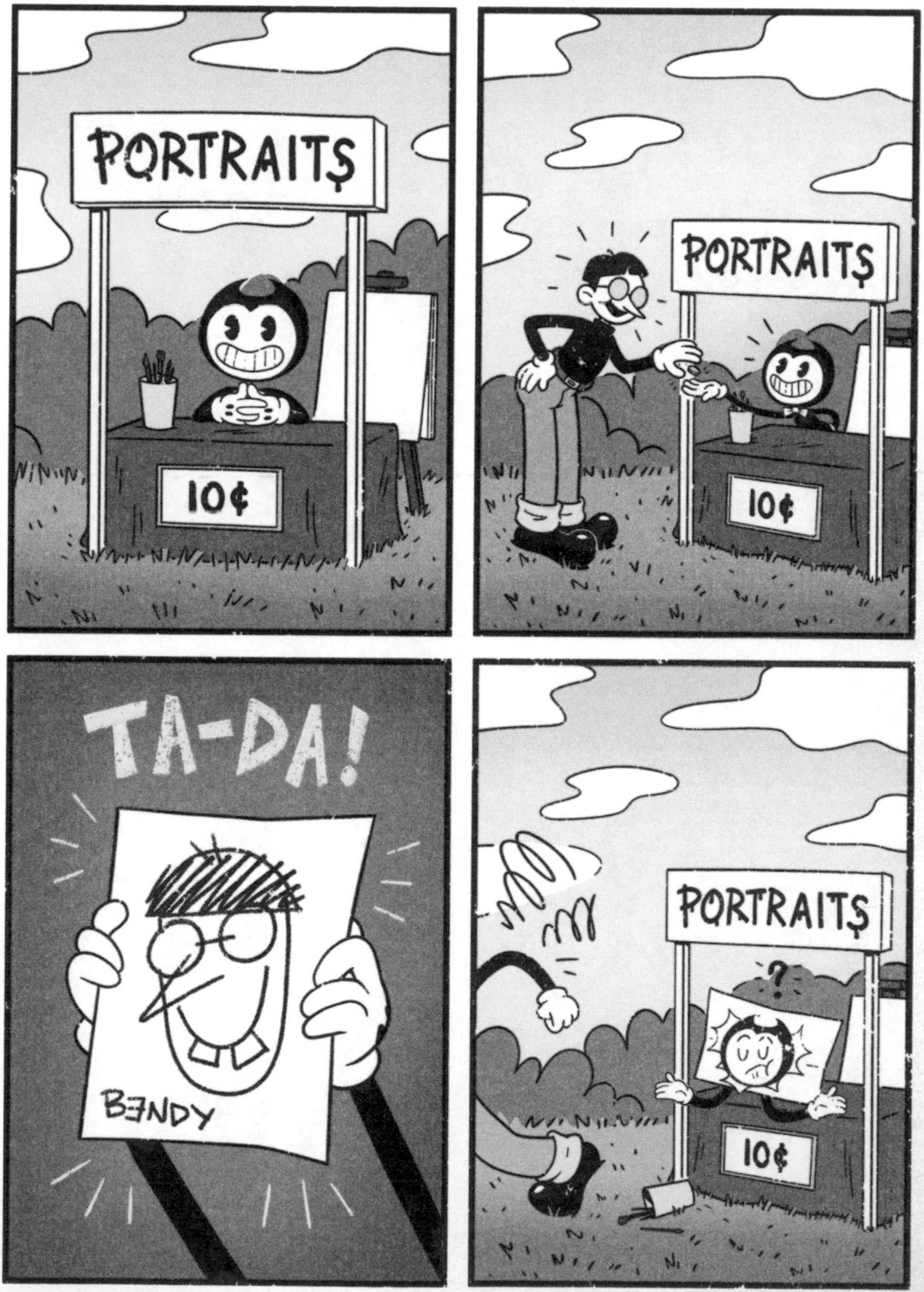

PORTRAITS
10¢
PORTRAITS
10¢
TA-DA!
BENDY
PORTRAITS
?
10¢

Cats and Dogs • May 4, 1932

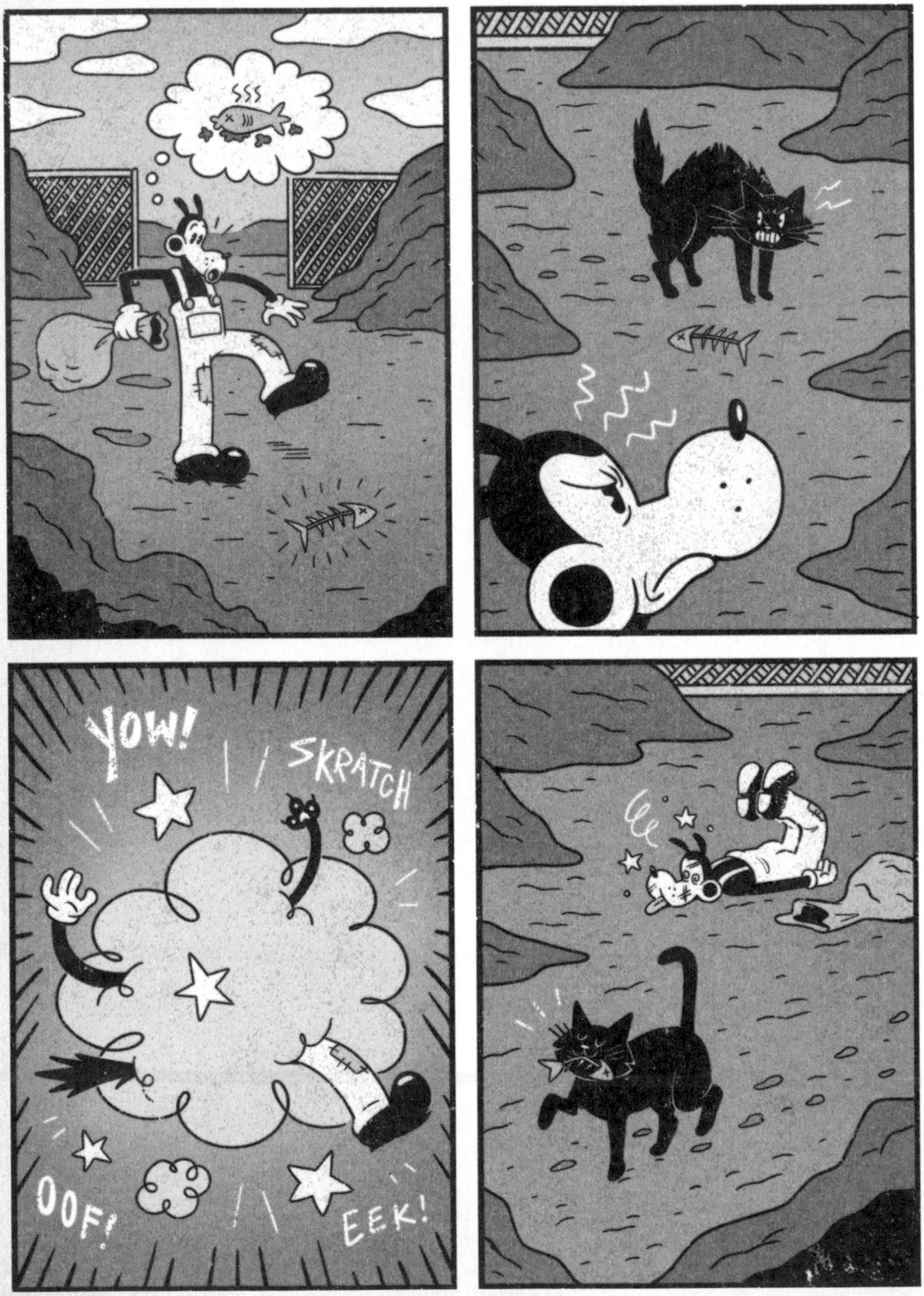
YOW!
SKRATCH
OOF!
EEK!

Two for One • September 22, 1932

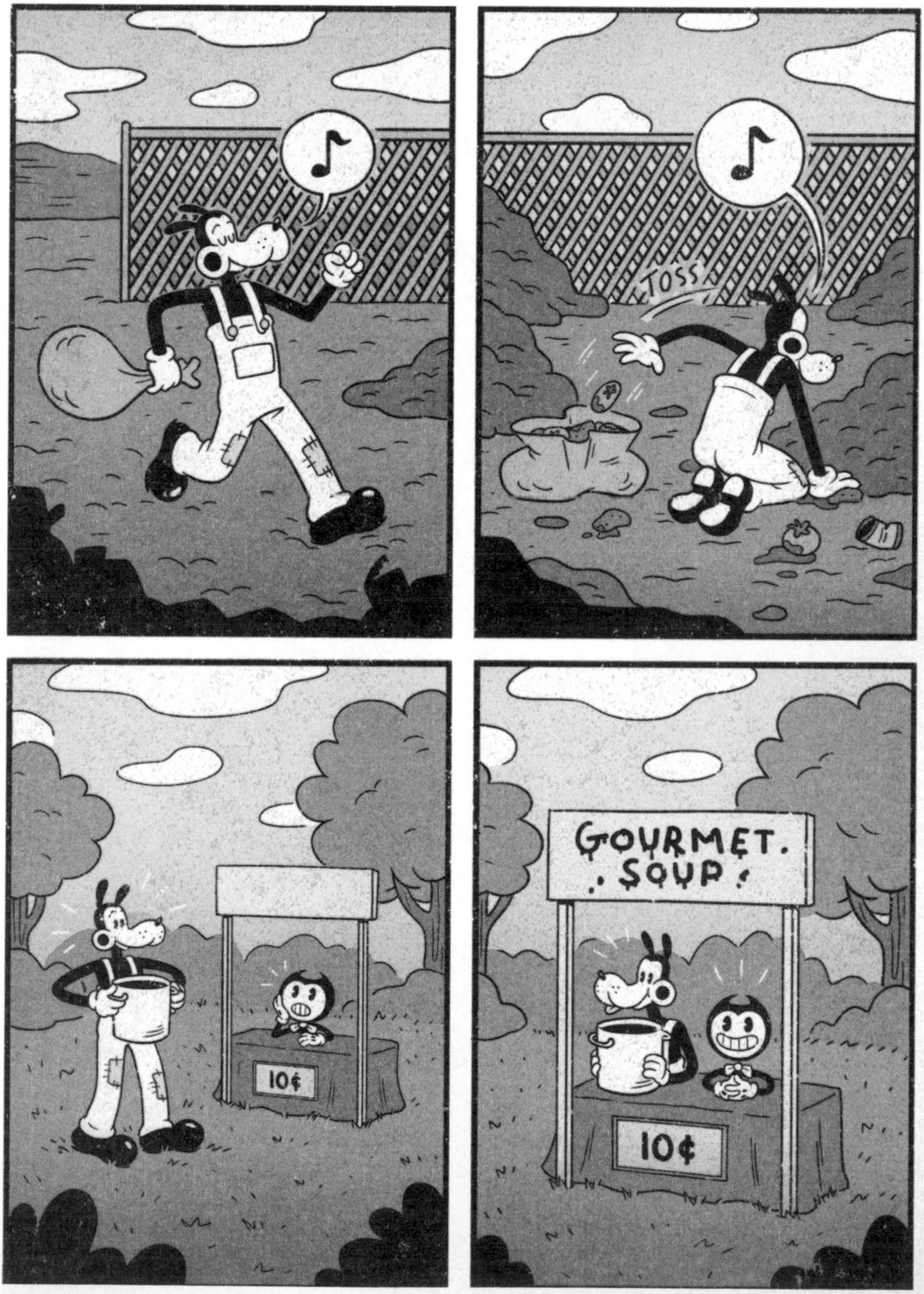
TOSS
10¢
GOURMET.
SOUP
10¢

Rain, Rain, Go Away • October 2, 1932

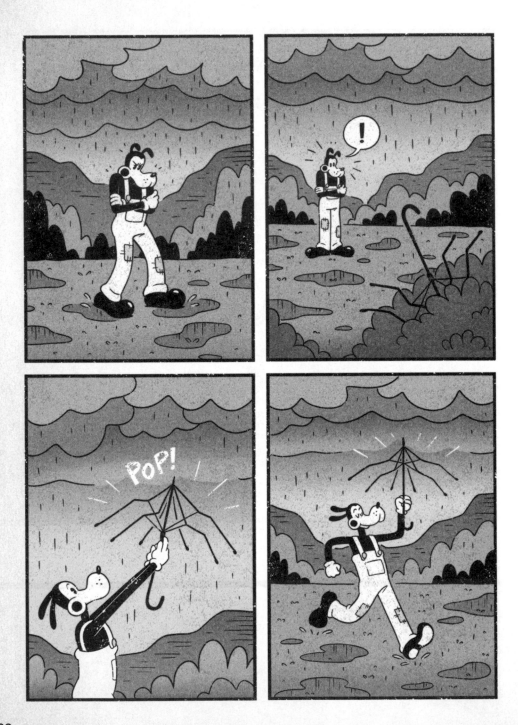

Bright Idea • October 3, 1932

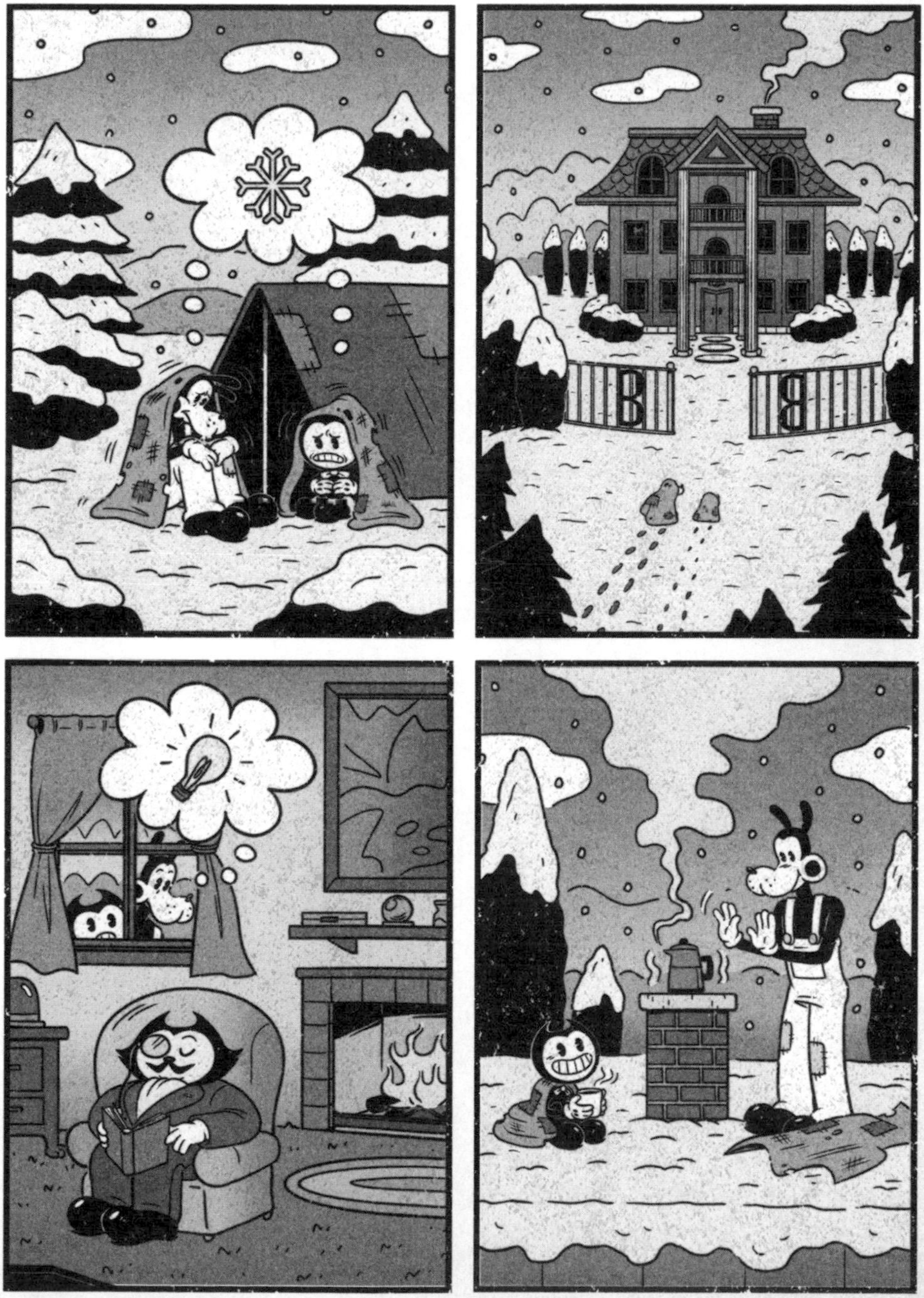
B
B

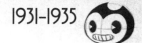

Counting Sheep • November 10, 1932

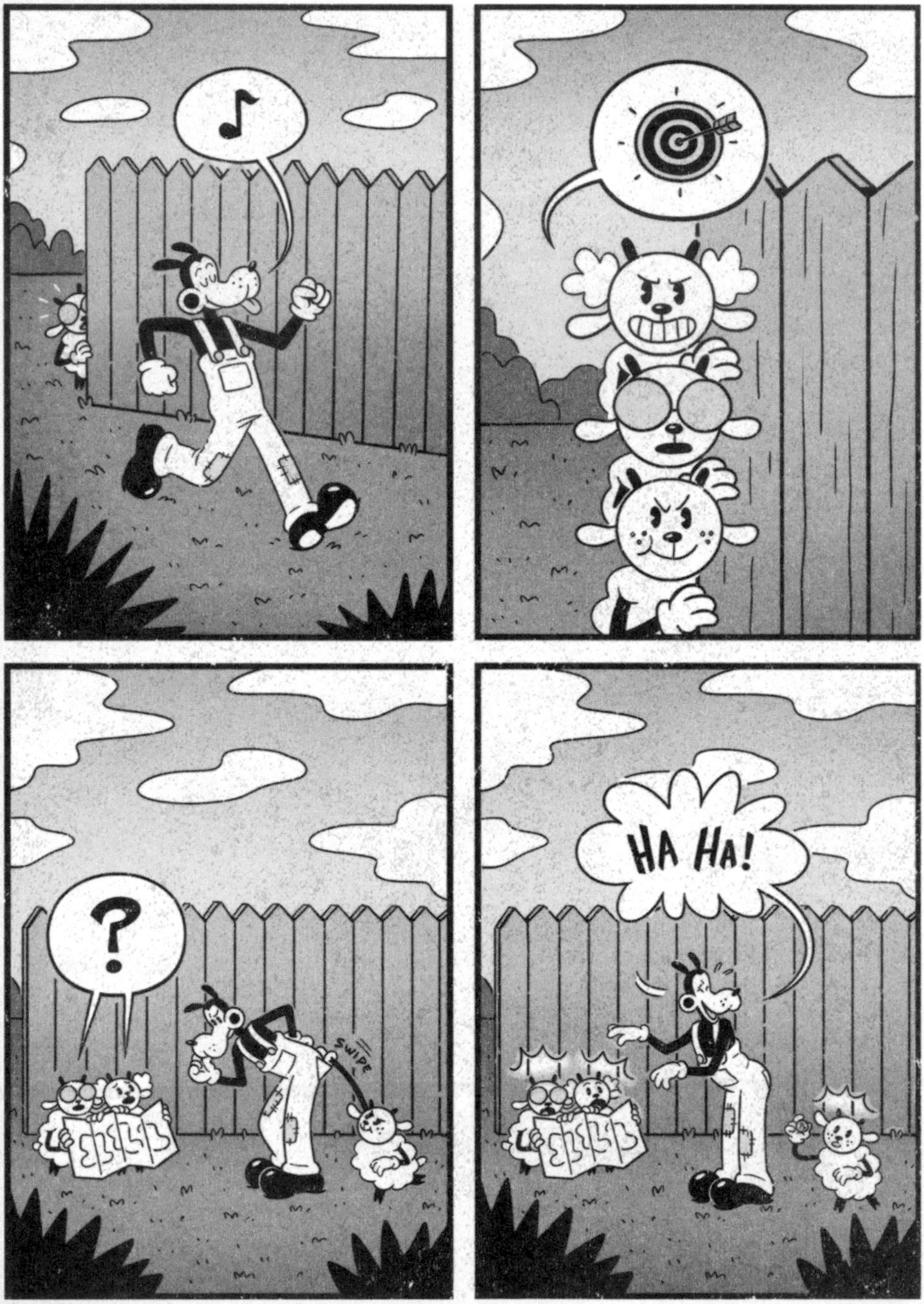
?
SWIPE
HA HA!

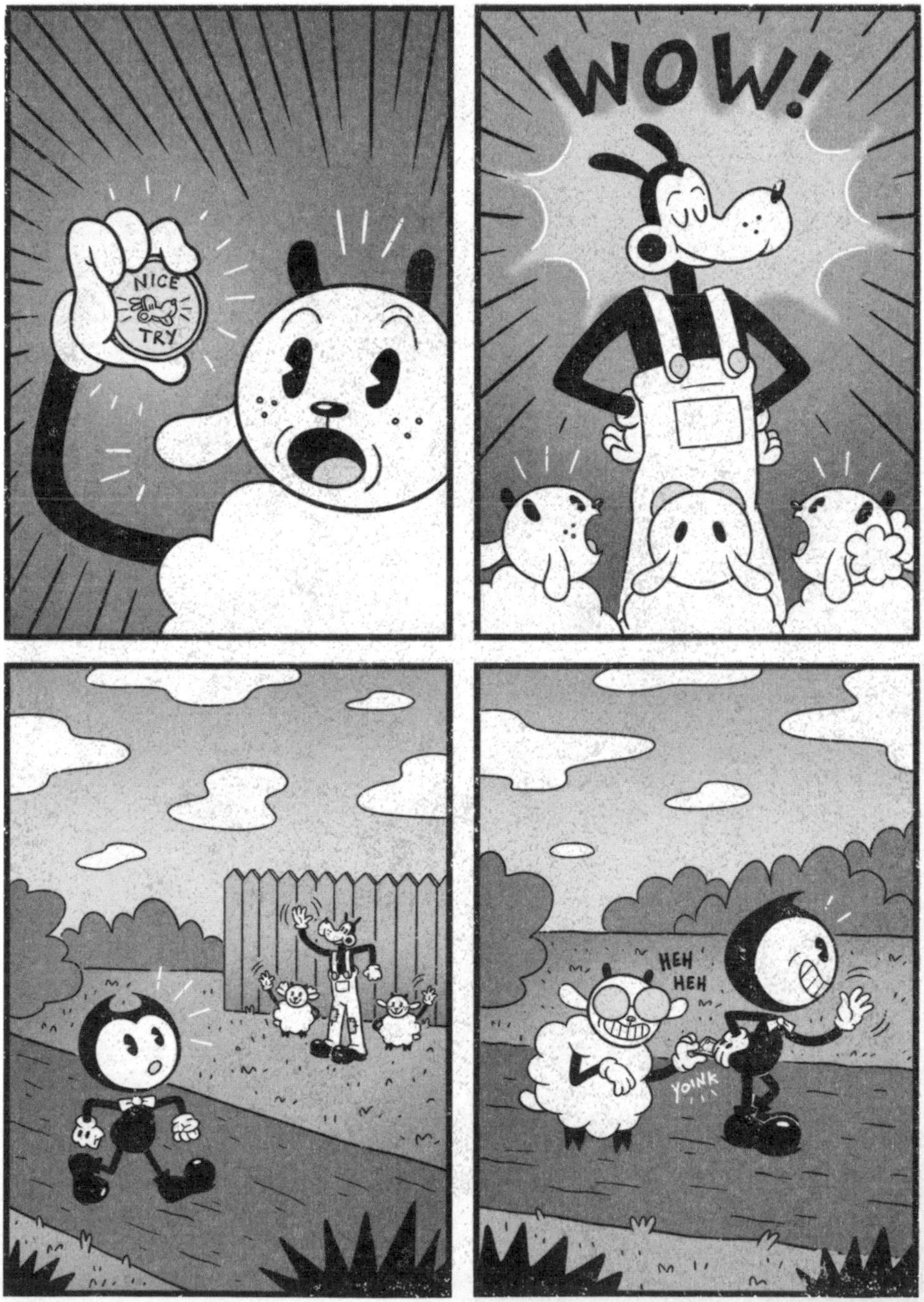
NICE
TRY
WOW!
HEH
HEH
YOINK

Hands Off • December 16, 1932

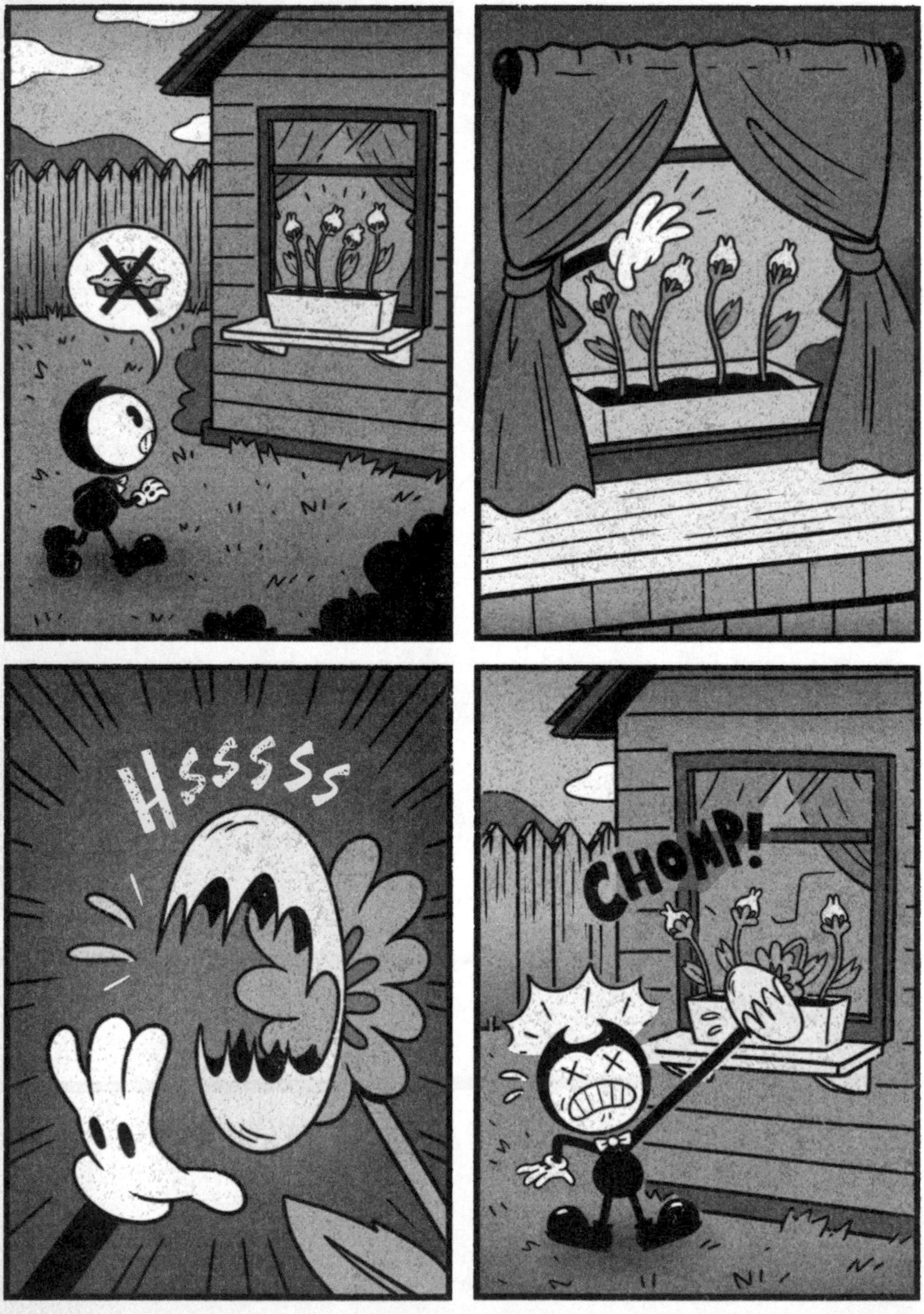
HSSSSS
CHOMP!

F for Effort • January 3, 1933

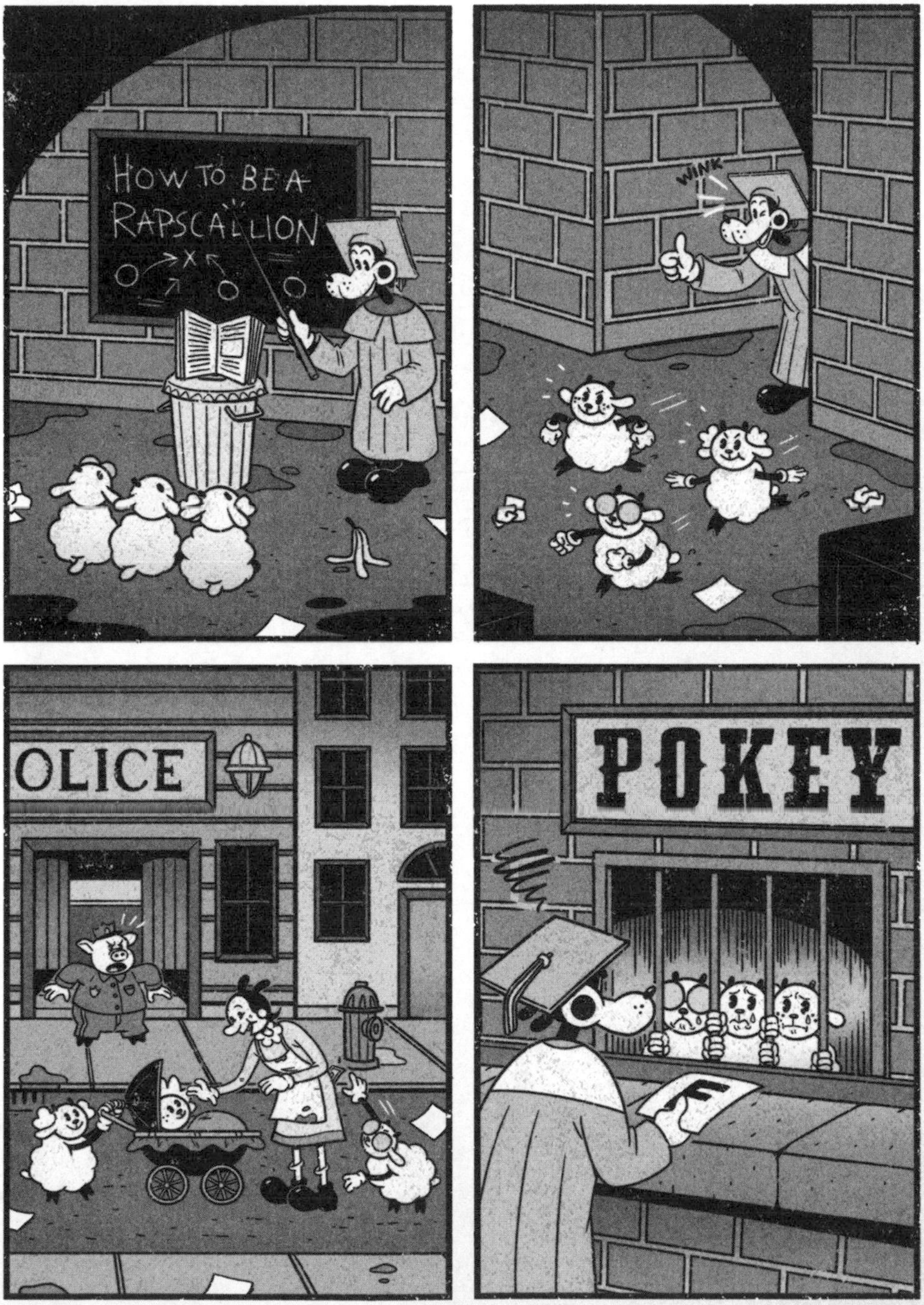
HOW TO BE A
RAPSCALLION
WINK
OLICE
POKEY
F

How Not To • January 10, 1933

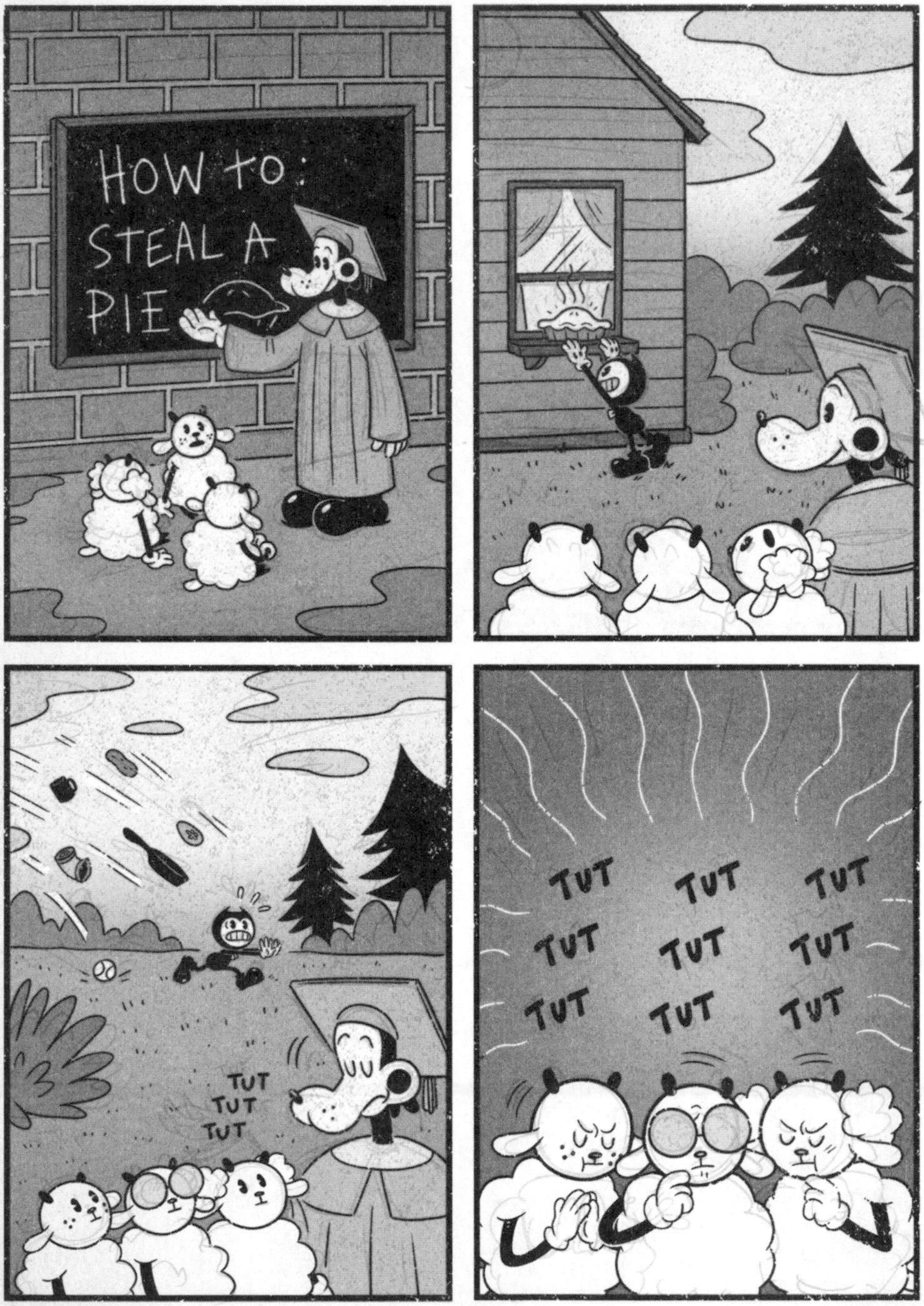
HOW TO:
STEAL A
PIE
TUT
TUT
TUT
TUT TUT TUT
TUT TUT TUT
TUT TUT TUT

Rocks Cream • February 10, 1933

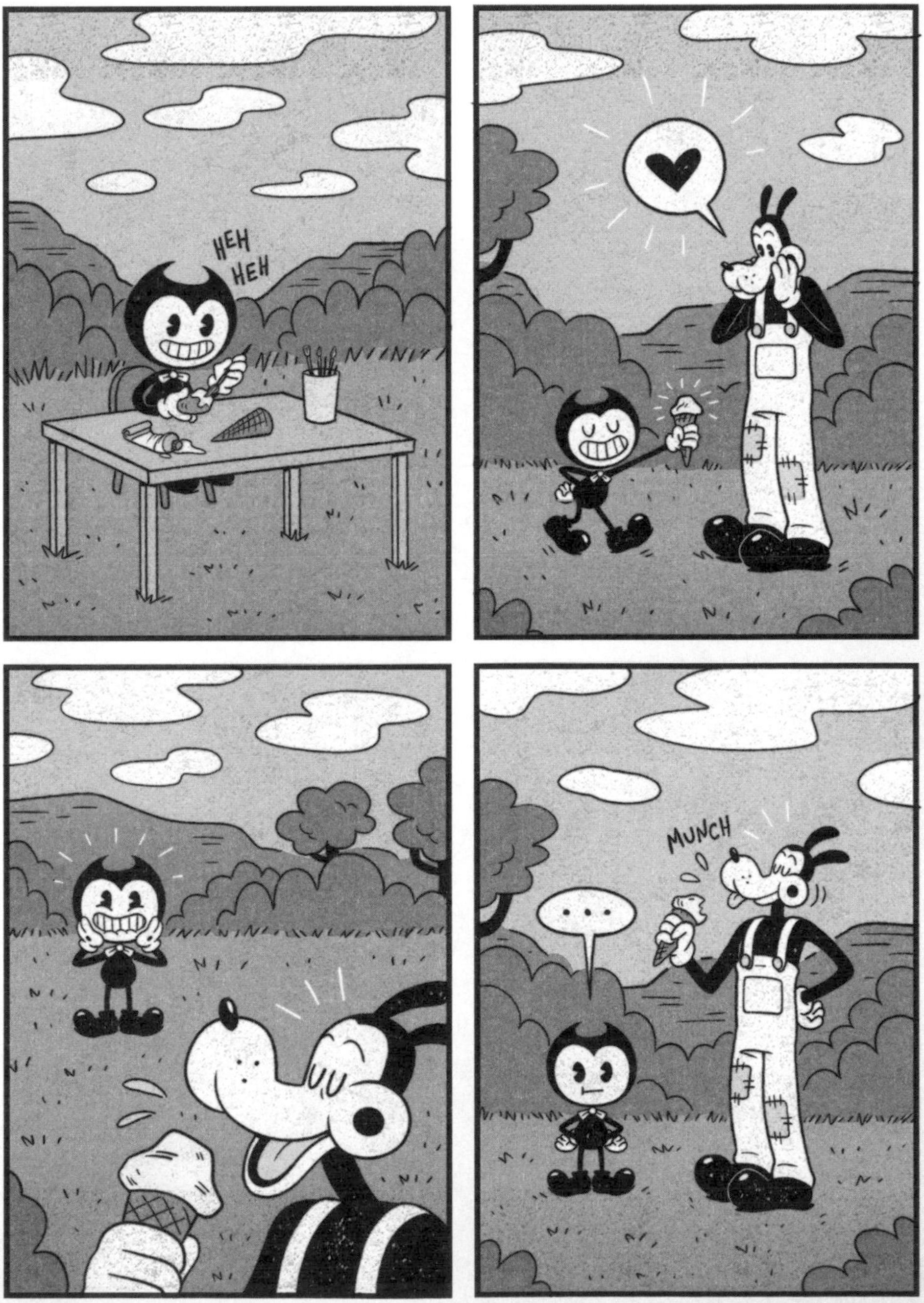
HEH
HEH
...
MUNCH

Batter's Eye • April 12, 1933

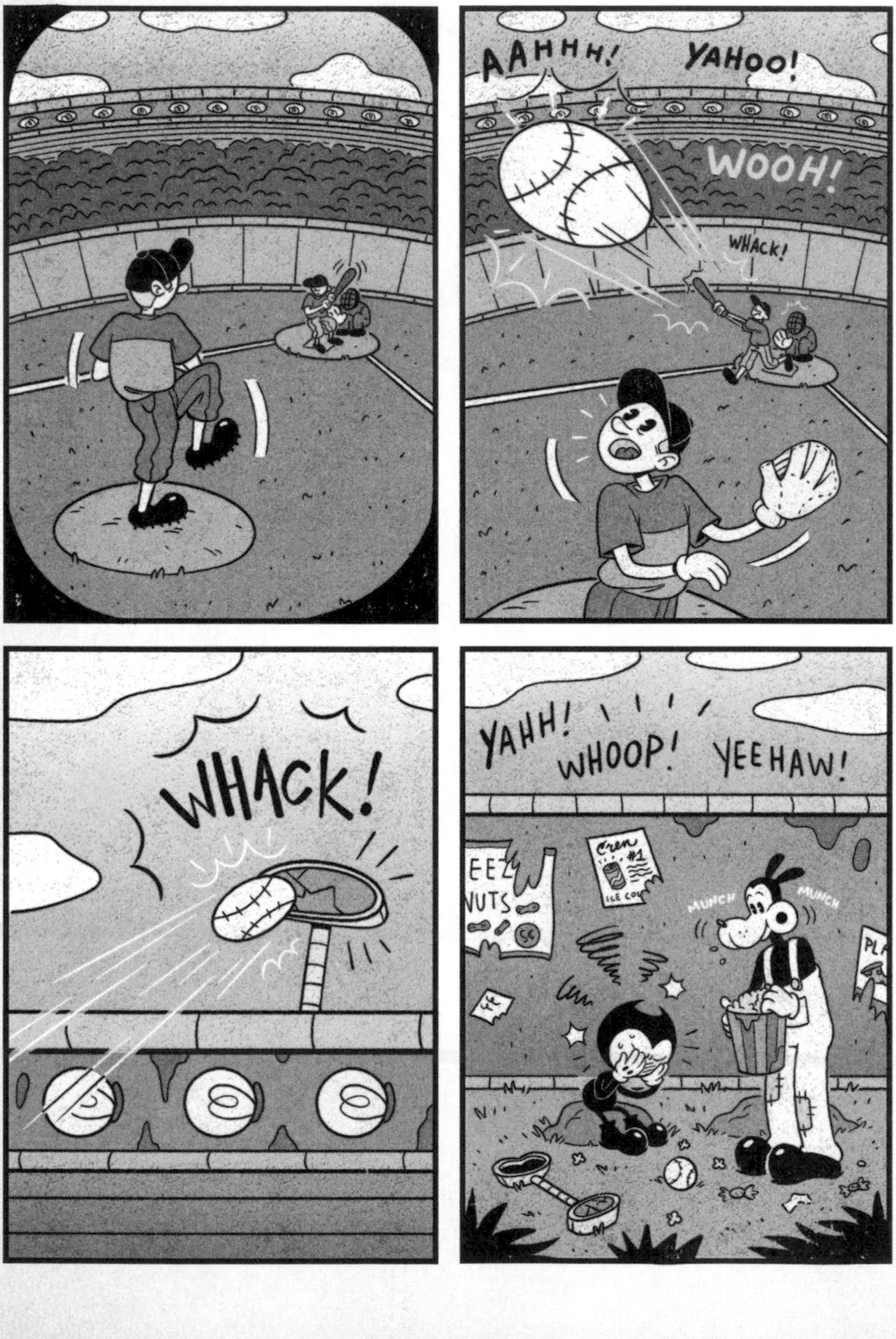
AAHHHH!
YAHOO!
WOOH!
WHACK!
WHACK!
YAHH!
WHOOP!
YEEHAW!
MUNCH
MUNCH

Pig Sty • April 5, 1933

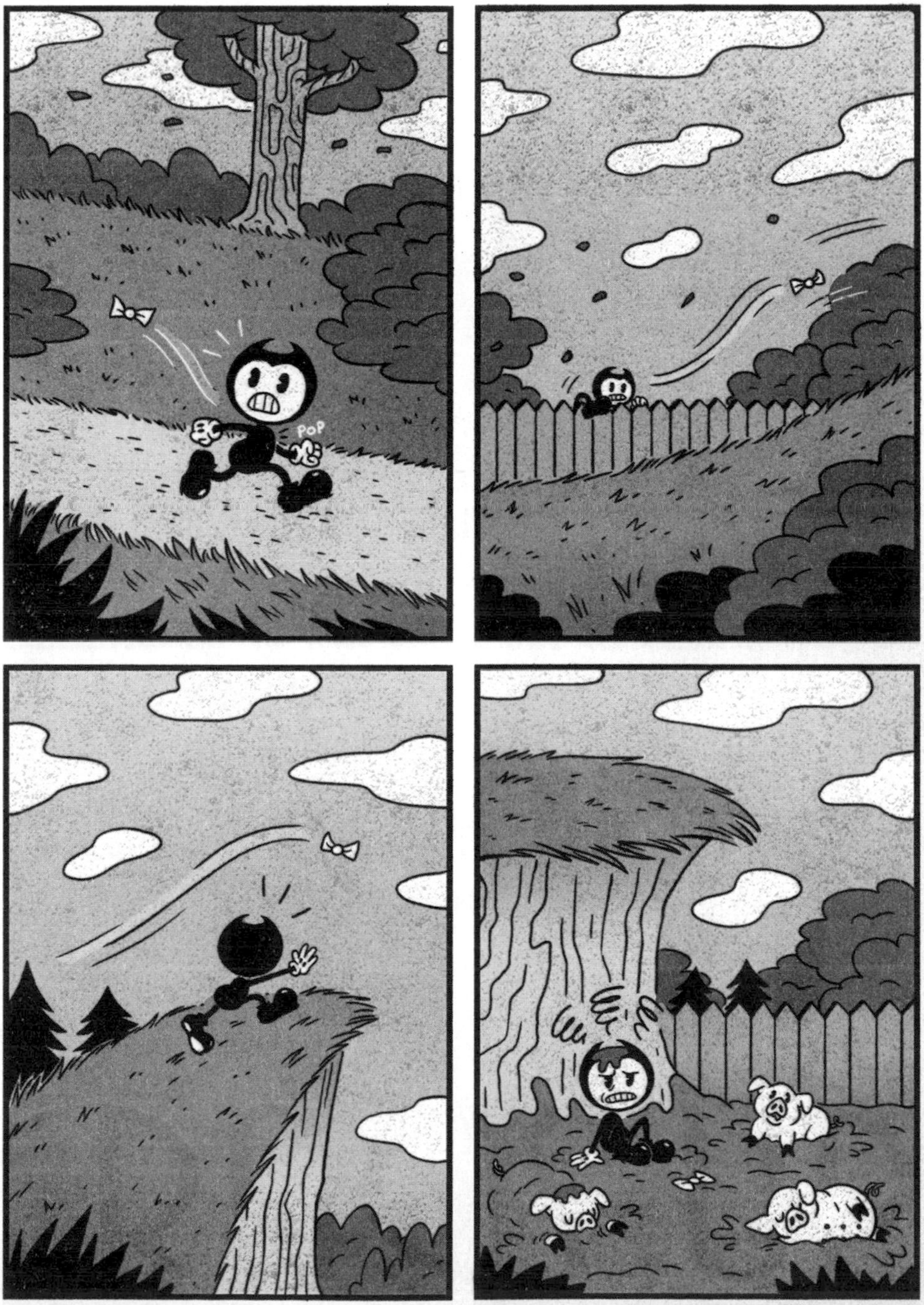
POP

Stink or Swim • June 7, 1933

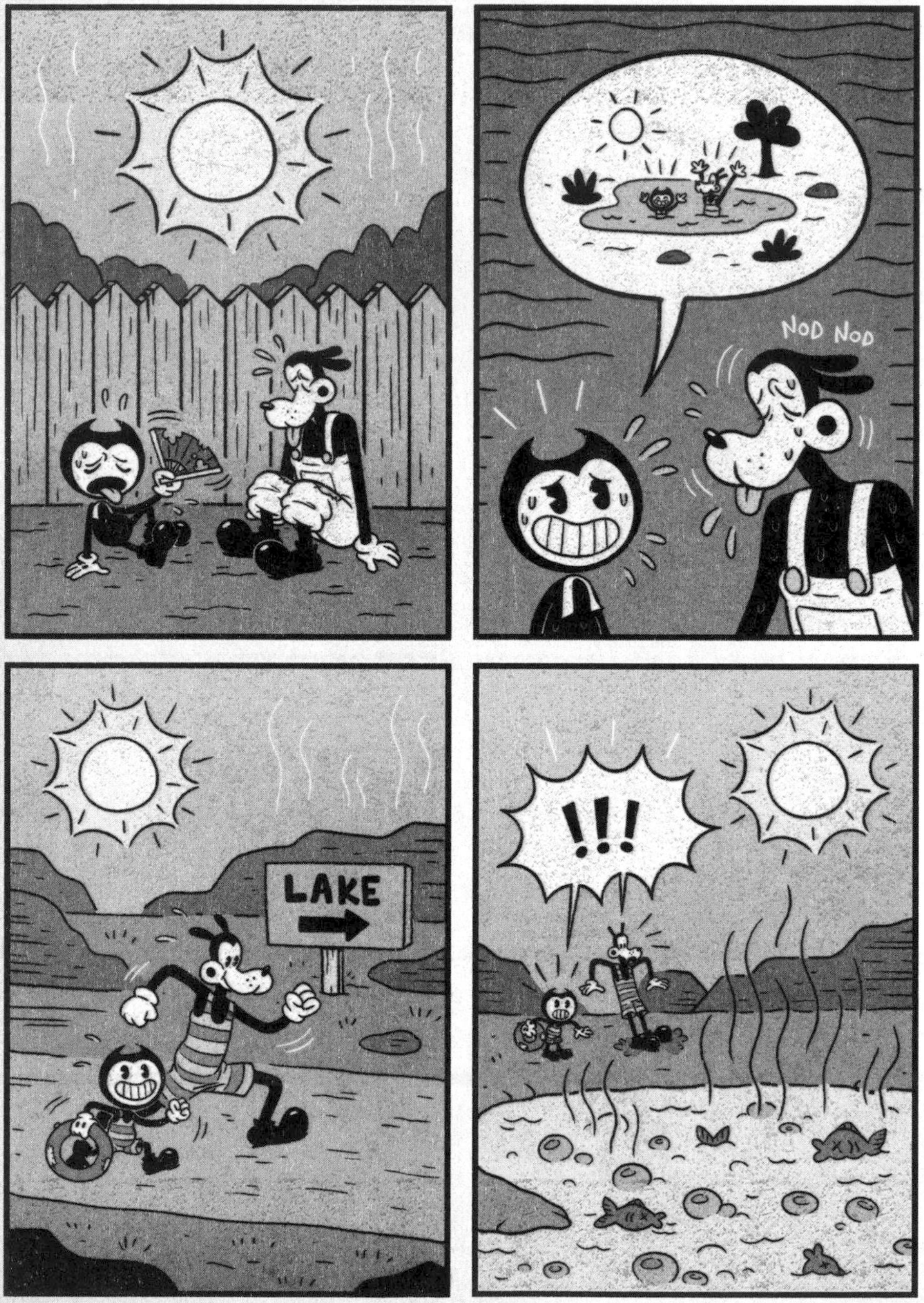
NOD NOD
LAKE
!!!

Bon Appe-Sneak • June 10, 1933

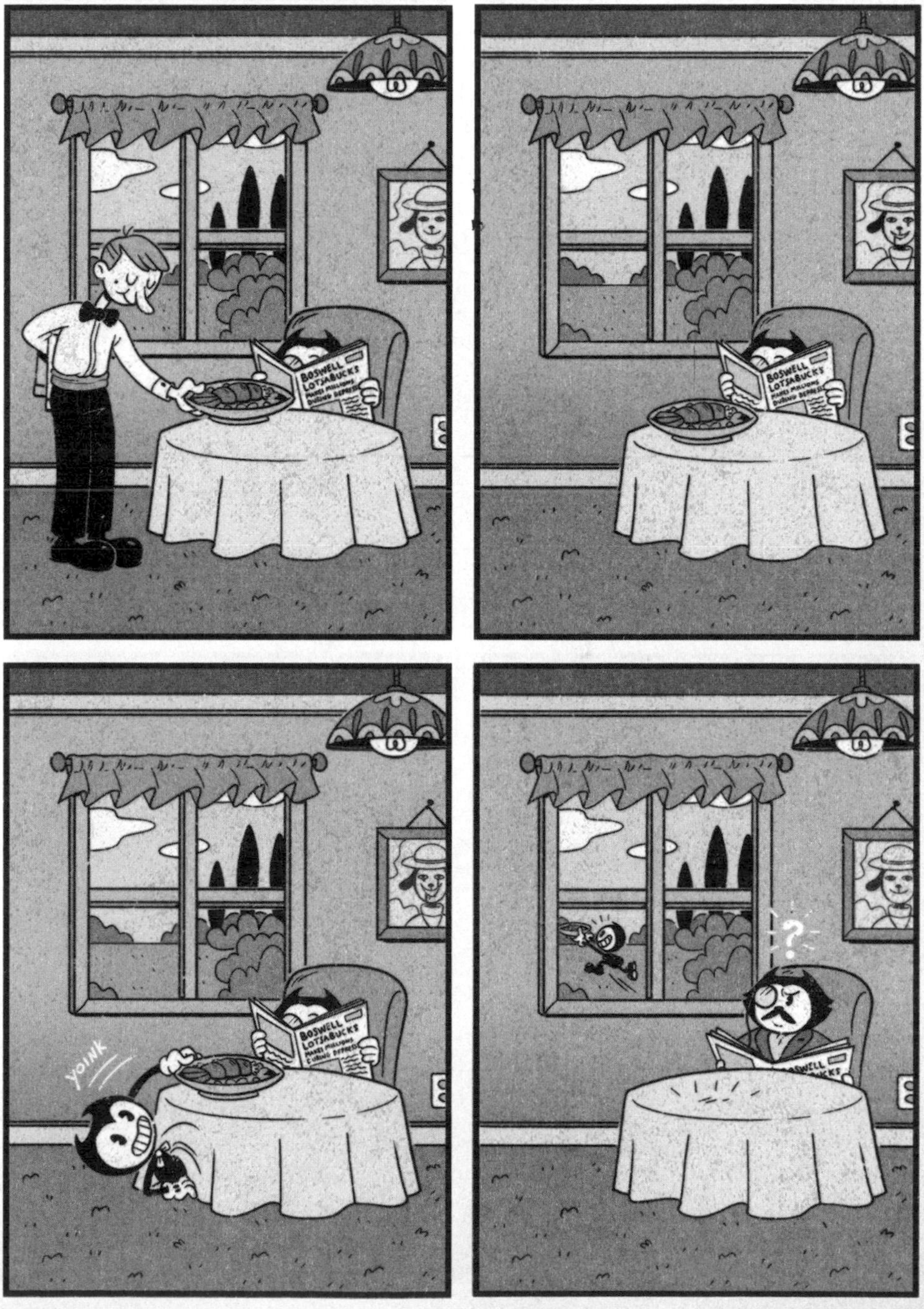
BOSWELL LOTSABUCKS
BOSWELL LOTSABUCKS
YOINK
BOSWELL LOTSABUCKS
?

Ode to Reuben • July 10, 1933

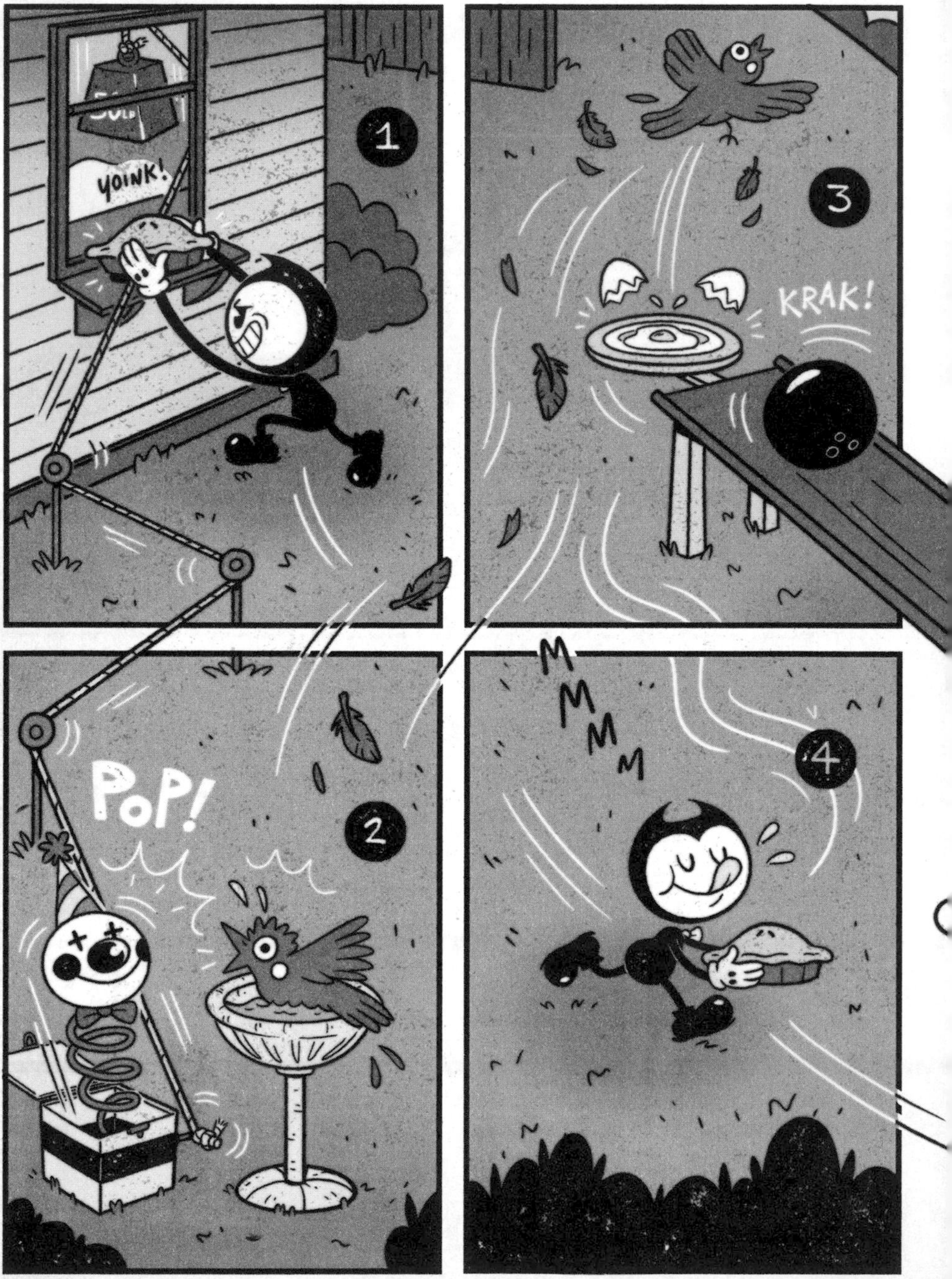
1
YOINK!
2
POP!
3
KRAK!
MMMM
4

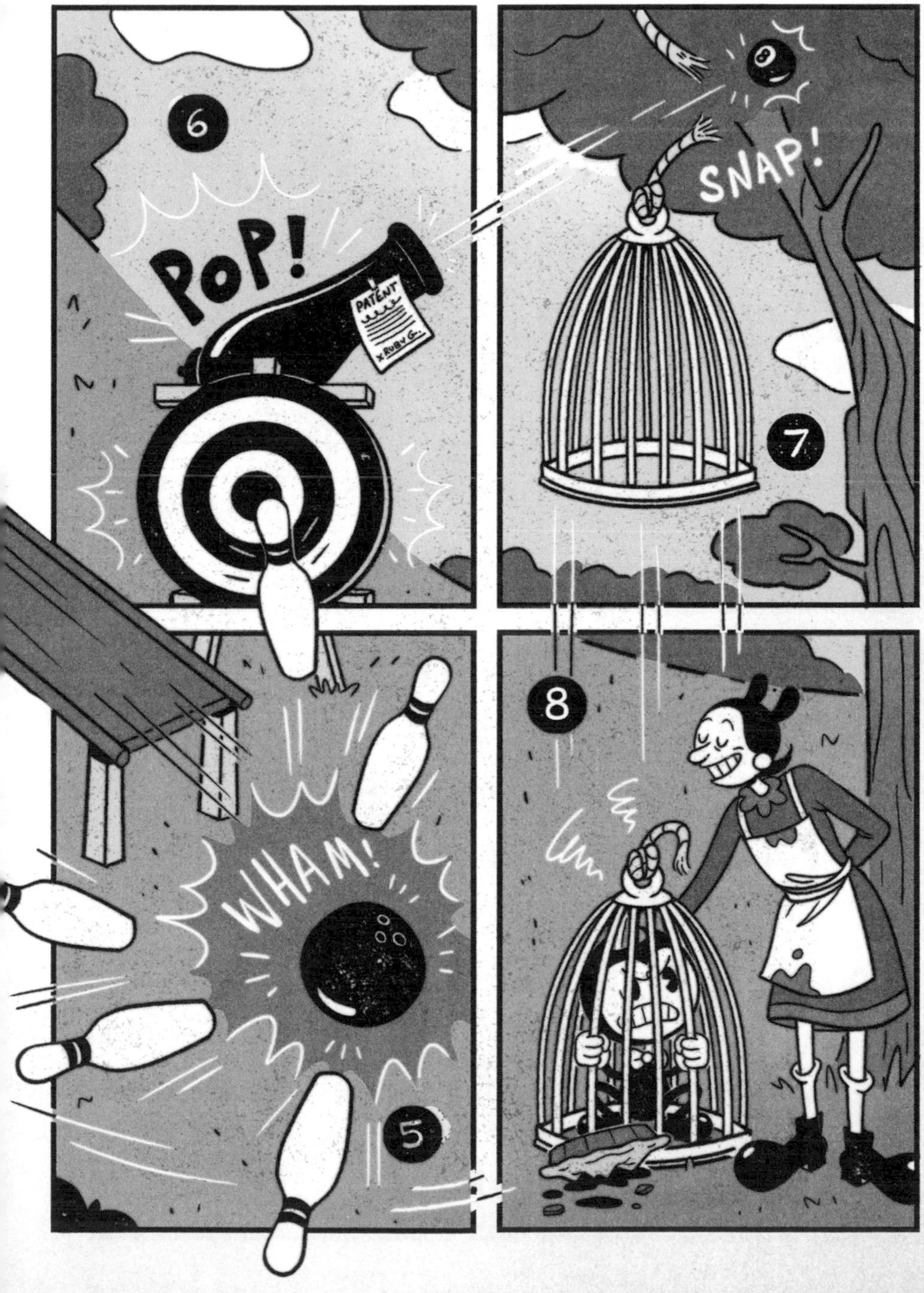
6
POP!
PATENT
x RUBY G.
SNAP!
7
8
WHAM!
5

Mutt Cuts • October 5, 1933

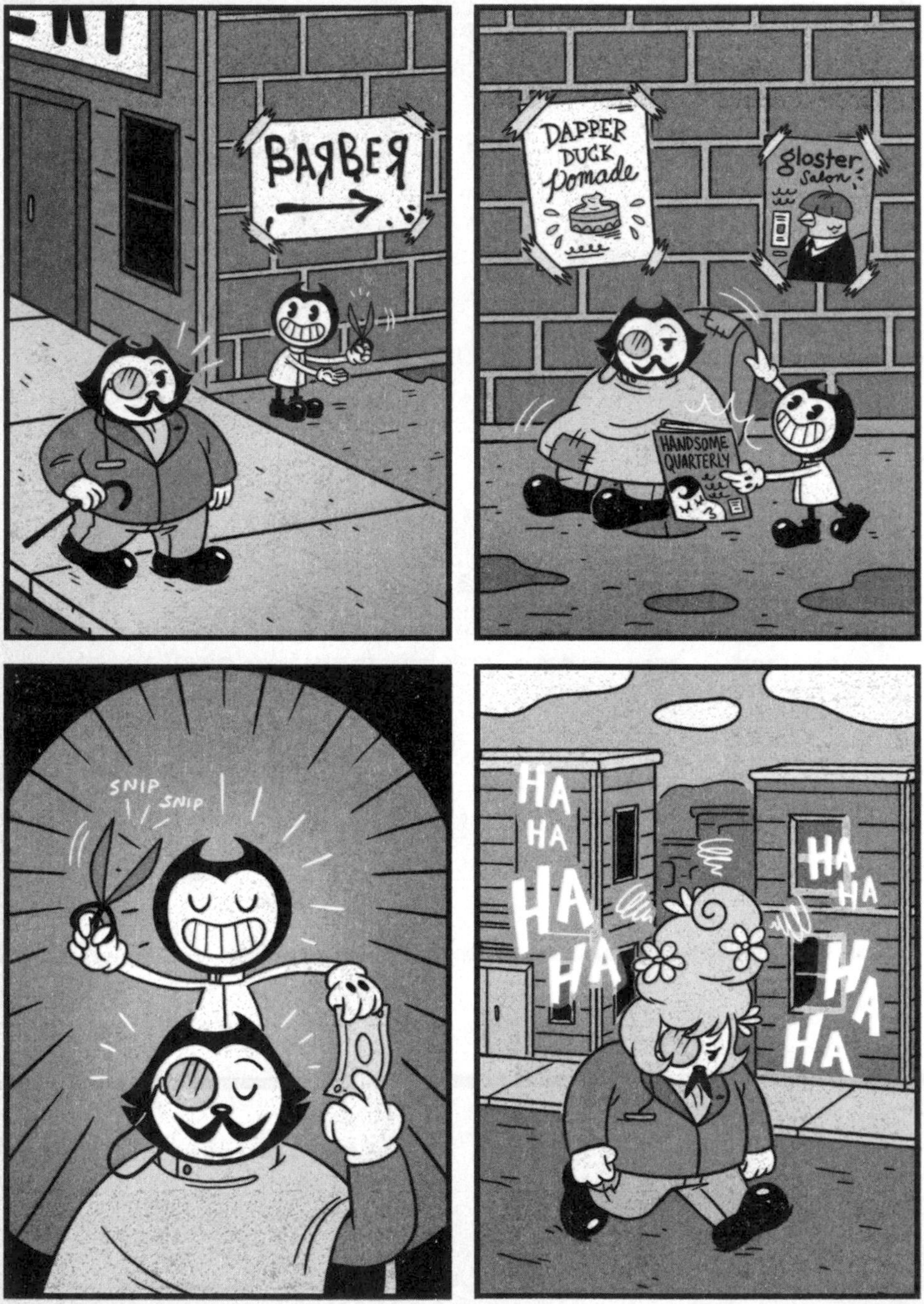
BARBER
DAPPER DUCK pomade
gloster Salon
HANDSOME QUARTERLY
SNIP SNIP
HA HA HA HA
HA HA HA HA

Sticky Situation • October 8, 1933

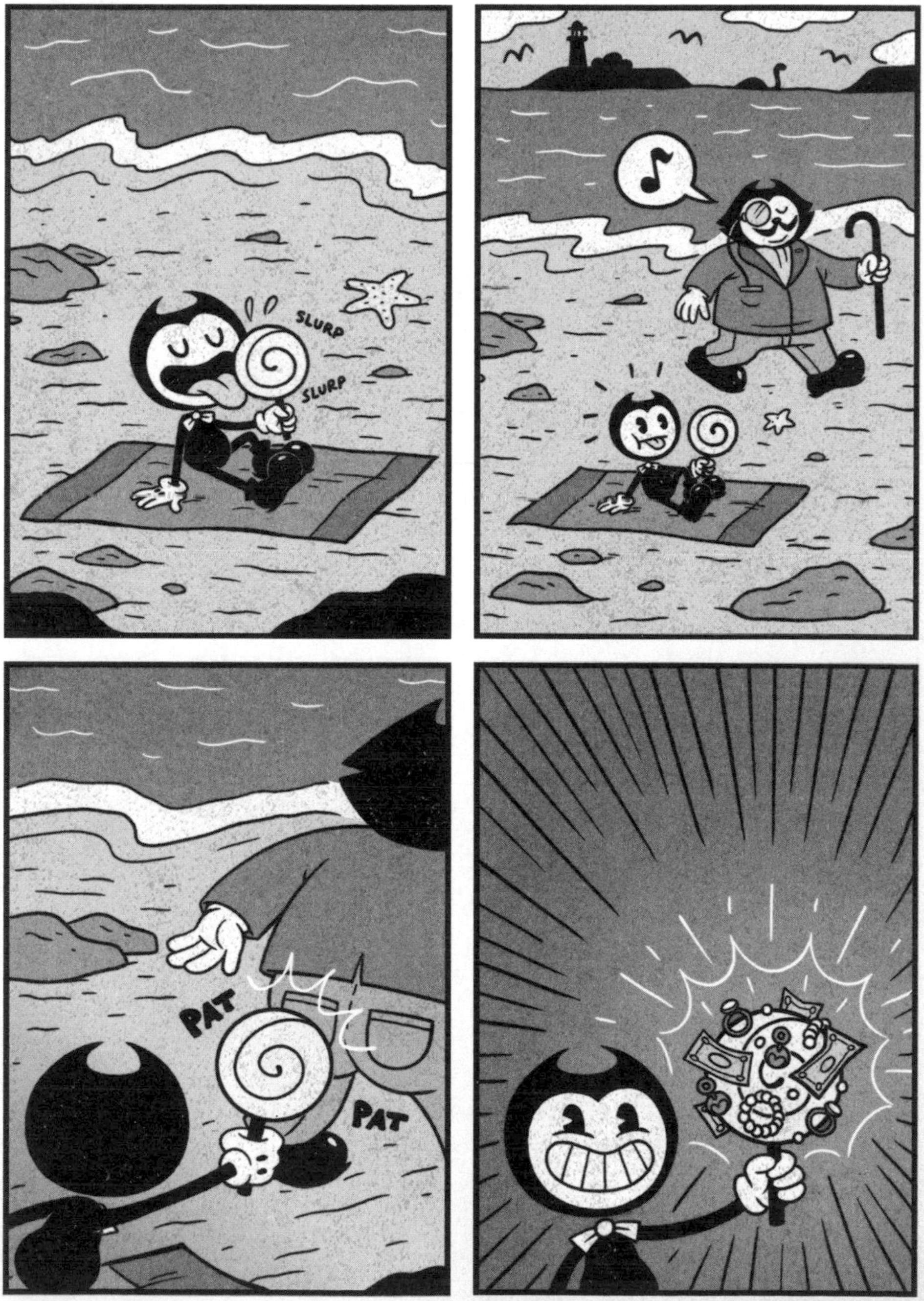
SLURP
SLURP
PAT
PAT

On Cloud 9 · January 10, 1933

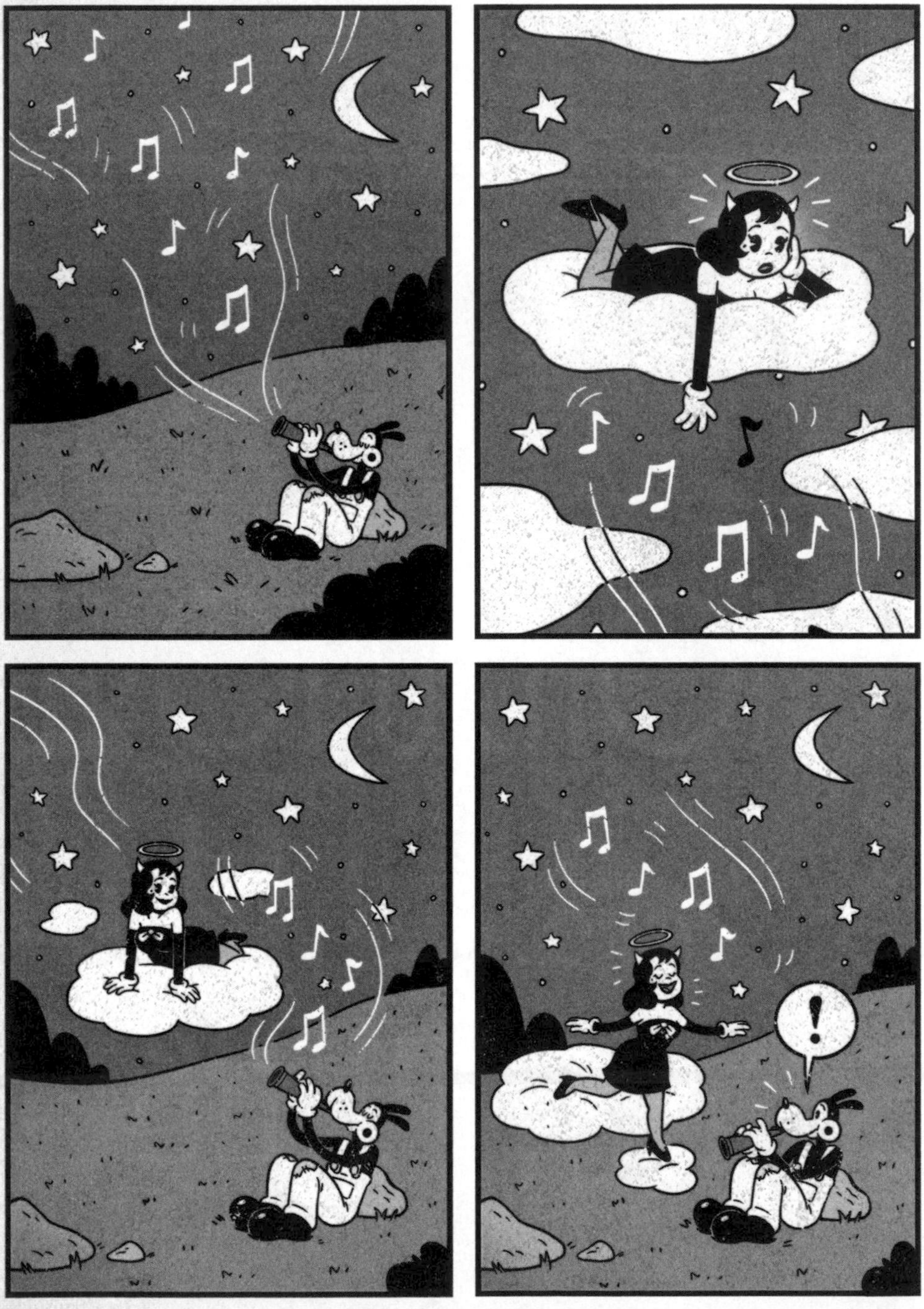
!

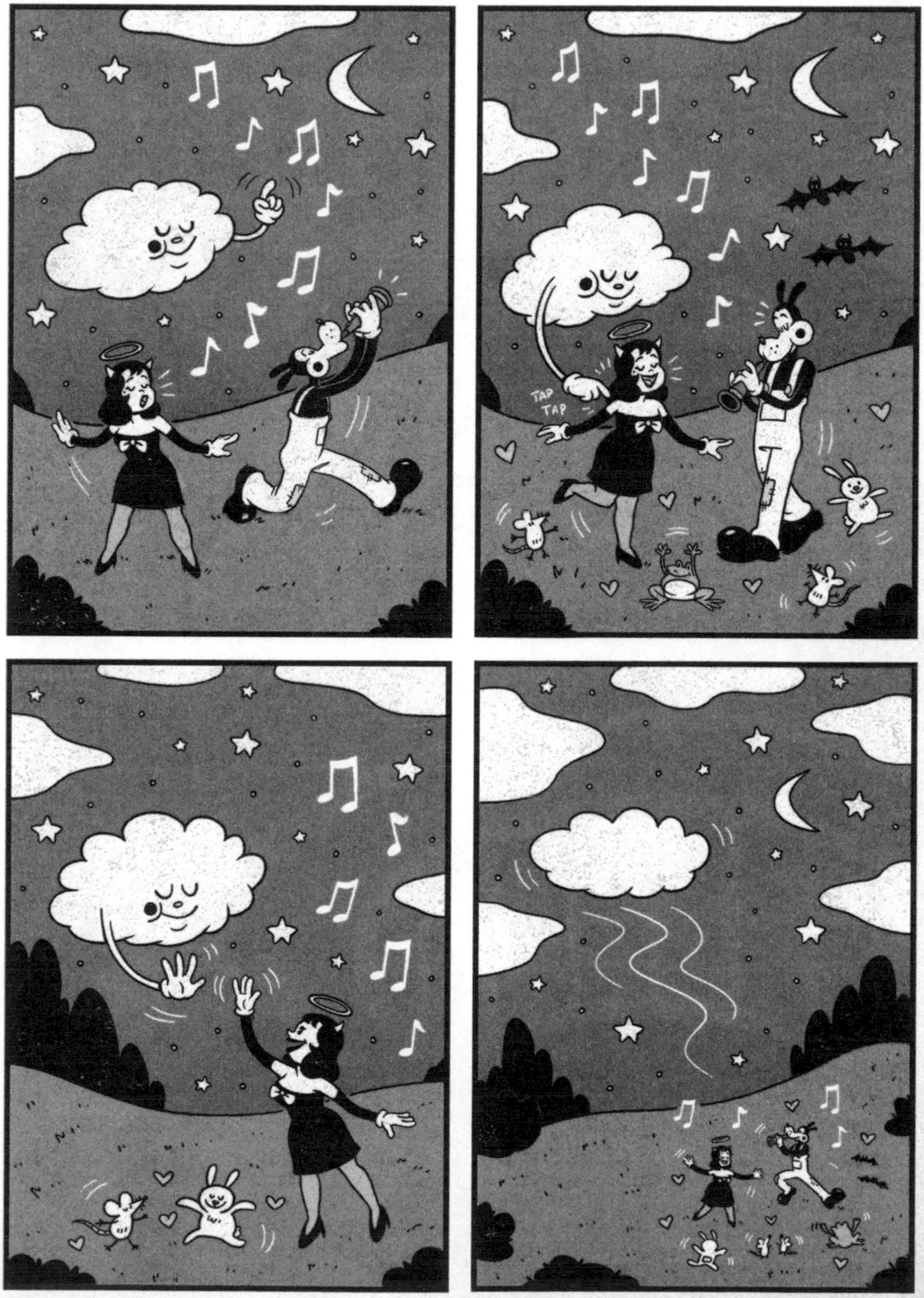
TAP
TAP

Mice Try • February 14, 1933

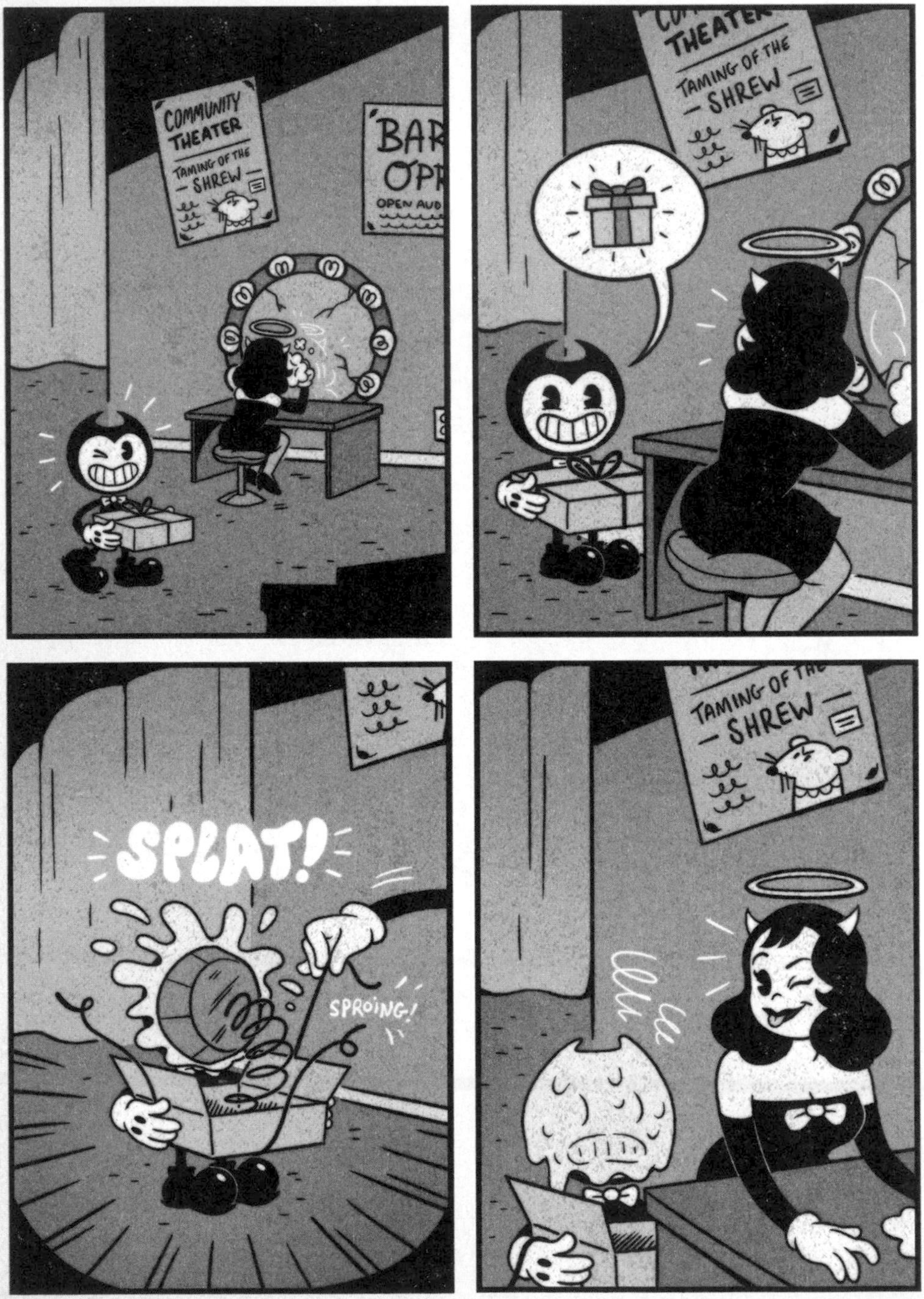
COMMUNITY THEATER
TAMING OF THE SHREW
BAR
OPR
OPEN AUD
THEATER
TAMING OF THE SHREW
SPLAT!
SPROING!
TAMING OF THE SHREW

Opening Act • May 6, 1933

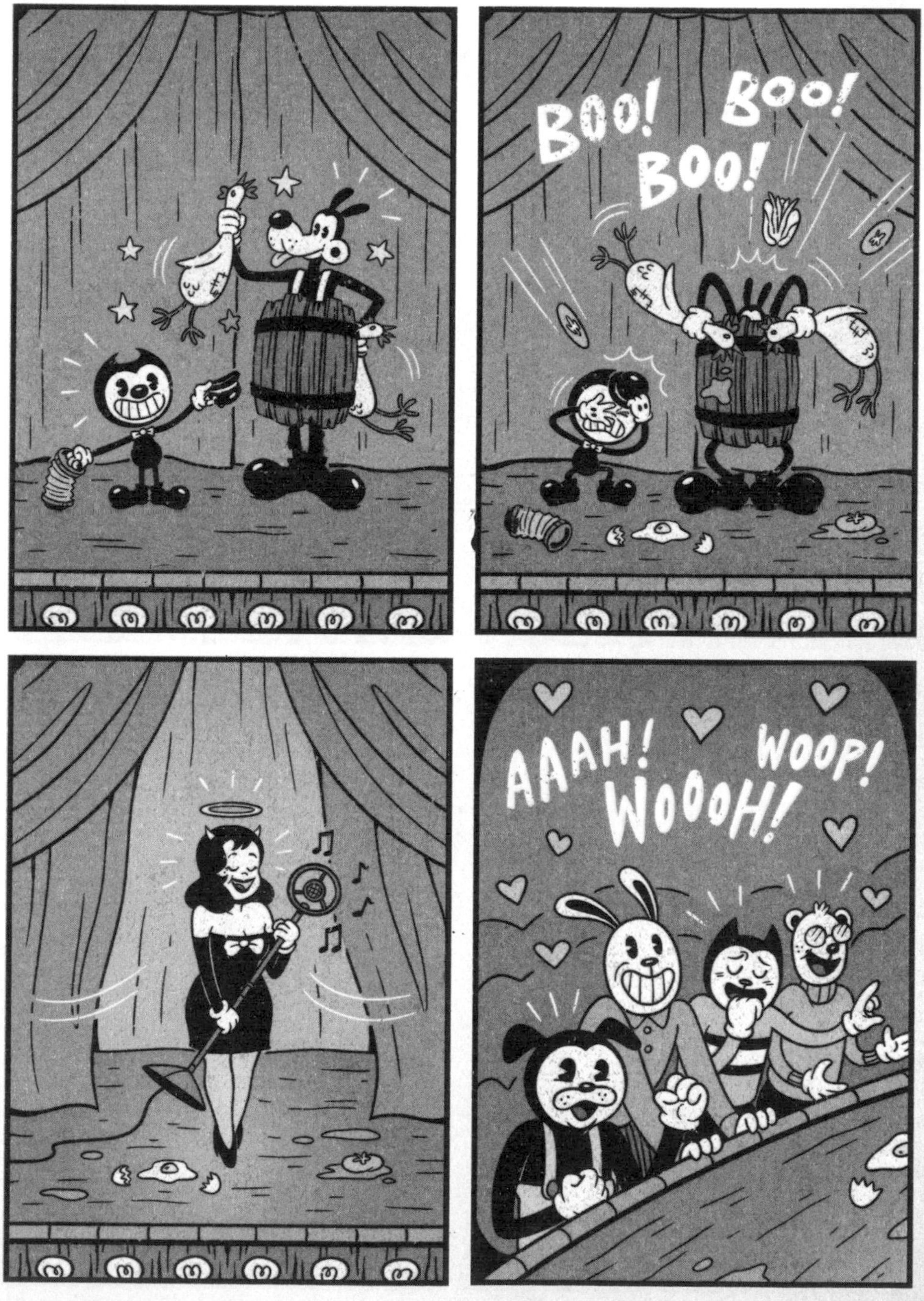
BOO! BOO!
BOO!
AAAH! WOOP!
WOOOH!

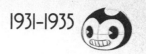

True Love • July 23, 1933

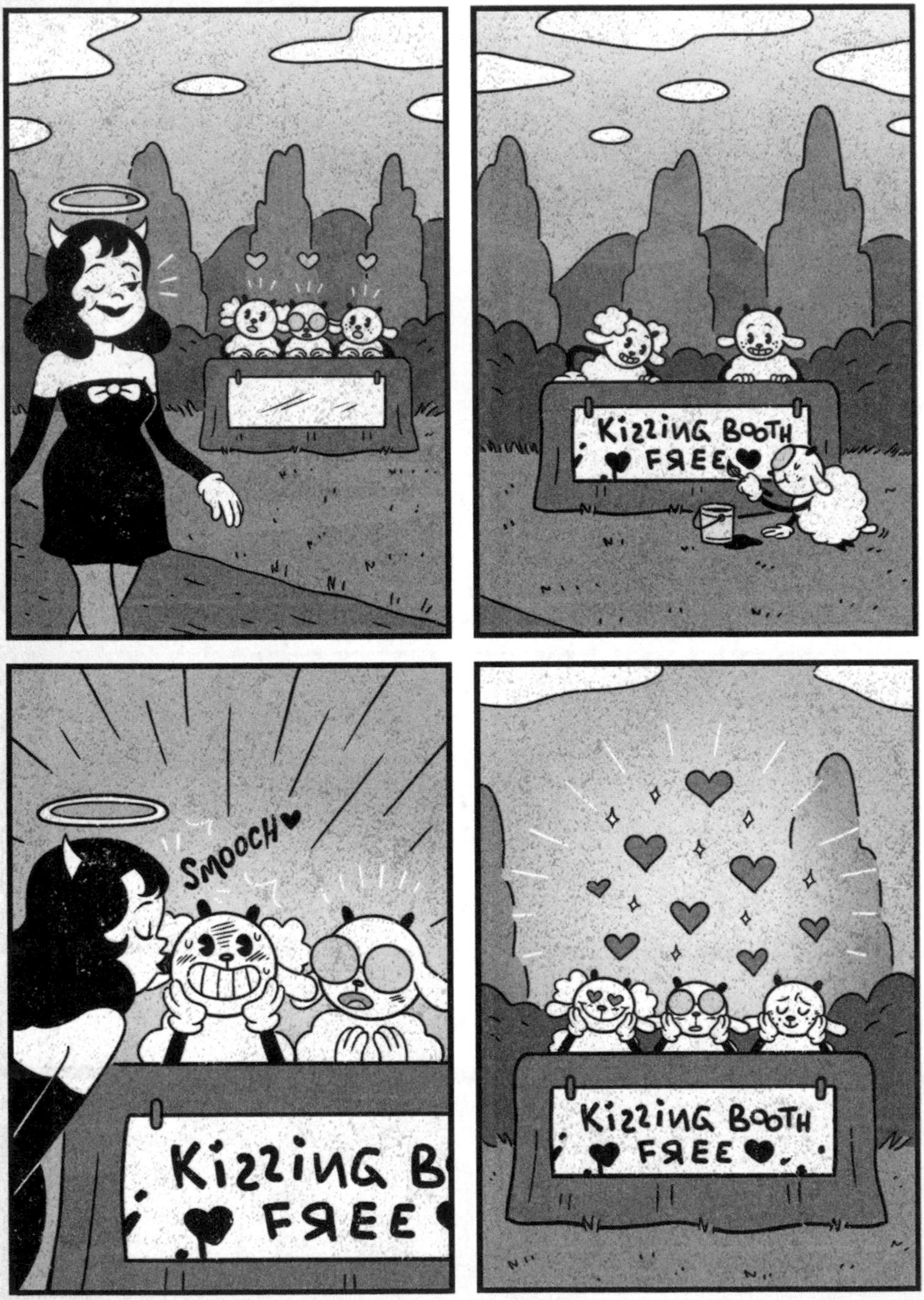
KiZZiNG BOOTH
FREE
SMOOCH
KiZZiNG B
FREE
KiZZiNG BOOTH
FREE

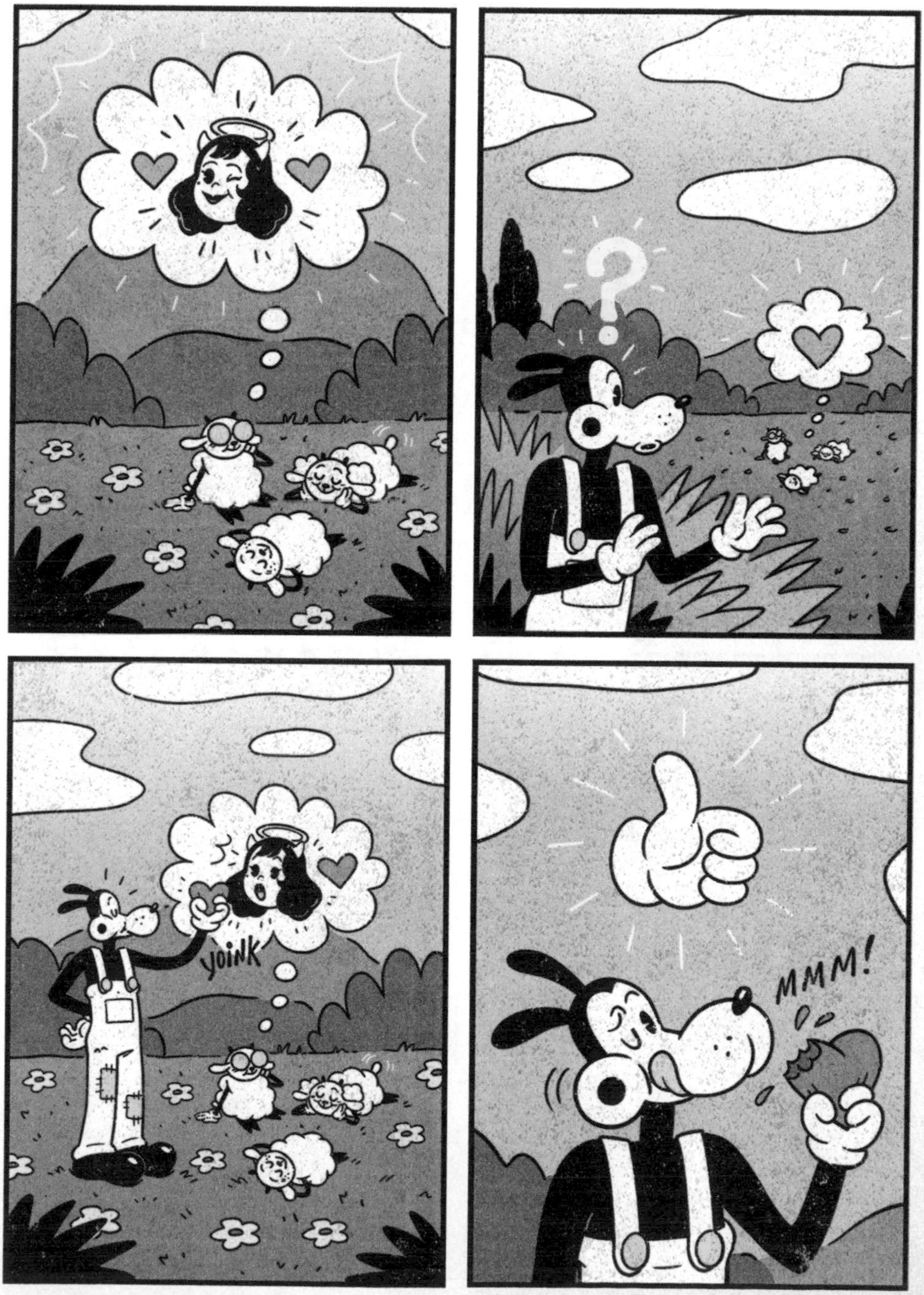
YOINK
MMM!

Encore • November 6, 1933

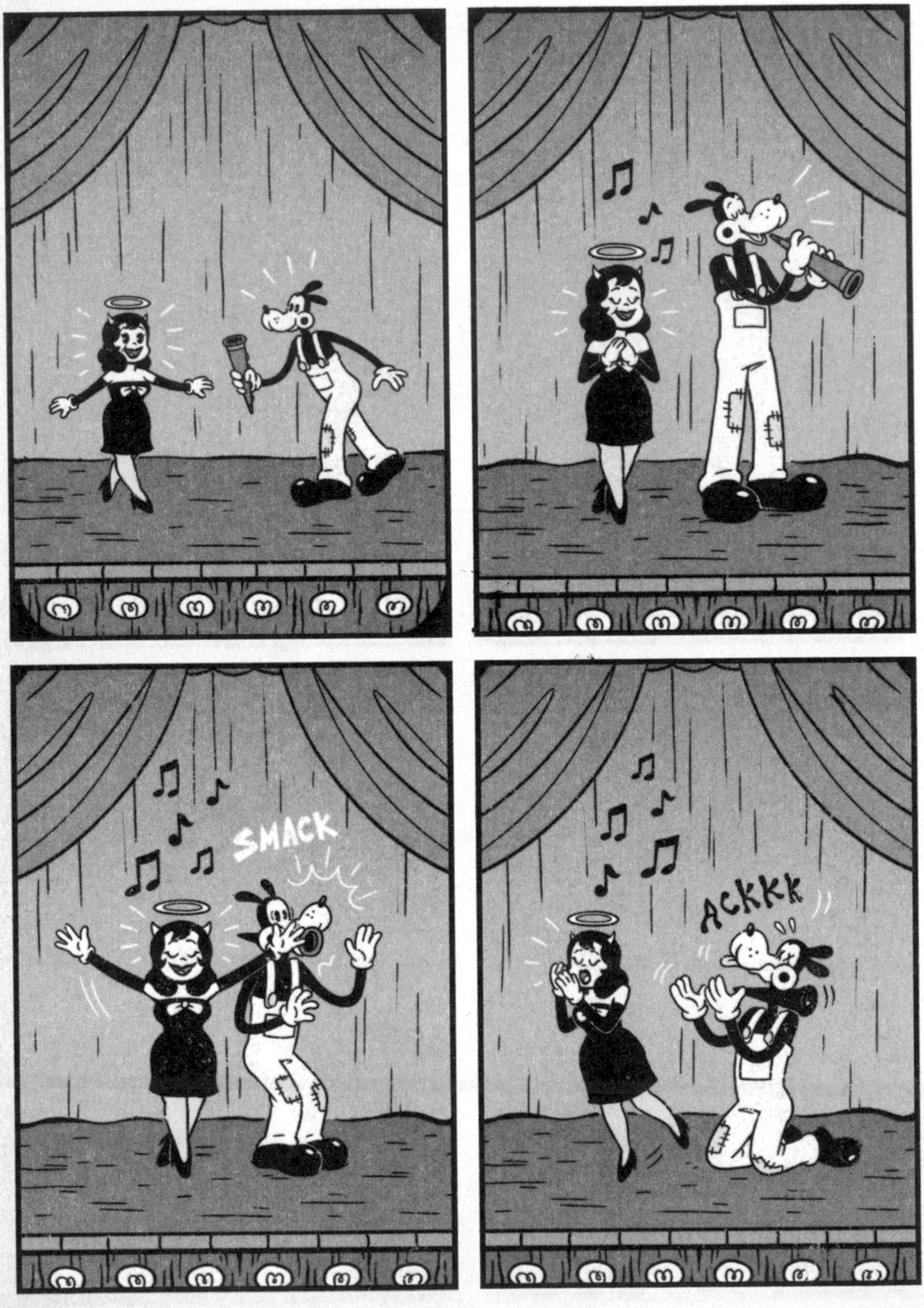
SMACK
ACKKK

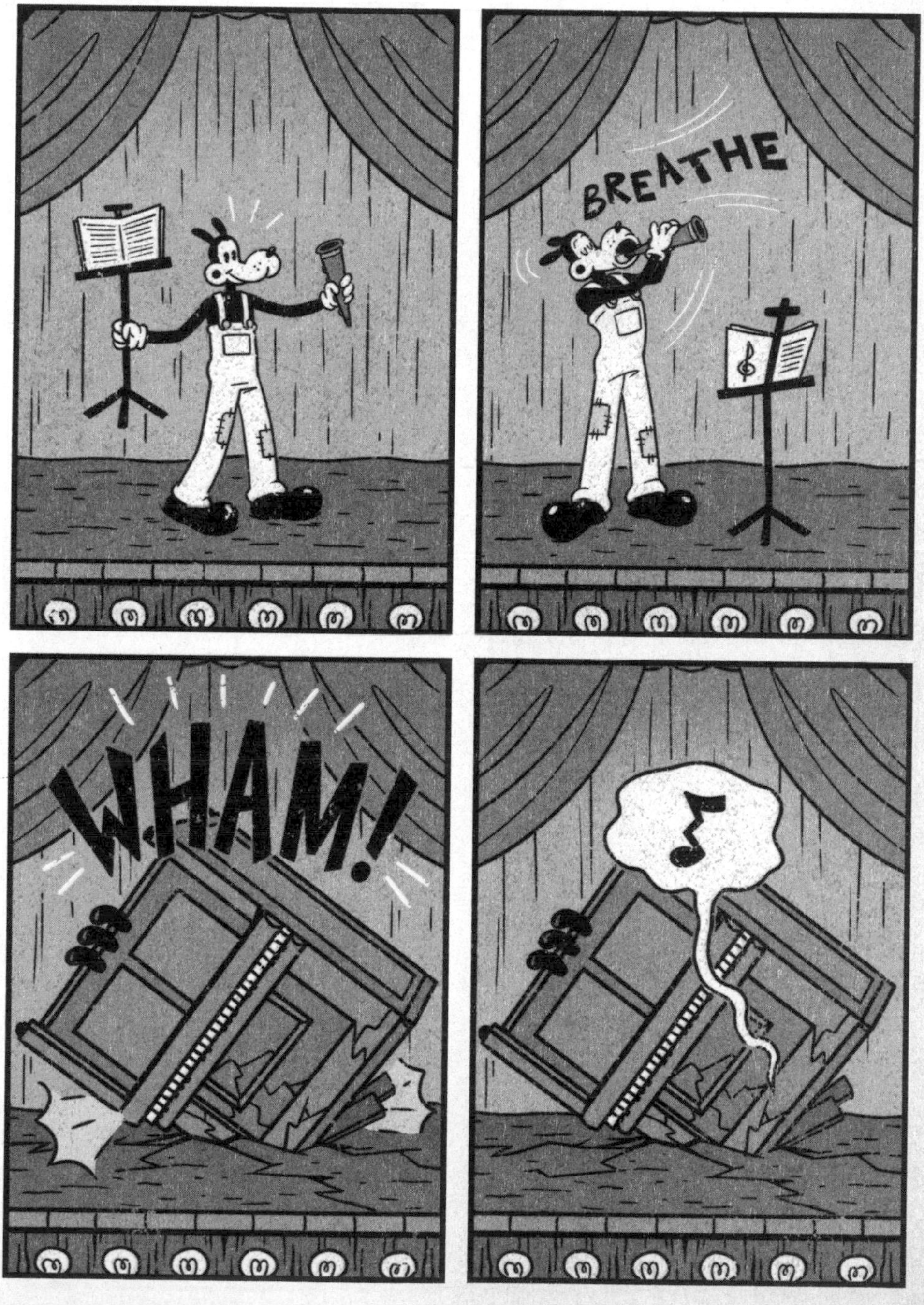
BREATHE
WHAM!

Fleas and Z's • February 18, 1934

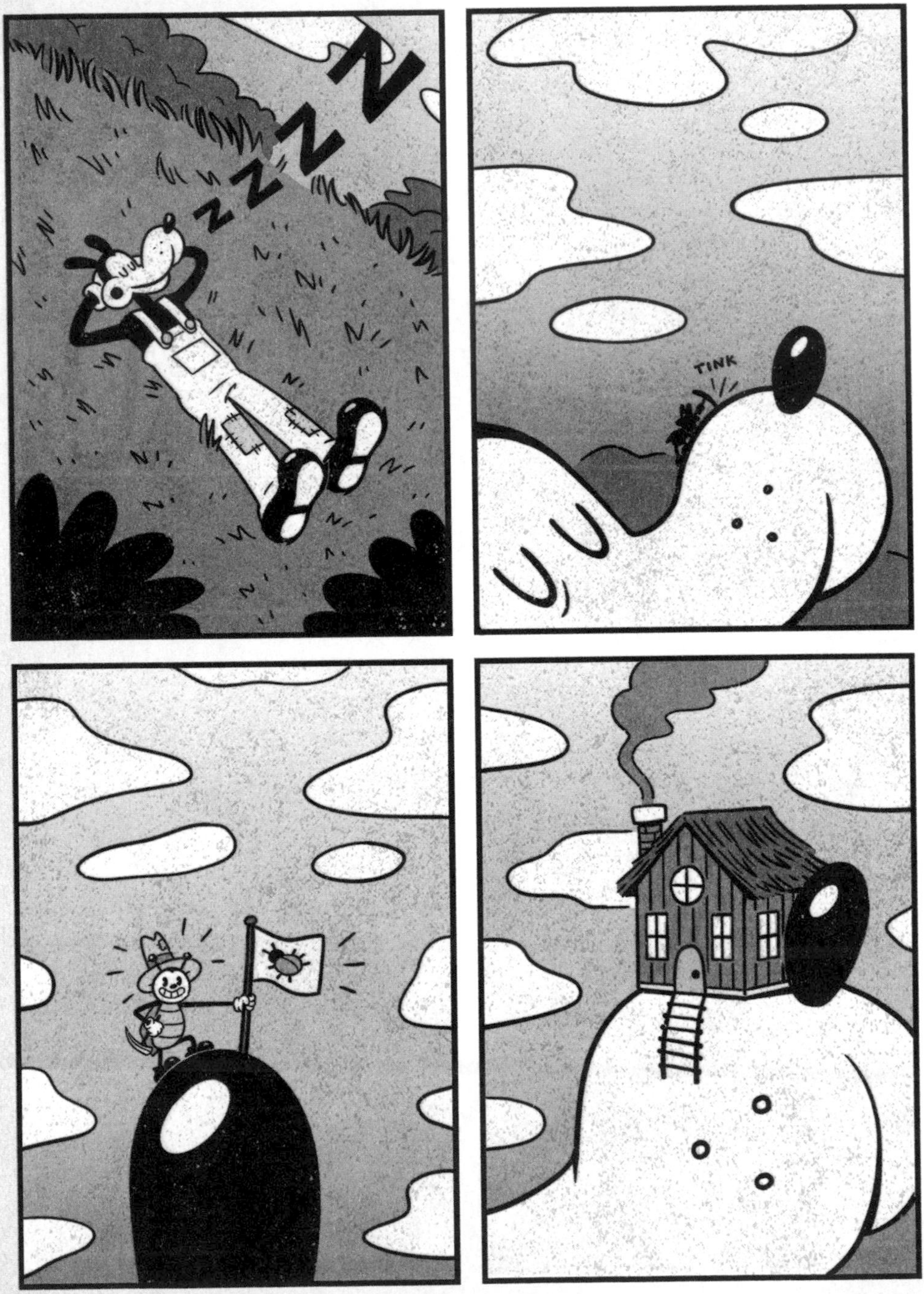
TINK

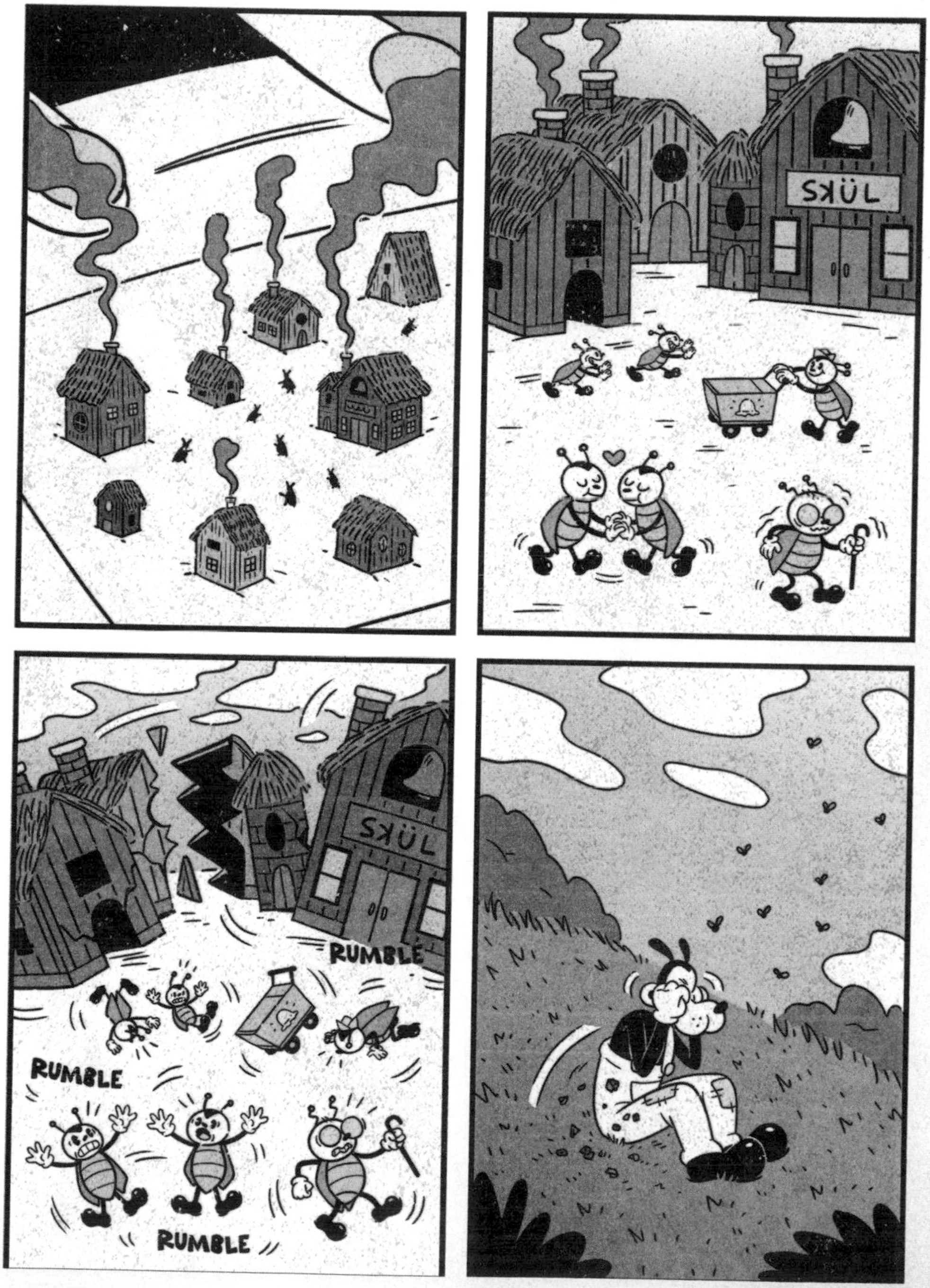

SKÜL
SKÜL
RUMBLE
RUMBLE
RUMBLE

Nothing is Free • May 18, 1934

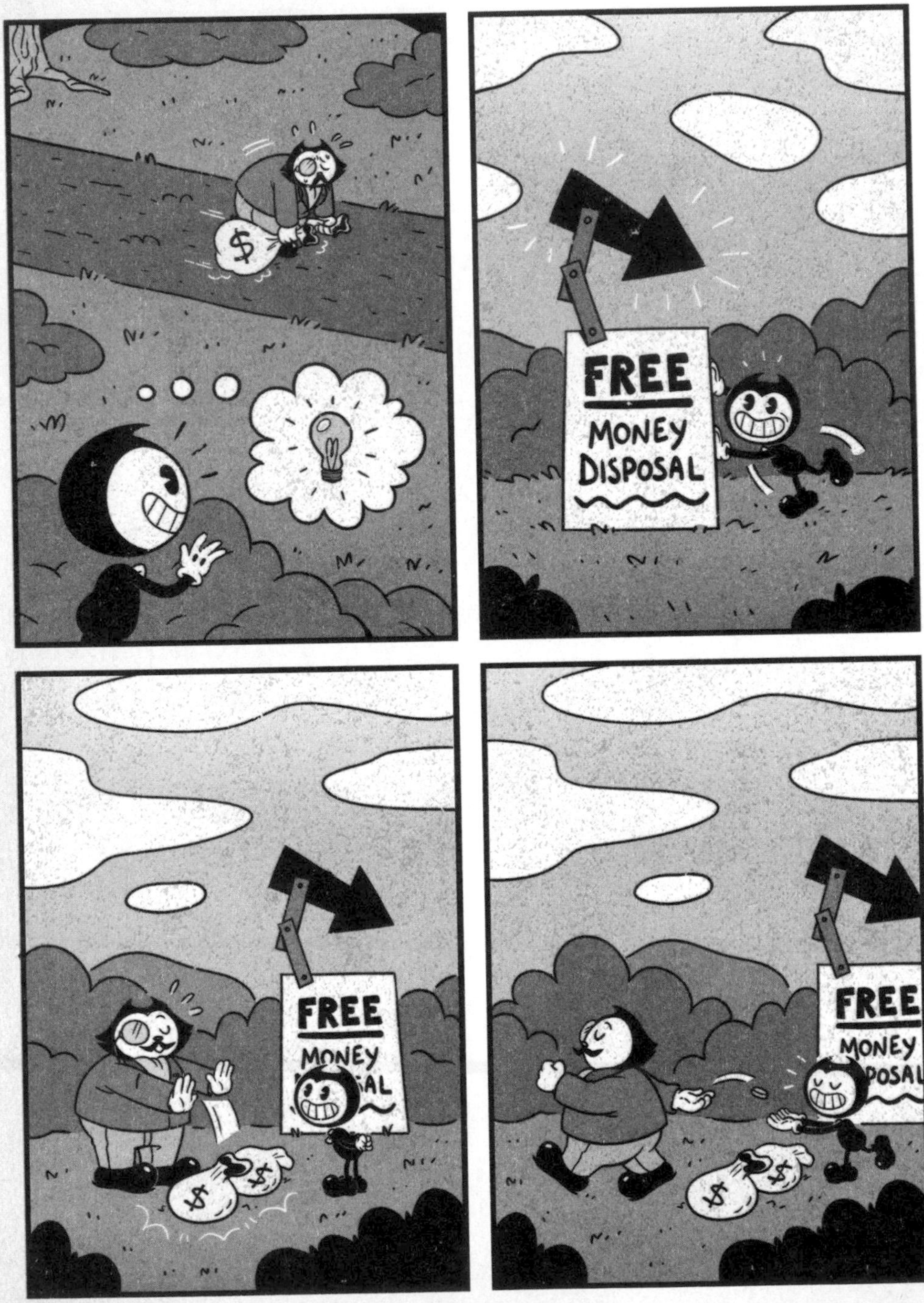
FREE
MONEY
DISPOSAL
FREE
MONEY
FREE
MONEY

Three for One • June 16, 1934

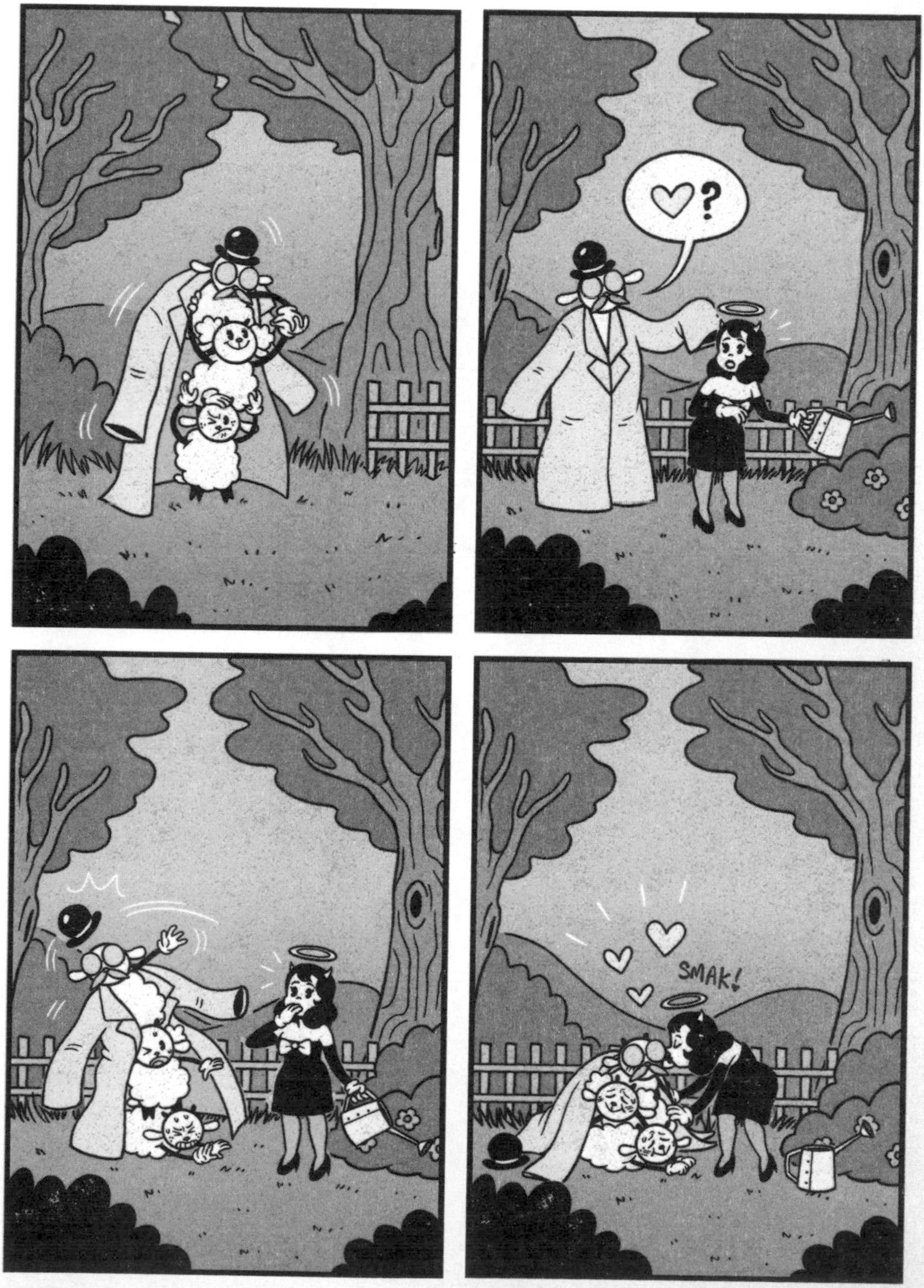
♡?
SMAK!

The Money will roll right in • August 10, 1934

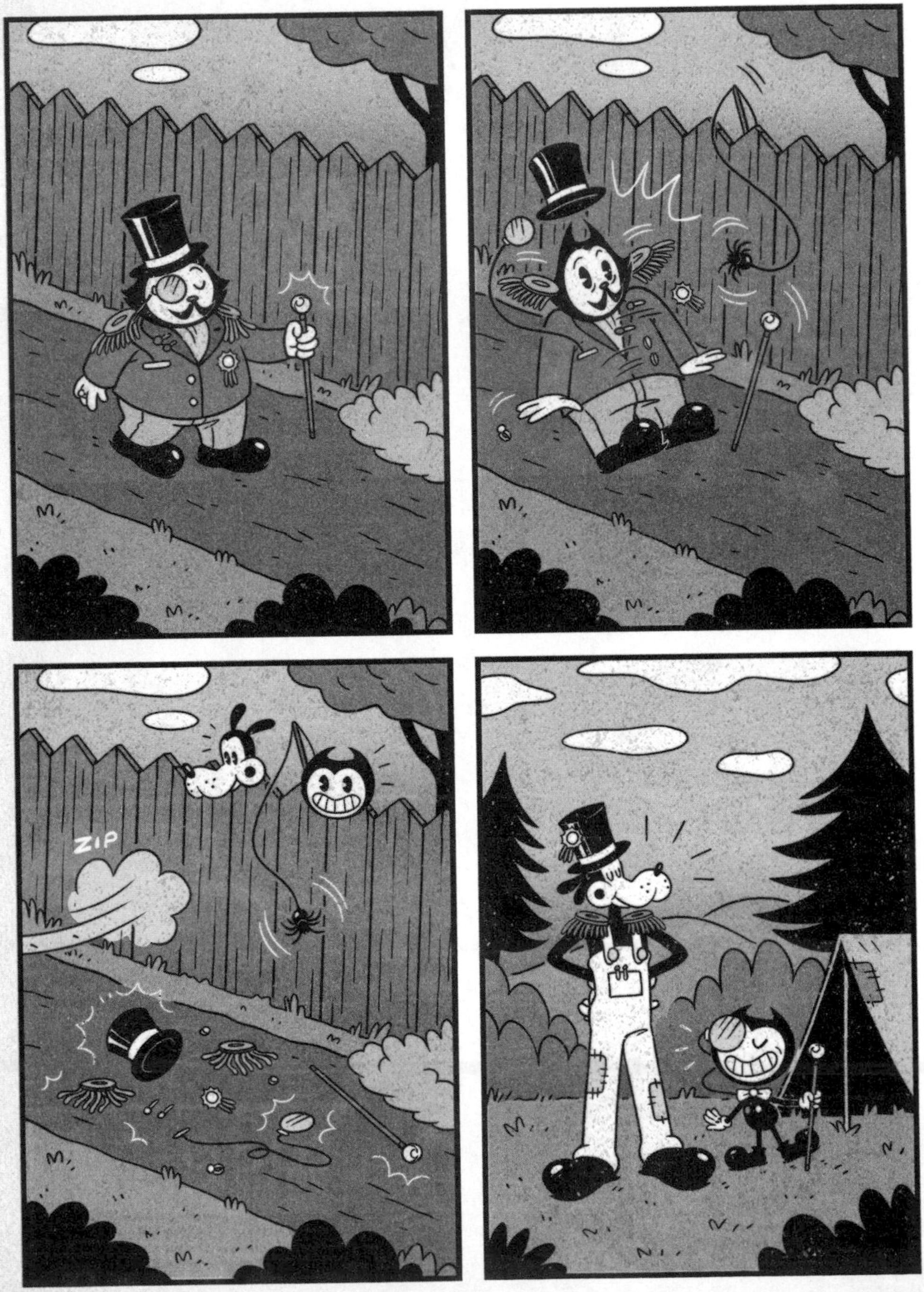
ZIP

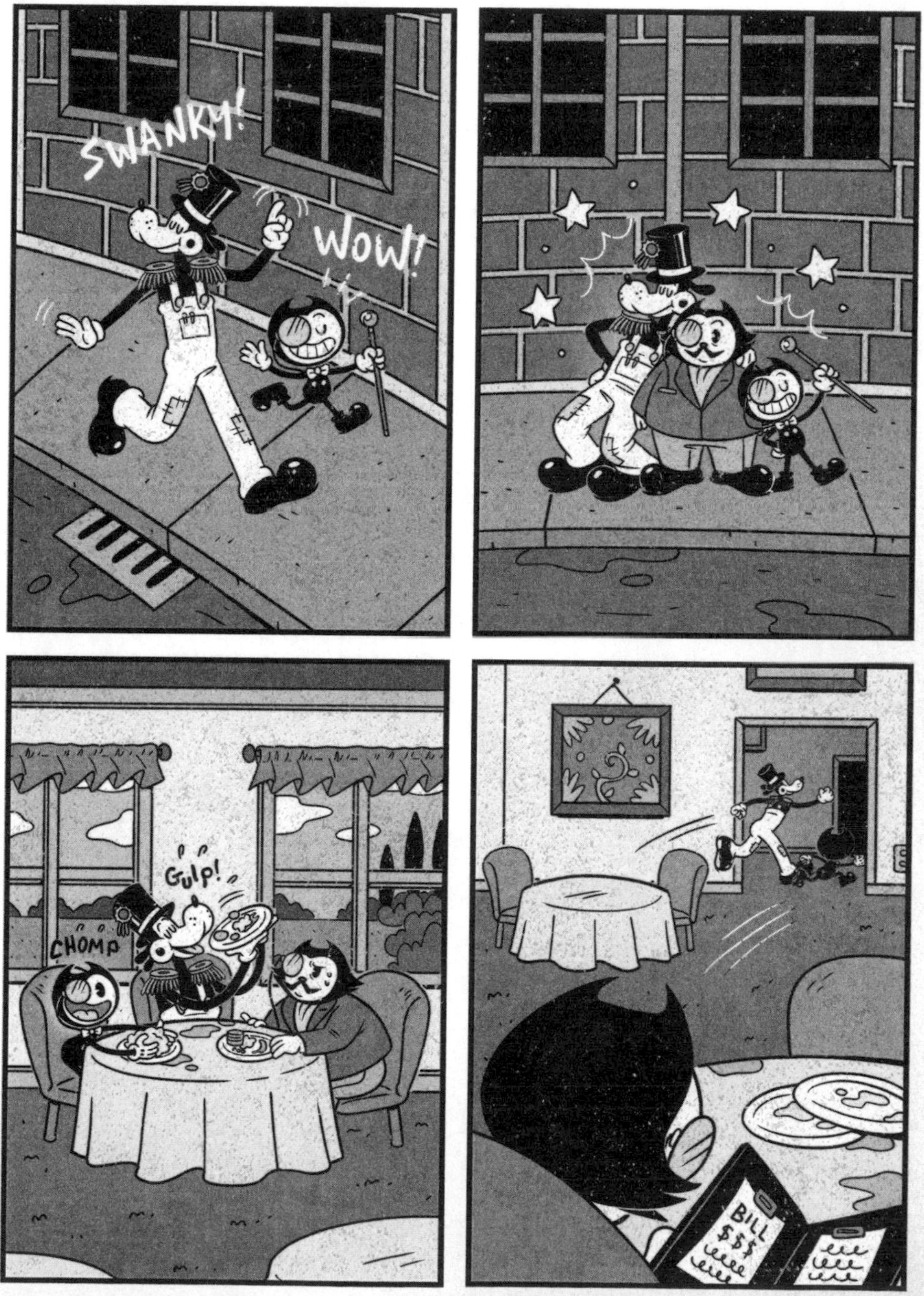
SWANKY!
WOW!
GULP!
CHOMP
BILL
$$$

Poor Yorick • November 20, 1934

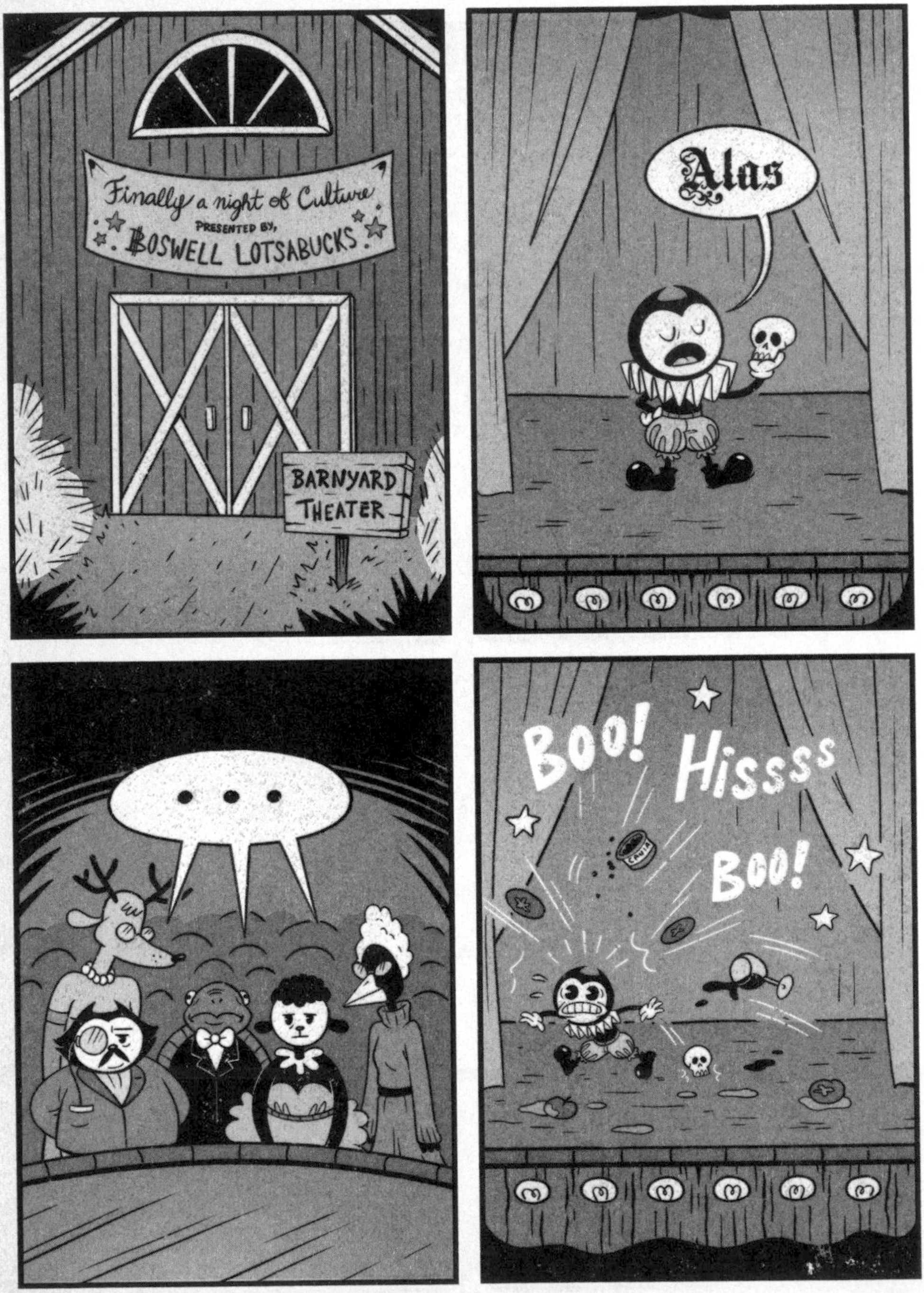
Finally a night of Culture
PRESENTED BY,
BOSWELL LOTSABUCKS
BARNYARD THEATER
Alas
• • •
BOO!
Hissss
BOO!

Graduation Day • December 5, 1934

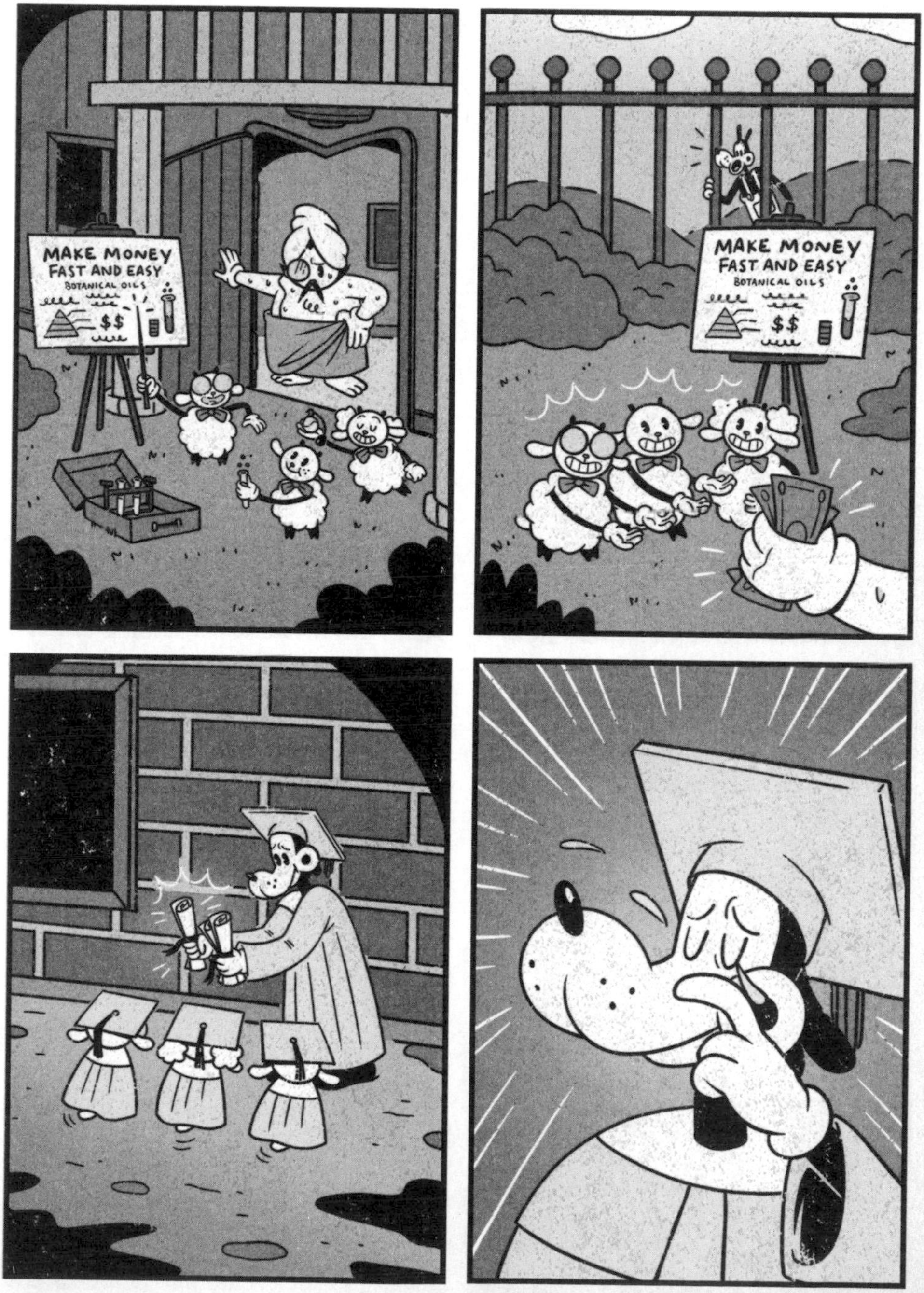
MAKE MONEY
FAST AND EASY
BOTANICAL OILS
$$
MAKE MONEY
FAST AND EASY
BOTANICAL OILS
$$

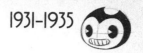

Pie and the Sky • March 10, 1935

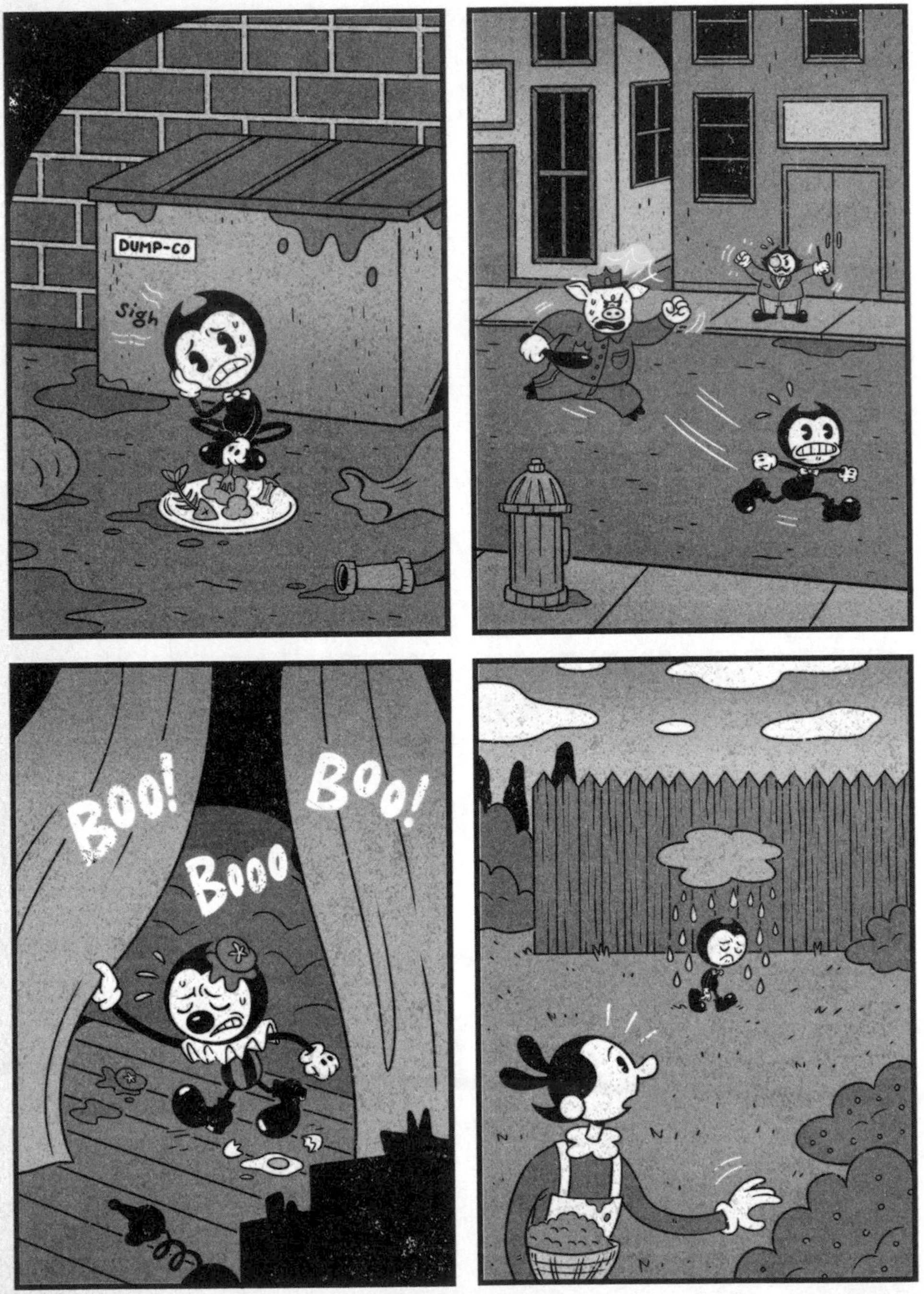
DUMP-CO
Sigh
BOO!
BOO!
BOOO

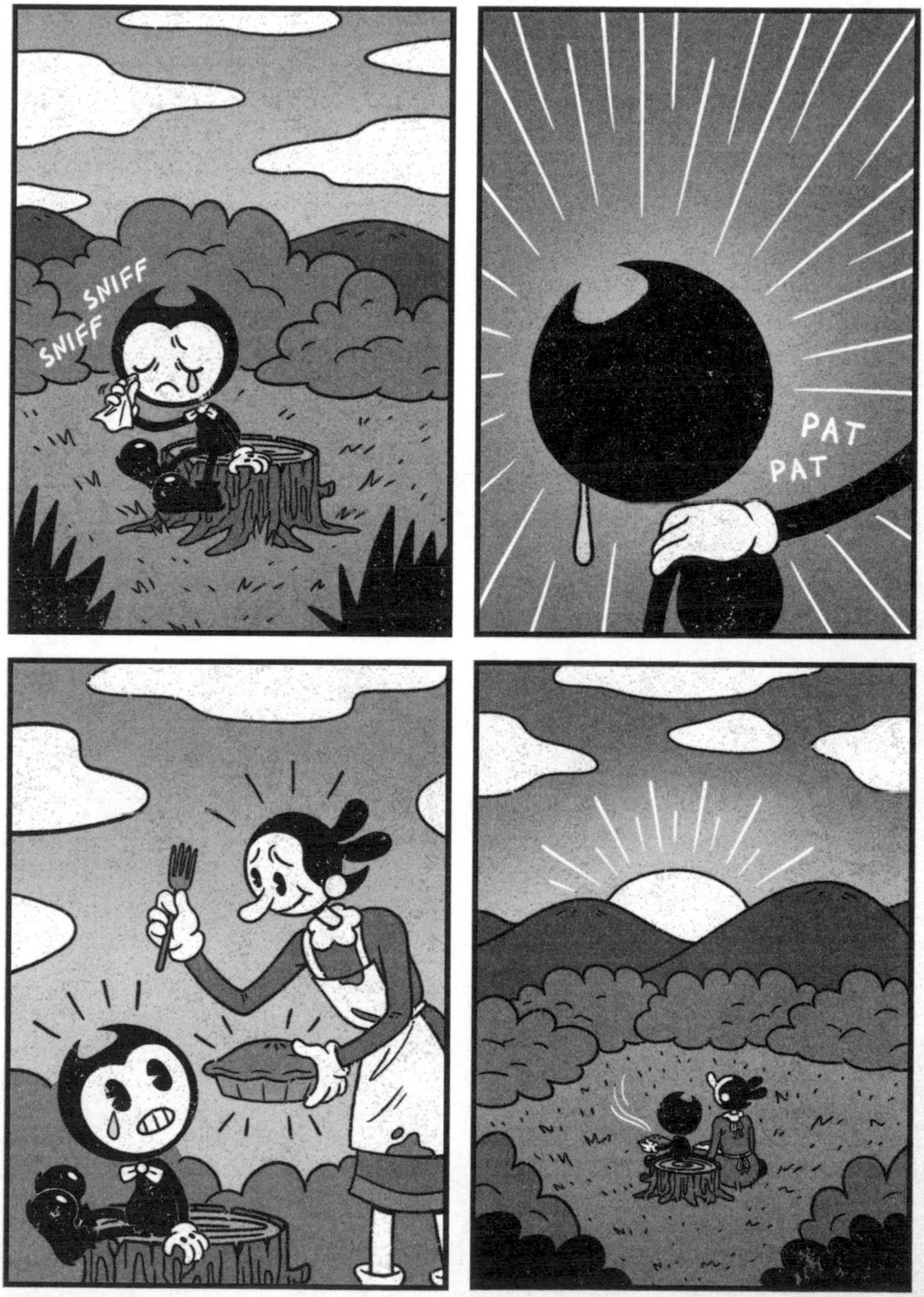
SNIFF
SNIFF
PAT
PAT

Automo-steal • May 3, 1935

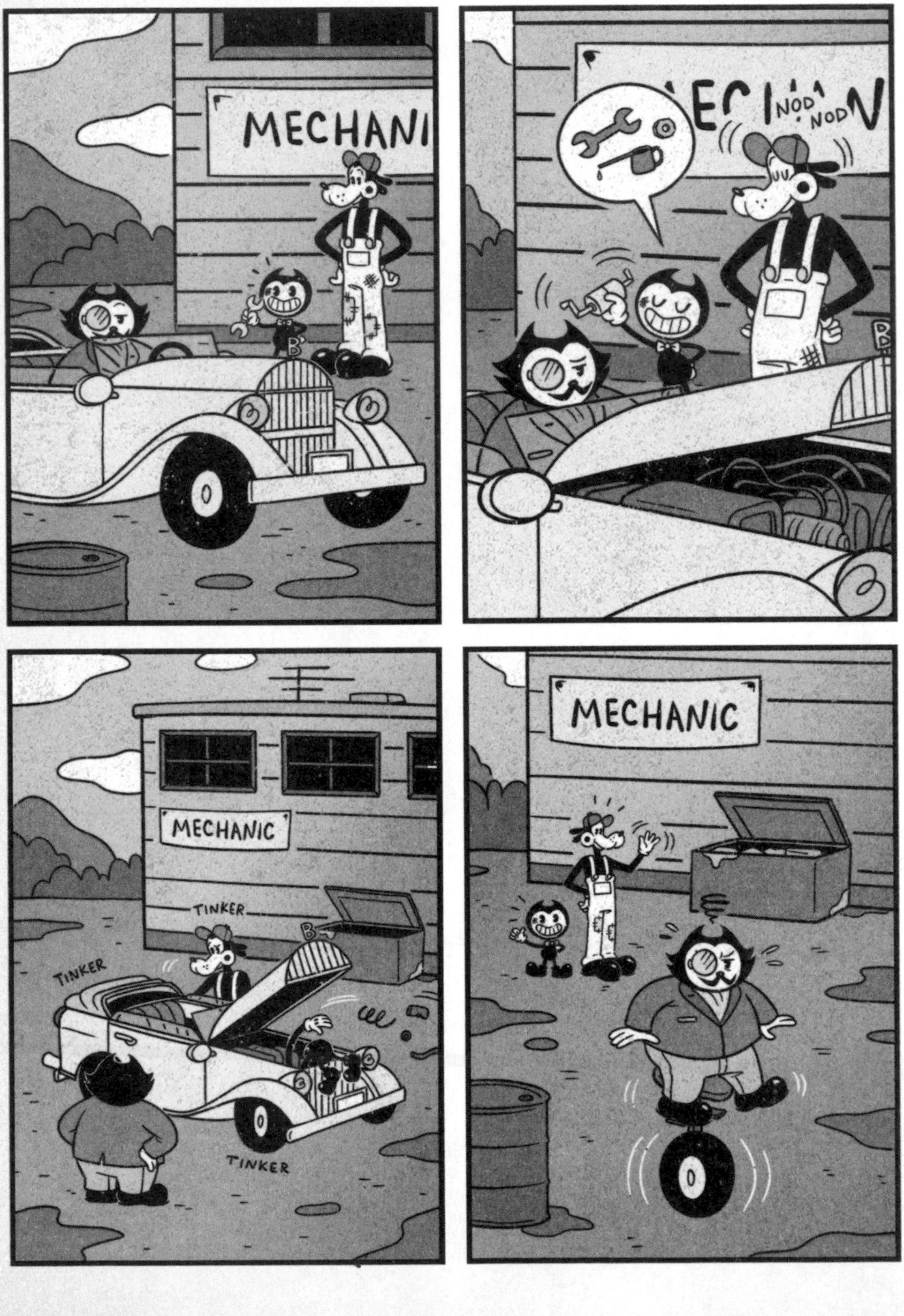
MECHANI
NOD NOD
MECHANIC
TINKER
TINKER
TINKER
MECHANIC

Opposites Attract • May 11, 1935

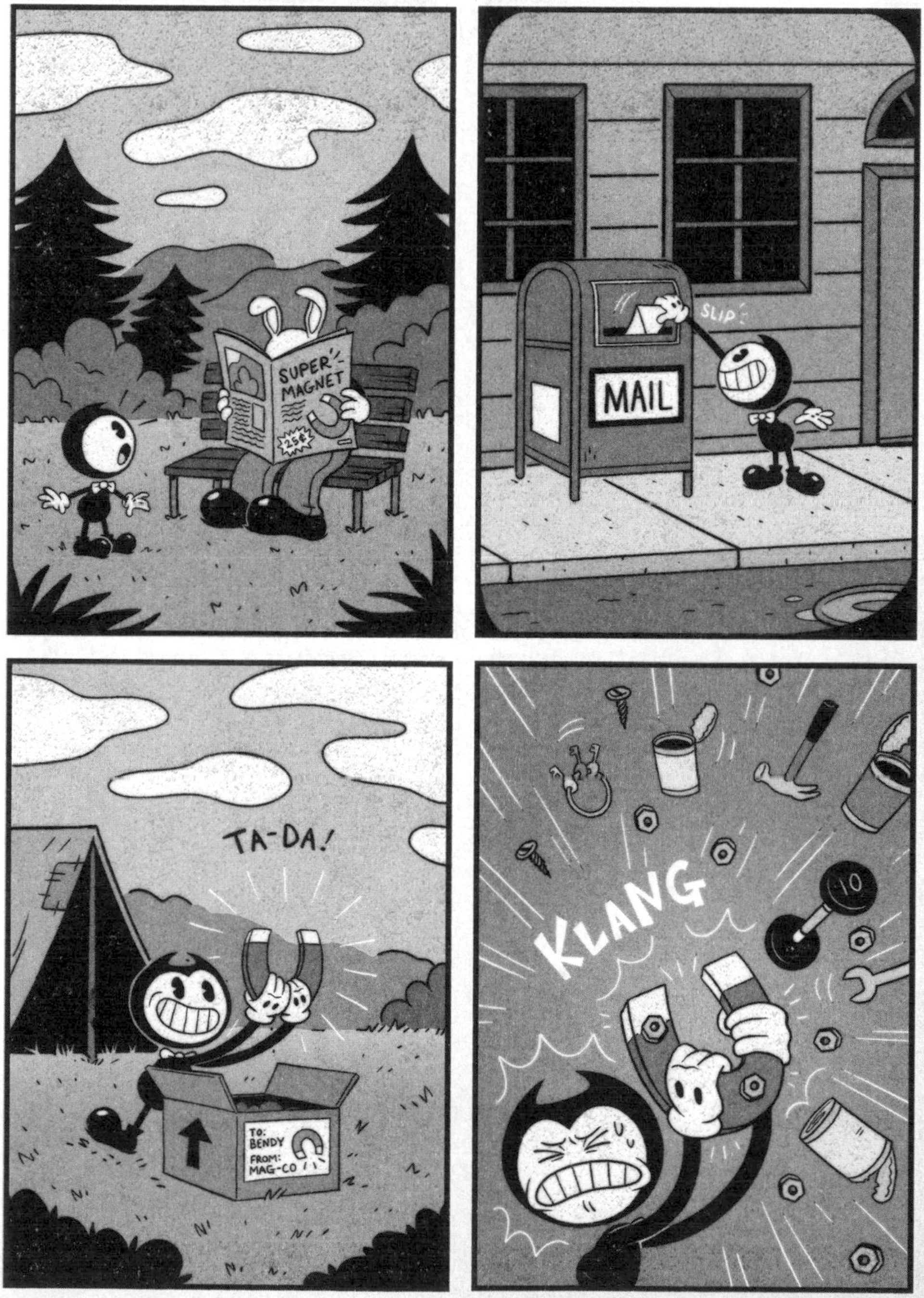
SUPER MAGNET
25¢
MAIL
SLIP
TA-DA!
TO: BENDY
FROM: MAG-CO
KLANG
10

DIME-STORE

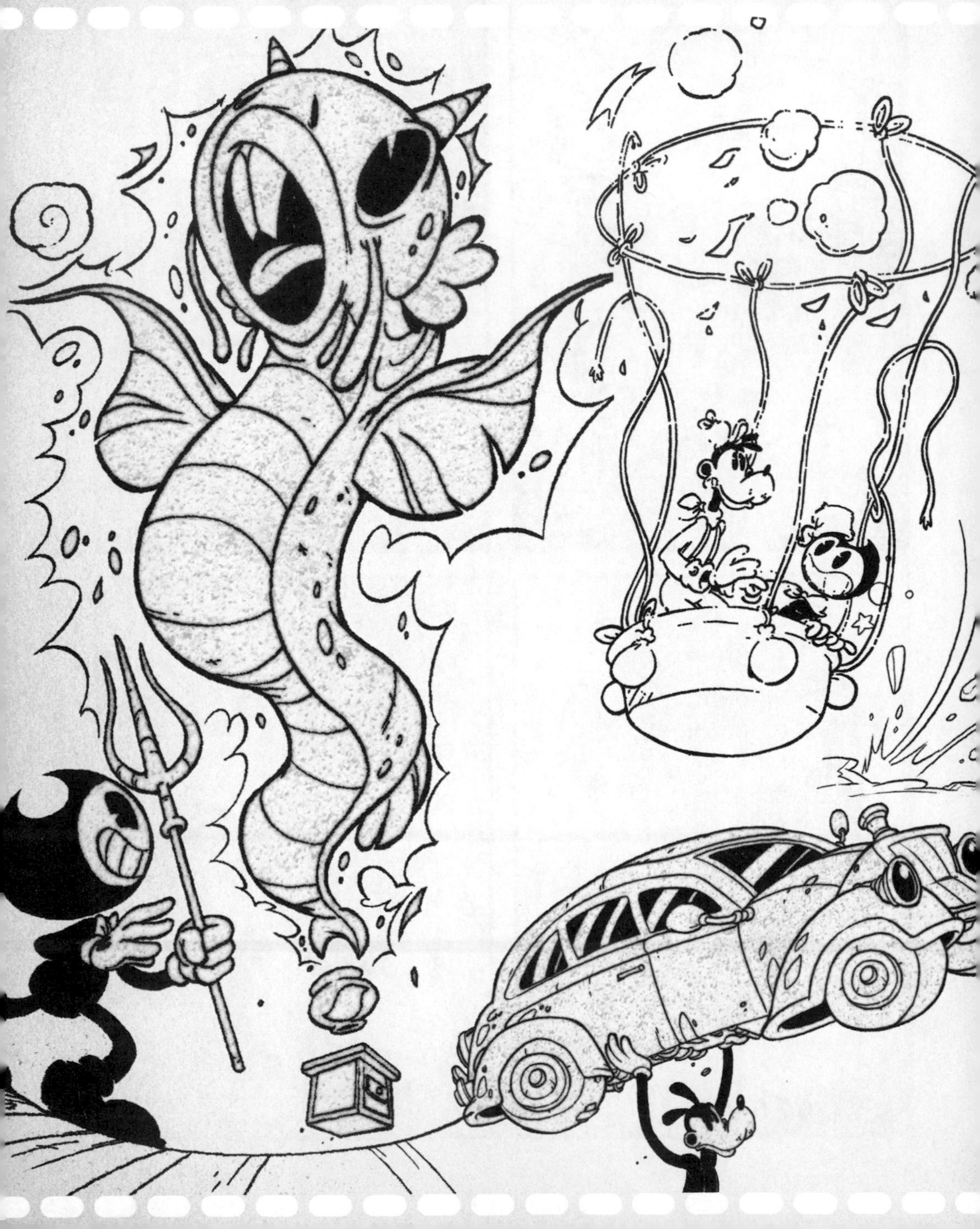

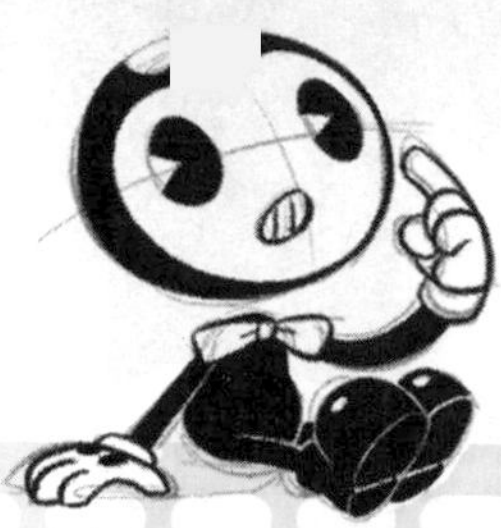

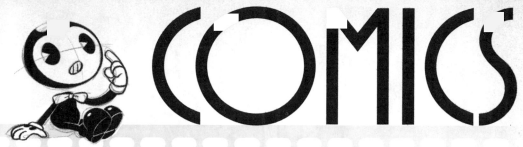

COMICS

1936–1940

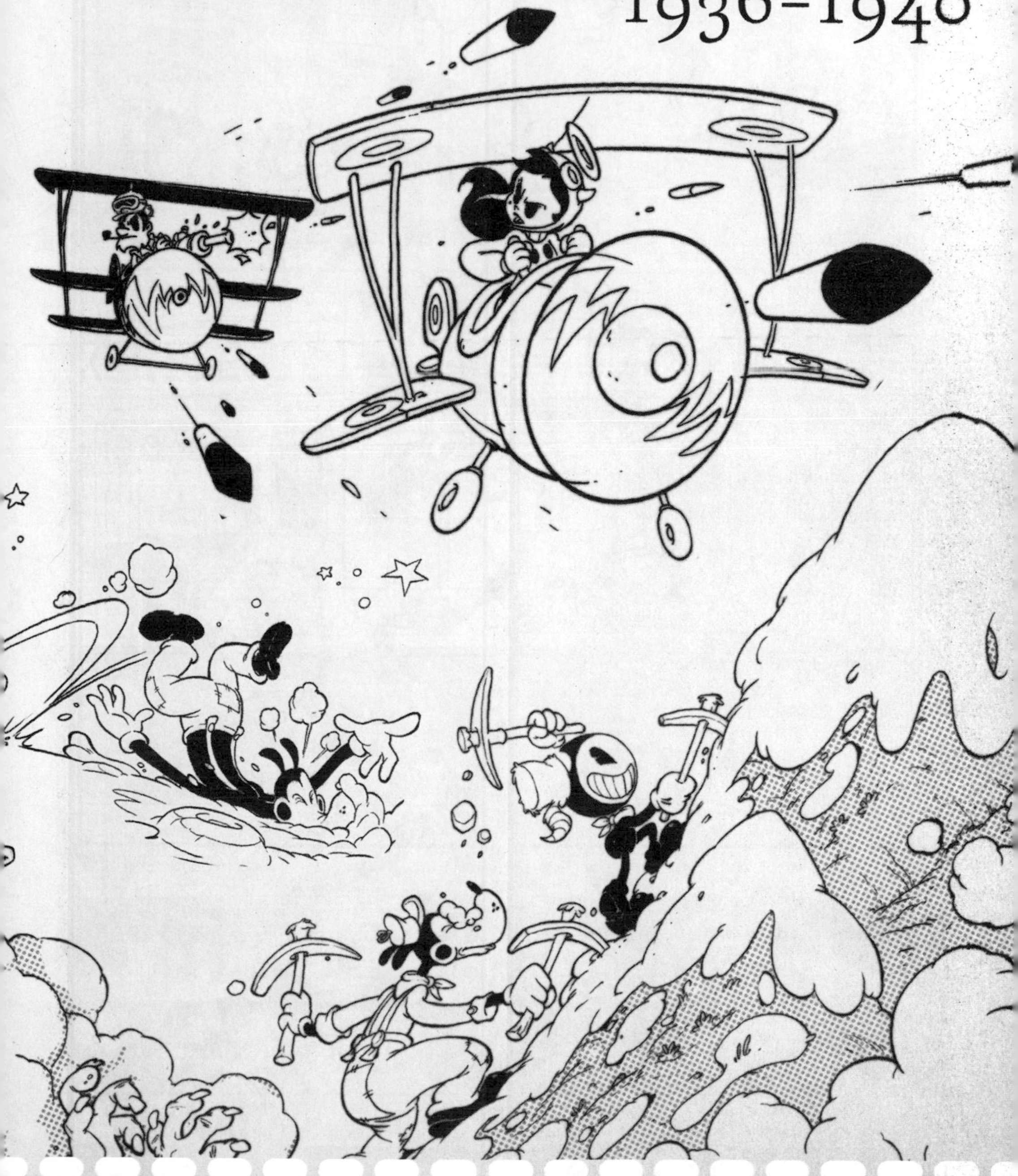

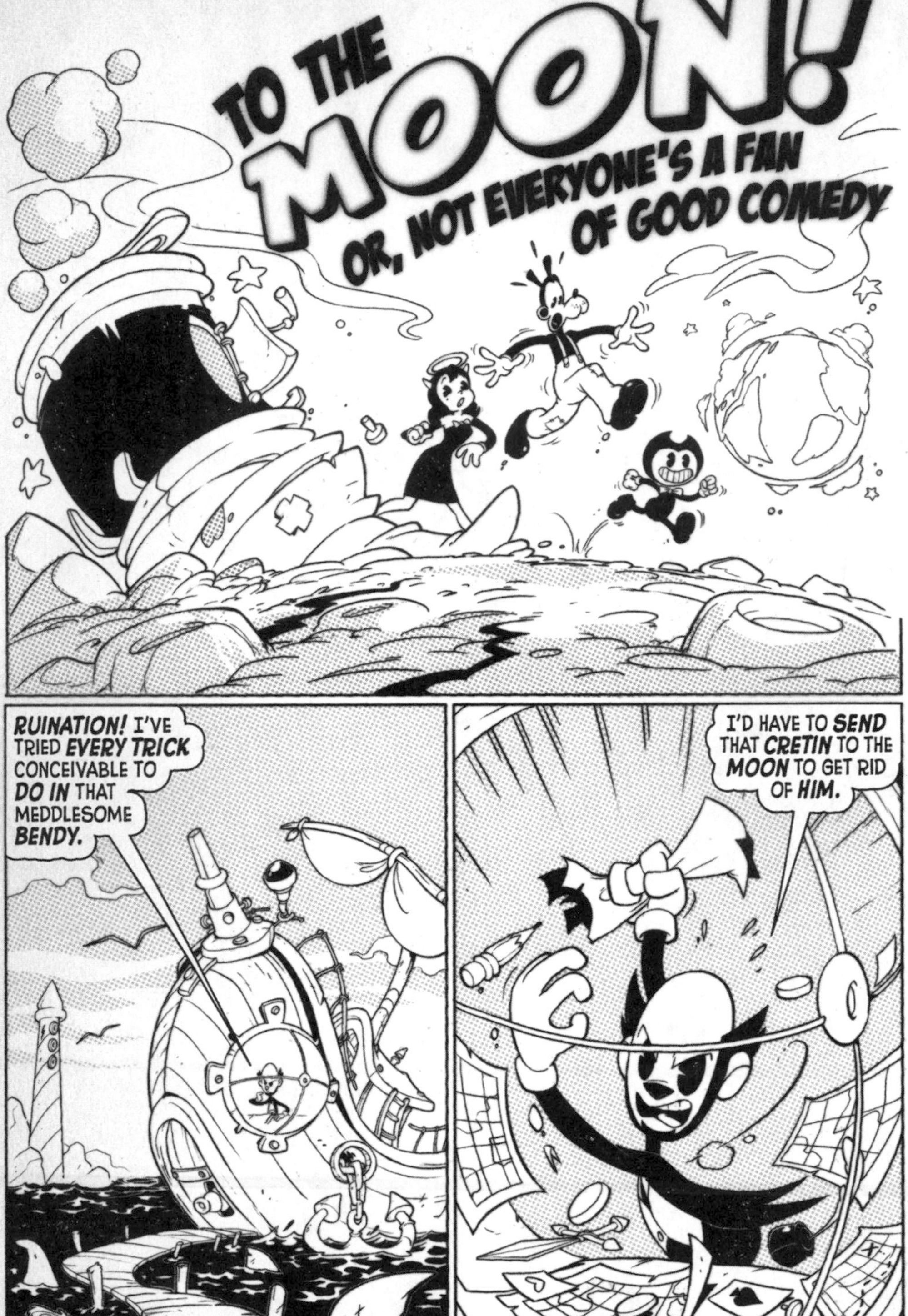
TO THE MOON!
OR, NOT EVERYONE'S A FAN OF GOOD COMEDY
RUINATION! I'VE TRIED EVERY TRICK CONCEIVABLE TO DO IN THAT MEDDLESOME BENDY.
I'D HAVE TO SEND THAT CRETIN TO THE MOON TO GET RID OF HIM.

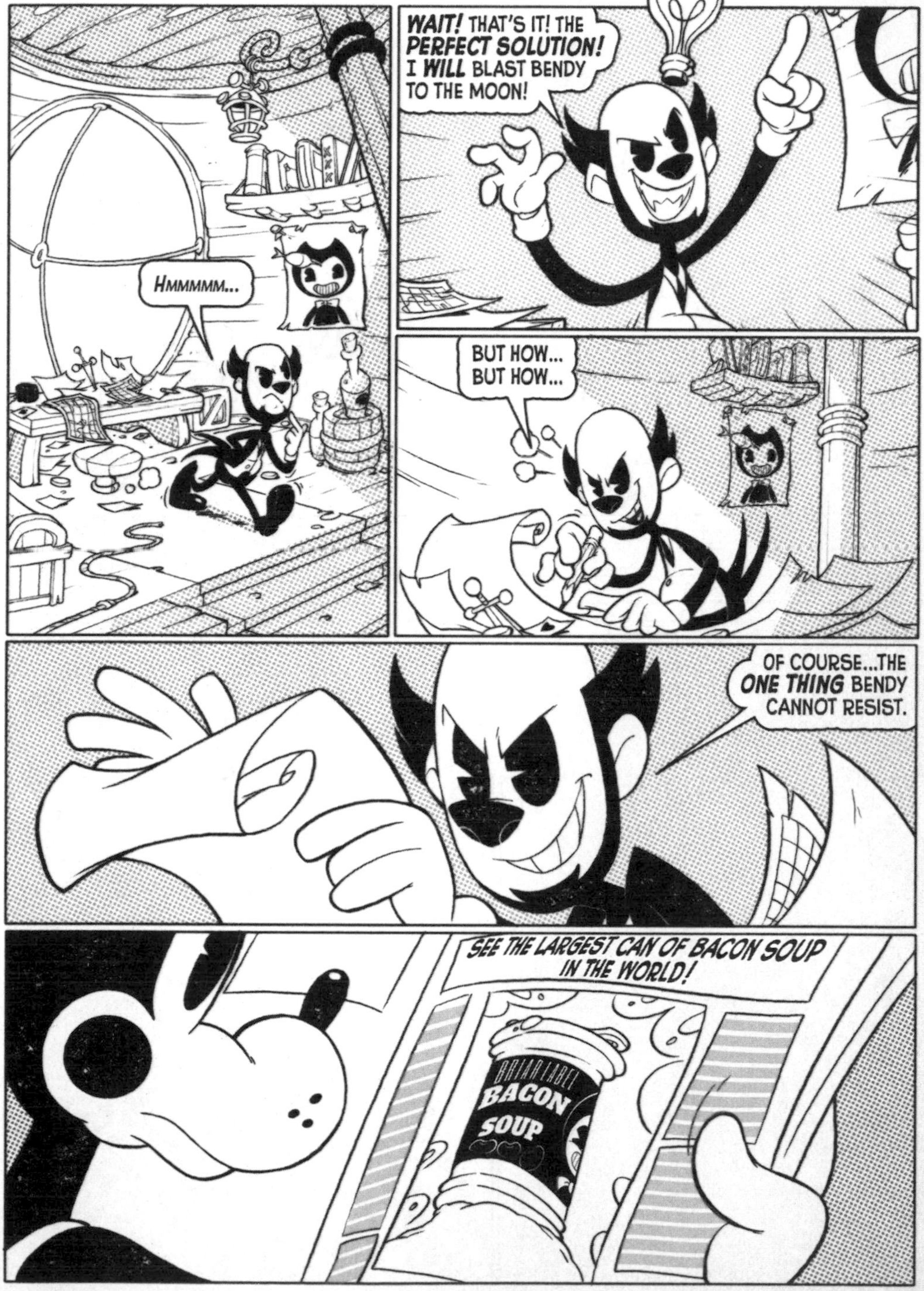
HMMMMM...
WAIT! THAT'S IT! THE PERFECT SOLUTION! I WILL BLAST BENDY TO THE MOON!
BUT HOW... BUT HOW...
OF COURSE...THE ONE THING BENDY CANNOT RESIST.
SEE THE LARGEST CAN OF BACON SOUP IN THE WORLD!
BRIAR LABEL
BACON SOUP

To the Moon! Or, Not Everyone's a Fan of Good Comedy

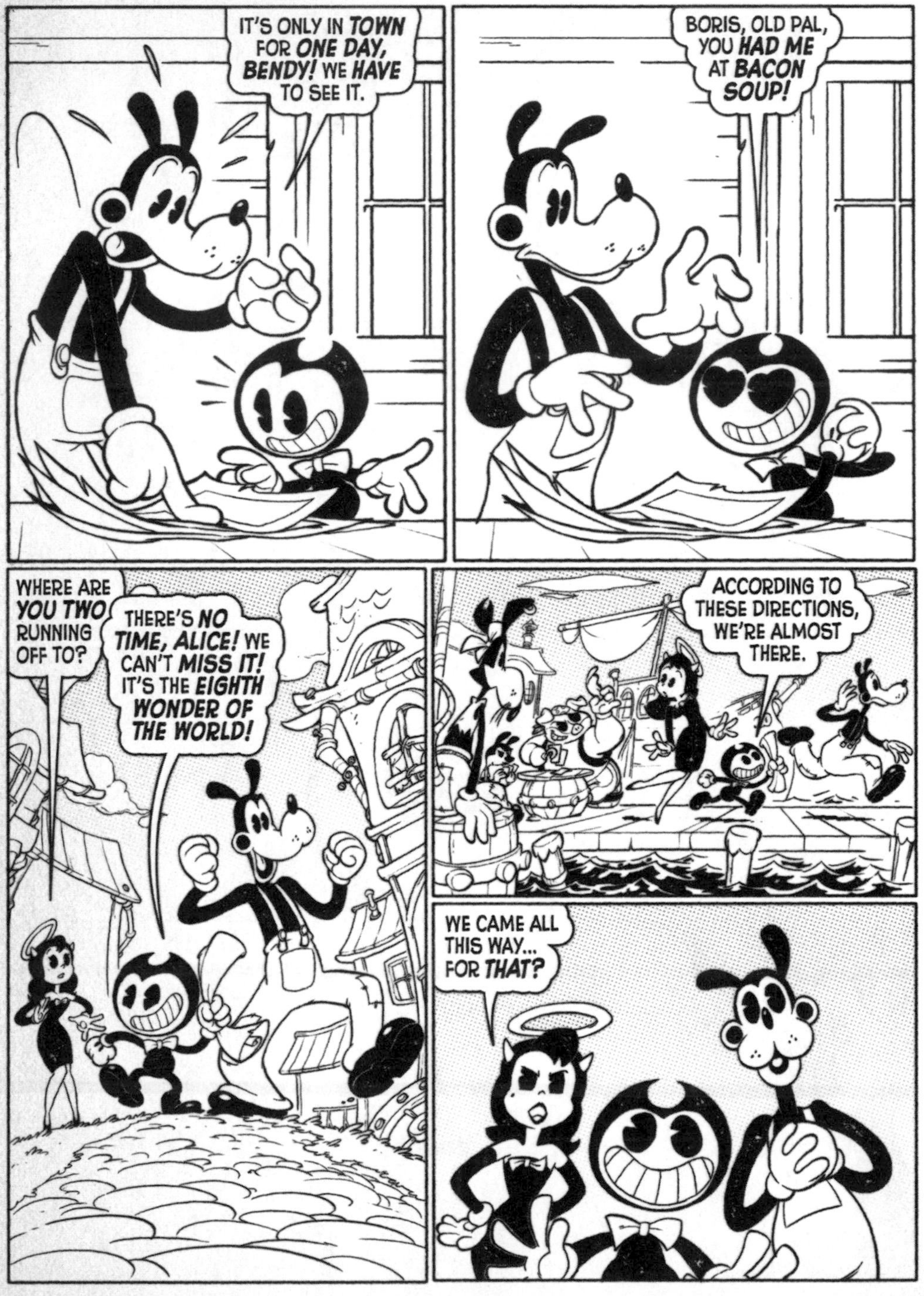
IT'S ONLY IN TOWN FOR ONE DAY, BENDY! WE HAVE TO SEE IT.
BORIS, OLD PAL, YOU HAD ME AT BACON SOUP!
WHERE ARE YOU TWO RUNNING OFF TO?
THERE'S NO TIME, ALICE! WE CAN'T MISS IT! IT'S THE EIGHTH WONDER OF THE WORLD!
ACCORDING TO THESE DIRECTIONS, WE'RE ALMOST THERE.
WE CAME ALL THIS WAY... FOR THAT?

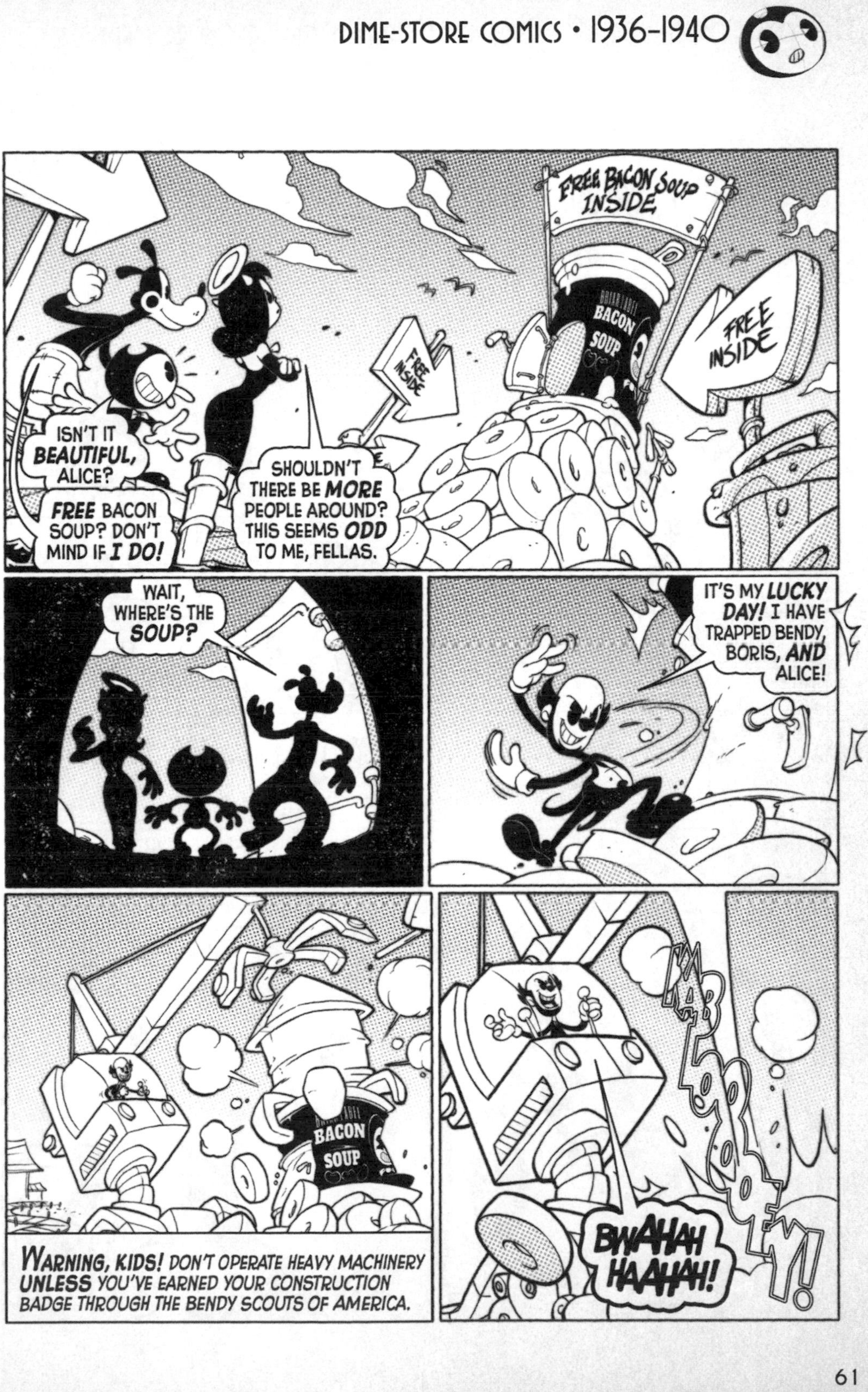
FREE BACON SOUP INSIDE
FREE INSIDE
BACON SOUP
FREE INSIDE
ISN'T IT **BEAUTIFUL**, ALICE?
FREE BACON SOUP? DON'T MIND IF ***I DO!***
SHOULDN'T THERE BE ***MORE*** PEOPLE AROUND? THIS SEEMS ***ODD*** TO ME, FELLAS.
WAIT, WHERE'S THE ***SOUP?***
IT'S MY ***LUCKY DAY!*** I HAVE TRAPPED BENDY, BORIS, ***AND*** ALICE!
BACON SOUP
WARNING, KIDS! *DON'T OPERATE HEAVY MACHINERY* ***UNLESS*** *YOU'VE EARNED YOUR CONSTRUCTION BADGE THROUGH THE BENDY SCOUTS OF AMERICA.*
KABLOOOOEY!
BWAHAH HAAHAH!

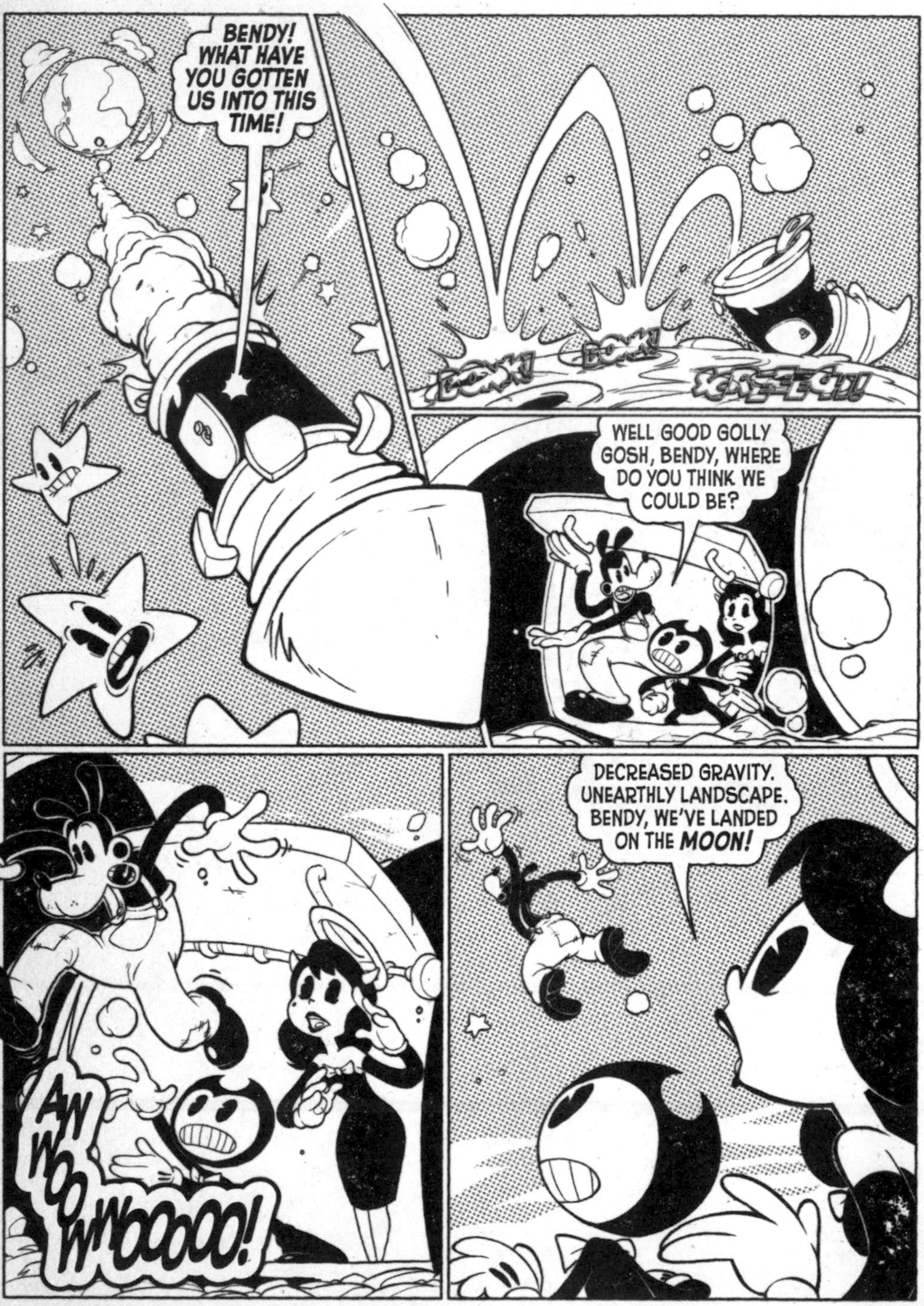
BENDY! WHAT HAVE YOU GOTTEN US INTO THIS TIME!
BONK!
BONK!
WELL GOOD GOLLY GOSH, BENDY, WHERE DO YOU THINK WE COULD BE?
AWWOOWWOOOOO!
DECREASED GRAVITY. UNEARTHLY LANDSCAPE. BENDY, WE'VE LANDED ON THE MOON!

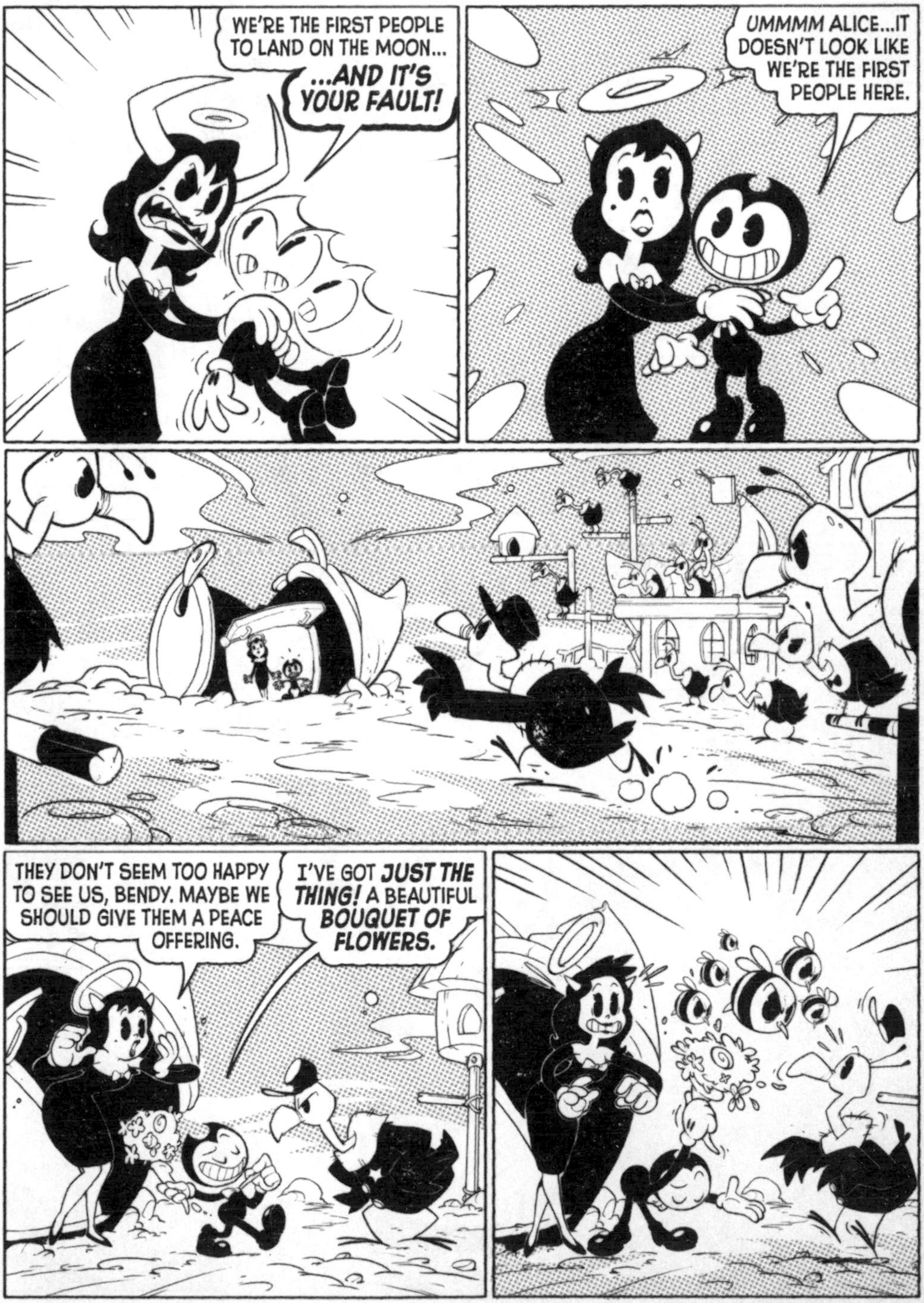
WE'RE THE FIRST PEOPLE TO LAND ON THE MOON...
...AND IT'S YOUR FAULT!
UMMMM ALICE...IT DOESN'T LOOK LIKE WE'RE THE FIRST PEOPLE HERE.
THEY DON'T SEEM TOO HAPPY TO SEE US, BENDY. MAYBE WE SHOULD GIVE THEM A PEACE OFFERING.
I'VE GOT JUST THE THING! A BEAUTIFUL BOUQUET OF FLOWERS.

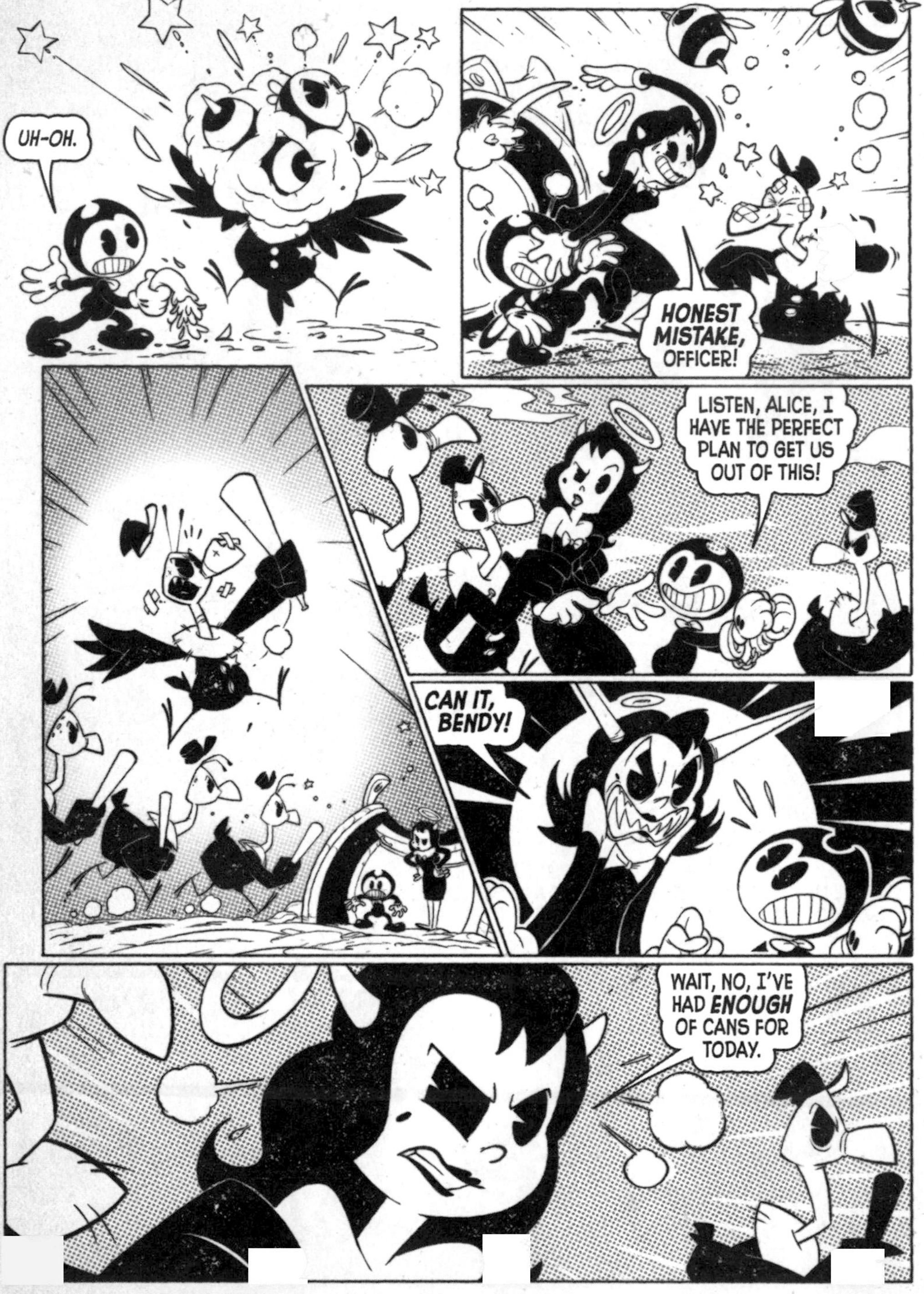
UH-OH.
HONEST MISTAKE, OFFICER!
LISTEN, ALICE, I HAVE THE PERFECT PLAN TO GET US OUT OF THIS!
CAN IT, BENDY!
WAIT, NO, I'VE HAD ENOUGH OF CANS FOR TODAY.

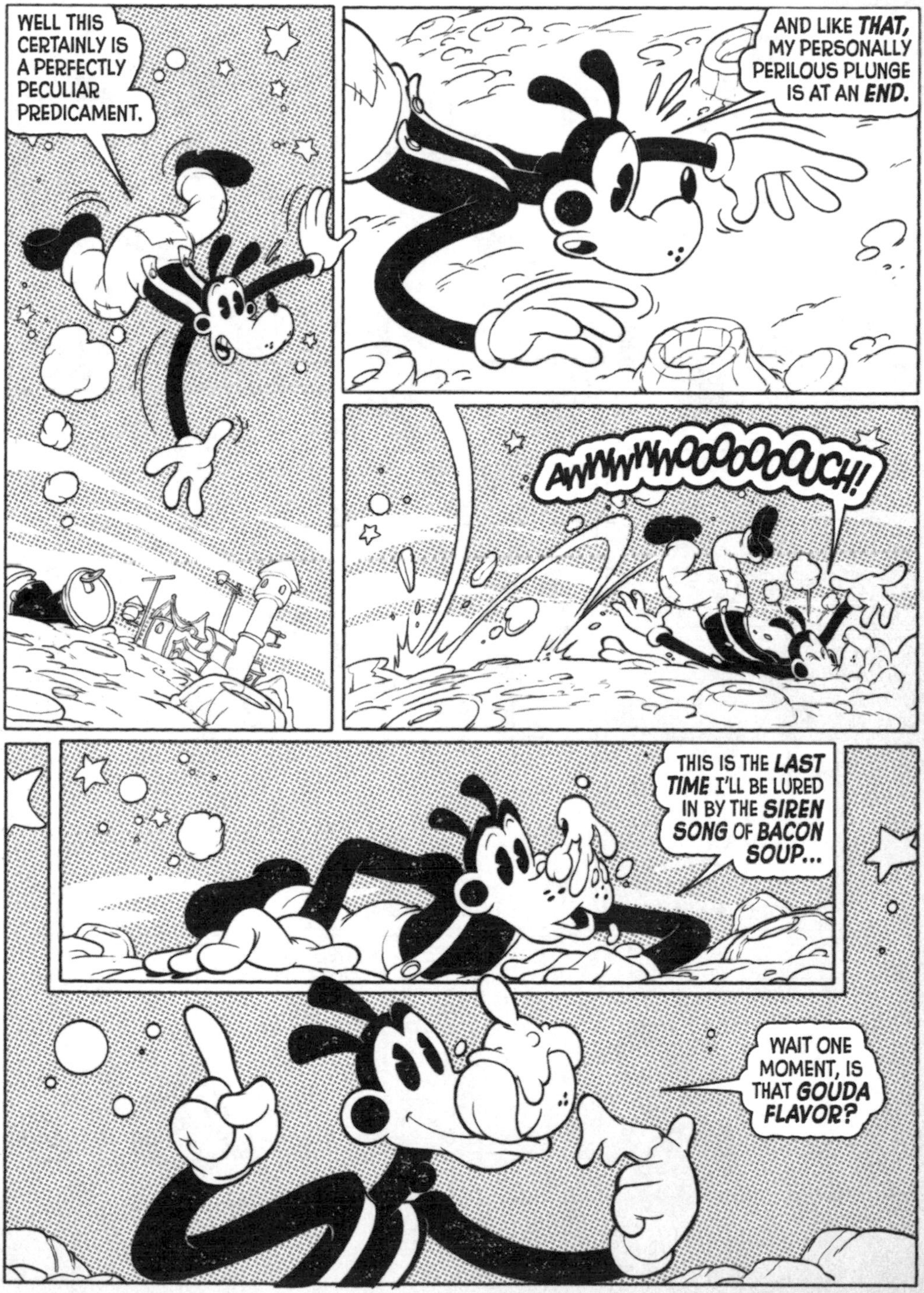
WELL THIS CERTAINLY IS A PERFECTLY PECULIAR PREDICAMENT.
AND LIKE THAT, MY PERSONALLY PERILOUS PLUNGE IS AT AN END.
AWWWWWOOOOOOOUCH!
THIS IS THE LAST TIME I'LL BE LURED IN BY THE SIREN SONG OF BACON SOUP...
WAIT ONE MOMENT, IS THAT GOUDA FLAVOR?

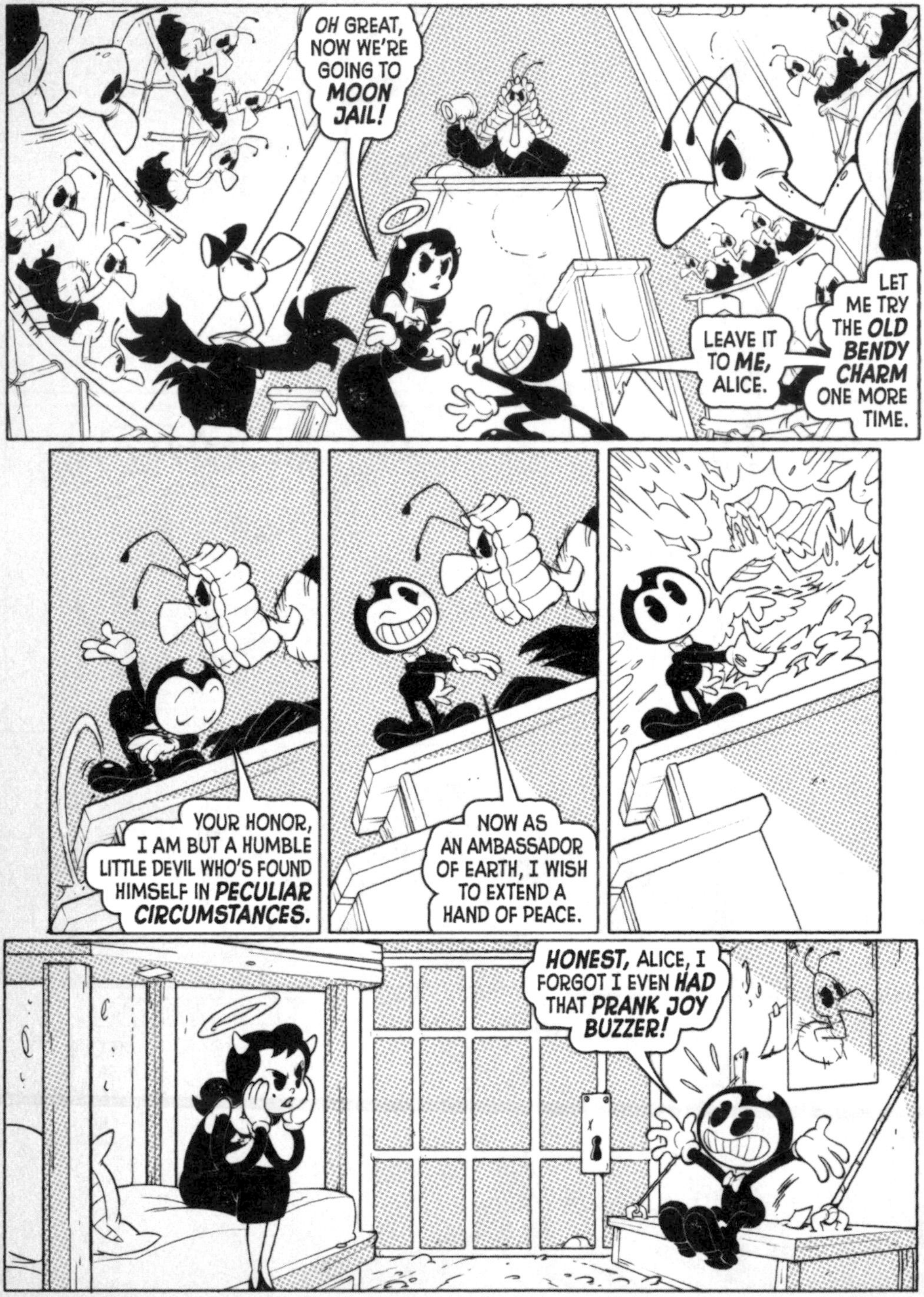
OH GREAT, NOW WE'RE GOING TO MOON JAIL!
LEAVE IT TO ME, ALICE.
LET ME TRY THE OLD BENDY CHARM ONE MORE TIME.
YOUR HONOR, I AM BUT A HUMBLE LITTLE DEVIL WHO'S FOUND HIMSELF IN PECULIAR CIRCUMSTANCES.
NOW AS AN AMBASSADOR OF EARTH, I WISH TO EXTEND A HAND OF PEACE.
HONEST, ALICE, I FORGOT I EVEN HAD THAT PRANK JOY BUZZER!

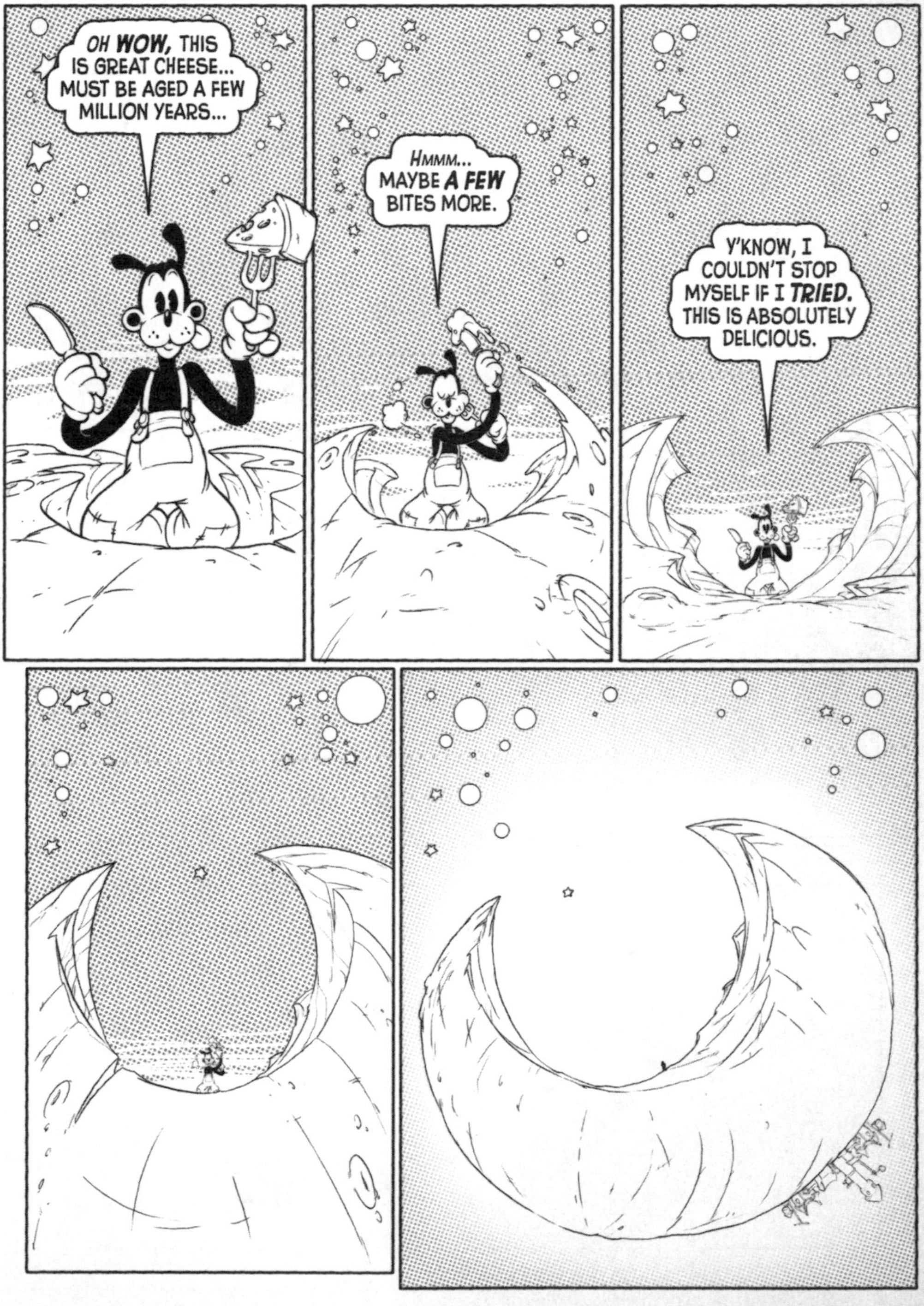
OH WOW, THIS IS GREAT CHEESE... MUST BE AGED A FEW MILLION YEARS...
HMMM... MAYBE A FEW BITES MORE.
Y'KNOW, I COULDN'T STOP MYSELF IF I TRIED. THIS IS ABSOLUTELY DELICIOUS.

To the Moon! Or, Not Everyone's a Fan of Good Comedy

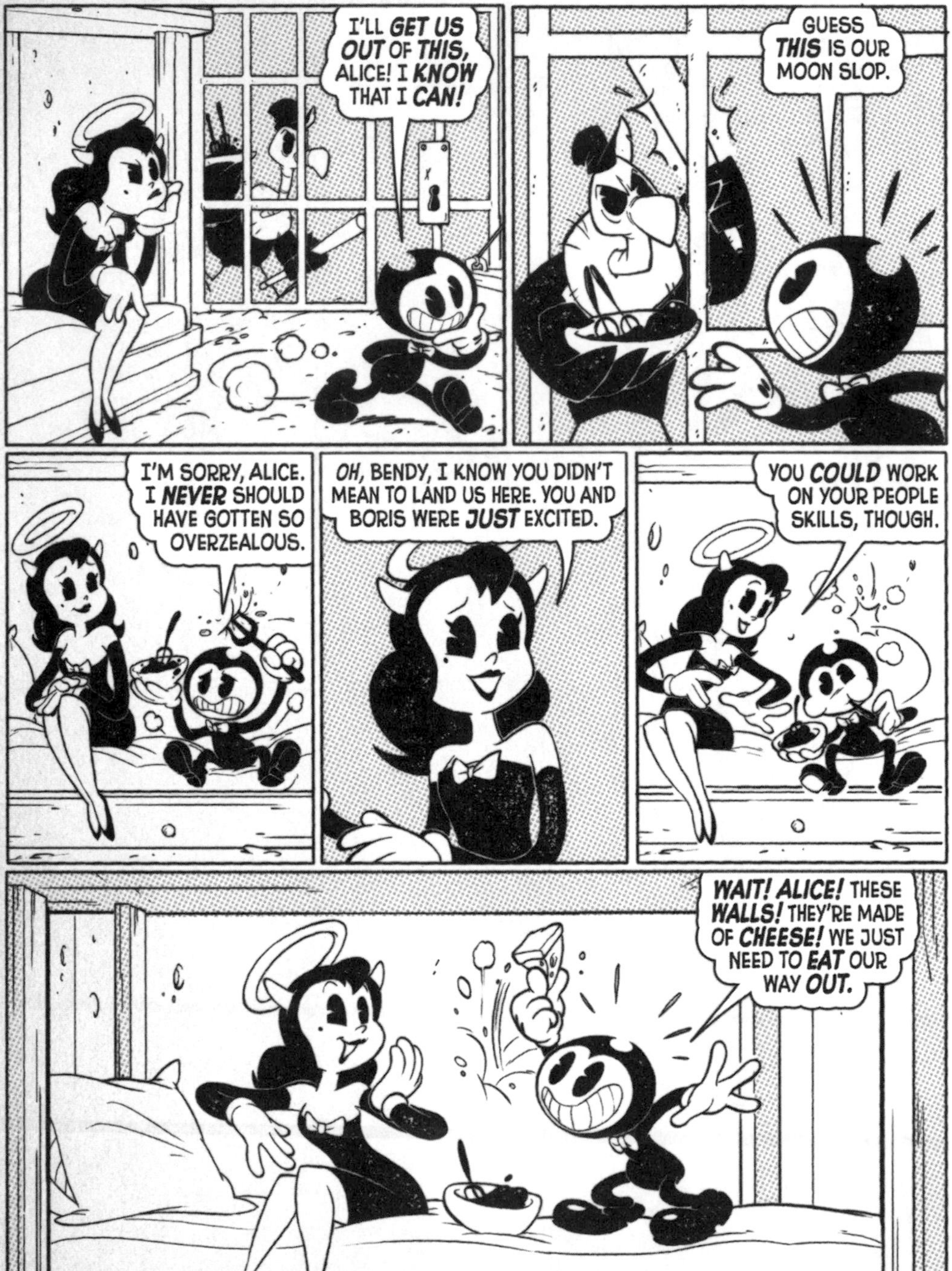

I'LL GET US OUT OF THIS, ALICE! I KNOW THAT I CAN!
GUESS THIS IS OUR MOON SLOP.
I'M SORRY, ALICE. I NEVER SHOULD HAVE GOTTEN SO OVERZEALOUS.
OH, BENDY, I KNOW YOU DIDN'T MEAN TO LAND US HERE. YOU AND BORIS WERE JUST EXCITED.
YOU COULD WORK ON YOUR PEOPLE SKILLS, THOUGH.
WAIT! ALICE! THESE WALLS! THEY'RE MADE OF CHEESE! WE JUST NEED TO EAT OUR WAY OUT.

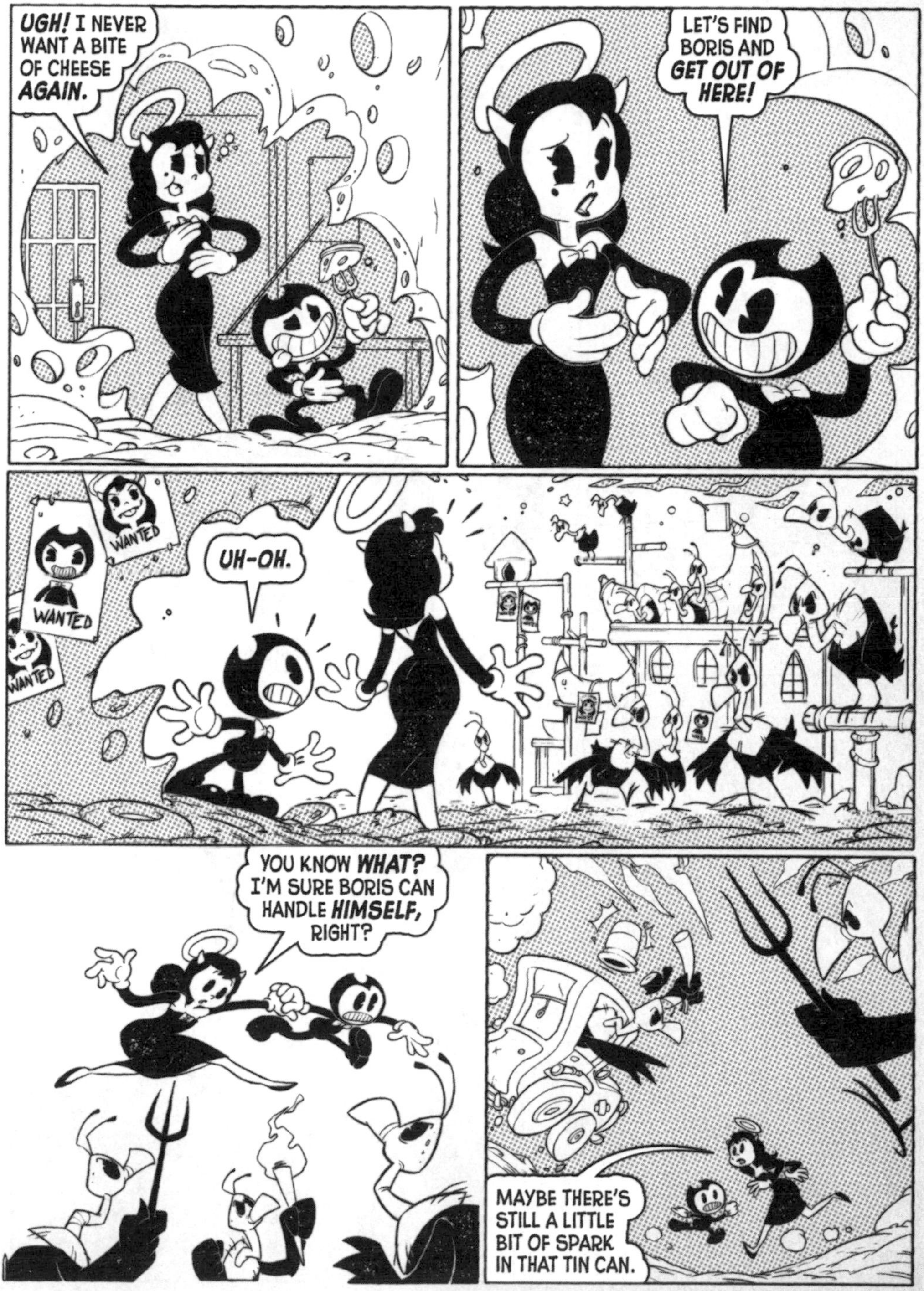
UGH! I NEVER WANT A BITE OF CHEESE AGAIN.
LET'S FIND BORIS AND GET OUT OF HERE!
WANTED
WANTED
WANTED
UH-OH.
YOU KNOW WHAT? I'M SURE BORIS CAN HANDLE HIMSELF, RIGHT?
MAYBE THERE'S STILL A LITTLE BIT OF SPARK IN THAT TIN CAN.

To the Moon! Or, Not Everyone's a Fan of Good Comedy

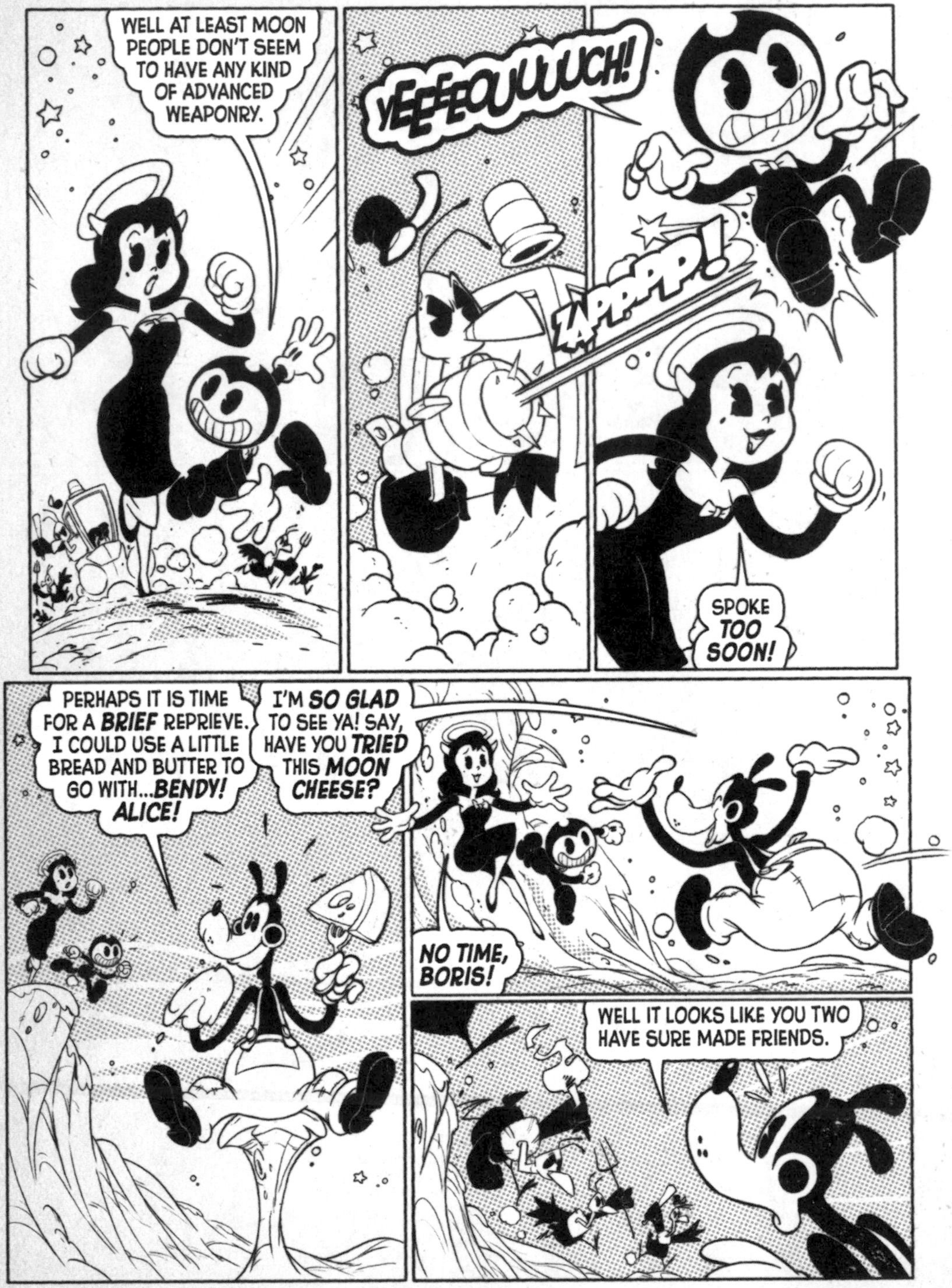
WELL AT LEAST MOON PEOPLE DON'T SEEM TO HAVE ANY KIND OF ADVANCED WEAPONRY.
YEEEEOUUUCH!
ZAPPPPP!
SPOKE TOO SOON!
PERHAPS IT IS TIME FOR A BRIEF REPRIEVE. I COULD USE A LITTLE BREAD AND BUTTER TO GO WITH...BENDY! ALICE!
I'M SO GLAD TO SEE YA! SAY, HAVE YOU TRIED THIS MOON CHEESE?
NO TIME, BORIS!
WELL IT LOOKS LIKE YOU TWO HAVE SURE MADE FRIENDS.

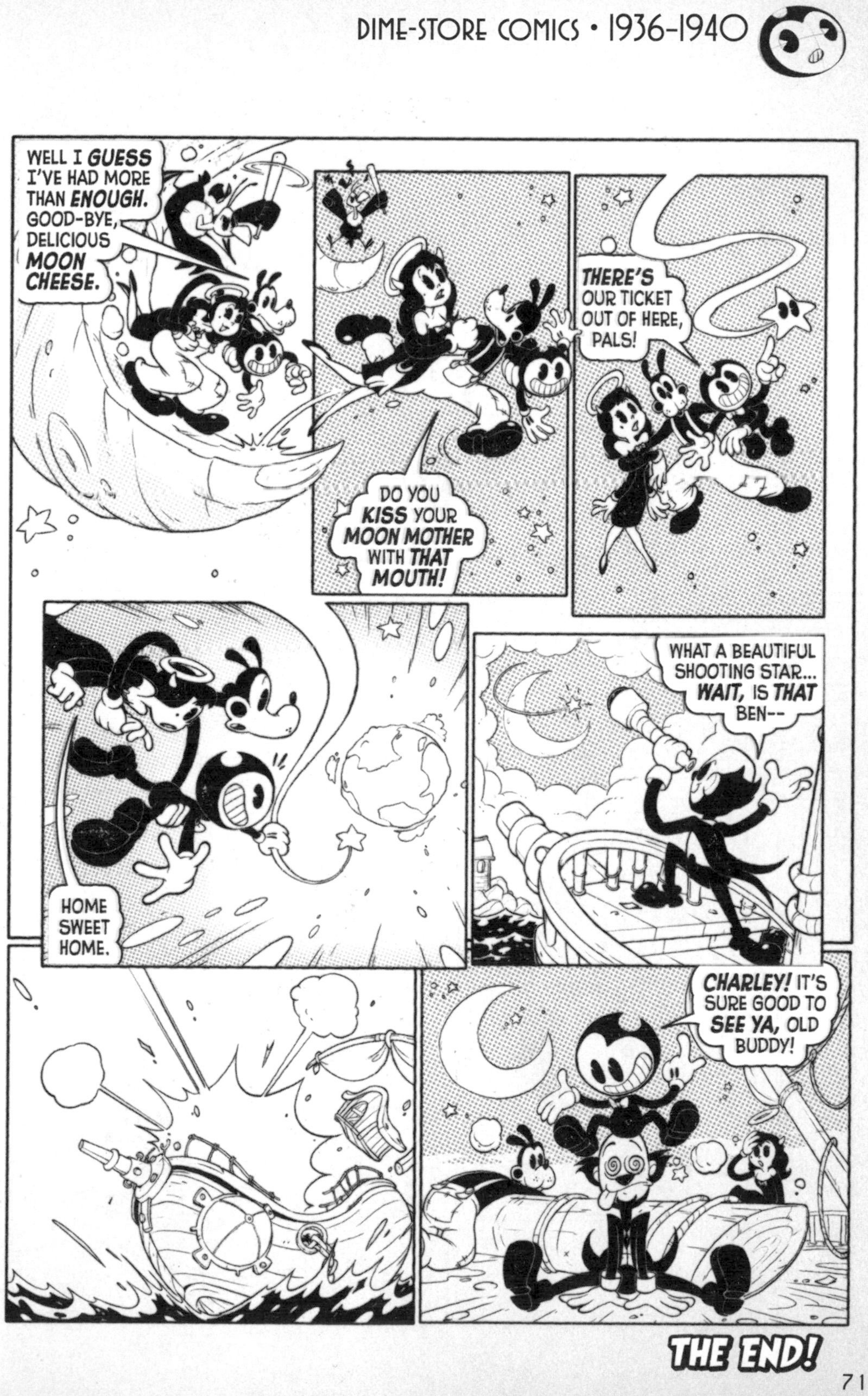
WELL I GUESS I'VE HAD MORE THAN ENOUGH. GOOD-BYE, DELICIOUS MOON CHEESE.
DO YOU KISS YOUR MOON MOTHER WITH THAT MOUTH!
THERE'S OUR TICKET OUT OF HERE, PALS!
HOME SWEET HOME.
WHAT A BEAUTIFUL SHOOTING STAR... WAIT, IS THAT BEN--
CHARLEY! IT'S SURE GOOD TO SEE YA, OLD BUDDY!

THE END!

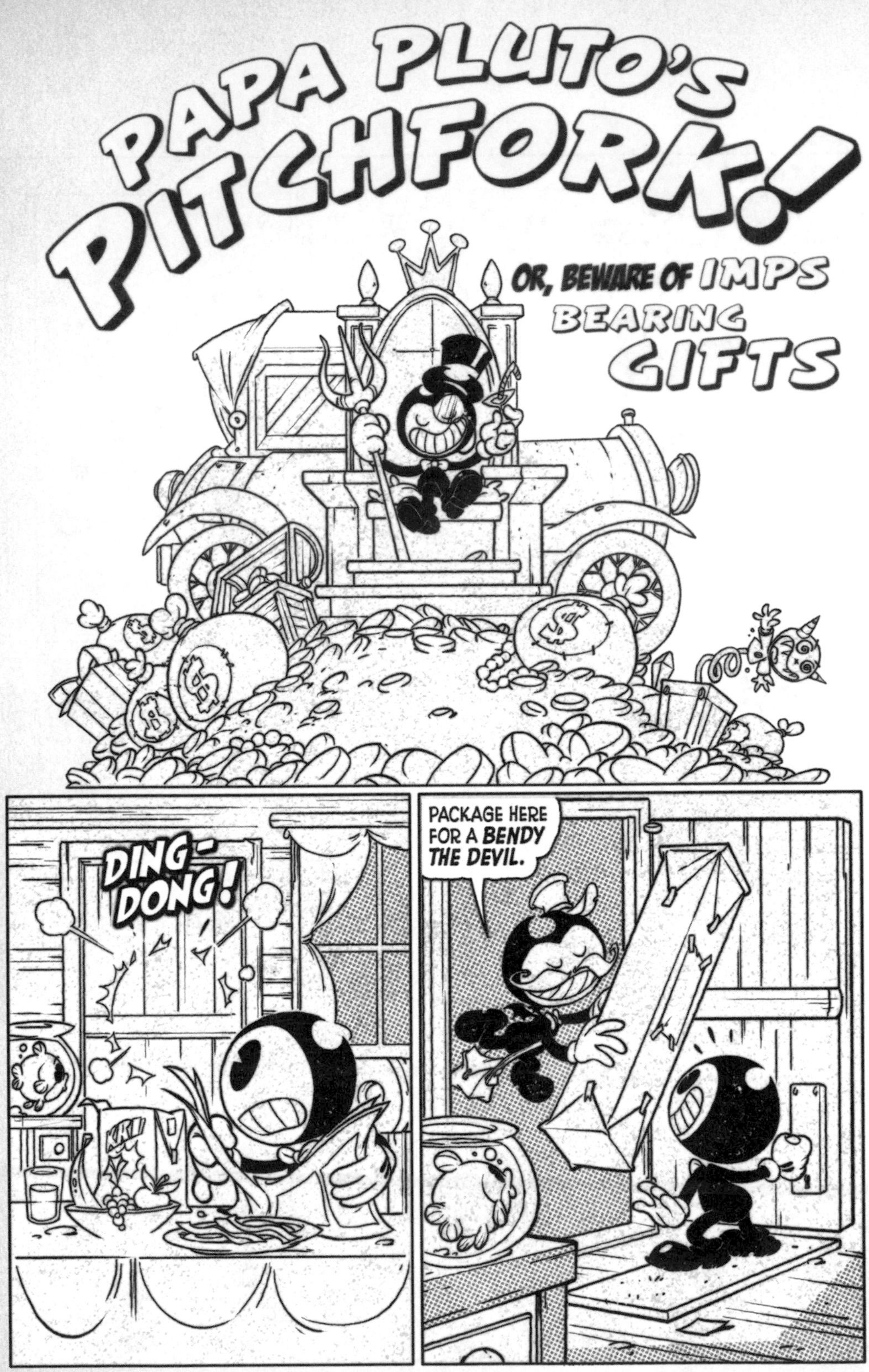
PAPA PLUTO'S PITCHFORK!
OR, BEWARE OF IMPS BEARING GIFTS
DING-DONG!
PACKAGE HERE FOR A BENDY THE DEVIL.

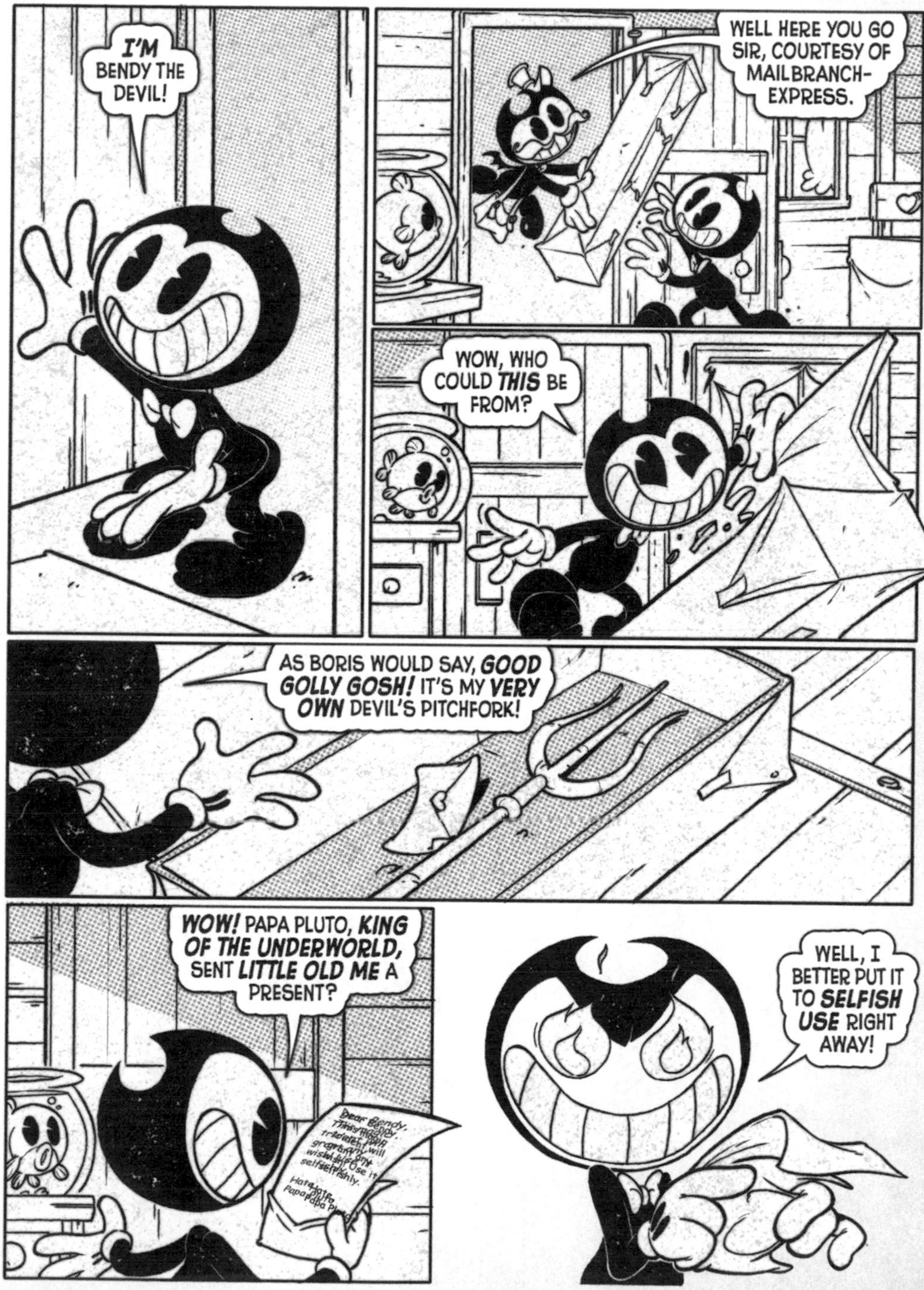
I'M BENDY THE DEVIL!
WELL HERE YOU GO SIR, COURTESY OF MAILBRANCH-EXPRESS.
WOW, WHO COULD THIS BE FROM?
AS BORIS WOULD SAY, GOOD GOLLY GOSH! IT'S MY VERY OWN DEVIL'S PITCHFORK!
WOW! PAPA PLUTO, KING OF THE UNDERWORLD, SENT LITTLE OLD ME A PRESENT?
WELL, I BETTER PUT IT TO SELFISH USE RIGHT AWAY!

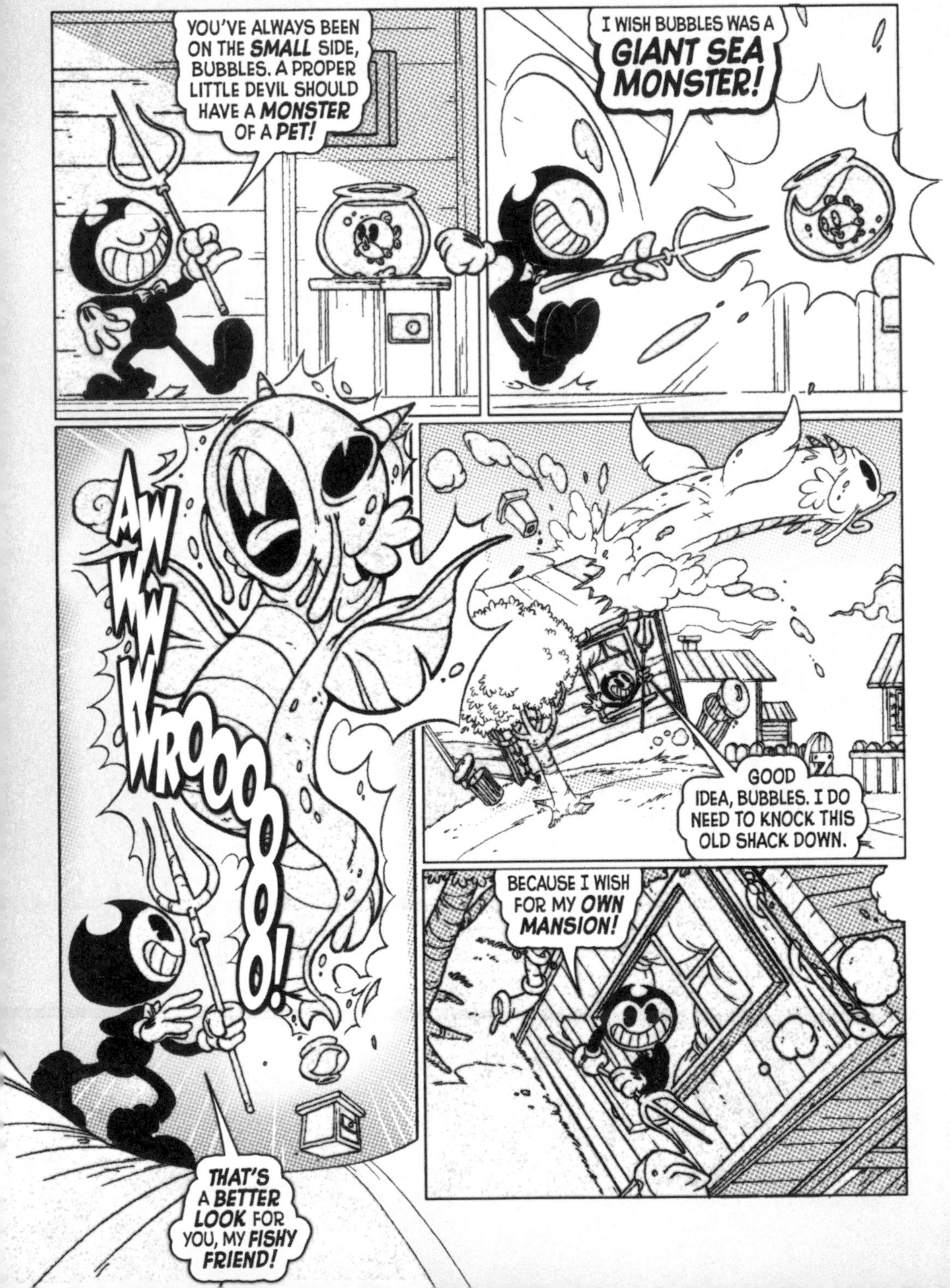
YOU'VE ALWAYS BEEN ON THE SMALL SIDE, BUBBLES. A PROPER LITTLE DEVIL SHOULD HAVE A MONSTER OF A PET!
I WISH BUBBLES WAS A GIANT SEA MONSTER!
AWWWWWWROOOOOOOOO8!
THAT'S A BETTER LOOK FOR YOU, MY FISHY FRIEND!
GOOD IDEA, BUBBLES. I DO NEED TO KNOCK THIS OLD SHACK DOWN.
BECAUSE I WISH FOR MY OWN MANSION!

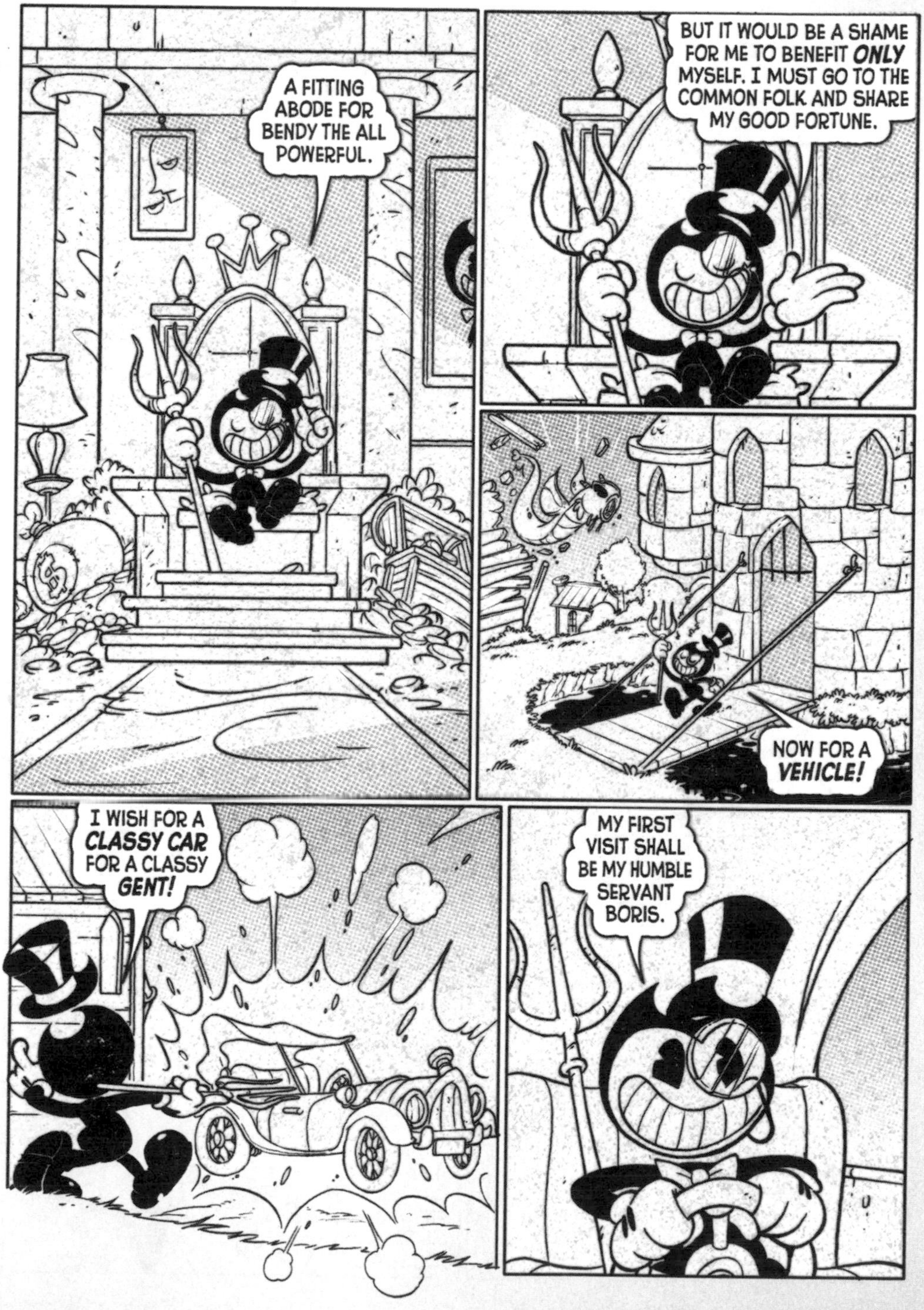
A FITTING ABODE FOR BENDY THE ALL POWERFUL.
BUT IT WOULD BE A SHAME FOR ME TO BENEFIT ONLY MYSELF. I MUST GO TO THE COMMON FOLK AND SHARE MY GOOD FORTUNE.
NOW FOR A VEHICLE!
I WISH FOR A CLASSY CAR FOR A CLASSY GENT!
MY FIRST VISIT SHALL BE MY HUMBLE SERVANT BORIS.

Papa Pluto's Pitchfork! Or, Beware of Imps Bearing Gifts

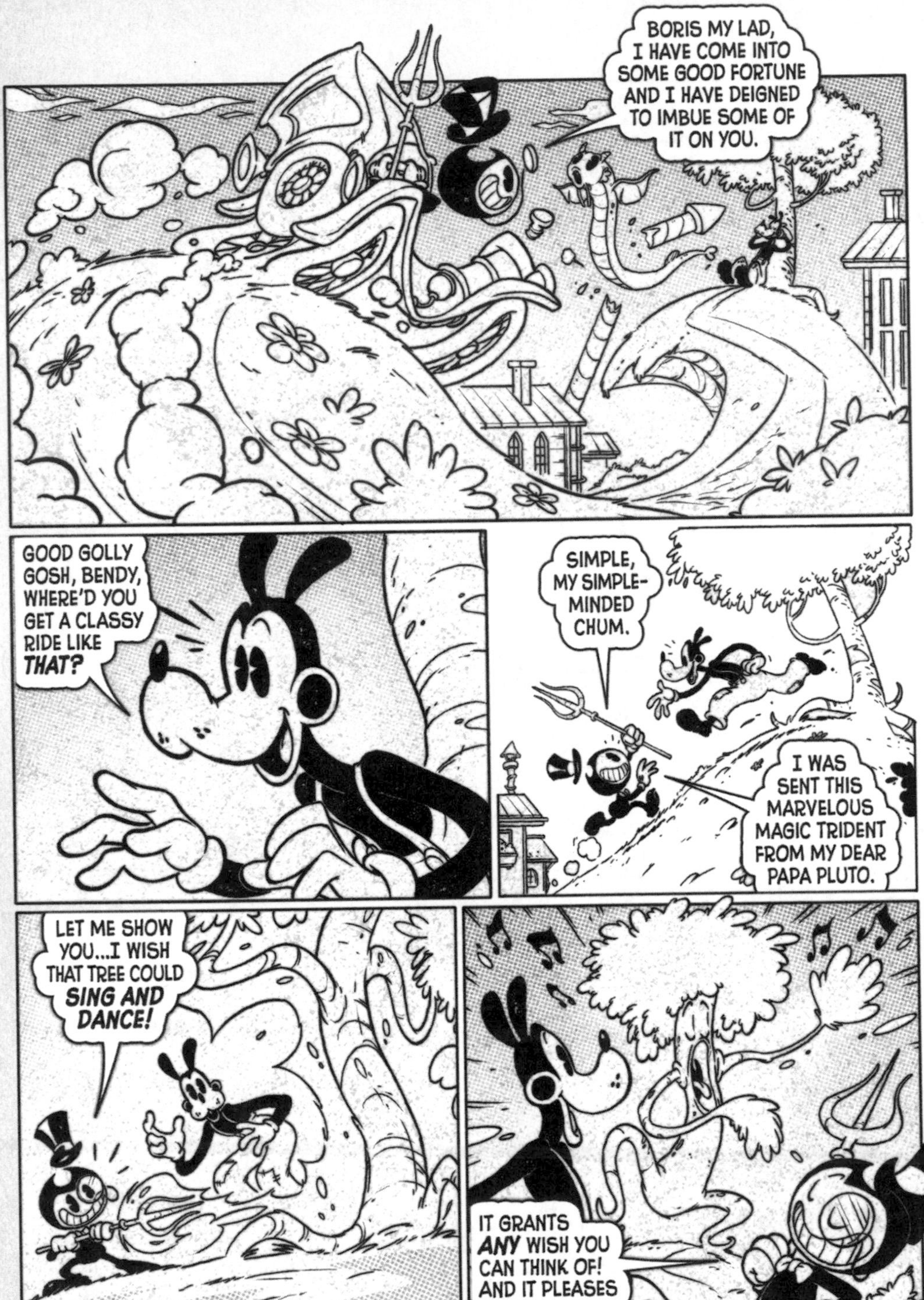
BORIS MY LAD, I HAVE COME INTO SOME GOOD FORTUNE AND I HAVE DEIGNED TO IMBUE SOME OF IT ON YOU.
GOOD GOLLY GOSH, BENDY, WHERE'D YOU GET A CLASSY RIDE LIKE *THAT?*
SIMPLE, MY SIMPLE-MINDED CHUM.
I WAS SENT THIS MARVELOUS MAGIC TRIDENT FROM MY DEAR PAPA PLUTO.
LET ME SHOW YOU...I WISH THAT TREE COULD *SING AND DANCE!*
IT GRANTS *ANY* WISH YOU CAN THINK OF! AND IT PLEASES ME TO BLESS YOU WITH ONE.

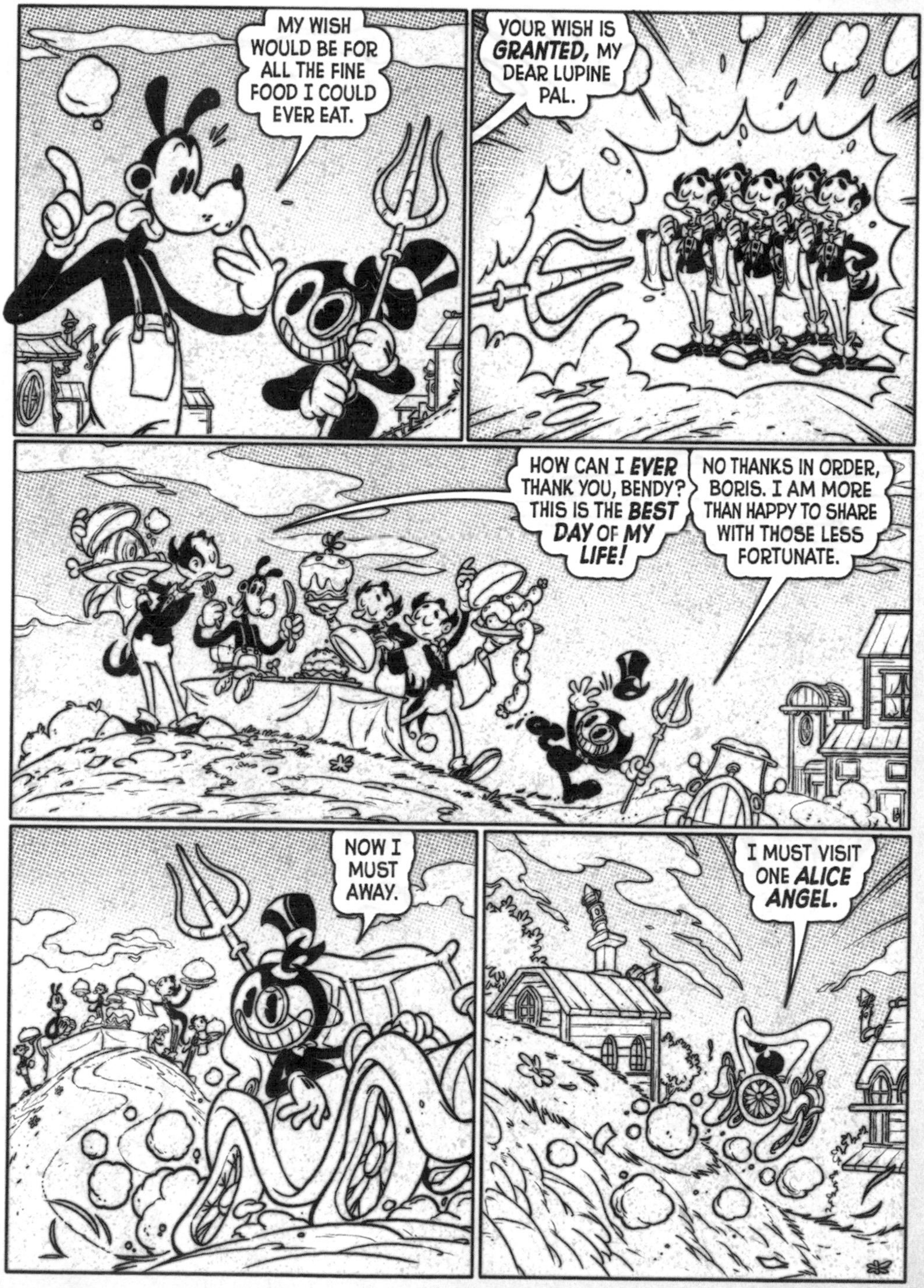
MY WISH WOULD BE FOR ALL THE FINE FOOD I COULD EVER EAT.
YOUR WISH IS GRANTED, MY DEAR LUPINE PAL.
HOW CAN I EVER THANK YOU, BENDY? THIS IS THE BEST DAY OF MY LIFE!
NO THANKS IN ORDER, BORIS. I AM MORE THAN HAPPY TO SHARE WITH THOSE LESS FORTUNATE.
NOW I MUST AWAY.
I MUST VISIT ONE ALICE ANGEL.

Papa Pluto's Pitchfork! Or, Beware of Imps Bearing Gifts

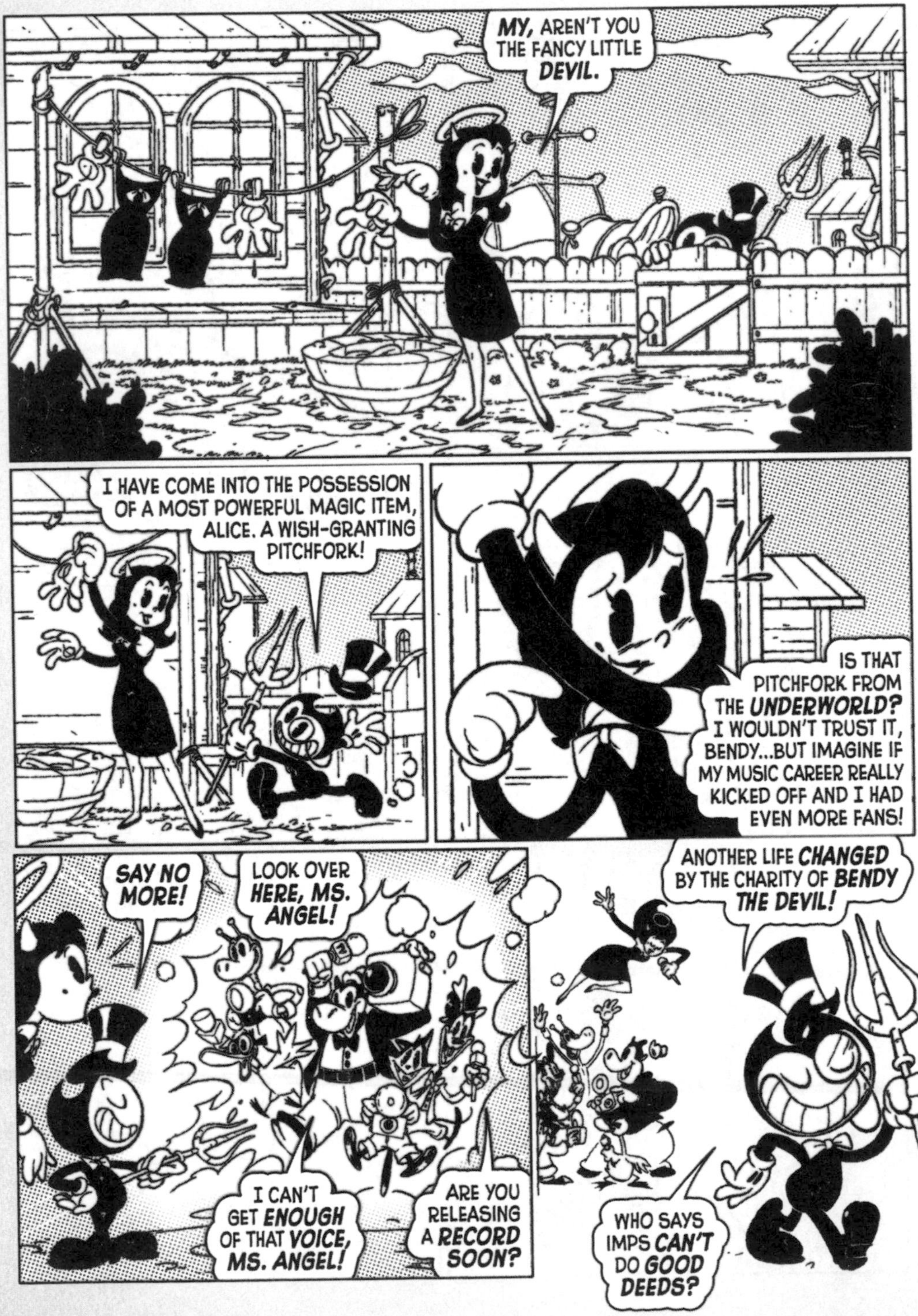
MY, AREN'T YOU THE FANCY LITTLE DEVIL.
I HAVE COME INTO THE POSSESSION OF A MOST POWERFUL MAGIC ITEM, ALICE. A WISH-GRANTING PITCHFORK!
IS THAT PITCHFORK FROM THE UNDERWORLD? I WOULDN'T TRUST IT, BENDY...BUT IMAGINE IF MY MUSIC CAREER REALLY KICKED OFF AND I HAD EVEN MORE FANS!
SAY NO MORE!
LOOK OVER HERE, MS. ANGEL!
I CAN'T GET ENOUGH OF THAT VOICE, MS. ANGEL!
ARE YOU RELEASING A RECORD SOON?
ANOTHER LIFE CHANGED BY THE CHARITY OF BENDY THE DEVIL!
WHO SAYS IMPS CAN'T DO GOOD DEEDS?

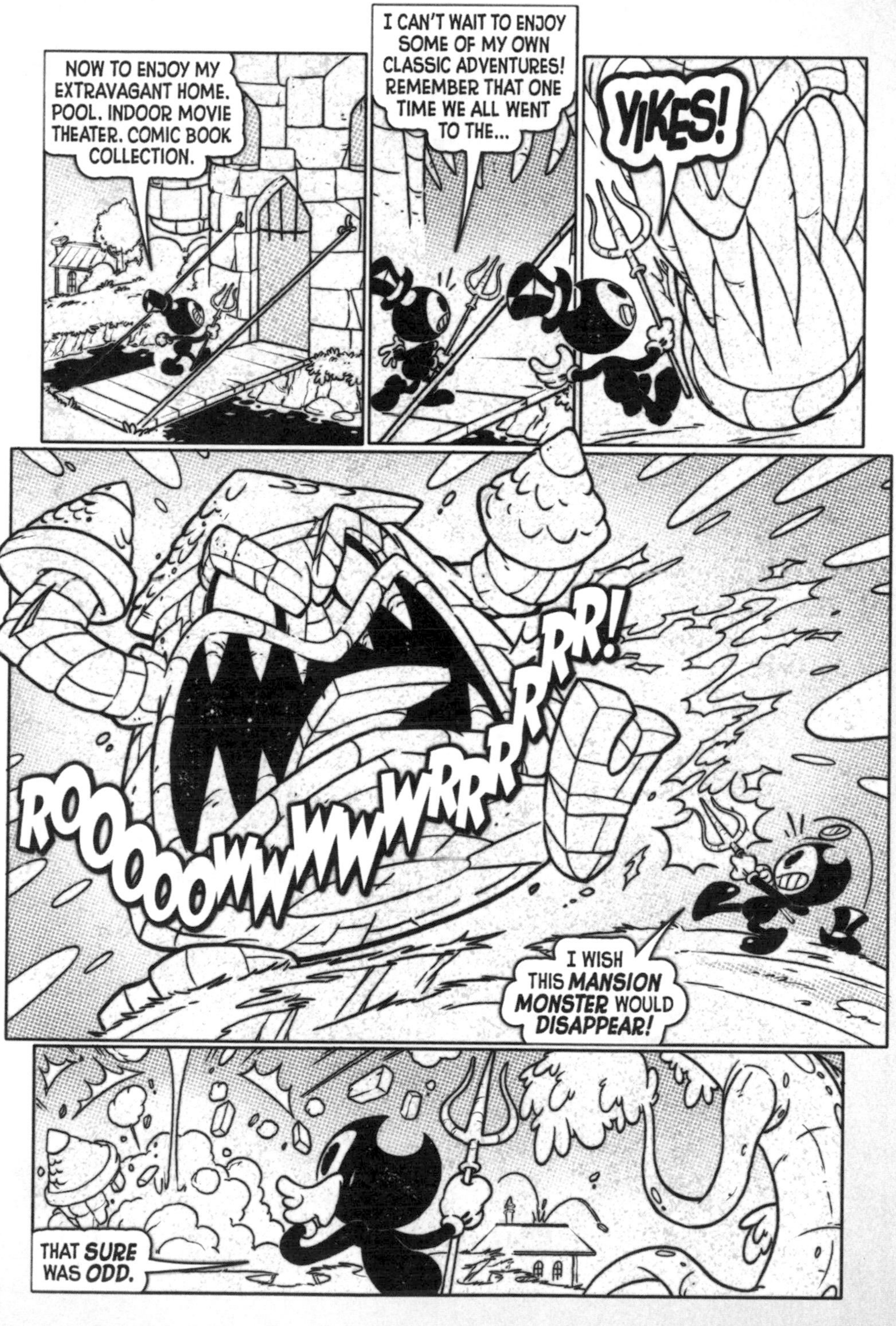
NOW TO ENJOY MY EXTRAVAGANT HOME. POOL. INDOOR MOVIE THEATER. COMIC BOOK COLLECTION.
I CAN'T WAIT TO ENJOY SOME OF MY OWN CLASSIC ADVENTURES! REMEMBER THAT ONE TIME WE ALL WENT TO THE...
YIKES!
ROOOOOOWWWWWRRRRRRRRR!
I WISH THIS MANSION MONSTER WOULD DISAPPEAR!
THAT SURE WAS ODD.

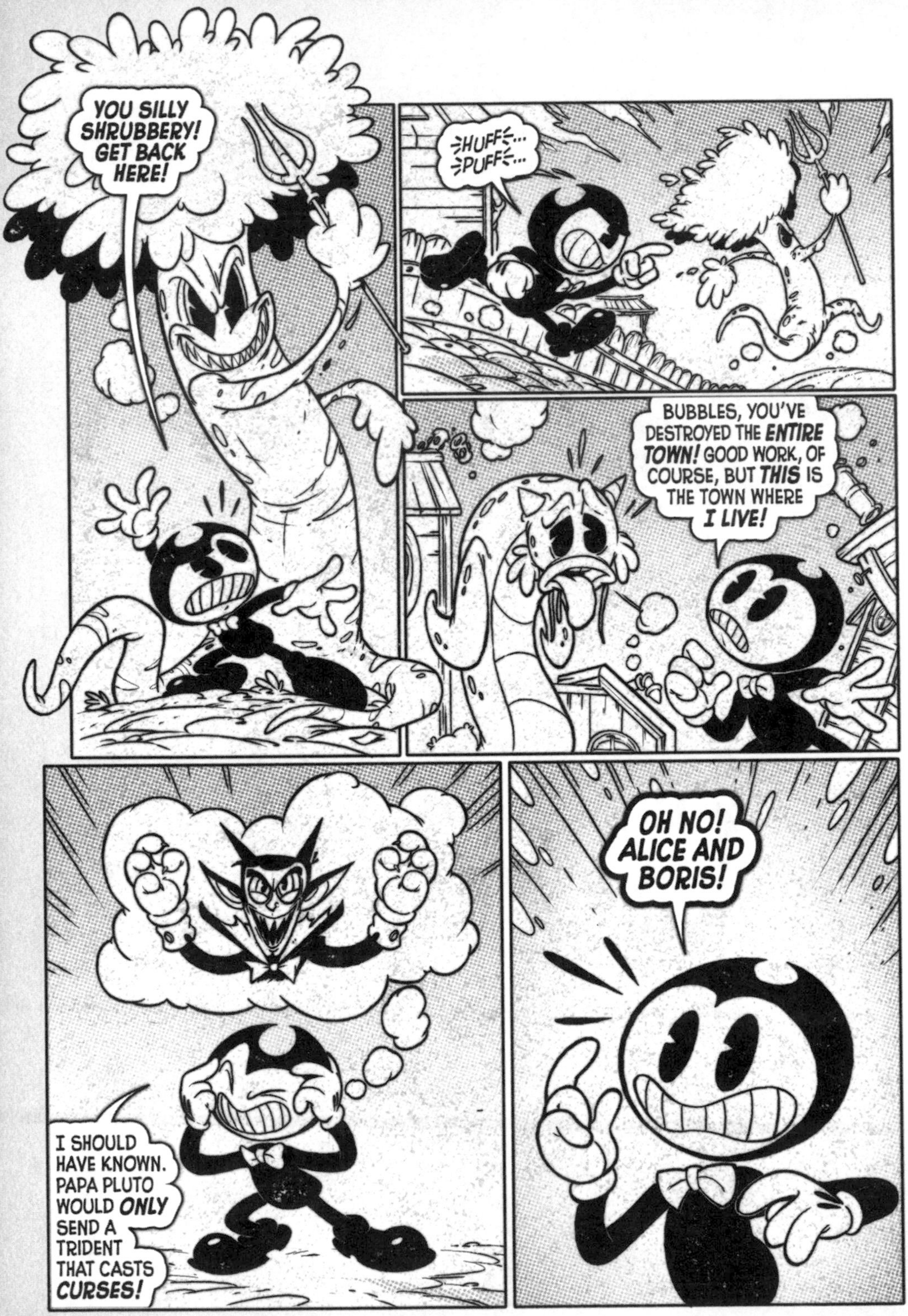
YOU SILLY SHRUBBERY! GET BACK HERE!
HUFF... PUFF...
BUBBLES, YOU'VE DESTROYED THE ENTIRE TOWN! GOOD WORK, OF COURSE, BUT THIS IS THE TOWN WHERE I LIVE!
I SHOULD HAVE KNOWN. PAPA PLUTO WOULD ONLY SEND A TRIDENT THAT CASTS CURSES!
OH NO! ALICE AND BORIS!

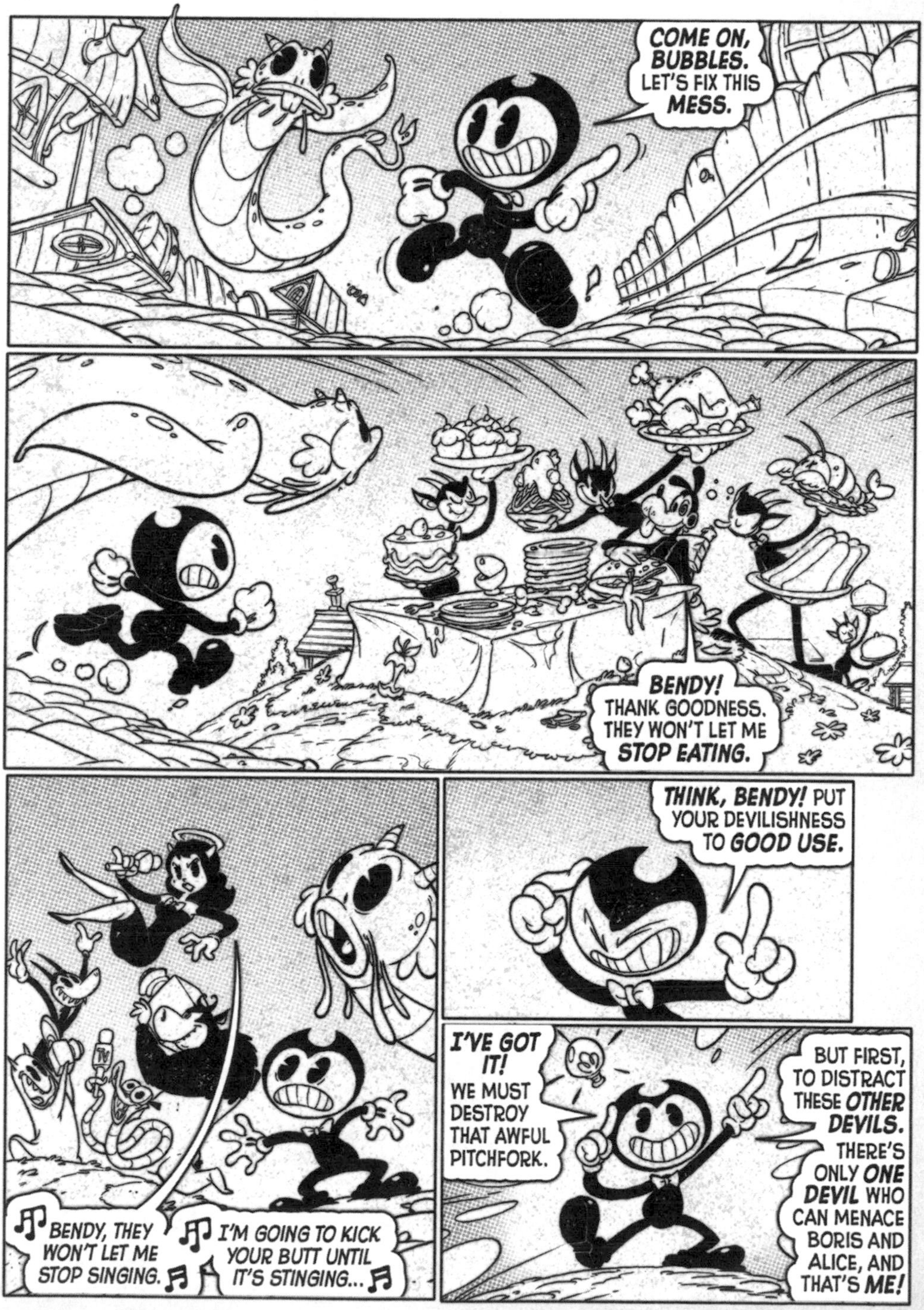
COME ON, BUBBLES. LET'S FIX THIS MESS.
BENDY! THANK GOODNESS. THEY WON'T LET ME STOP EATING.
BENDY, THEY WON'T LET ME STOP SINGING.
I'M GOING TO KICK YOUR BUTT UNTIL IT'S STINGING...
THINK, BENDY! PUT YOUR DEVILISHNESS TO GOOD USE.
I'VE GOT IT! WE MUST DESTROY THAT AWFUL PITCHFORK.
BUT FIRST, TO DISTRACT THESE OTHER DEVILS. THERE'S ONLY ONE DEVIL WHO CAN MENACE BORIS AND ALICE, AND THAT'S ME!

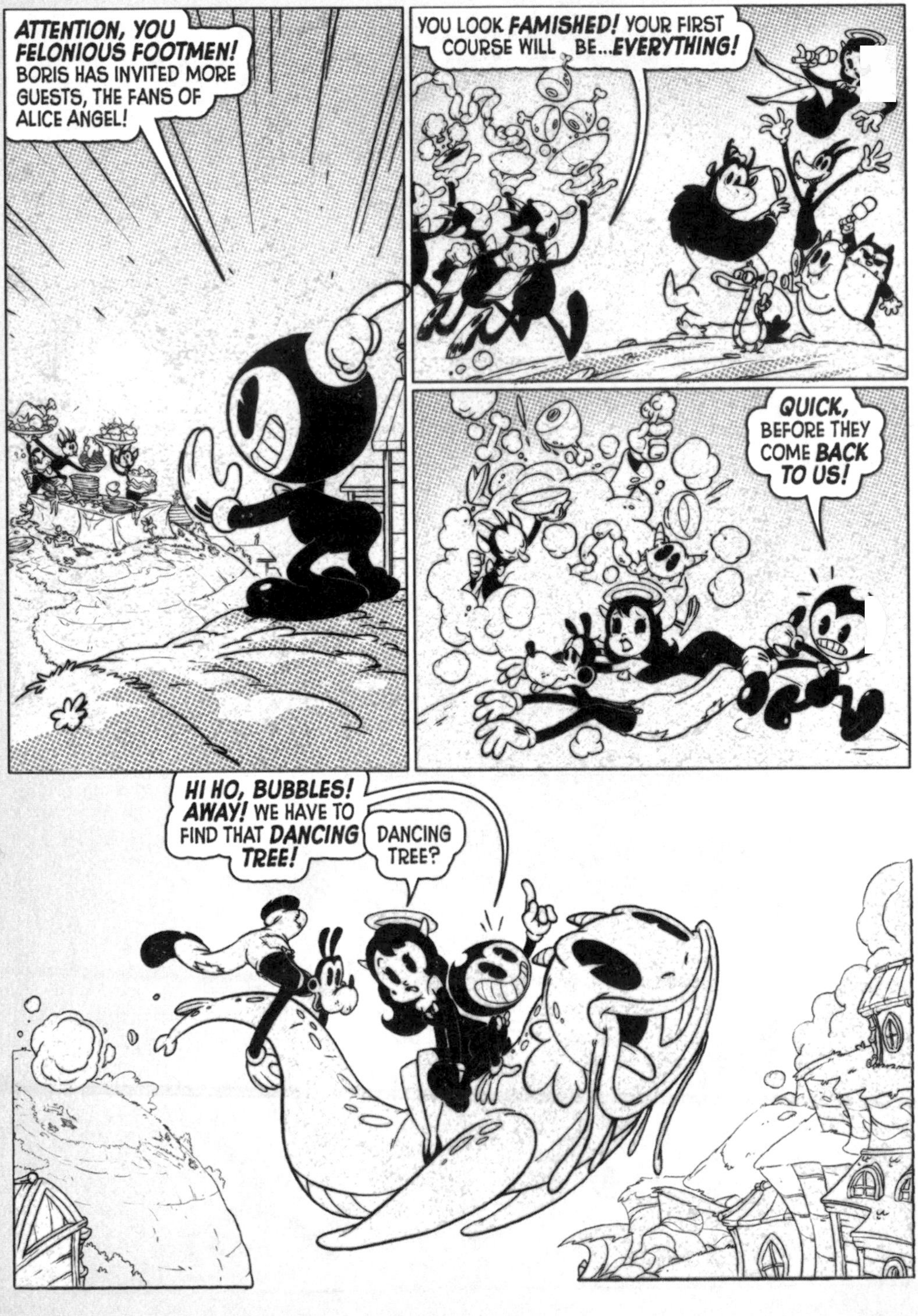
ATTENTION, YOU FELONIOUS FOOTMEN! BORIS HAS INVITED MORE GUESTS, THE FANS OF ALICE ANGEL!
YOU LOOK FAMISHED! YOUR FIRST COURSE WILL BE...EVERYTHING!
QUICK, BEFORE THEY COME BACK TO US!
HI HO, BUBBLES! AWAY! WE HAVE TO FIND THAT DANCING TREE!
DANCING TREE?

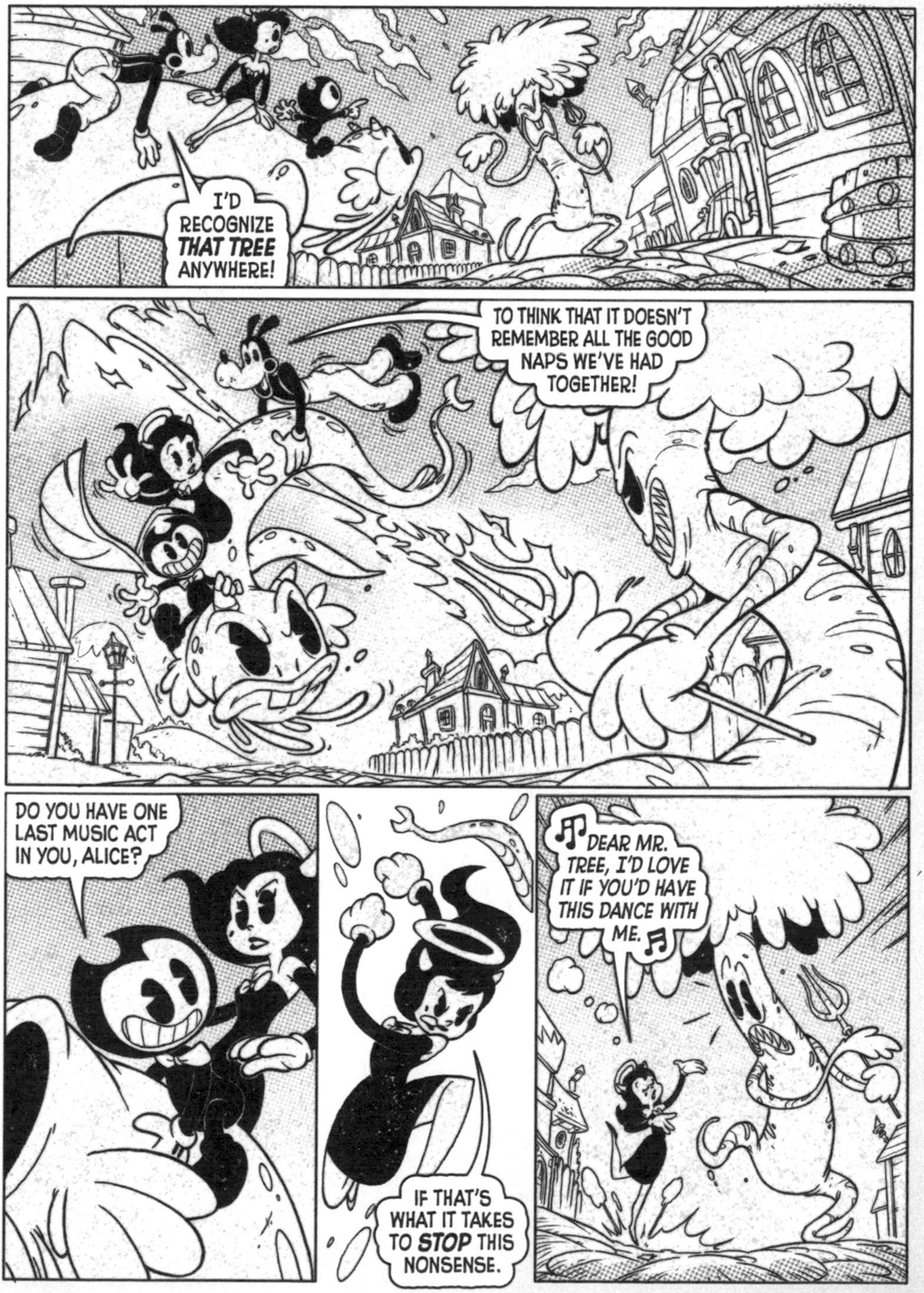
I'D RECOGNIZE THAT TREE ANYWHERE!
TO THINK THAT IT DOESN'T REMEMBER ALL THE GOOD NAPS WE'VE HAD TOGETHER!
DO YOU HAVE ONE LAST MUSIC ACT IN YOU, ALICE?
IF THAT'S WHAT IT TAKES TO STOP THIS NONSENSE.
DEAR MR. TREE, I'D LOVE IT IF YOU'D HAVE THIS DANCE WITH ME.

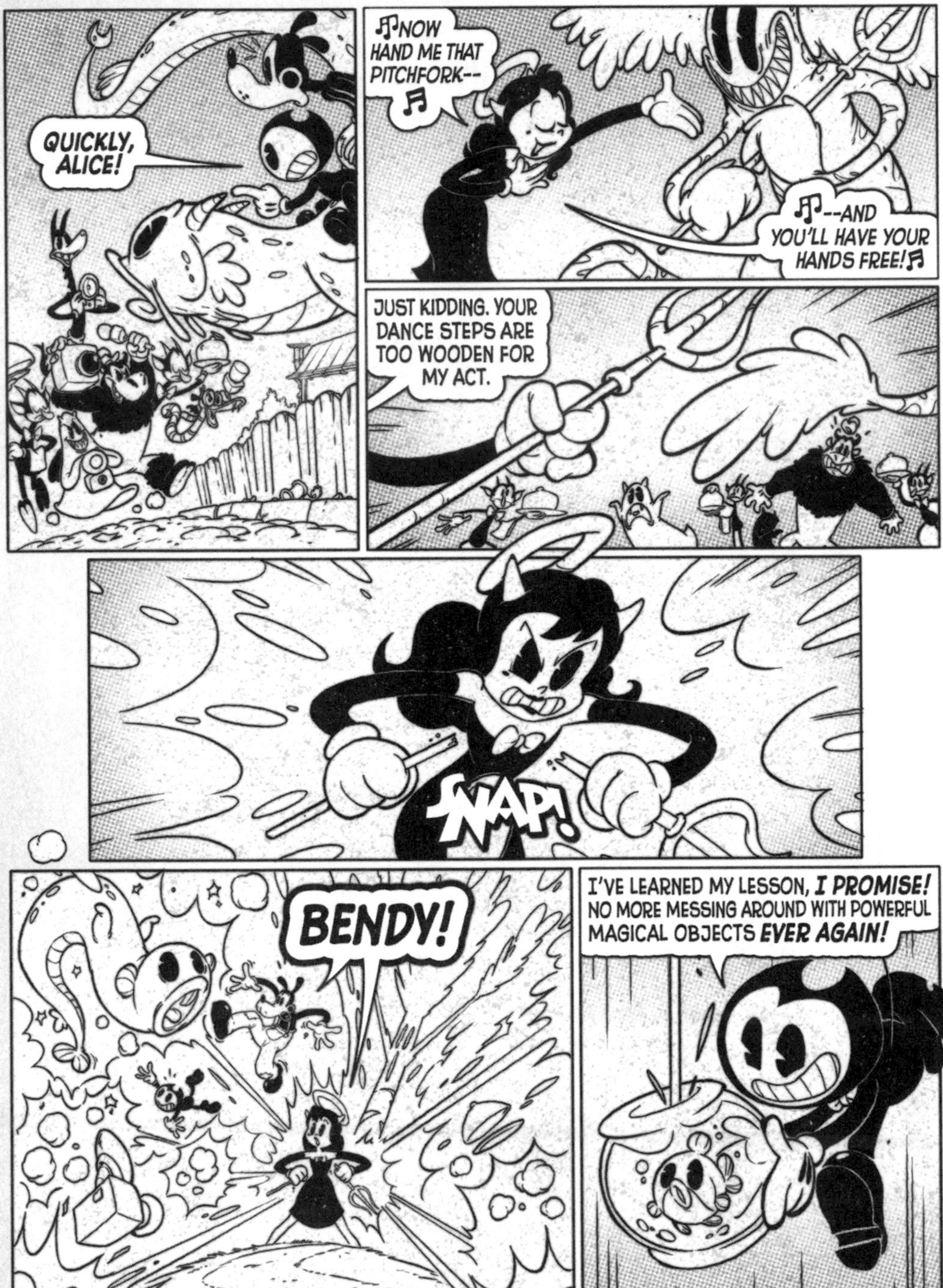
QUICKLY, ALICE!
♫NOW HAND ME THAT PITCHFORK-- ♫
♫--AND YOU'LL HAVE YOUR HANDS FREE!♫
JUST KIDDING. YOUR DANCE STEPS ARE TOO WOODEN FOR MY ACT.
SNAP!
BENDY!
I'VE LEARNED MY LESSON, I PROMISE! NO MORE MESSING AROUND WITH POWERFUL MAGICAL OBJECTS EVER AGAIN!

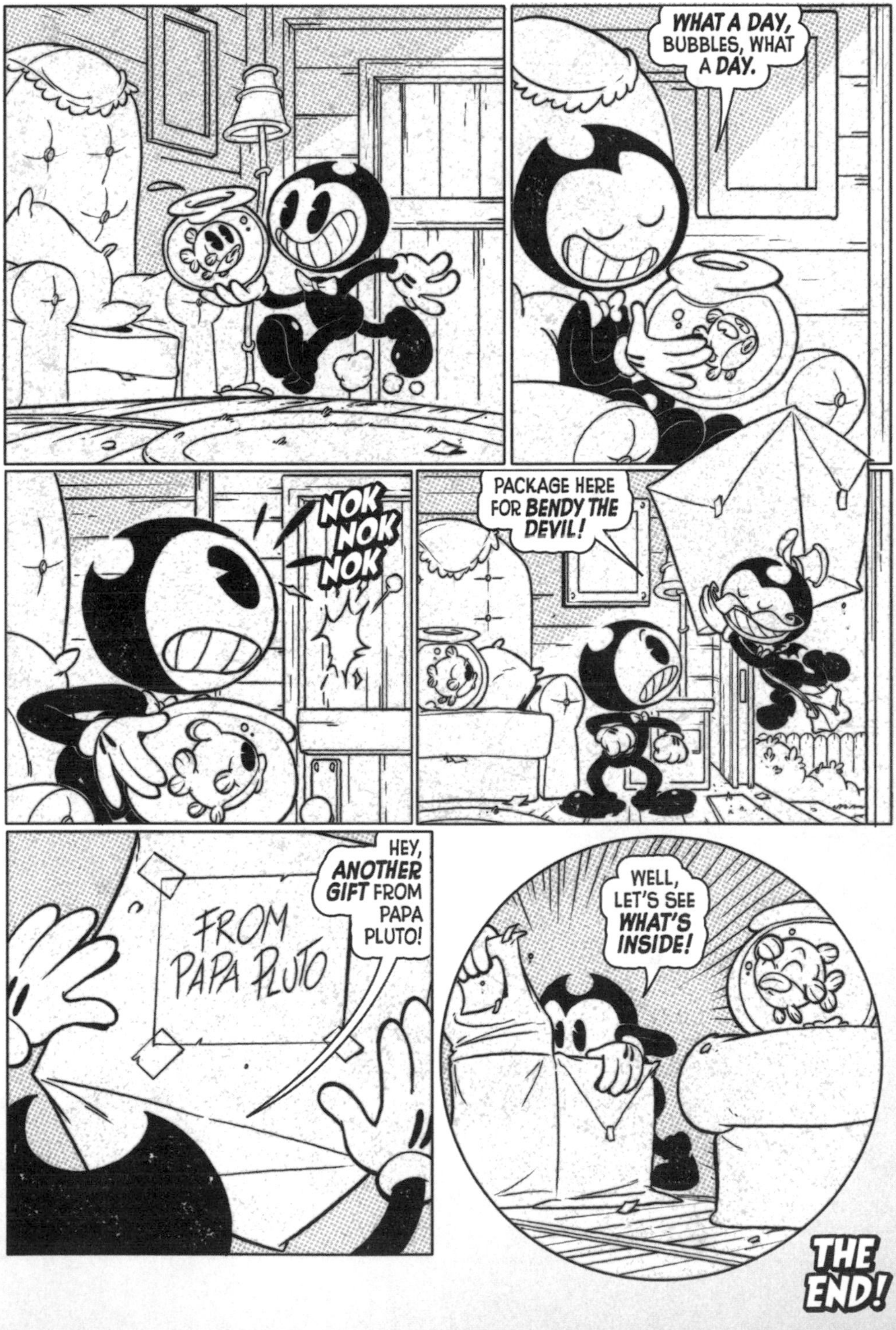
WHAT A DAY, BUBBLES, WHAT A DAY.
NOK NOK NOK
PACKAGE HERE FOR BENDY THE DEVIL!
FROM PAPA PLUTO
HEY, ANOTHER GIFT FROM PAPA PLUTO!
WELL, LET'S SEE WHAT'S INSIDE!
THE END!

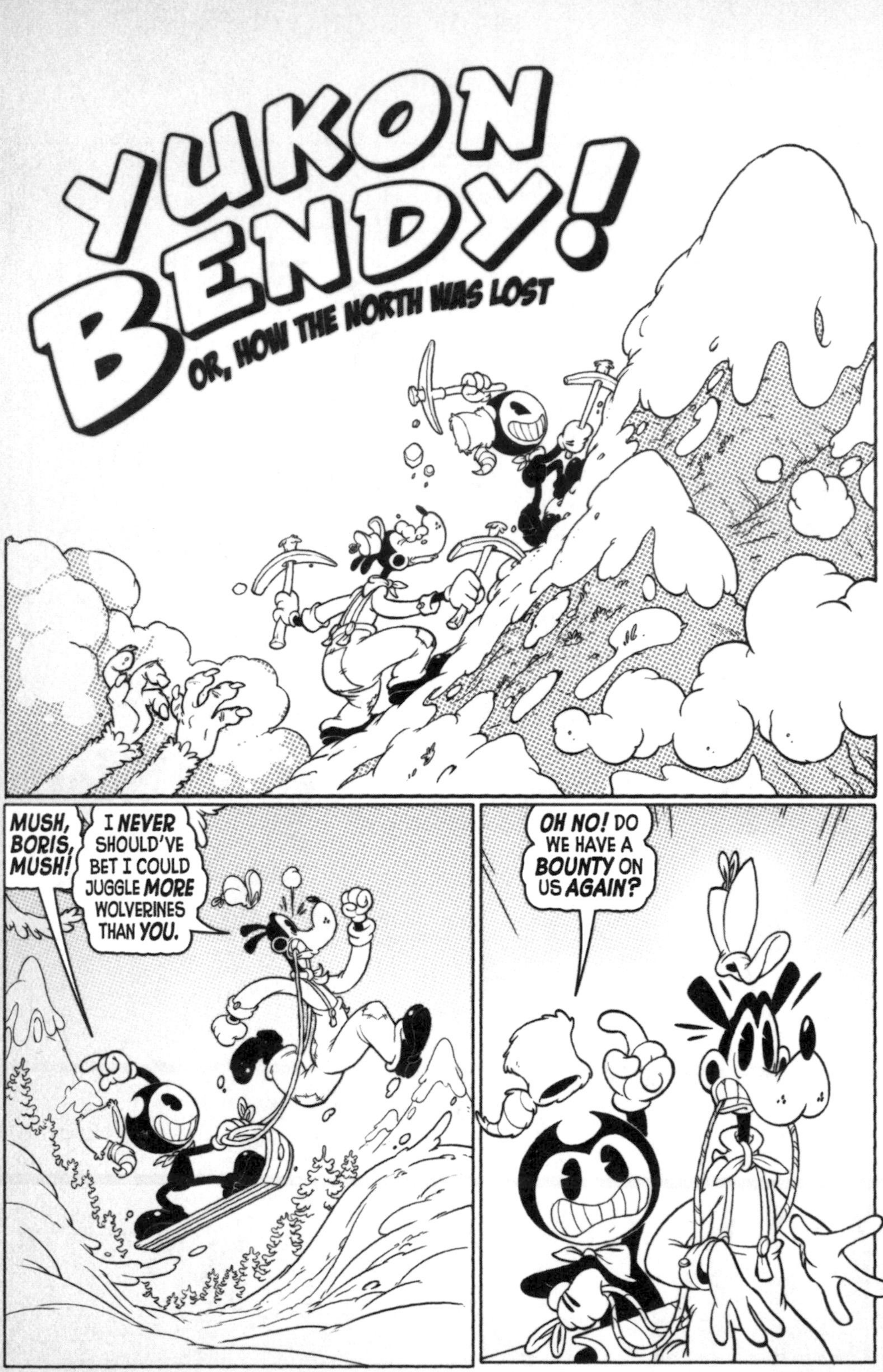
YUKON BENDY!
OR, HOW THE NORTH WAS LOST
MUSH, BORIS, MUSH!
I NEVER SHOULD'VE BET I COULD JUGGLE MORE WOLVERINES THAN YOU.
OH NO! DO WE HAVE A BOUNTY ON US AGAIN?

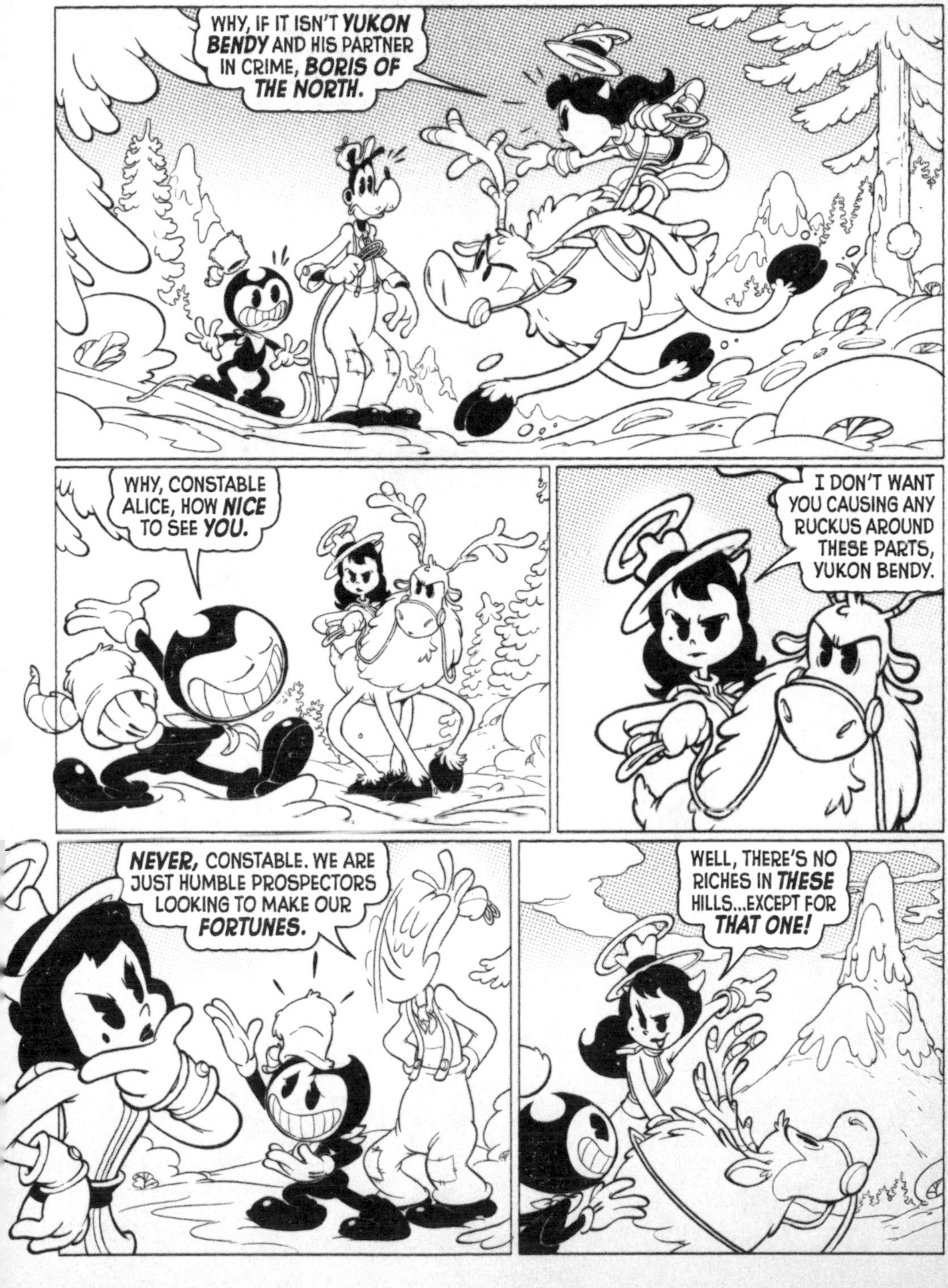
WHY, IF IT ISN'T *YUKON BENDY* AND HIS PARTNER IN CRIME, *BORIS OF THE NORTH.*
WHY, CONSTABLE ALICE, HOW *NICE* TO SEE *YOU.*
I DON'T WANT YOU CAUSING ANY RUCKUS AROUND THESE PARTS, YUKON BENDY.
NEVER, CONSTABLE. WE ARE JUST HUMBLE PROSPECTORS LOOKING TO MAKE OUR *FORTUNES.*
WELL, THERE'S NO RICHES IN *THESE* HILLS...EXCEPT FOR *THAT ONE!*

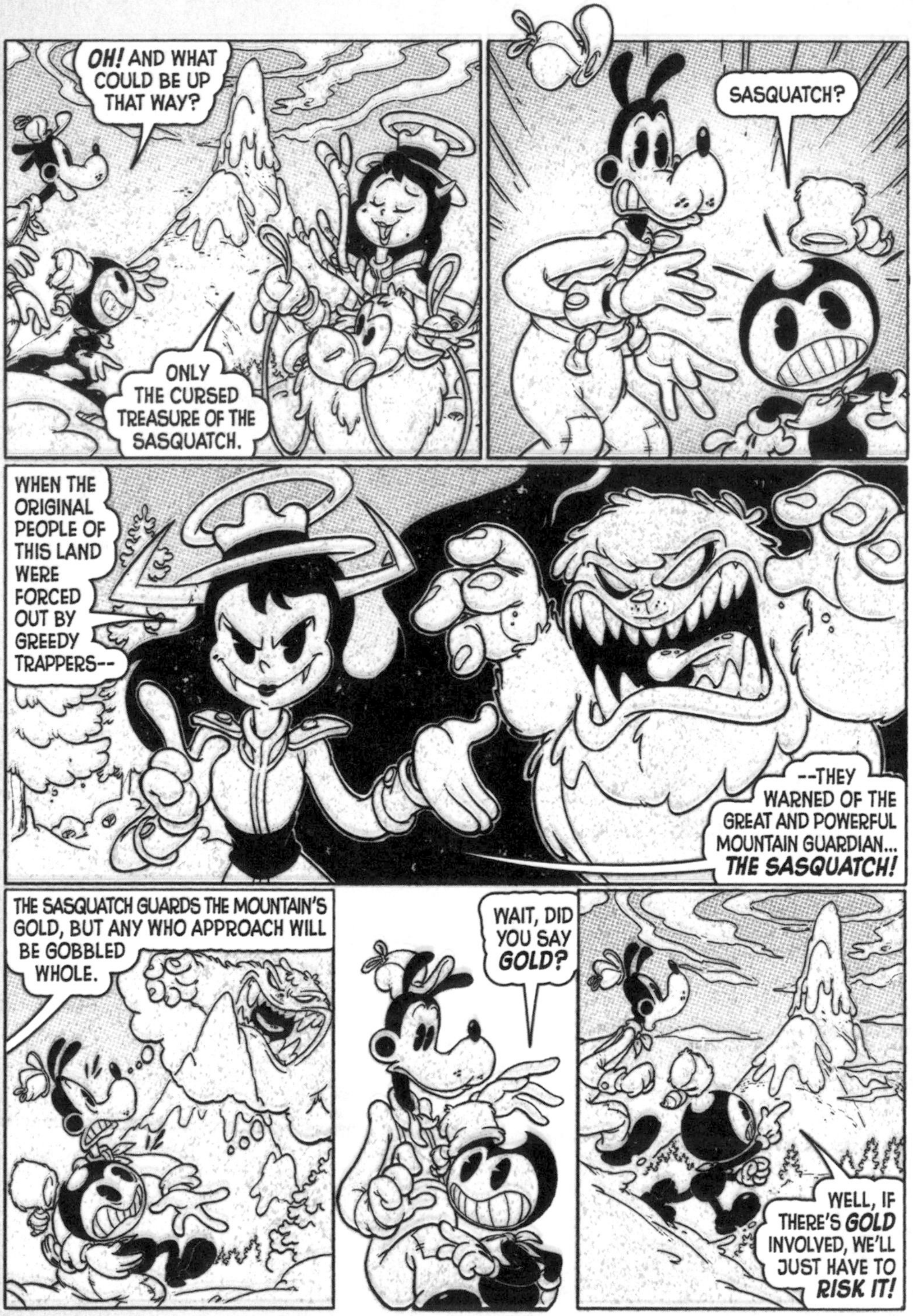
OH! AND WHAT COULD BE UP THAT WAY?
ONLY THE CURSED TREASURE OF THE SASQUATCH.
SASQUATCH?
WHEN THE ORIGINAL PEOPLE OF THIS LAND WERE FORCED OUT BY GREEDY TRAPPERS--
--THEY WARNED OF THE GREAT AND POWERFUL MOUNTAIN GUARDIAN... THE SASQUATCH!
THE SASQUATCH GUARDS THE MOUNTAIN'S GOLD, BUT ANY WHO APPROACH WILL BE GOBBLED WHOLE.
WAIT, DID YOU SAY GOLD?
WELL, IF THERE'S GOLD INVOLVED, WE'LL JUST HAVE TO RISK IT!

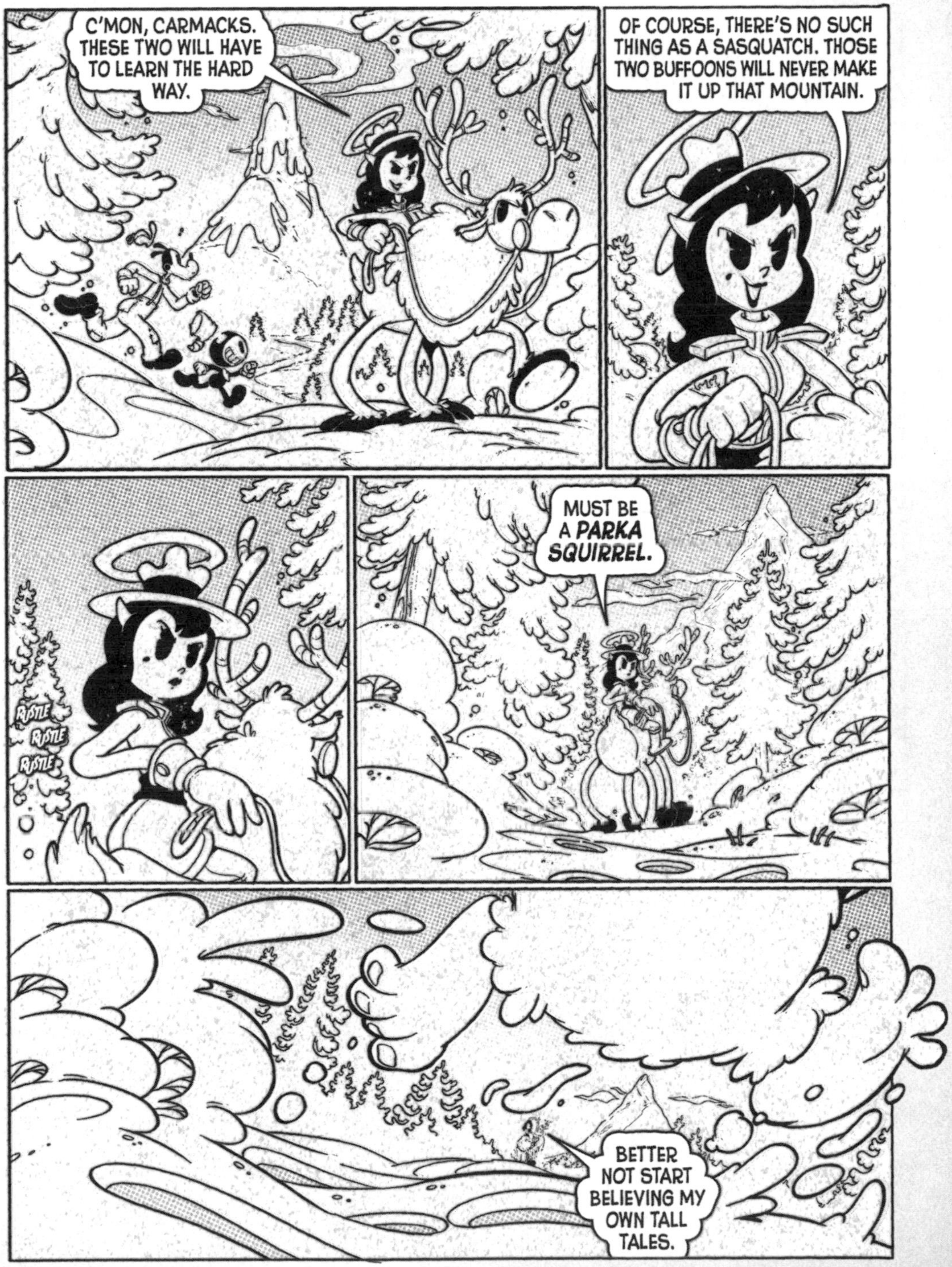
C'MON, CARMACKS. THESE TWO WILL HAVE TO LEARN THE HARD WAY.
OF COURSE, THERE'S NO SUCH THING AS A SASQUATCH. THOSE TWO BUFFOONS WILL NEVER MAKE IT UP THAT MOUNTAIN.
RUSTLE
RUSTLE
RUSTLE
MUST BE A **PARKA SQUIRREL.**
BETTER NOT START BELIEVING MY OWN TALL TALES.

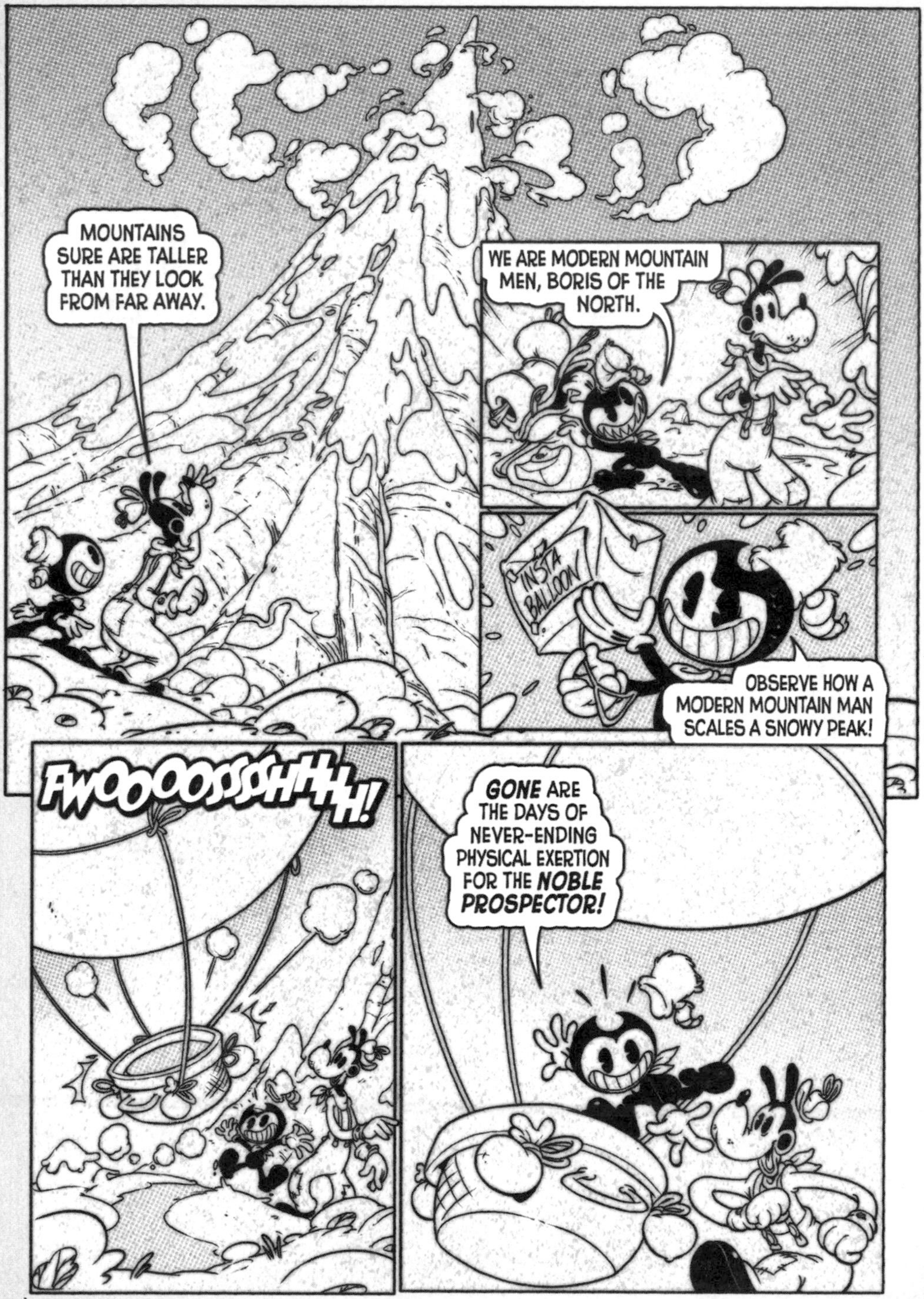
MOUNTAINS SURE ARE TALLER THAN THEY LOOK FROM FAR AWAY.
WE ARE MODERN MOUNTAIN MEN, BORIS OF THE NORTH.
INSTA BALLOON
OBSERVE HOW A MODERN MOUNTAIN MAN SCALES A SNOWY PEAK!
FWOOOOOSSSSHHHHH!
GONE ARE THE DAYS OF NEVER-ENDING PHYSICAL EXERTION FOR THE NOBLE PROSPECTOR!

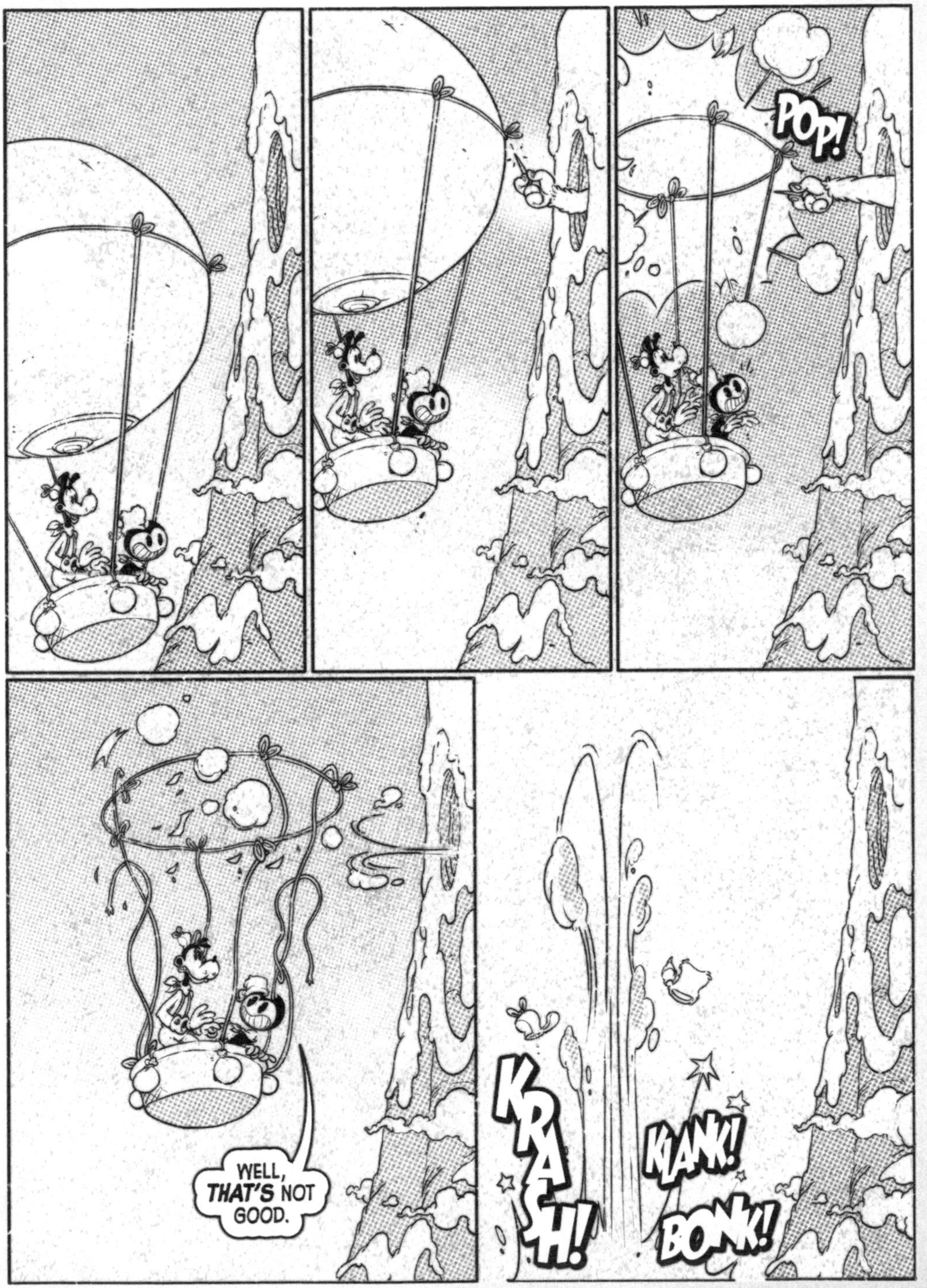
POP!
WELL, THAT'S NOT GOOD.
KRASH!
KLANK!
BONK!

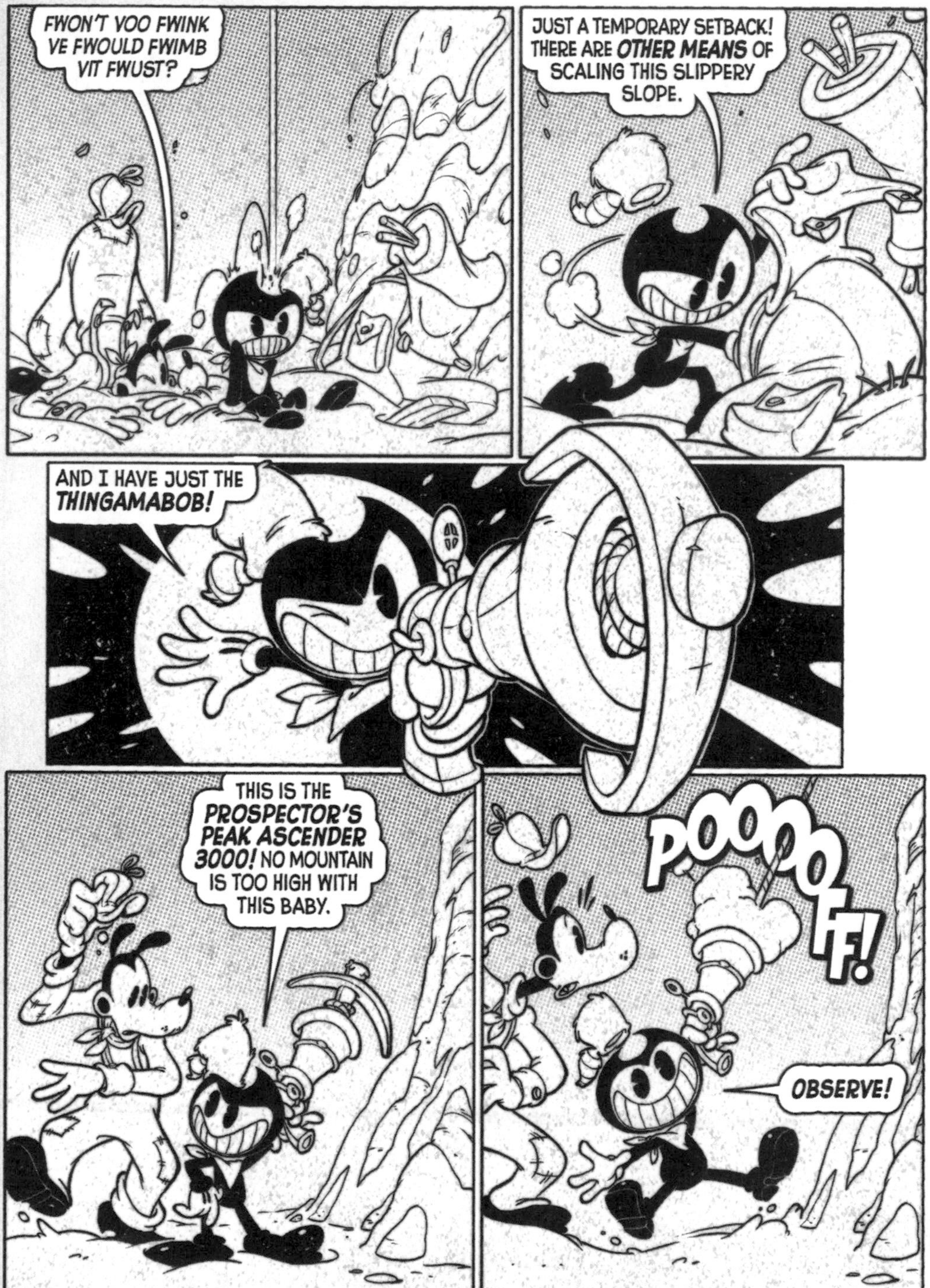
FWON'T VOO FWINK VE FWOULD FWIMB VIT FWUST?
JUST A TEMPORARY SETBACK! THERE ARE OTHER MEANS OF SCALING THIS SLIPPERY SLOPE.
AND I HAVE JUST THE THINGAMABOB!
THIS IS THE PROSPECTOR'S PEAK ASCENDER 3000! NO MOUNTAIN IS TOO HIGH WITH THIS BABY.
POOOOOFF!
OBSERVE!

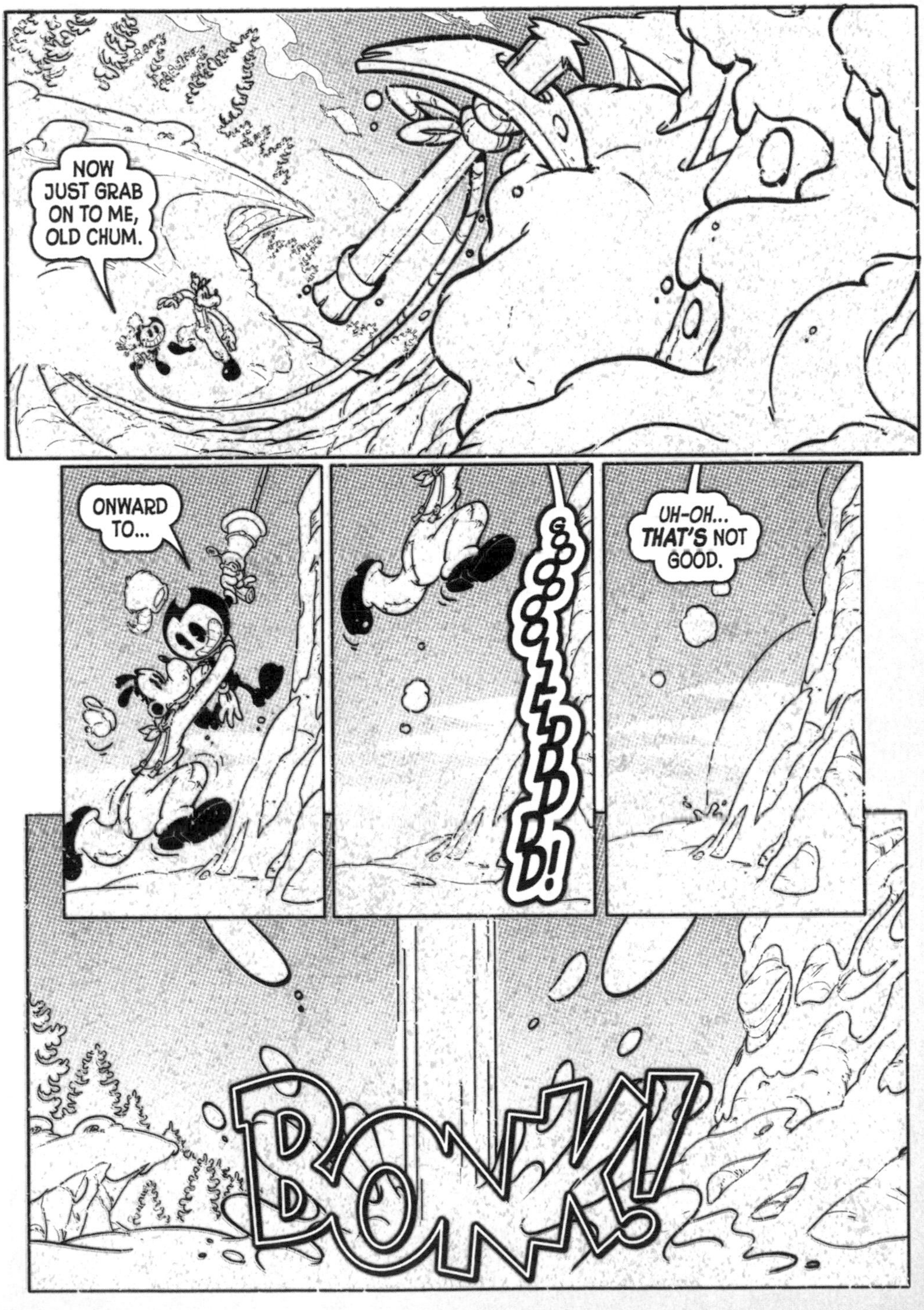
NOW JUST GRAB ON TO ME, OLD CHUM.
ONWARD TO...
GOOOOOLLLDDDD!
UH-OH... THAT'S NOT GOOD.
BONK!
BONK!

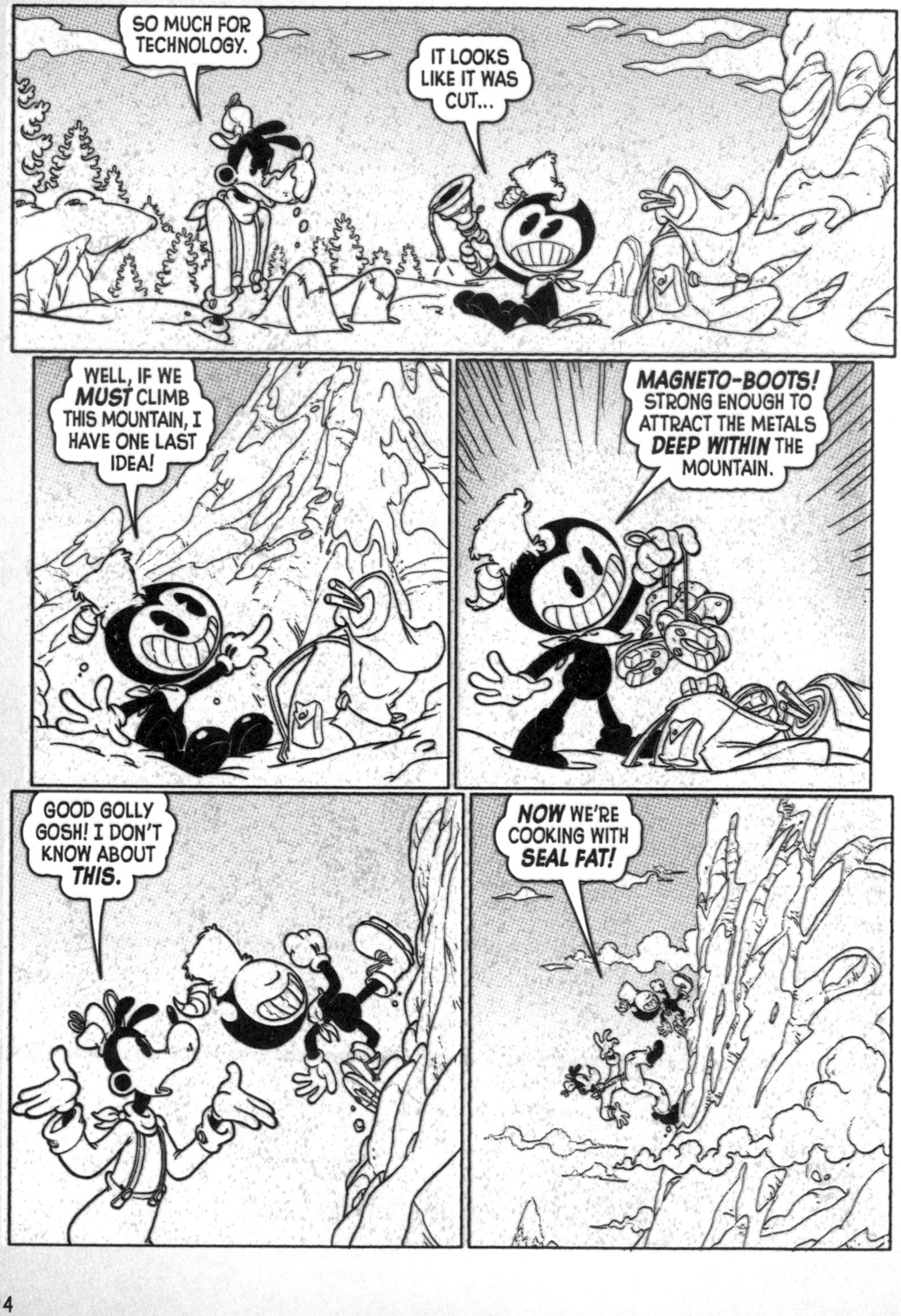
SO MUCH FOR TECHNOLOGY.
IT LOOKS LIKE IT WAS CUT...
WELL, IF WE MUST CLIMB THIS MOUNTAIN, I HAVE ONE LAST IDEA!
MAGNETO-BOOTS! STRONG ENOUGH TO ATTRACT THE METALS DEEP WITHIN THE MOUNTAIN.
GOOD GOLLY GOSH! I DON'T KNOW ABOUT THIS.
NOW WE'RE COOKING WITH SEAL FAT!

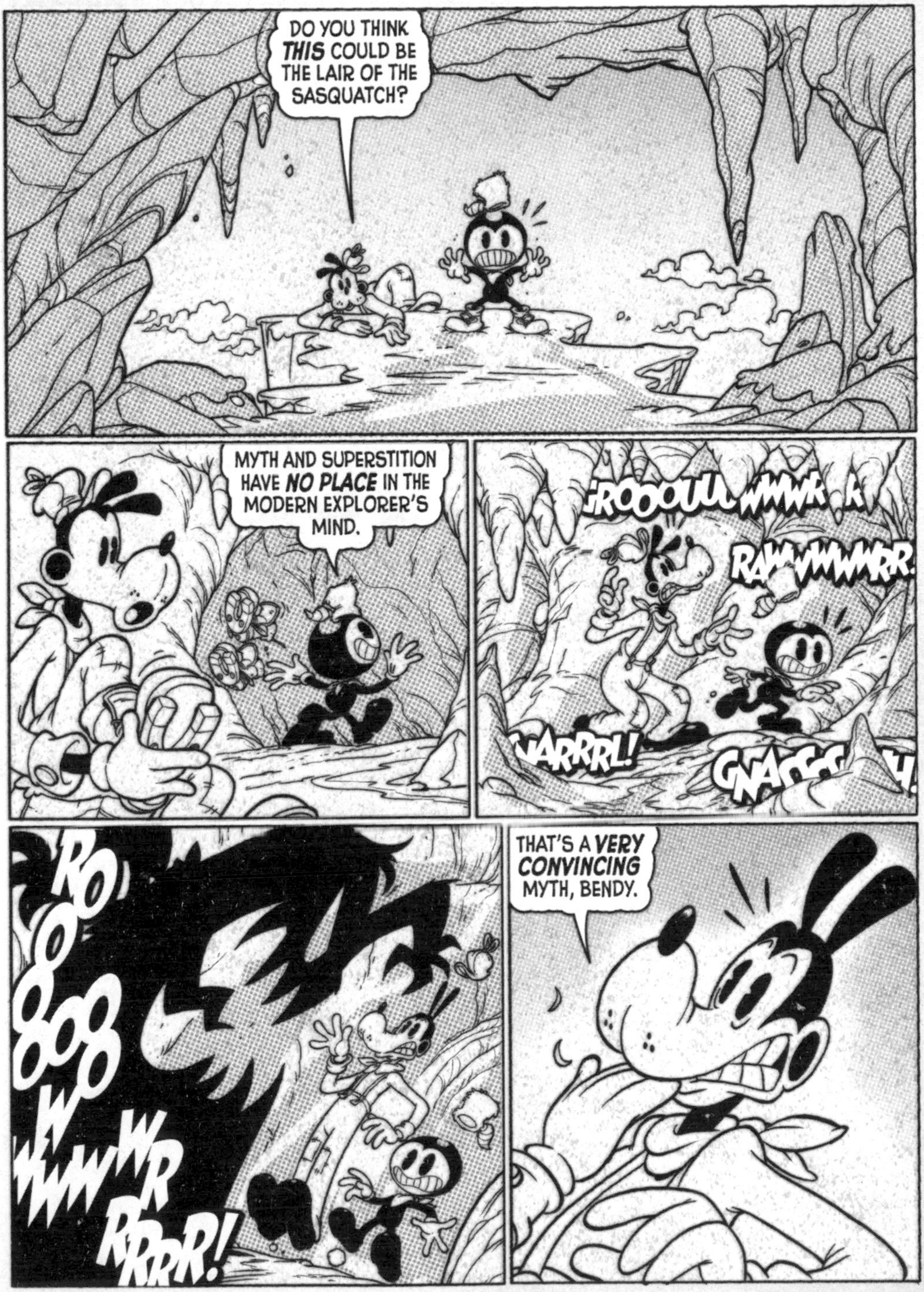
DO YOU THINK THIS COULD BE THE LAIR OF THE SASQUATCH?
MYTH AND SUPERSTITION HAVE NO PLACE IN THE MODERN EXPLORER'S MIND.
THAT'S A VERY CONVINCING MYTH, BENDY.

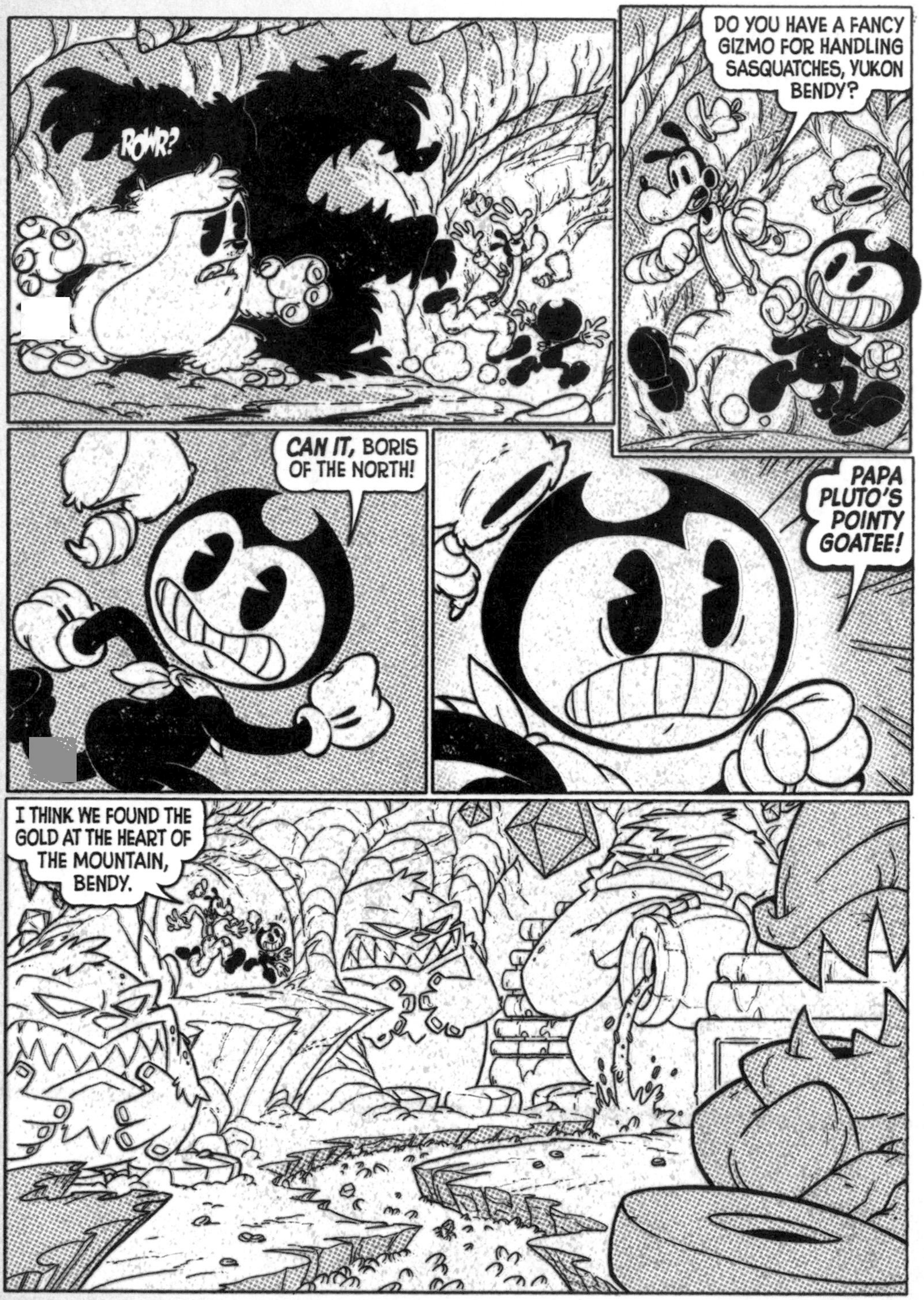
ROWR?
DO YOU HAVE A FANCY GIZMO FOR HANDLING SASQUATCHES, YUKON BENDY?
CAN IT, BORIS OF THE NORTH!
PAPA PLUTO'S POINTY GOATEE!
I THINK WE FOUND THE GOLD AT THE HEART OF THE MOUNTAIN, BENDY.

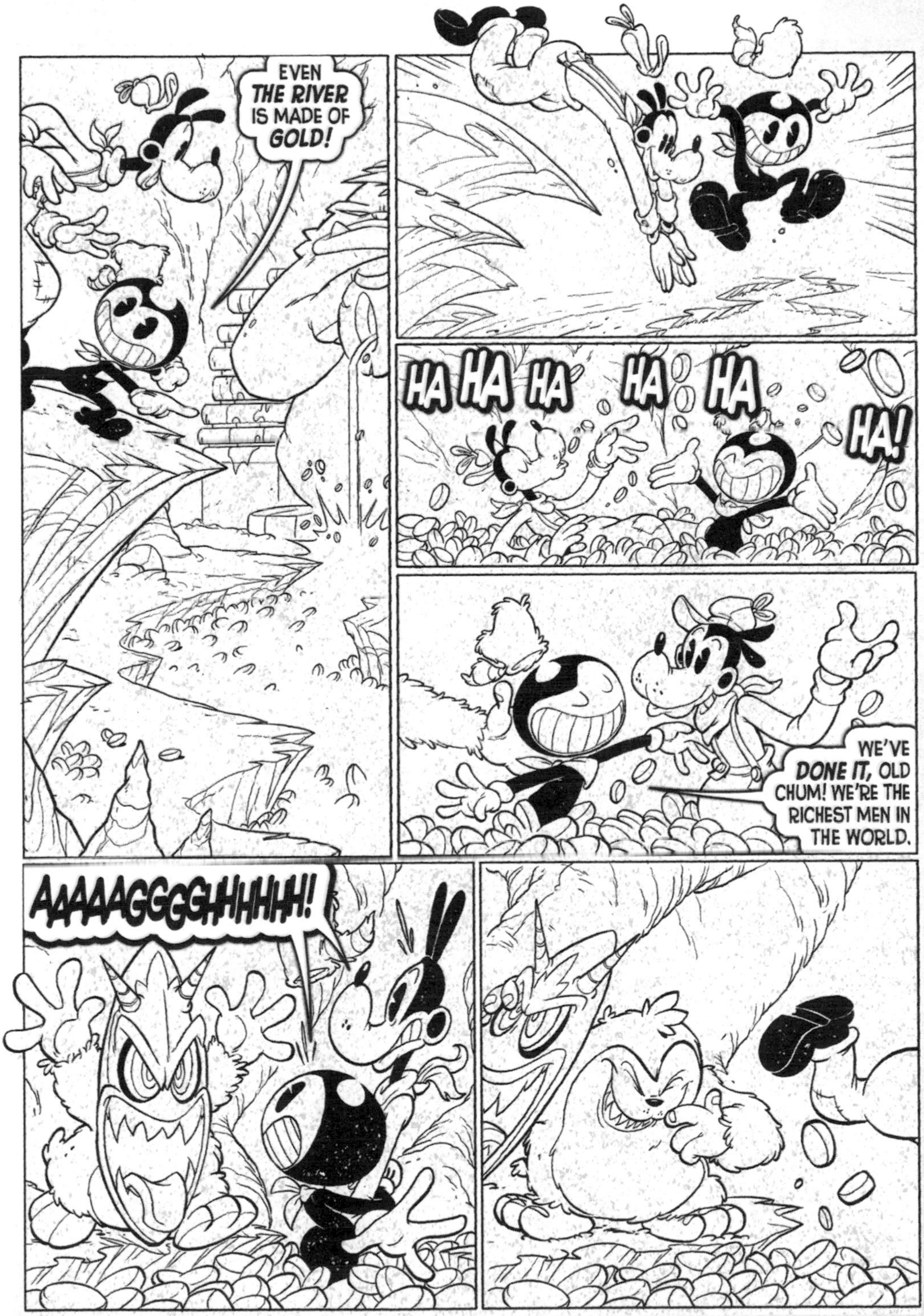
EVEN THE RIVER IS MADE OF GOLD!
HA HA HA HA HA HA!
WE'VE DONE IT, OLD CHUM! WE'RE THE RICHEST MEN IN THE WORLD.
AAAAAGGGGHHHHH!

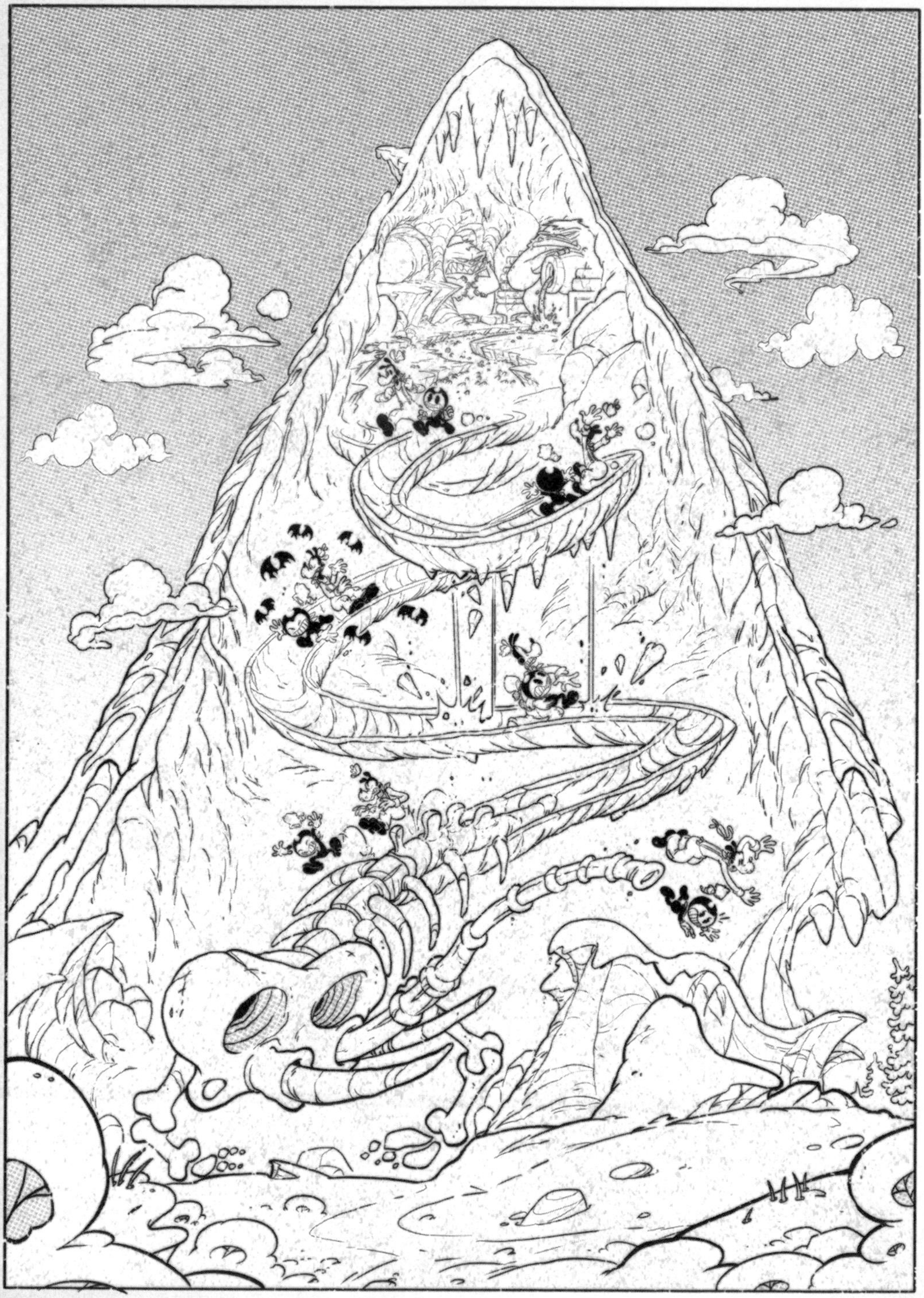

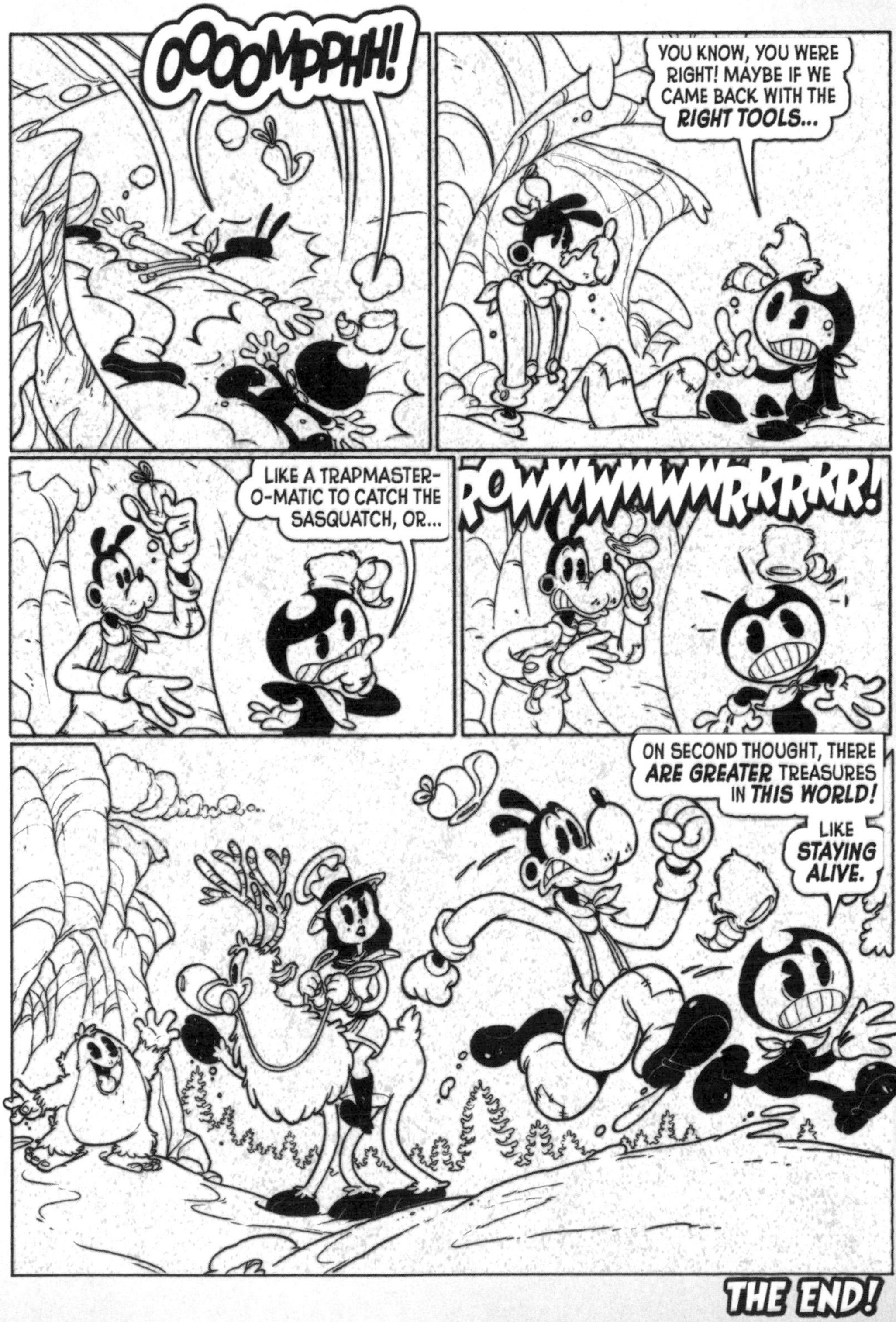
OOOOMPPHH!
YOU KNOW, YOU WERE RIGHT! MAYBE IF WE CAME BACK WITH THE RIGHT TOOLS...
LIKE A TRAPMASTER-O-MATIC TO CATCH THE SASQUATCH, OR...
ROWWWWWWRRRRR!
ON SECOND THOUGHT, THERE ARE GREATER TREASURES IN THIS WORLD!
LIKE STAYING ALIVE.
THE END!

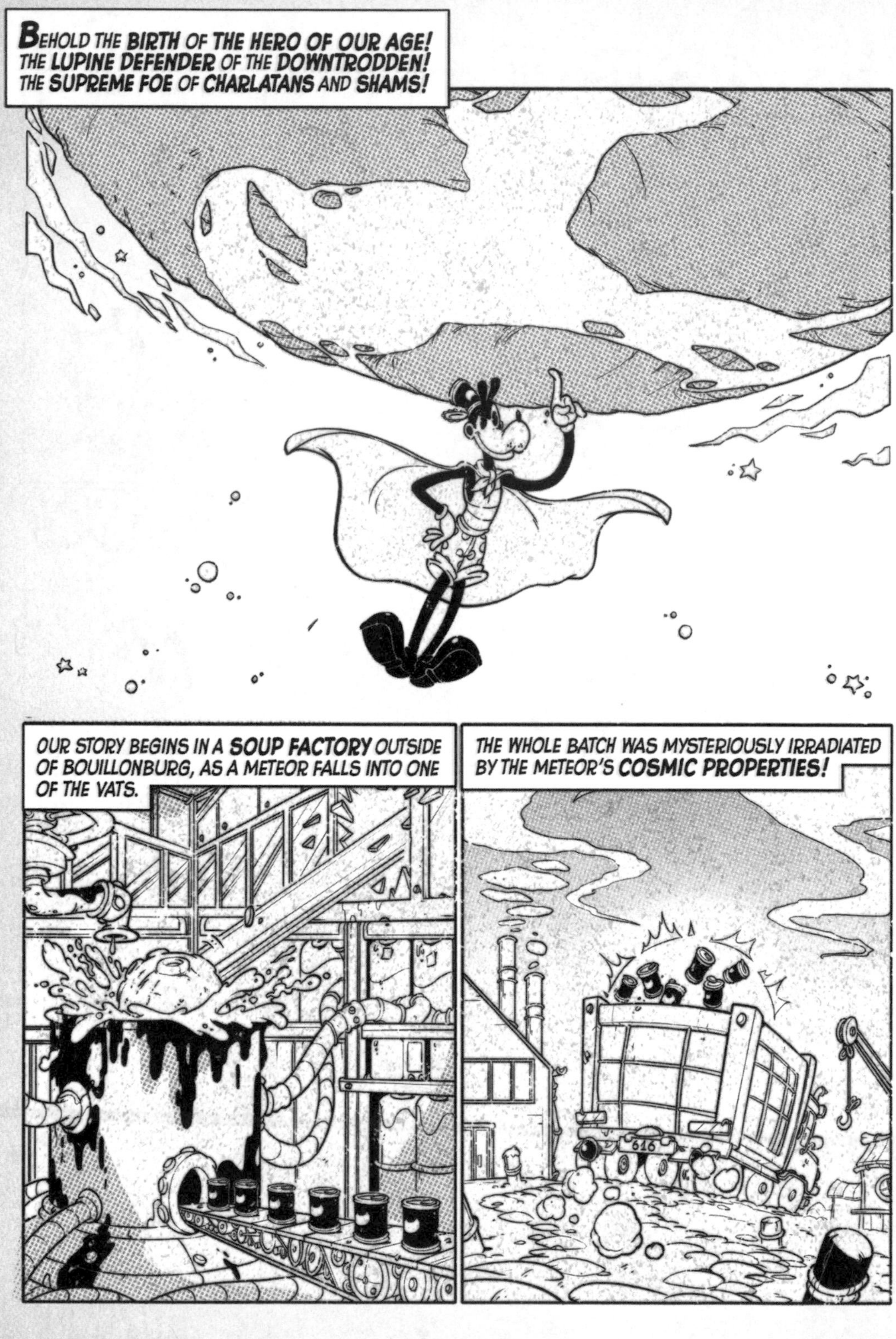
BEHOLD THE BIRTH OF THE HERO OF OUR AGE! THE LUPINE DEFENDER OF THE DOWNTRODDEN! THE SUPREME FOE OF CHARLATANS AND SHAMS!
OUR STORY BEGINS IN A SOUP FACTORY OUTSIDE OF BOUILLONBURG, AS A METEOR FALLS INTO ONE OF THE VATS.
THE WHOLE BATCH WAS MYSTERIOUSLY IRRADIATED BY THE METEOR'S COSMIC PROPERTIES!

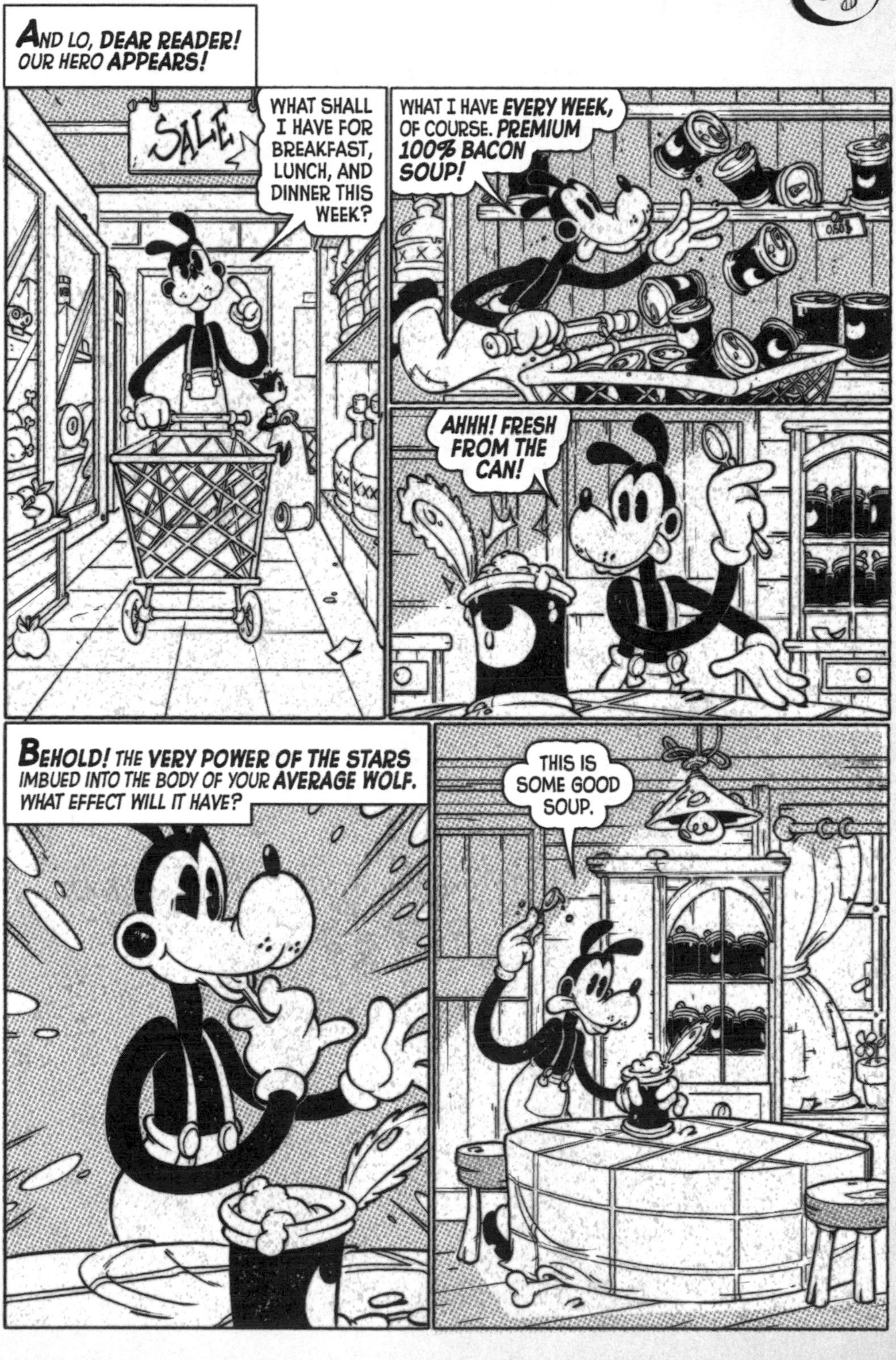
AND LO, DEAR READER! OUR HERO APPEARS!
SALE
WHAT SHALL I HAVE FOR BREAKFAST, LUNCH, AND DINNER THIS WEEK?
WHAT I HAVE EVERY WEEK, OF COURSE. PREMIUM 100% BACON SOUP!
AHHH! FRESH FROM THE CAN!
BEHOLD! THE VERY POWER OF THE STARS IMBUED INTO THE BODY OF YOUR AVERAGE WOLF. WHAT EFFECT WILL IT HAVE?
THIS IS SOME GOOD SOUP.

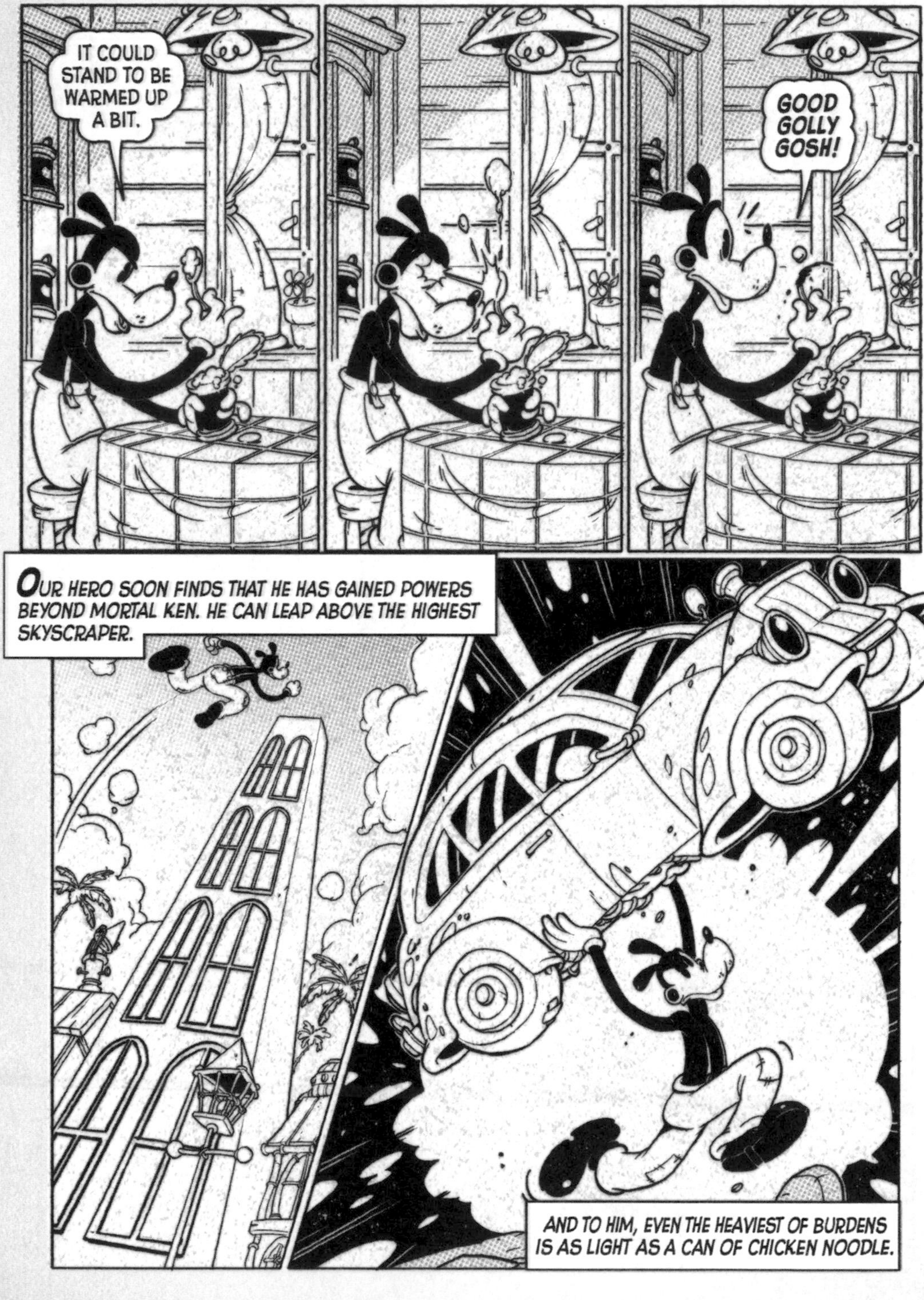
IT COULD STAND TO BE WARMED UP A BIT.
GOOD GOLLY GOSH!
OUR HERO SOON FINDS THAT HE HAS GAINED POWERS BEYOND MORTAL KEN. HE CAN LEAP ABOVE THE HIGHEST SKYSCRAPER.
AND TO HIM, EVEN THE HEAVIEST OF BURDENS IS AS LIGHT AS A CAN OF CHICKEN NOODLE.

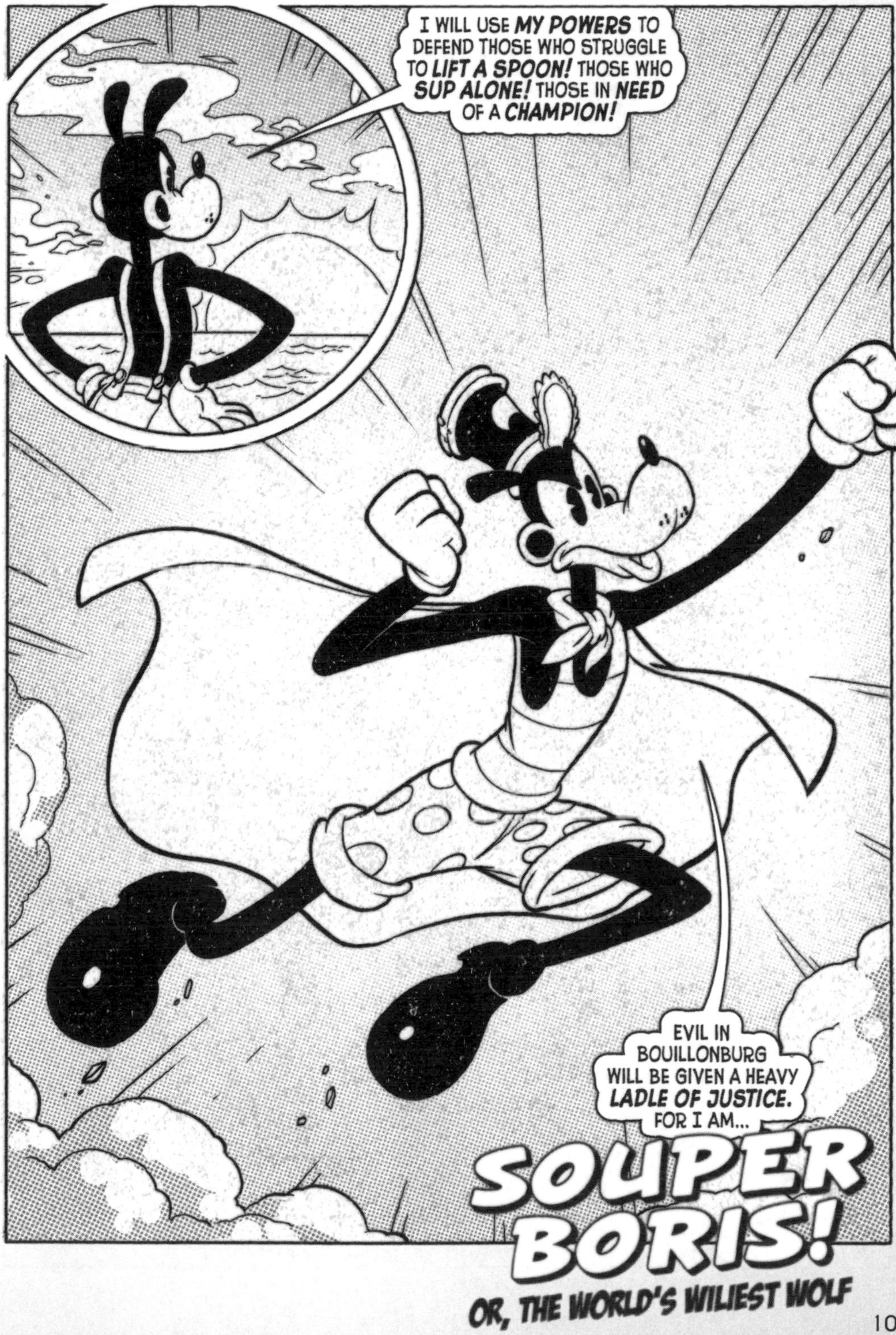
I WILL USE MY POWERS TO DEFEND THOSE WHO STRUGGLE TO LIFT A SPOON! THOSE WHO SUP ALONE! THOSE IN NEED OF A CHAMPION!
EVIL IN BOUILLONBURG WILL BE GIVEN A HEAVY LADLE OF JUSTICE. FOR I AM...
SOUPER BORIS!
OR, THE WORLD'S WILIEST WOLF

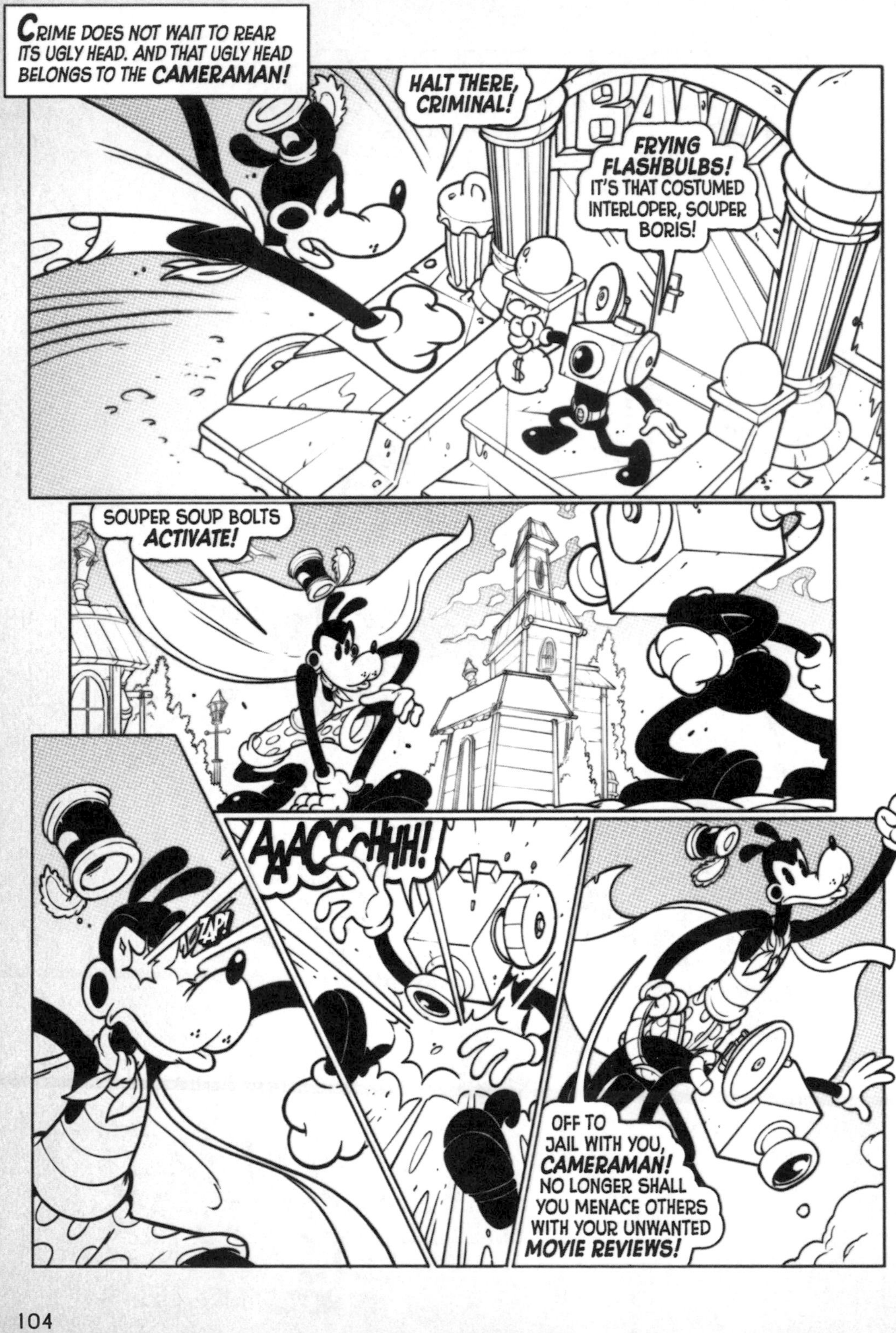
CRIME DOES NOT WAIT TO REAR ITS UGLY HEAD. AND THAT UGLY HEAD BELONGS TO THE CAMERAMAN!
HALT THERE, CRIMINAL!
FRYING FLASHBULBS! IT'S THAT COSTUMED INTERLOPER, SOUPER BORIS!
SOUPER SOUP BOLTS ACTIVATE!
ZAP!
AAACCCHHH!
OFF TO JAIL WITH YOU, CAMERAMAN! NO LONGER SHALL YOU MENACE OTHERS WITH YOUR UNWANTED MOVIE REVIEWS!

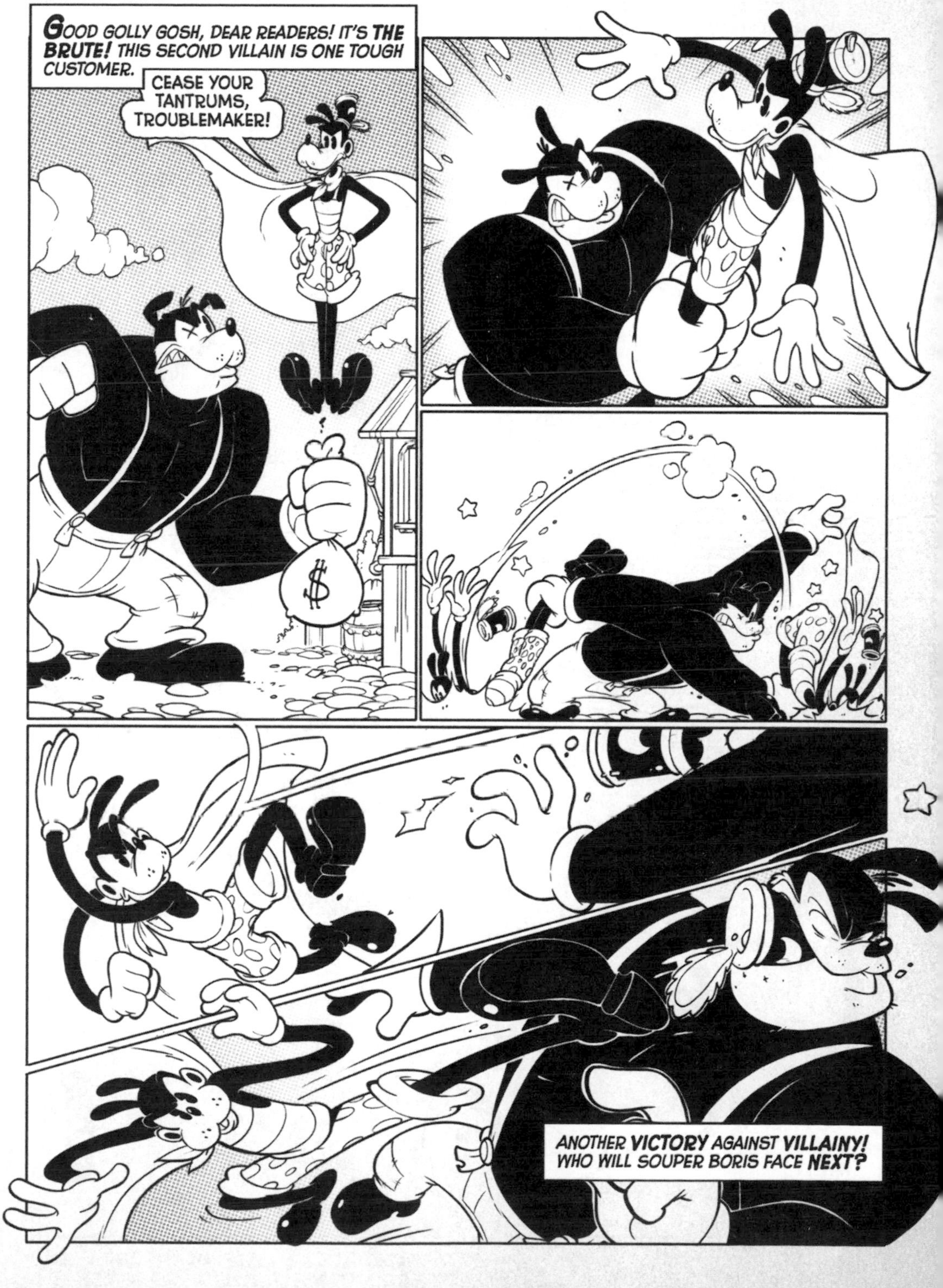
GOOD GOLLY GOSH, DEAR READERS! IT'S **THE BRUTE!** THIS SECOND VILLAIN IS ONE TOUGH CUSTOMER.
CEASE YOUR TANTRUMS, TROUBLEMAKER!
ANOTHER **VICTORY** AGAINST **VILLAINY!** WHO WILL SOUPER BORIS FACE **NEXT?**

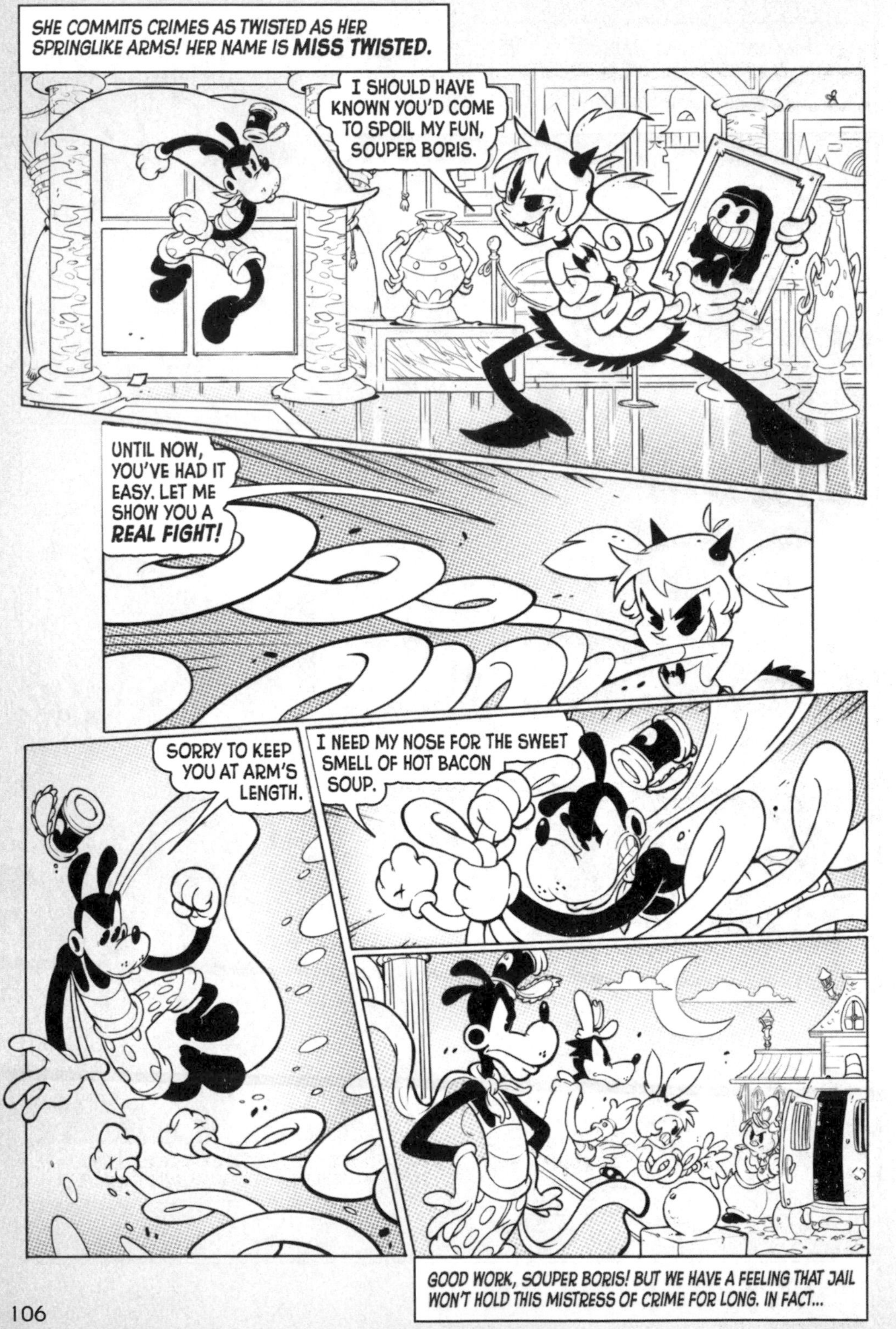
SHE COMMITS CRIMES AS TWISTED AS HER SPRINGLIKE ARMS! HER NAME IS **MISS TWISTED.**
I SHOULD HAVE KNOWN YOU'D COME TO SPOIL MY FUN, SOUPER BORIS.
UNTIL NOW, YOU'VE HAD IT EASY. LET ME SHOW YOU A ***REAL FIGHT!***
SORRY TO KEEP YOU AT ARM'S LENGTH.
I NEED MY NOSE FOR THE SWEET SMELL OF HOT BACON SOUP.
GOOD WORK, SOUPER BORIS! BUT WE HAVE A FEELING THAT JAIL WON'T HOLD THIS MISTRESS OF CRIME FOR LONG. IN FACT...

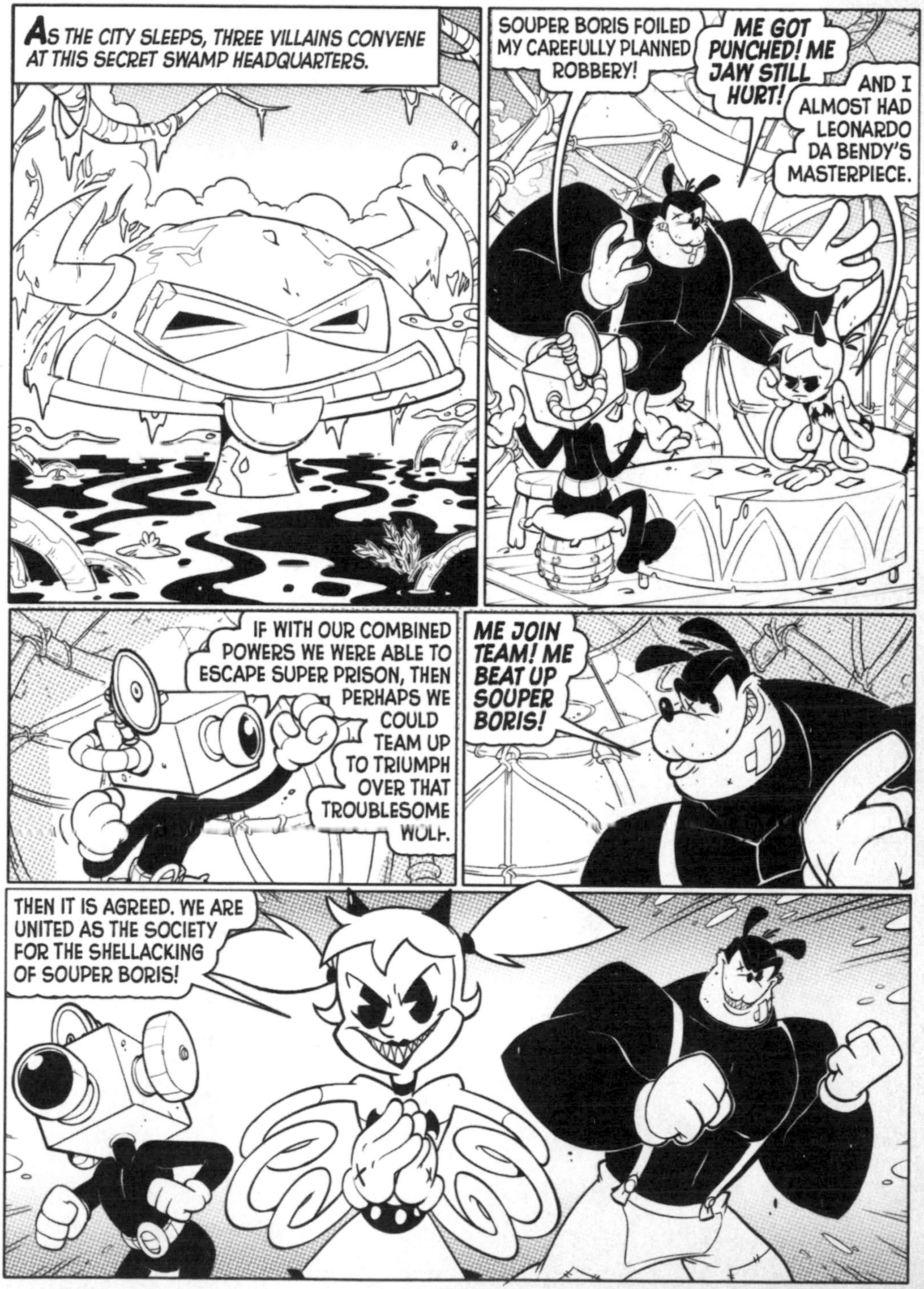
AS THE CITY SLEEPS, THREE VILLAINS CONVENE AT THIS SECRET SWAMP HEADQUARTERS.
SOUPER BORIS FOILED MY CAREFULLY PLANNED ROBBERY!
ME GOT PUNCHED! ME JAW STILL HURT!
AND I ALMOST HAD LEONARDO DA BENDY'S MASTERPIECE.
IF WITH OUR COMBINED POWERS WE WERE ABLE TO ESCAPE SUPER PRISON, THEN PERHAPS WE COULD TEAM UP TO TRIUMPH OVER THAT TROUBLESOME WOLF.
ME JOIN TEAM! ME BEAT UP SOUPER BORIS!
THEN IT IS AGREED. WE ARE UNITED AS THE SOCIETY FOR THE SHELLACKING OF SOUPER BORIS!

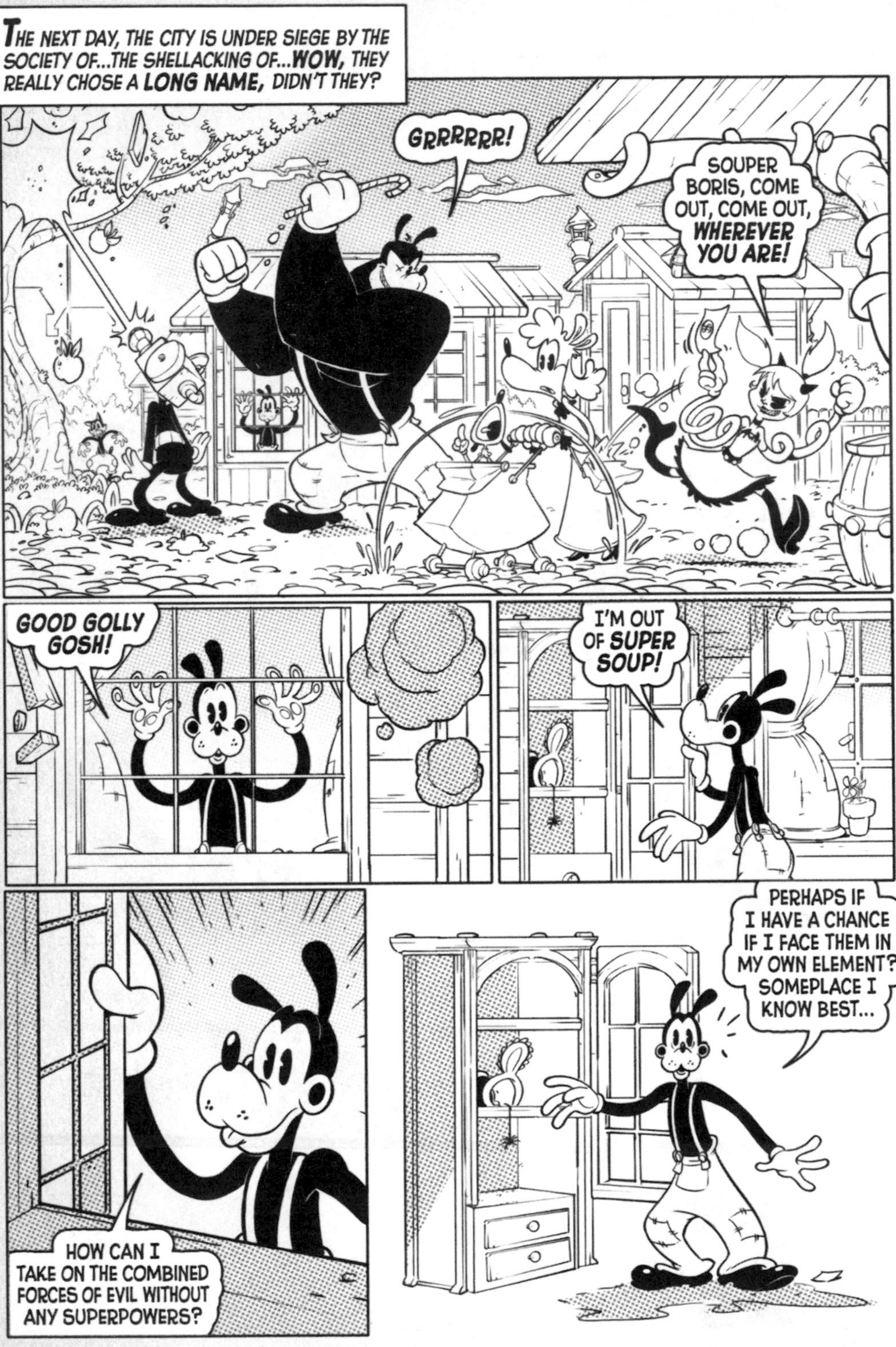
THE NEXT DAY, THE CITY IS UNDER SIEGE BY THE SOCIETY OF...THE SHELLACKING OF...WOW, THEY REALLY CHOSE A LONG NAME, DIDN'T THEY?
GRRRRRR!
SOUPER BORIS, COME OUT, COME OUT, WHEREVER YOU ARE!
GOOD GOLLY GOSH!
I'M OUT OF SUPER SOUP!
HOW CAN I TAKE ON THE COMBINED FORCES OF EVIL WITHOUT ANY SUPERPOWERS?
PERHAPS IF I HAVE A CHANCE IF I FACE THEM IN MY OWN ELEMENT? SOMEPLACE I KNOW BEST...

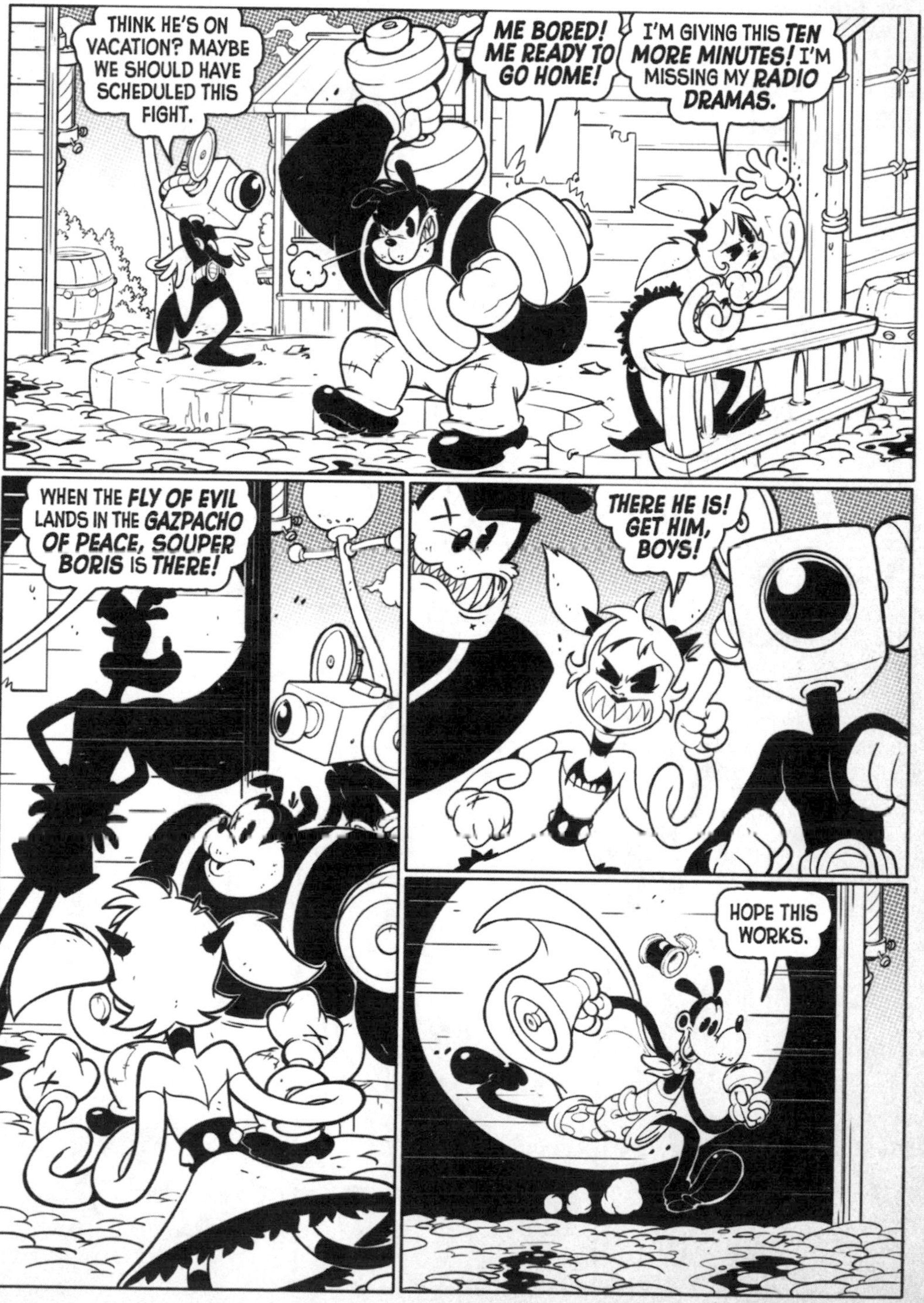
THINK HE'S ON VACATION? MAYBE WE SHOULD HAVE SCHEDULED THIS FIGHT.
ME BORED! ME READY TO GO HOME!
I'M GIVING THIS TEN MORE MINUTES! I'M MISSING MY RADIO DRAMAS.
WHEN THE FLY OF EVIL LANDS IN THE GAZPACHO OF PEACE, SOUPER BORIS IS THERE!
THERE HE IS! GET HIM, BOYS!
HOPE THIS WORKS.

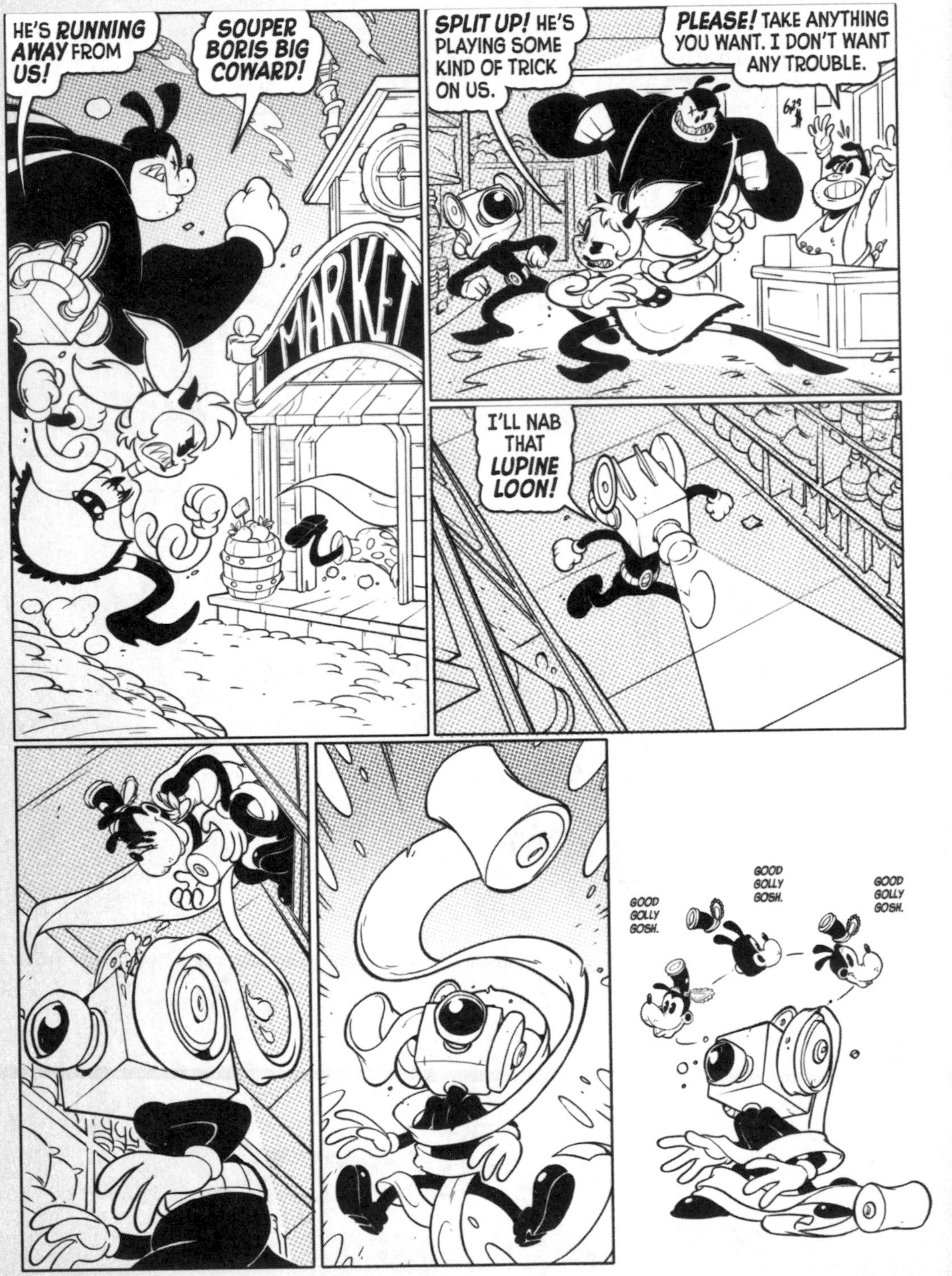
HE'S **RUNNING AWAY** FROM **US!**
SOUPER BORIS BIG COWARD!
MARKET
SPLIT UP! HE'S PLAYING SOME KIND OF TRICK ON US.
PLEASE! TAKE ANYTHING YOU WANT. I DON'T WANT ANY TROUBLE.
I'LL NAB THAT **LUPINE LOON!**
GOOD GOLLY GOSH.
GOOD GOLLY GOSH.
GOOD GOLLY GOSH.

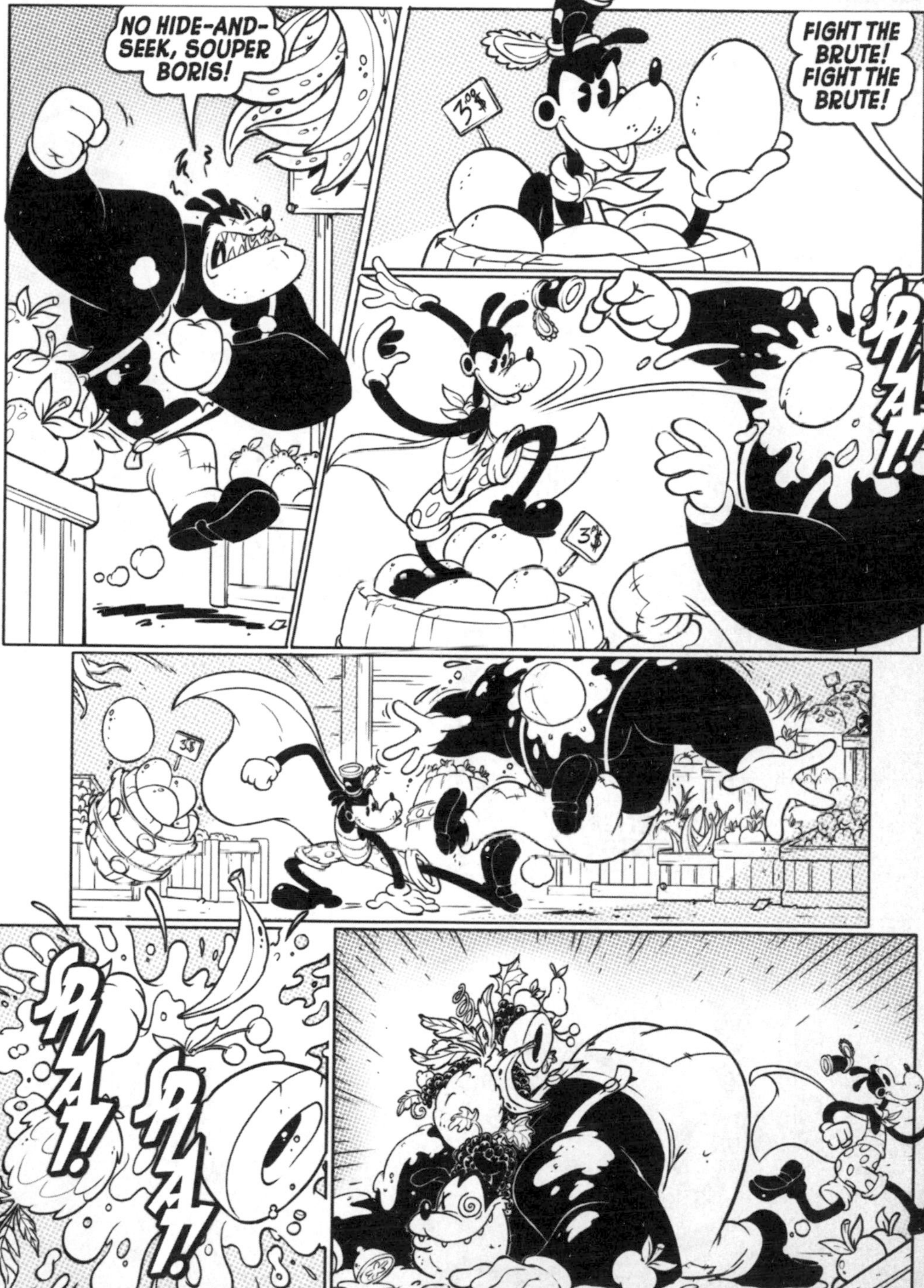
NO HIDE-AND-SEEK, SOUPER BORIS!
FIGHT THE BRUTE! FIGHT THE BRUTE!
SPLAT!
SPLAT!
SPLAT!

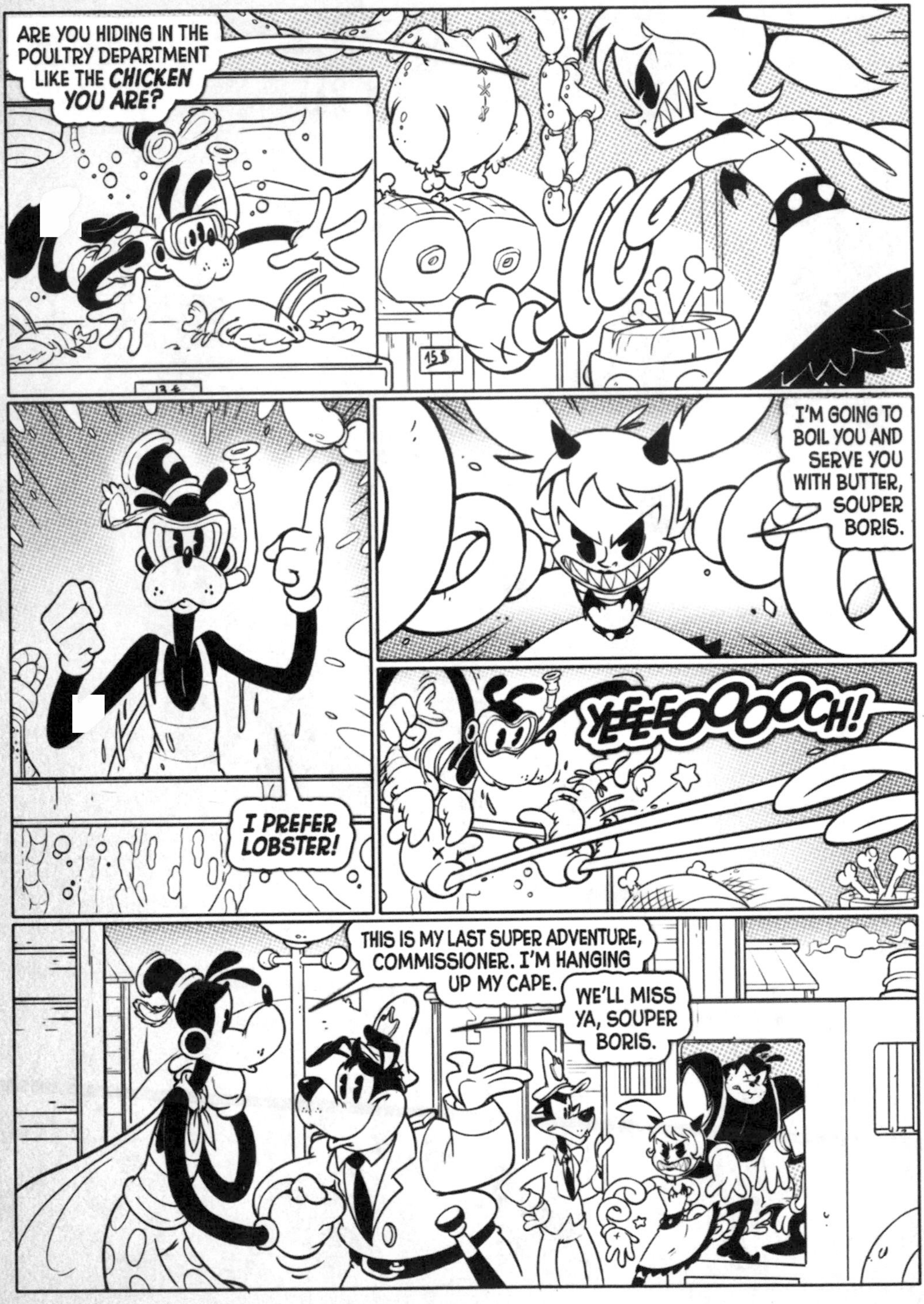
ARE YOU HIDING IN THE POULTRY DEPARTMENT LIKE THE CHICKEN YOU ARE?
15$
13$
I PREFER LOBSTER!
I'M GOING TO BOIL YOU AND SERVE YOU WITH BUTTER, SOUPER BORIS.
YEEEOOOOOCH!
THIS IS MY LAST SUPER ADVENTURE, COMMISSIONER. I'M HANGING UP MY CAPE.
WE'LL MISS YA, SOUPER BORIS.

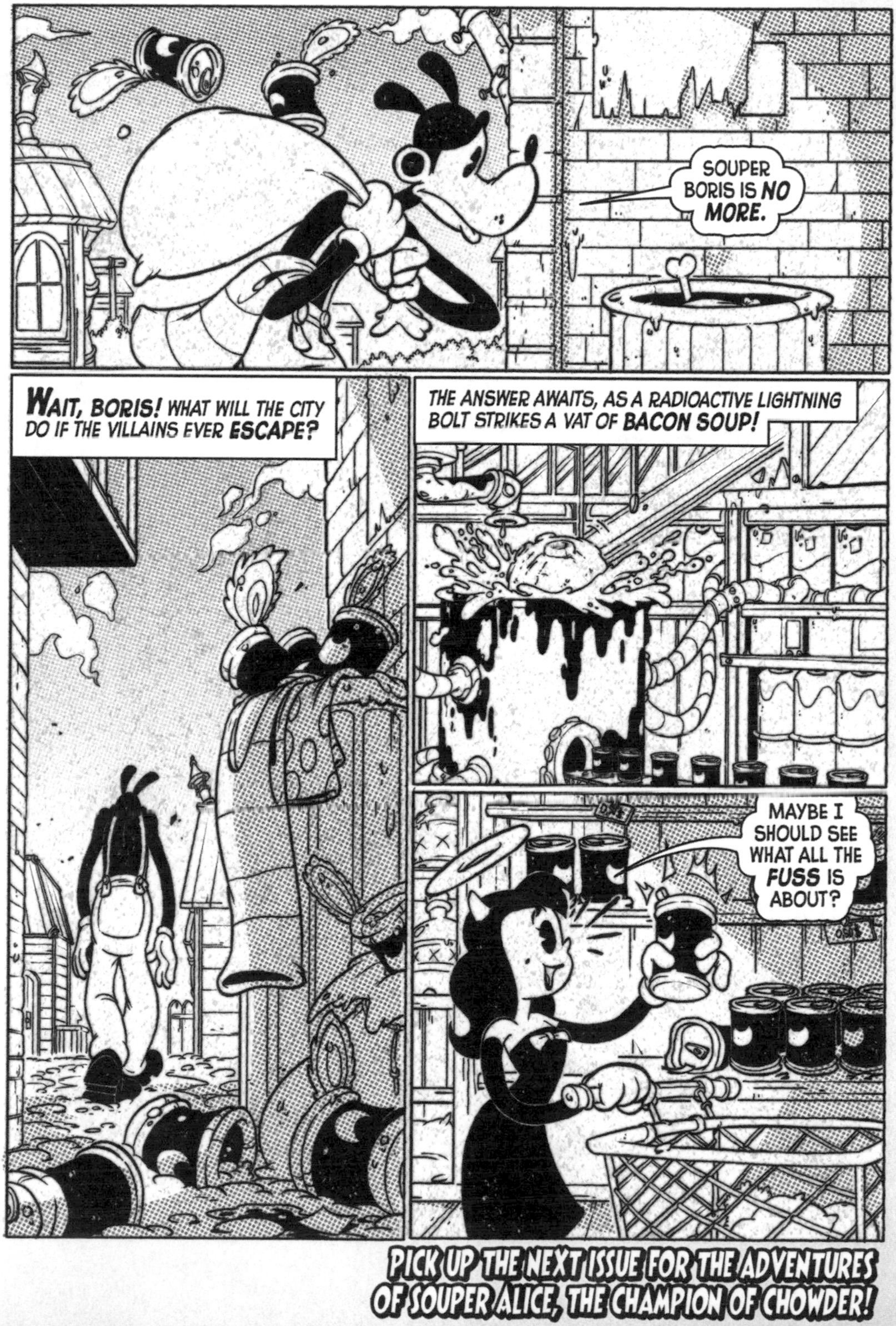
SOUPER BORIS IS NO MORE.
WAIT, BORIS! WHAT WILL THE CITY DO IF THE VILLAINS EVER ESCAPE?
THE ANSWER AWAITS, AS A RADIOACTIVE LIGHTNING BOLT STRIKES A VAT OF BACON SOUP!
MAYBE I SHOULD SEE WHAT ALL THE FUSS IS ABOUT?

PICK UP THE NEXT ISSUE FOR THE ADVENTURES OF SOUPER ALICE, THE CHAMPION OF CHOWDER!

Alice the Aviator! Or, Give Them Heck, Angel!

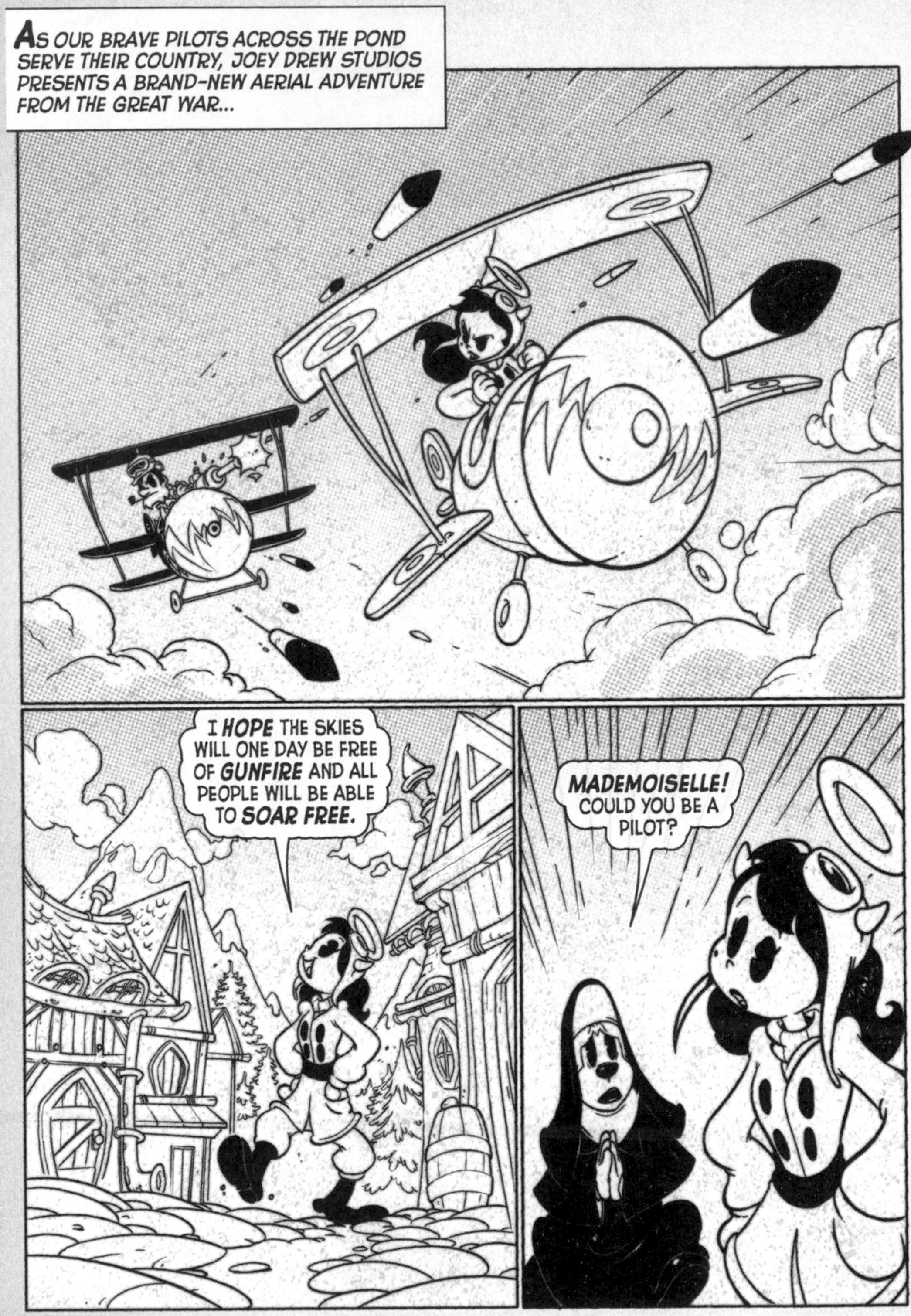
AS OUR BRAVE PILOTS ACROSS THE POND SERVE THEIR COUNTRY, JOEY DREW STUDIOS PRESENTS A BRAND-NEW AERIAL ADVENTURE FROM THE GREAT WAR...
I HOPE THE SKIES WILL ONE DAY BE FREE OF GUNFIRE AND ALL PEOPLE WILL BE ABLE TO SOAR FREE.
MADEMOISELLE! COULD YOU BE A PILOT?

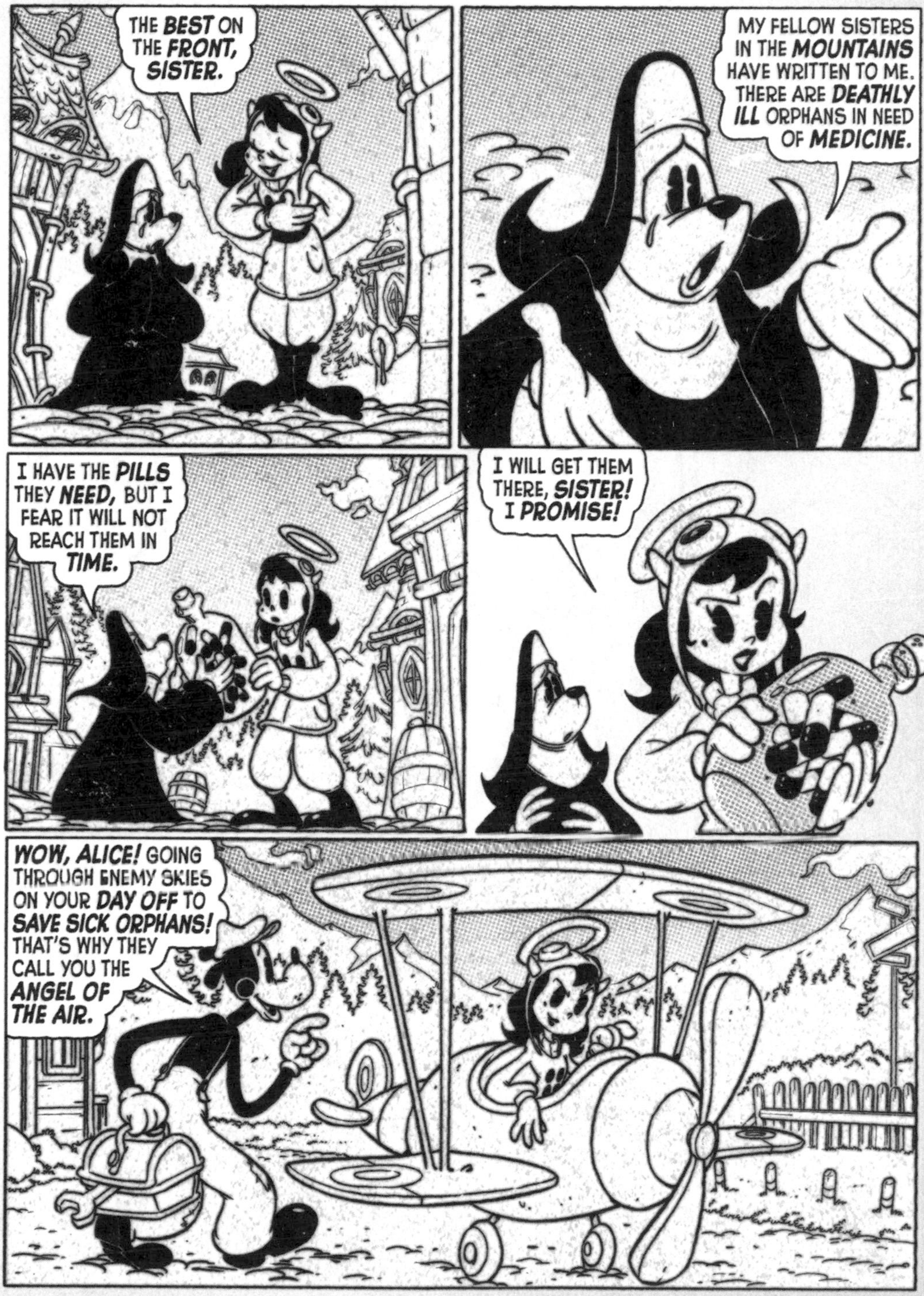
THE BEST ON THE FRONT, SISTER.
MY FELLOW SISTERS IN THE MOUNTAINS HAVE WRITTEN TO ME. THERE ARE DEATHLY ILL ORPHANS IN NEED OF MEDICINE.
I HAVE THE PILLS THEY NEED, BUT I FEAR IT WILL NOT REACH THEM IN TIME.
I WILL GET THEM THERE, SISTER! I PROMISE!
WOW, ALICE! GOING THROUGH ENEMY SKIES ON YOUR DAY OFF TO SAVE SICK ORPHANS! THAT'S WHY THEY CALL YOU THE ANGEL OF THE AIR.

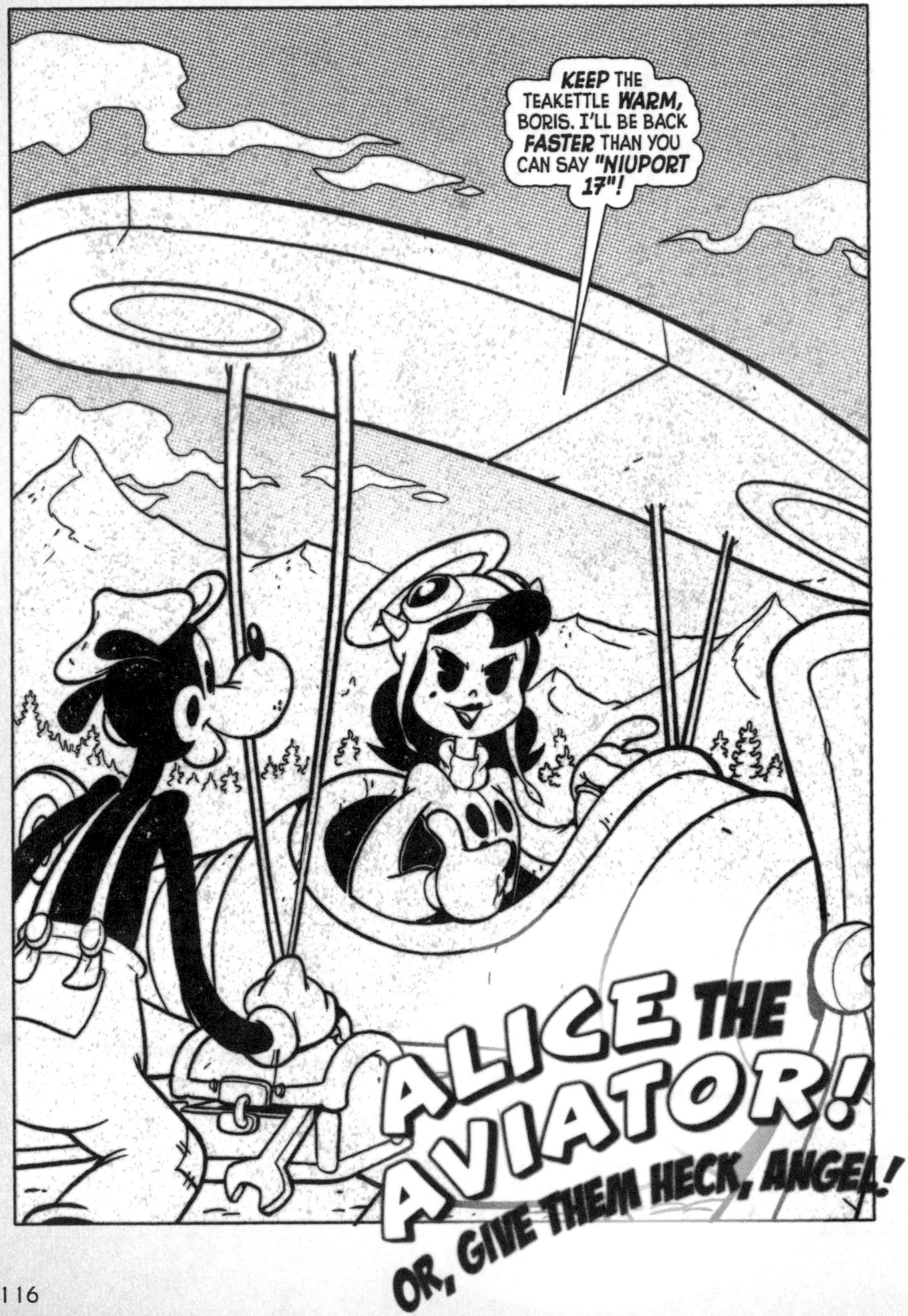
KEEP THE TEAKETTLE WARM, BORIS. I'LL BE BACK FASTER THAN YOU CAN SAY "NIUPORT 17"!
ALICE THE AVIATOR!
OR, GIVE THEM HECK, ANGEL!

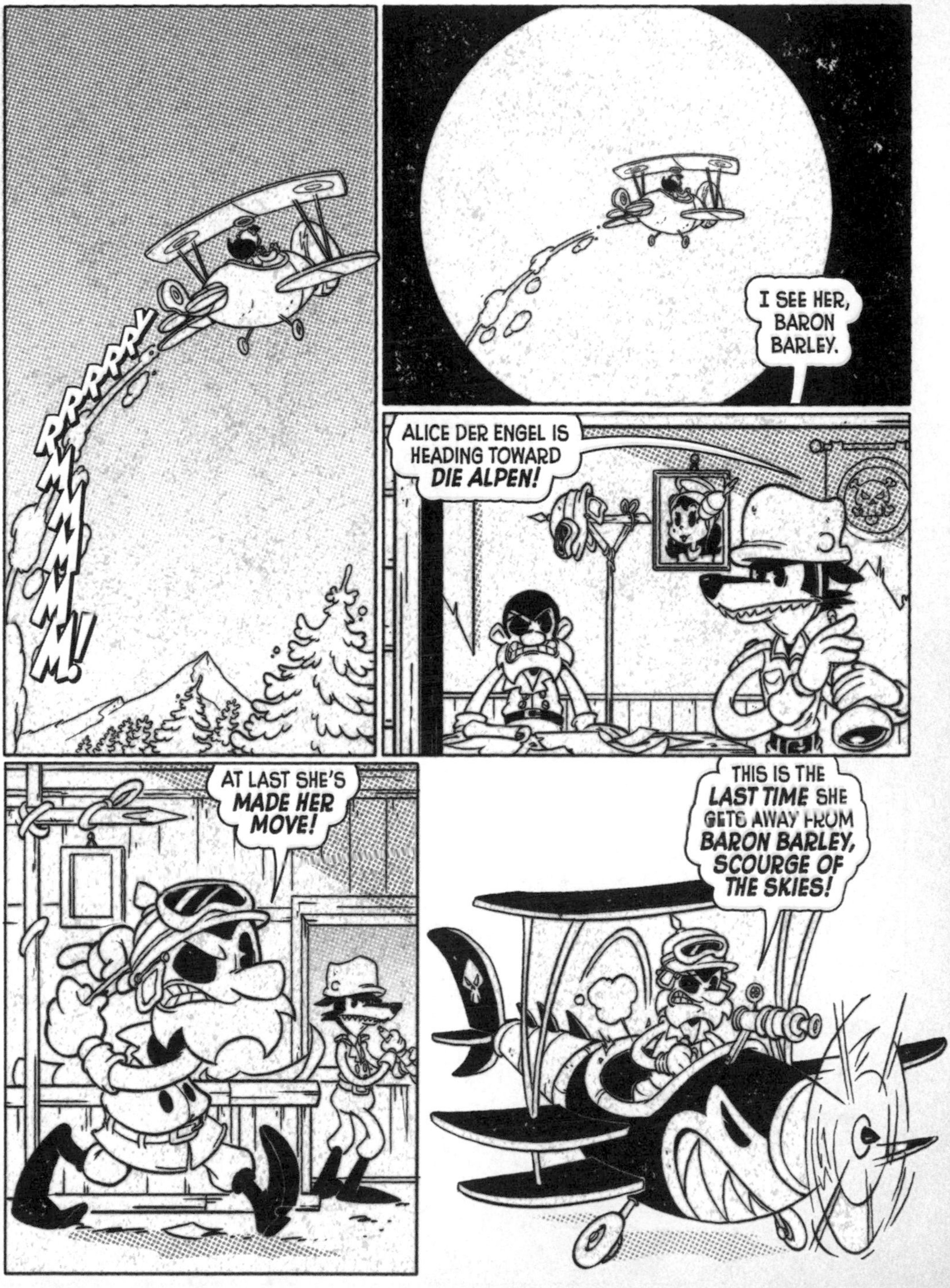
RRRRRRRRMMMMMMM!
I SEE HER, BARON BARLEY.
ALICE DER ENGEL IS HEADING TOWARD *DIE ALPEN!*
AT LAST SHE'S *MADE HER MOVE!*
THIS IS THE *LAST TIME* SHE GETS AWAY FROM *BARON BARLEY, SCOURGE OF THE SKIES!*

Alice the Aviator! Or, Give Them Heck, Angel!

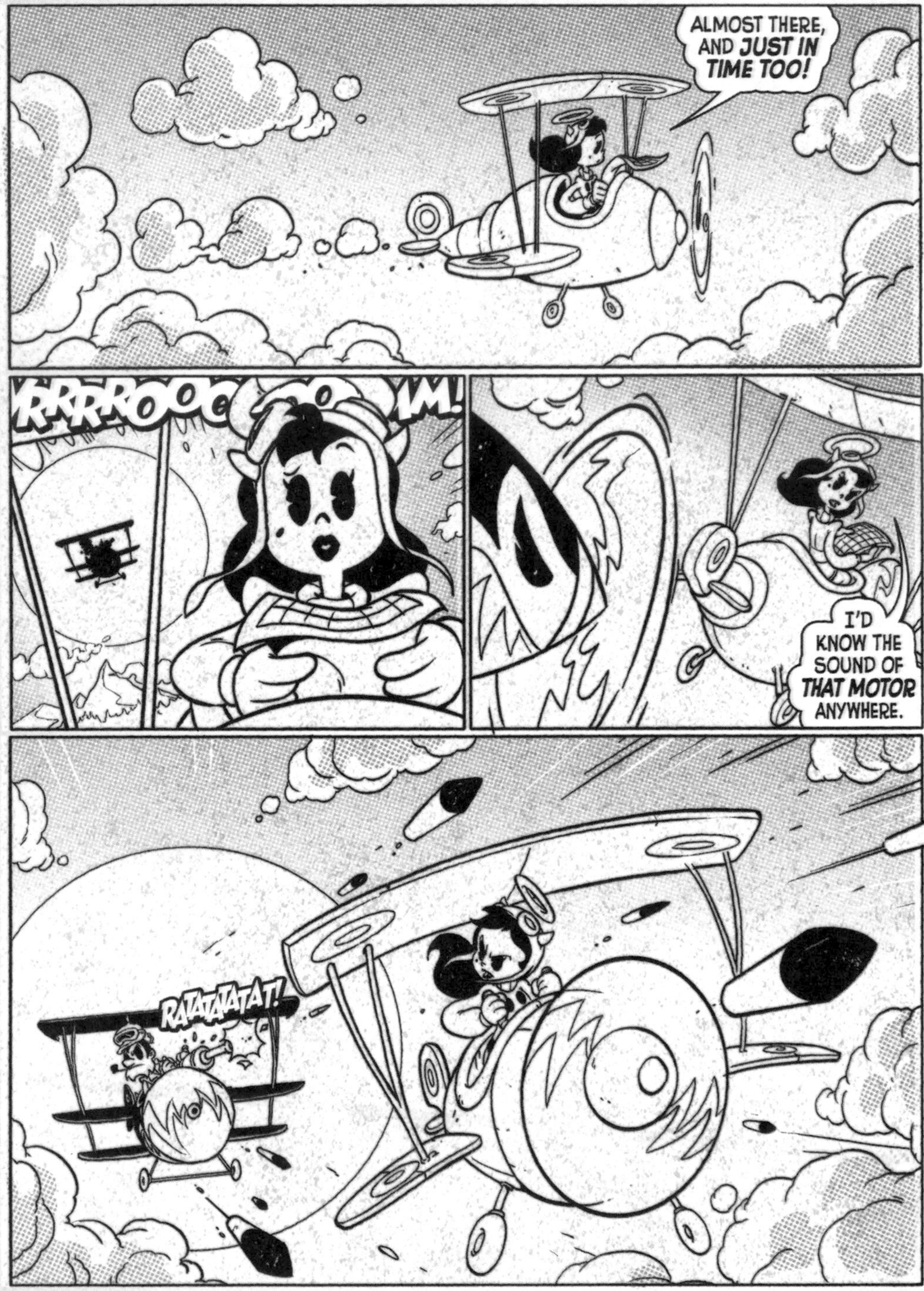
ALMOST THERE, AND JUST IN TIME TOO!
I'D KNOW THE SOUND OF THAT MOTOR ANYWHERE.
RATATATATAT!

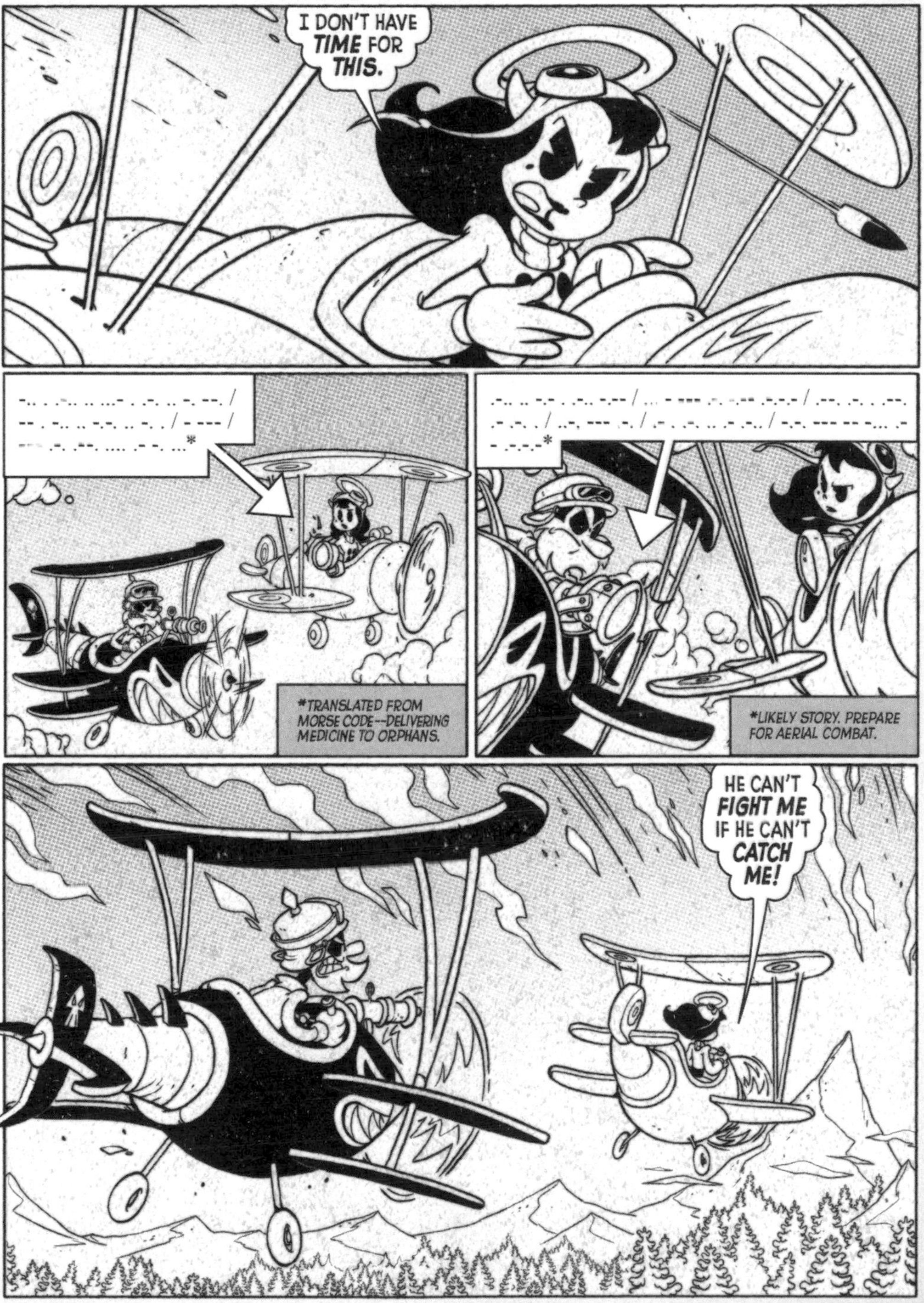
I DON'T HAVE TIME FOR THIS.
*TRANSLATED FROM MORSE CODE--DELIVERING MEDICINE TO ORPHANS.
*LIKELY STORY. PREPARE FOR AERIAL COMBAT.
HE CAN'T FIGHT ME IF HE CAN'T CATCH ME!

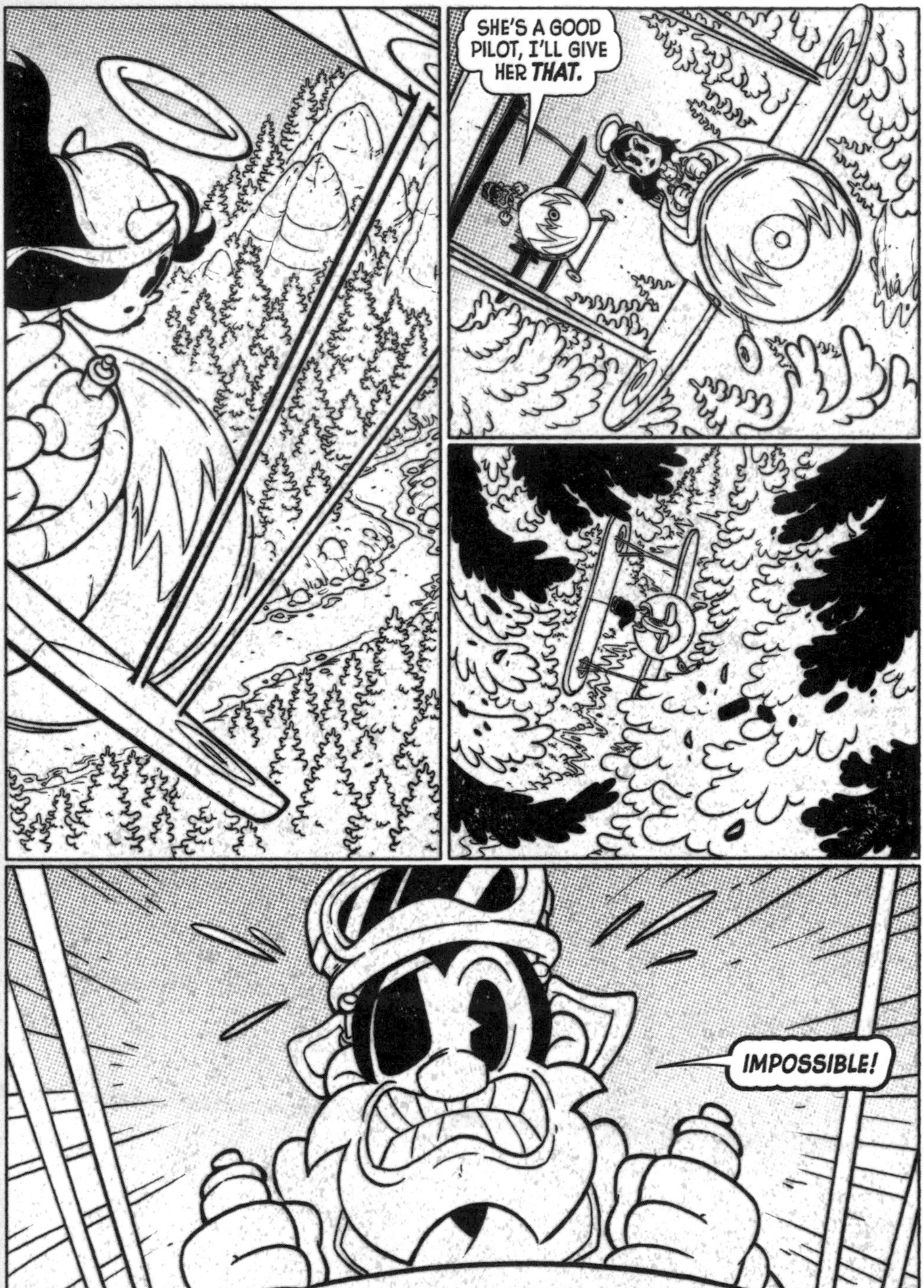
SHE'S A GOOD PILOT, I'LL GIVE HER *THAT.*
IMPOSSIBLE!

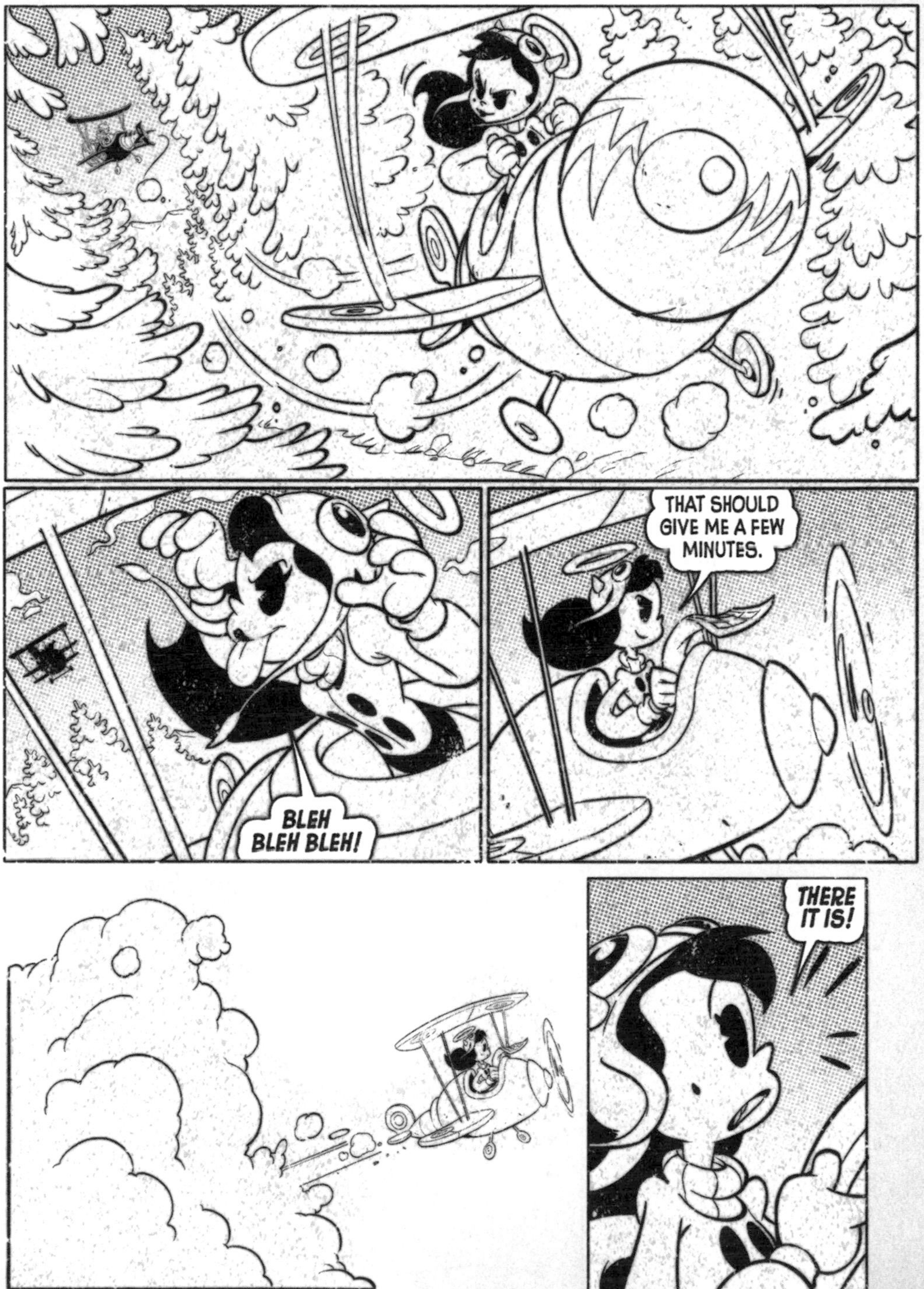
BLEH
BLEH BLEH!
THAT SHOULD GIVE ME A FEW MINUTES.
THERE IT IS!

Alice the Aviator! Or, Give Them Heck, Angel!

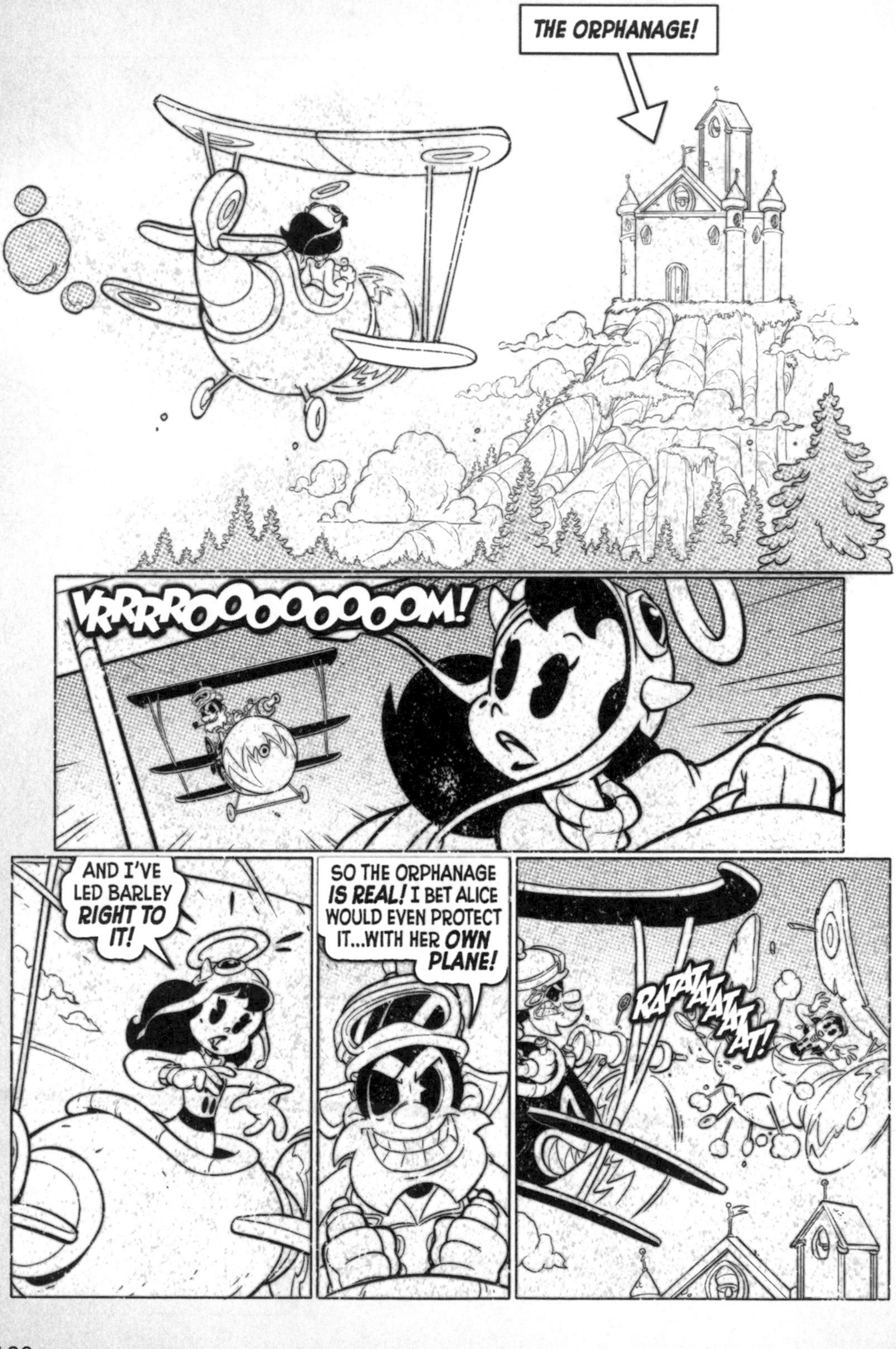

THE ORPHANAGE!
VRRRROOOOOOOOOM!
AND I'VE LED BARLEY RIGHT TO IT!
SO THE ORPHANAGE IS REAL! I BET ALICE WOULD EVEN PROTECT IT...WITH HER OWN PLANE!
RATATATATATAT!

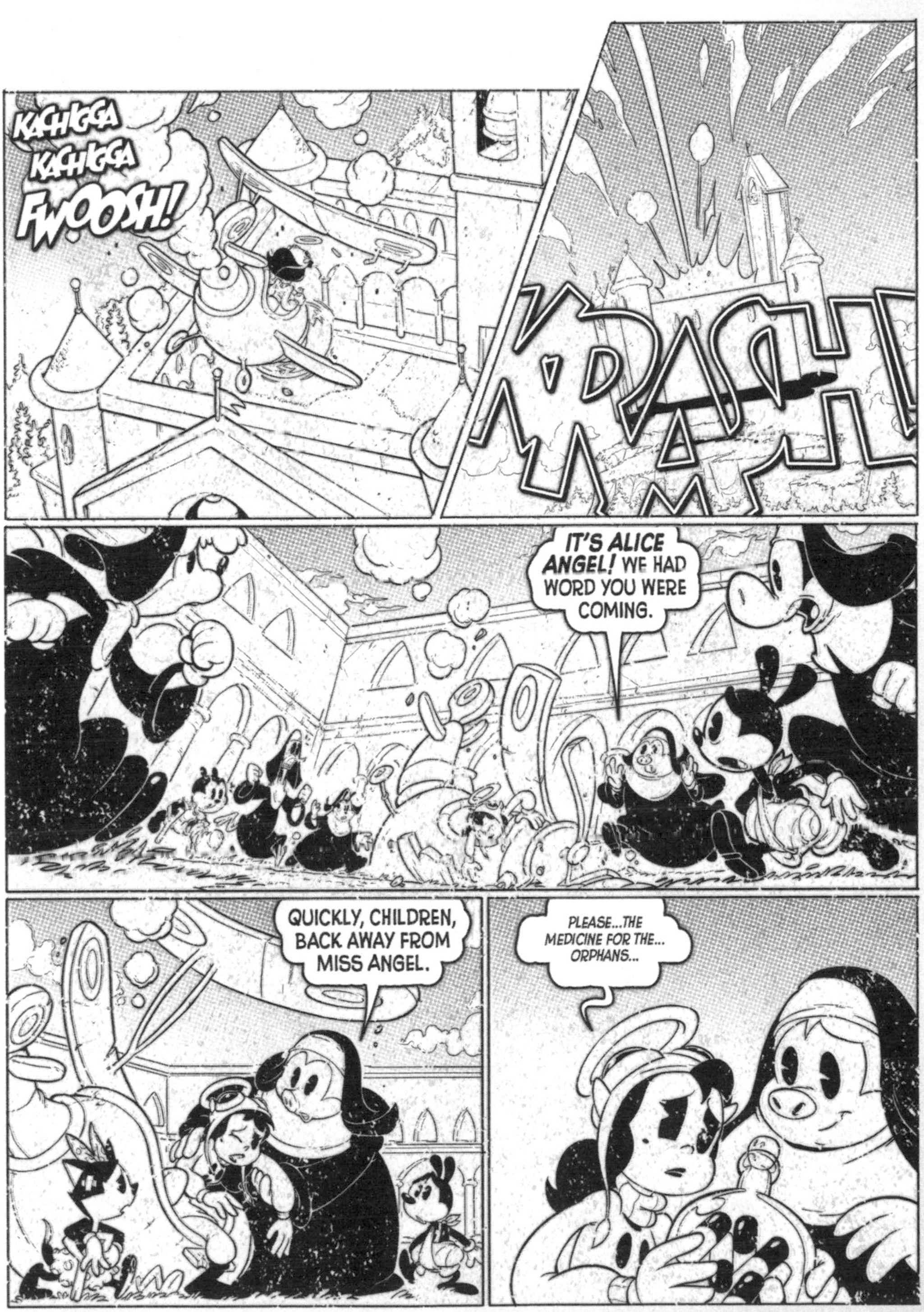
KACHIGGA
KACHIGGA
FWOOSH!
KRASH
IT'S ALICE ANGEL! WE HAD WORD YOU WERE COMING.
QUICKLY, CHILDREN, BACK AWAY FROM MISS ANGEL.
PLEASE...THE MEDICINE FOR THE... ORPHANS...

Alice the Aviator! Or, Give Them Heck, Angel!

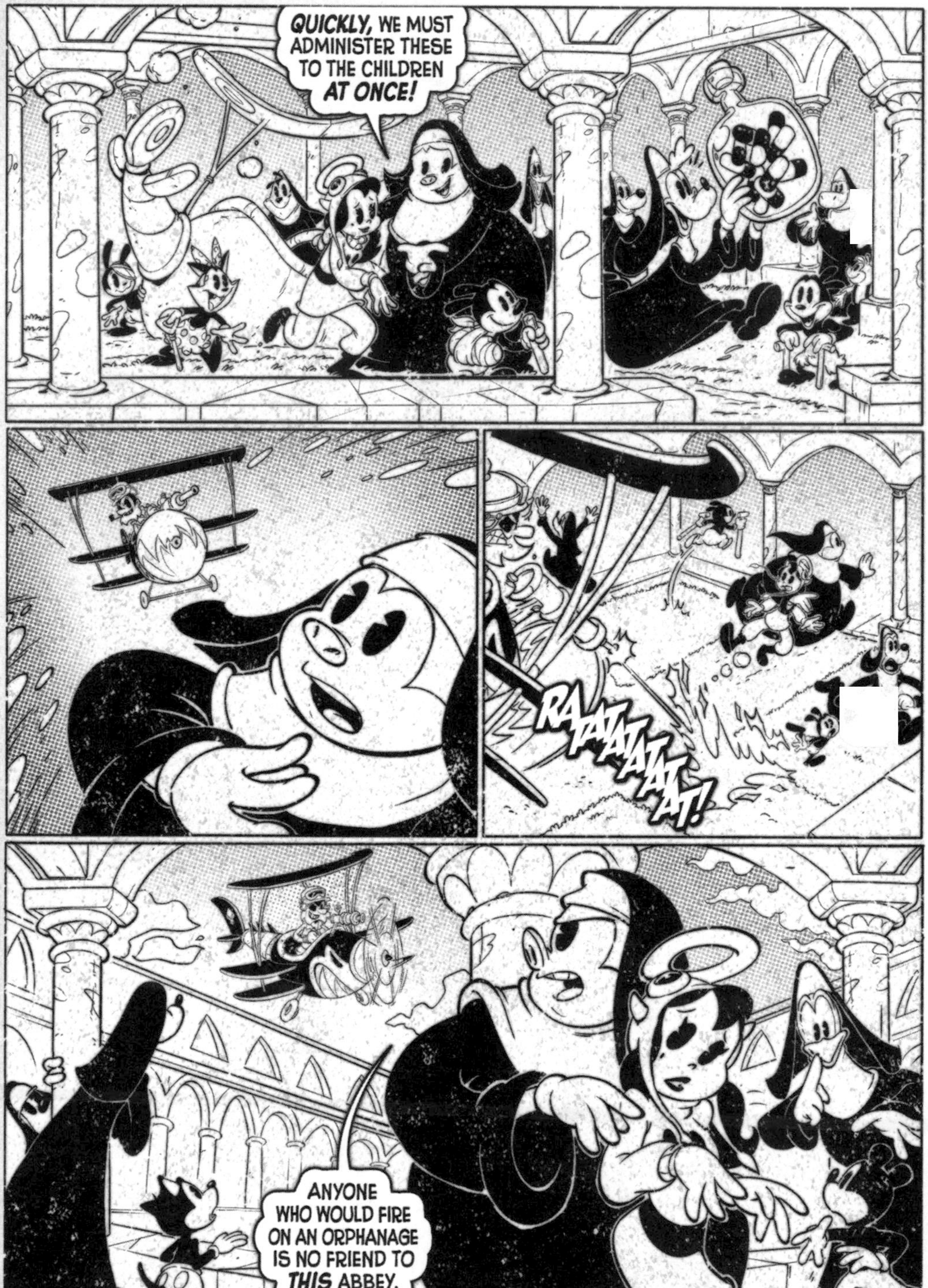
QUICKLY, WE MUST ADMINISTER THESE TO THE CHILDREN AT ONCE!
RATATATATATAT!
ANYONE WHO WOULD FIRE ON AN ORPHANAGE IS NO FRIEND TO THIS ABBEY.

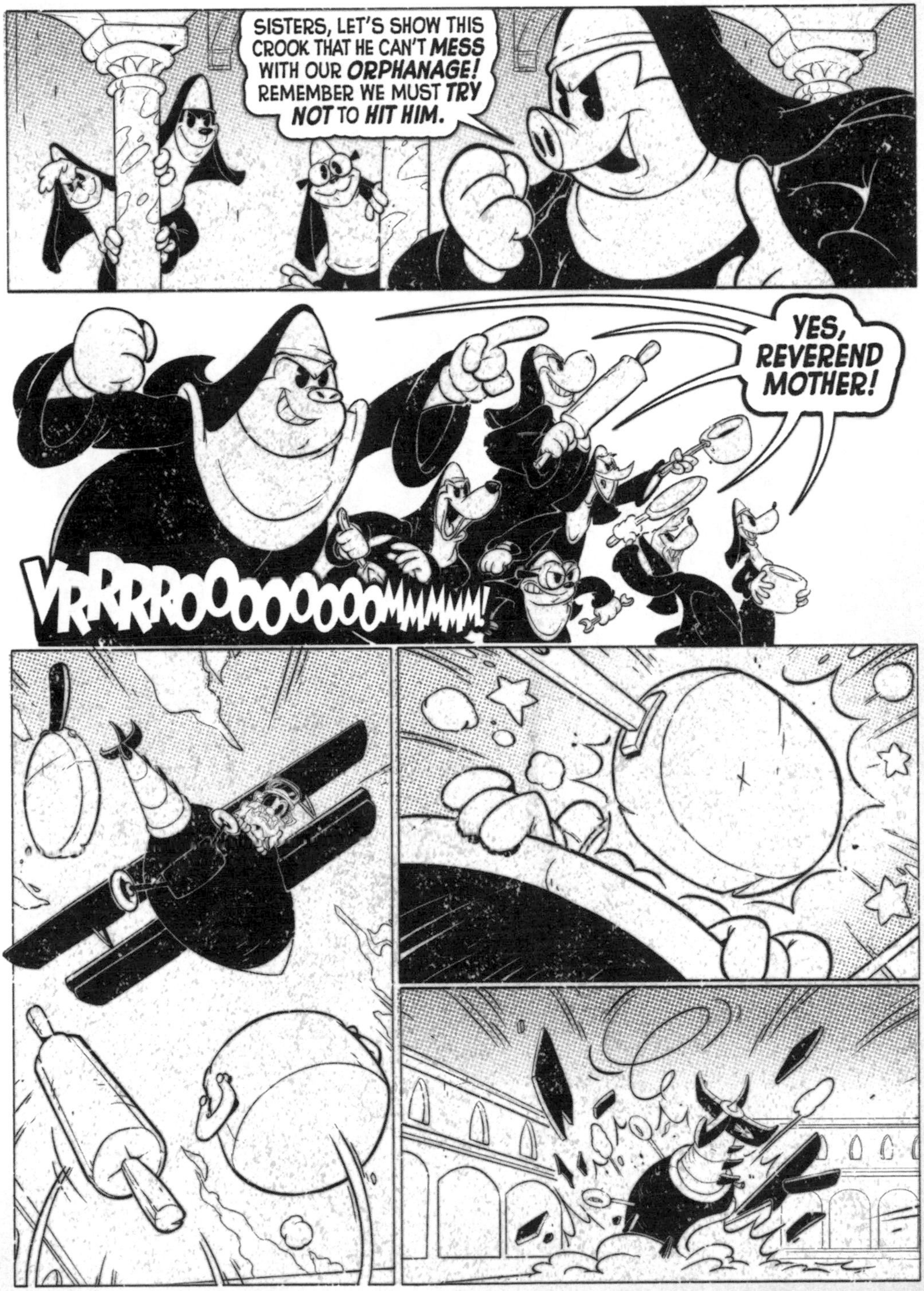
SISTERS, LET'S SHOW THIS CROOK THAT HE CAN'T MESS WITH OUR ORPHANAGE! REMEMBER WE MUST TRY NOT TO HIT HIM.
YES, REVEREND MOTHER!
VRRRROOOOOOOOMMMMM!

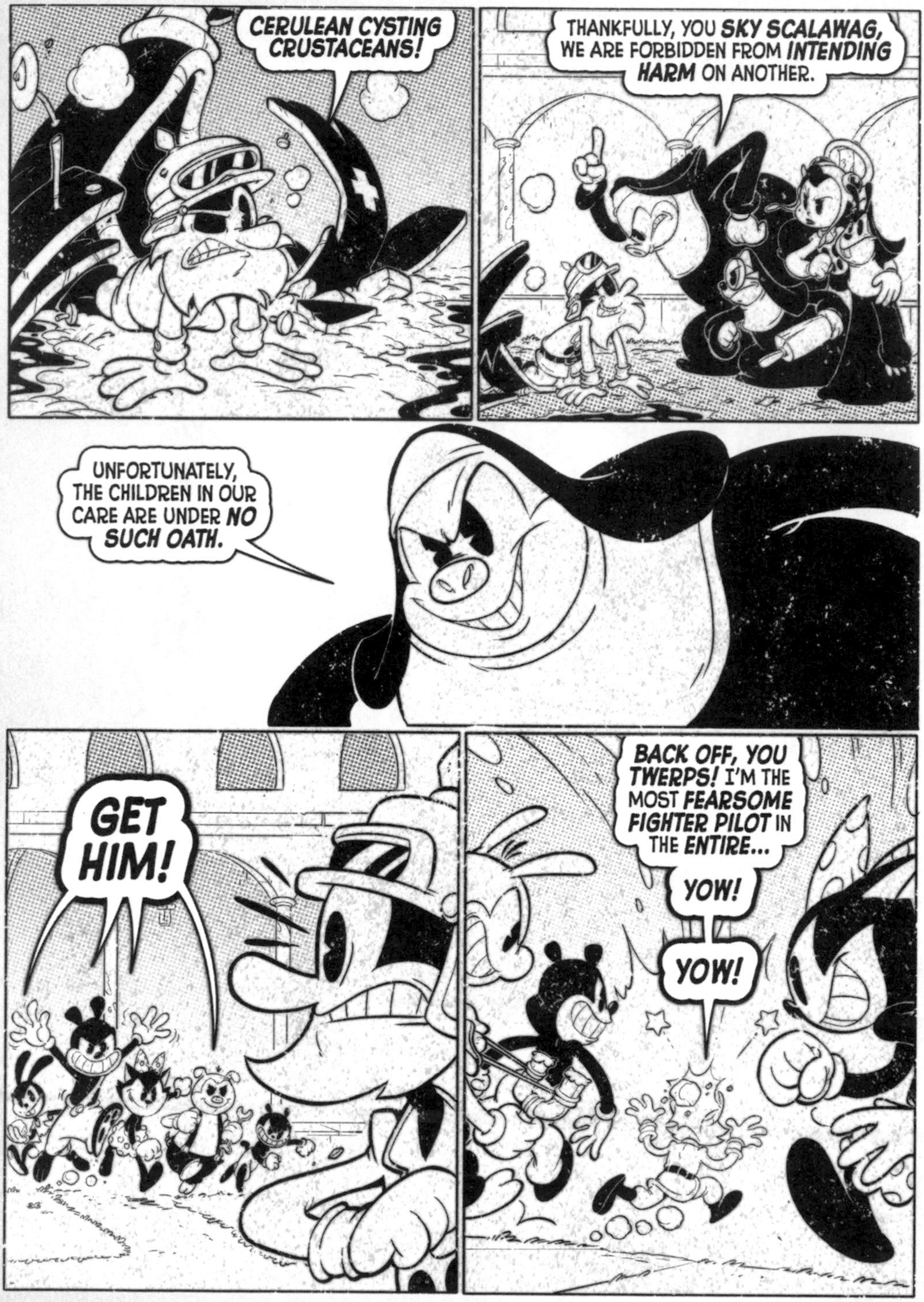
CERULEAN CYSTING CRUSTACEANS!
THANKFULLY, YOU SKY SCALAWAG, WE ARE FORBIDDEN FROM INTENDING HARM ON ANOTHER.
UNFORTUNATELY, THE CHILDREN IN OUR CARE ARE UNDER NO SUCH OATH.
GET HIM!
BACK OFF, YOU TWERPS! I'M THE MOST FEARSOME FIGHTER PILOT IN THE ENTIRE...
YOW!
YOW!

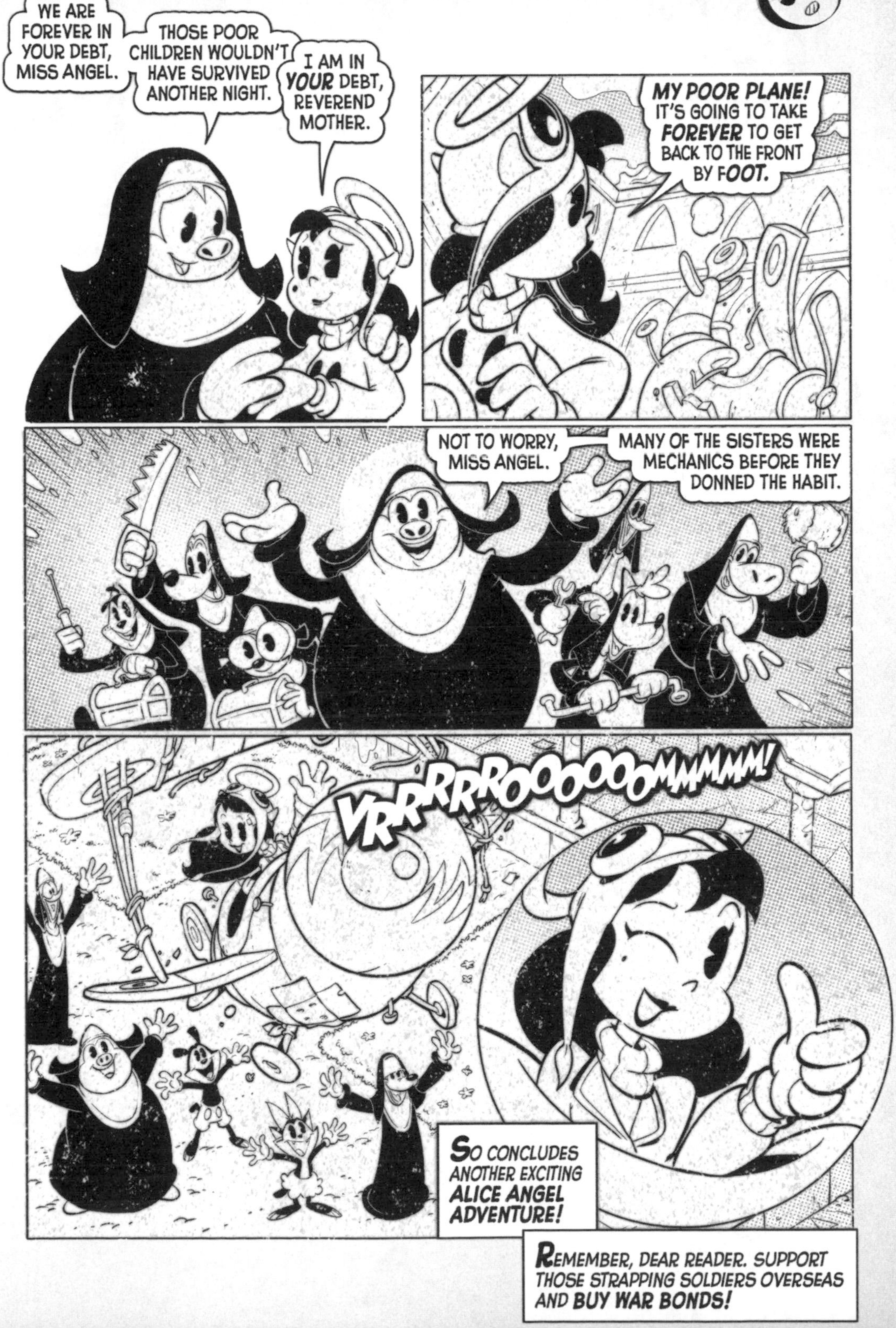
WE ARE FOREVER IN YOUR DEBT, MISS ANGEL.
THOSE POOR CHILDREN WOULDN'T HAVE SURVIVED ANOTHER NIGHT.
I AM IN YOUR DEBT, REVEREND MOTHER.
MY POOR PLANE! IT'S GOING TO TAKE FOREVER TO GET BACK TO THE FRONT BY FOOT.
NOT TO WORRY, MISS ANGEL.
MANY OF THE SISTERS WERE MECHANICS BEFORE THEY DONNED THE HABIT.
VRRRRROOOOOOMMMMM!
SO CONCLUDES ANOTHER EXCITING ALICE ANGEL ADVENTURE!
REMEMBER, DEAR READER. SUPPORT THOSE STRAPPING SOLDIERS OVERSEAS AND BUY WAR BONDS!

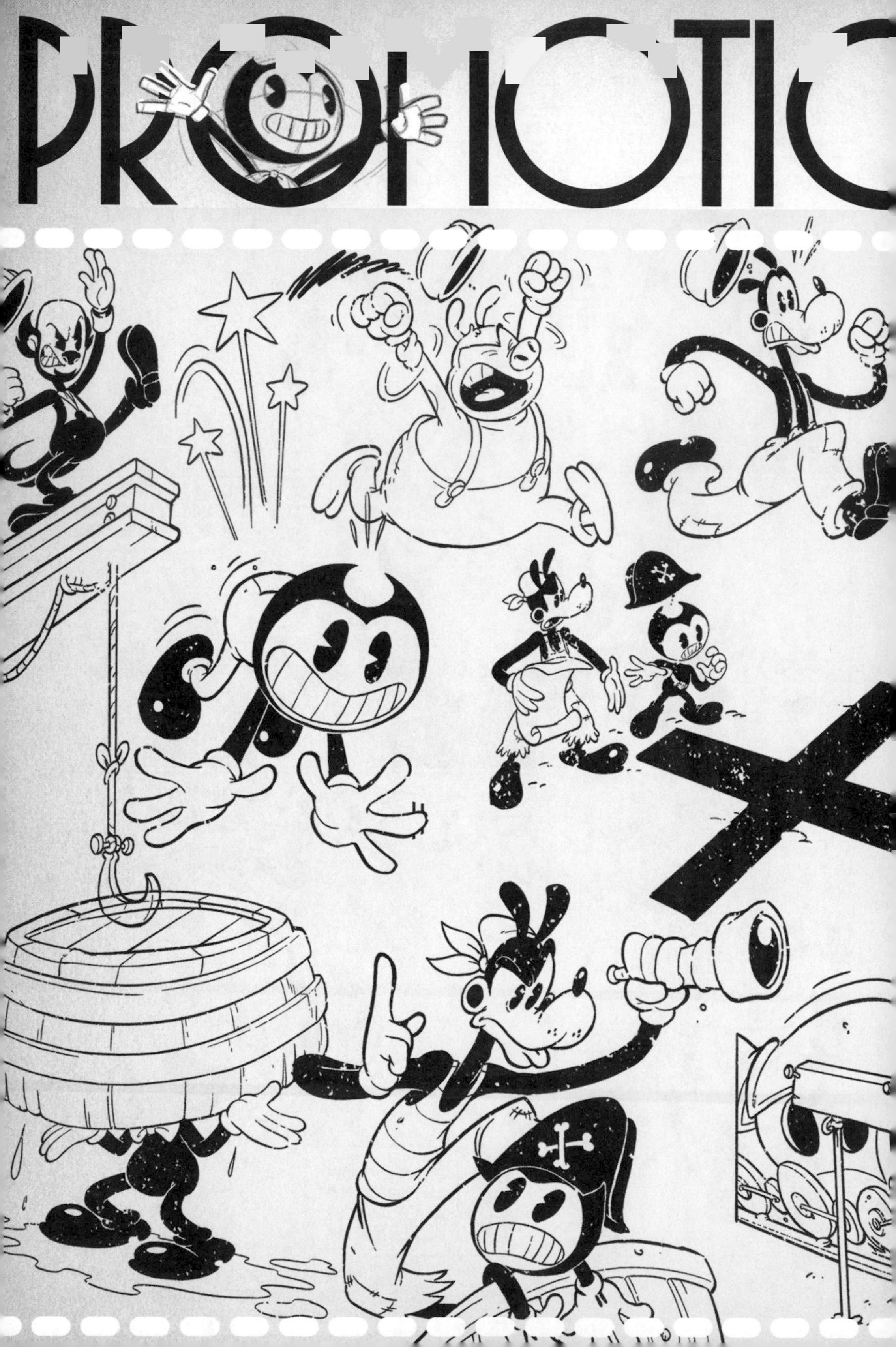
PROMOTIO

ONAL COMICS

1941–1946

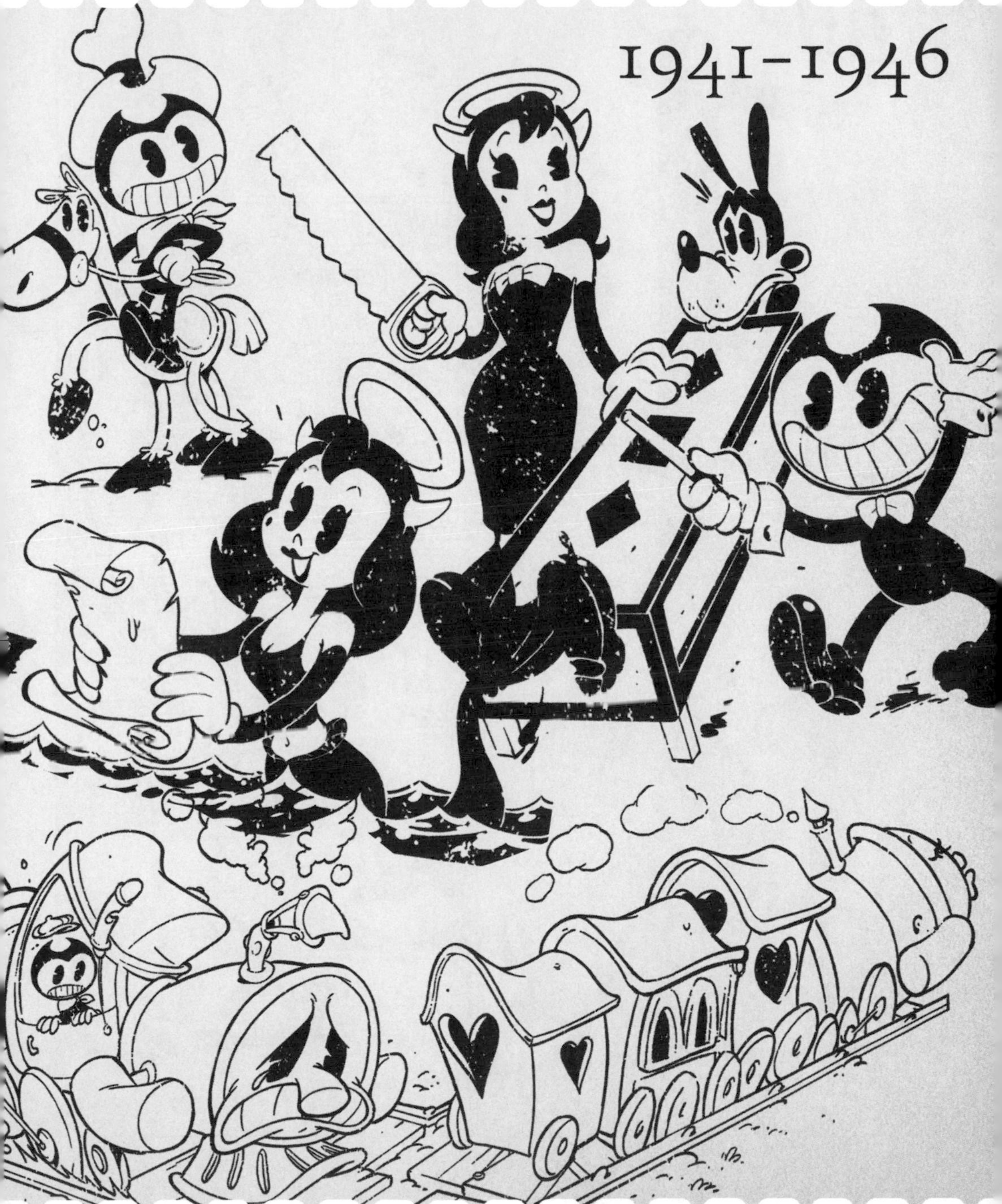

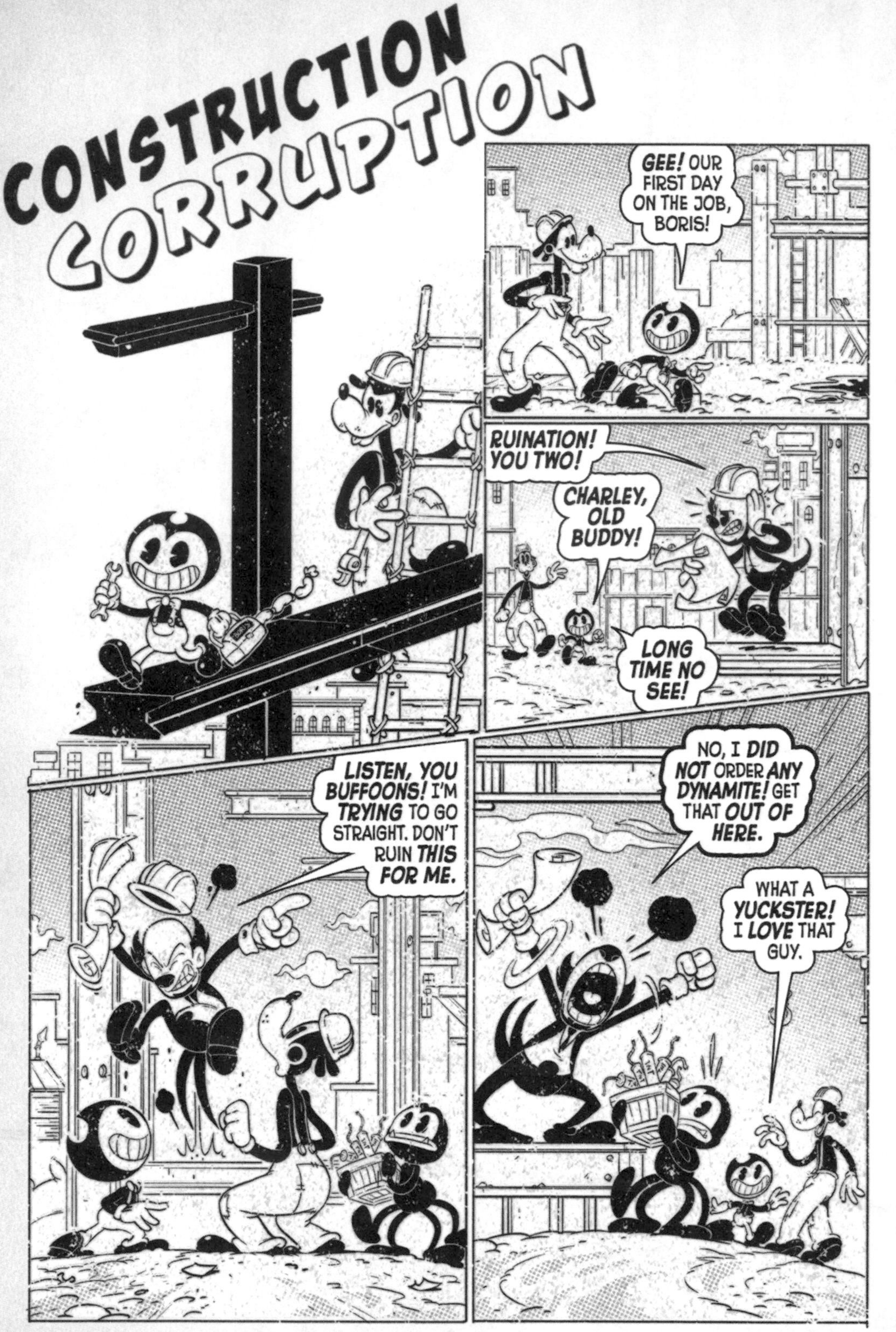
CONSTRUCTION CORRUPTION
GEE! OUR FIRST DAY ON THE JOB, BORIS!
RUINATION! YOU TWO!
CHARLEY, OLD BUDDY!
LONG TIME NO SEE!
LISTEN, YOU BUFFOONS! I'M TRYING TO GO STRAIGHT. DON'T RUIN THIS FOR ME.
NO, I DID NOT ORDER ANY DYNAMITE! GET THAT OUT OF HERE.
WHAT A YUCKSTER! I LOVE THAT GUY.

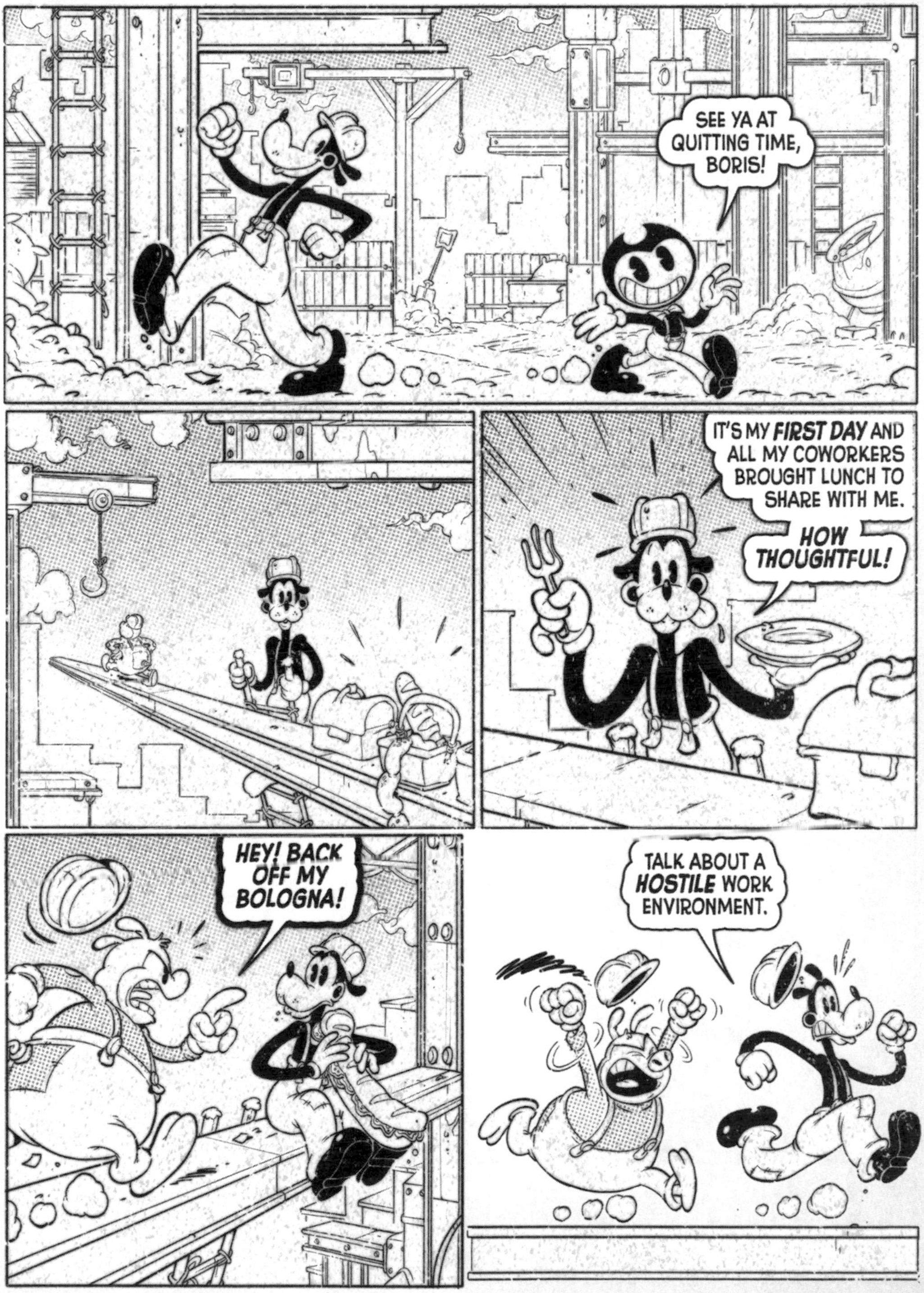
SEE YA AT QUITTING TIME, BORIS!
IT'S MY FIRST DAY AND ALL MY COWORKERS BROUGHT LUNCH TO SHARE WITH ME.
HOW THOUGHTFUL!
HEY! BACK OFF MY BOLOGNA!
TALK ABOUT A HOSTILE WORK ENVIRONMENT.

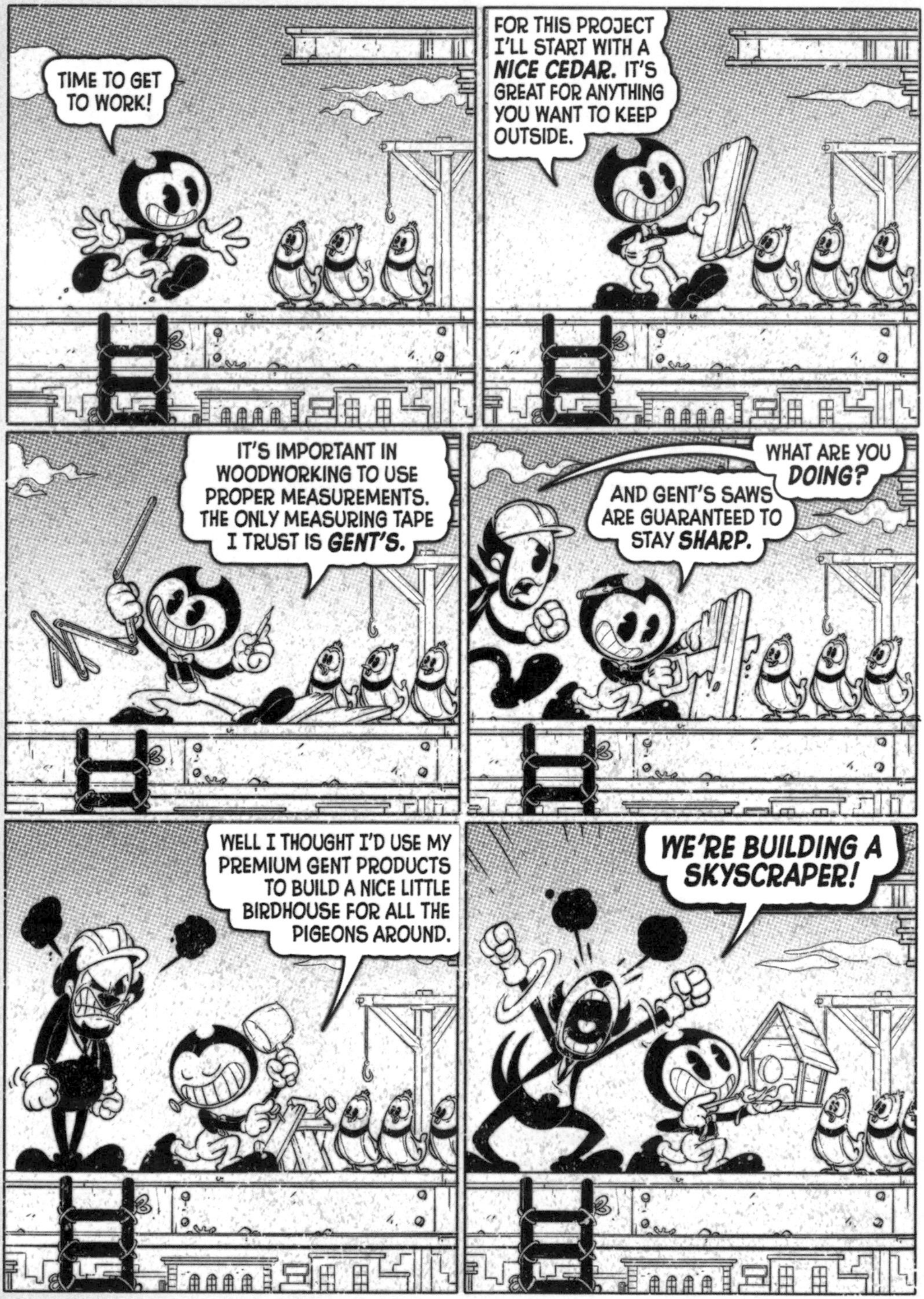
TIME TO GET TO WORK!
FOR THIS PROJECT I'LL START WITH A NICE CEDAR. IT'S GREAT FOR ANYTHING YOU WANT TO KEEP OUTSIDE.
IT'S IMPORTANT IN WOODWORKING TO USE PROPER MEASUREMENTS. THE ONLY MEASURING TAPE I TRUST IS GENT'S.
AND GENT'S SAWS ARE GUARANTEED TO STAY SHARP.
WHAT ARE YOU DOING?
WELL I THOUGHT I'D USE MY PREMIUM GENT PRODUCTS TO BUILD A NICE LITTLE BIRDHOUSE FOR ALL THE PIGEONS AROUND.
WE'RE BUILDING A SKYSCRAPER!

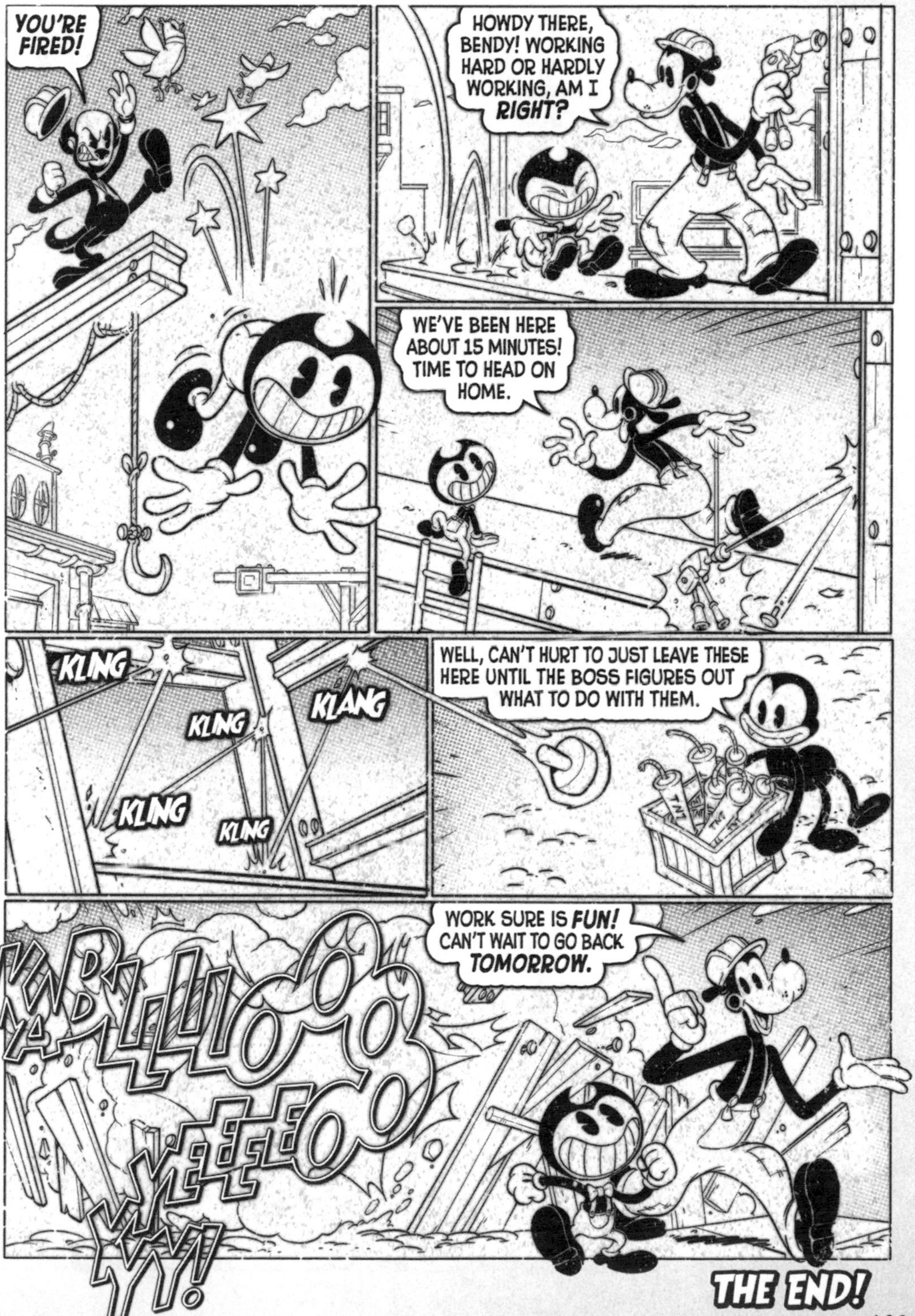
YOU'RE FIRED!
HOWDY THERE, BENDY! WORKING HARD OR HARDLY WORKING, AM I RIGHT?
WE'VE BEEN HERE ABOUT 15 MINUTES! TIME TO HEAD ON HOME.
KLING
KLANG
KLING
KLING
KLING
WELL, CAN'T HURT TO JUST LEAVE THESE HERE UNTIL THE BOSS FIGURES OUT WHAT TO DO WITH THEM.
WORK SURE IS FUN! CAN'T WAIT TO GO BACK TOMORROW.
THE END!

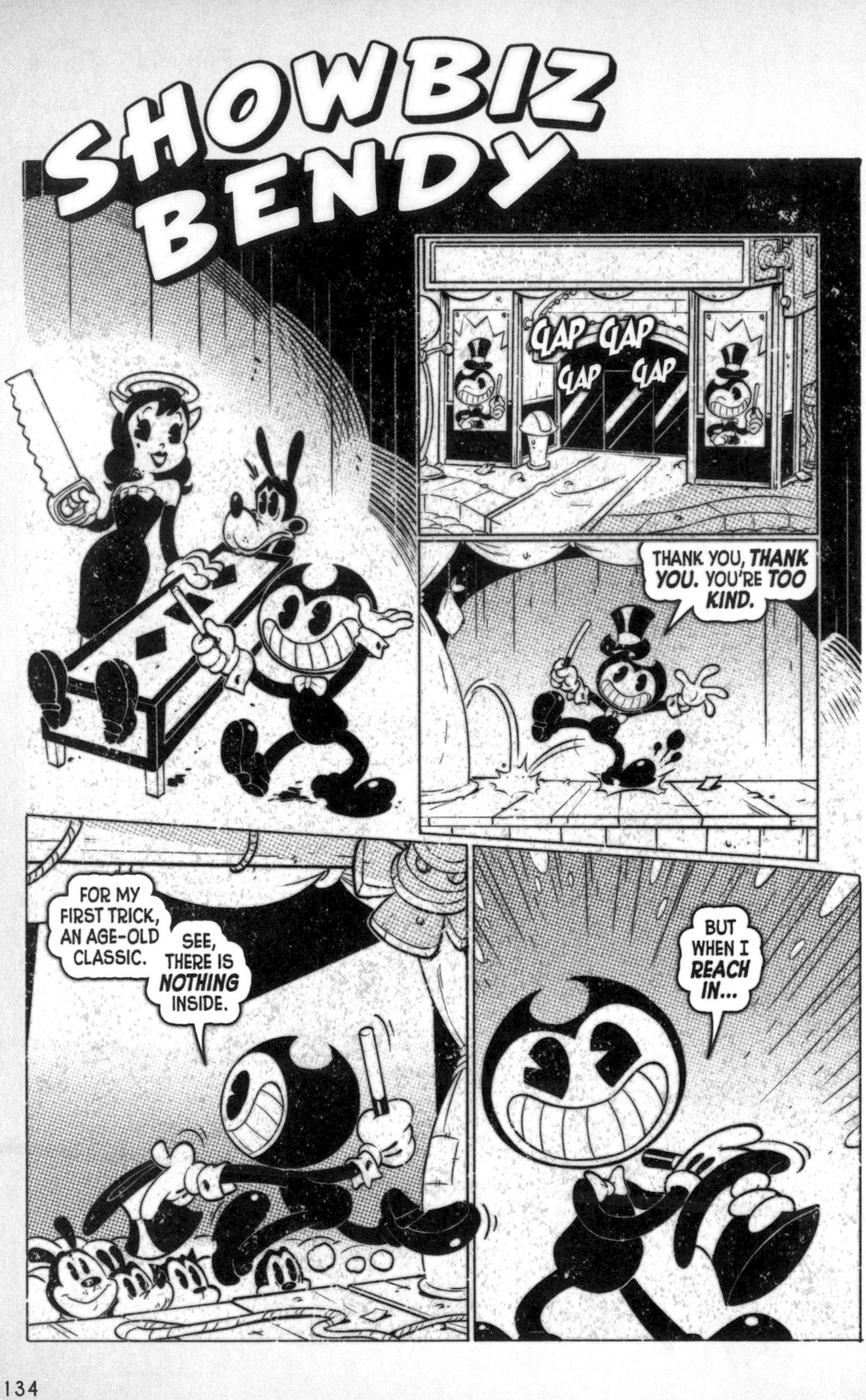
SHOWBIZ BENDY
CLAP CLAP
CLAP CLAP
THANK YOU, THANK YOU. YOU'RE TOO KIND.
FOR MY FIRST TRICK, AN AGE-OLD CLASSIC.
SEE, THERE IS NOTHING INSIDE.
BUT WHEN I REACH IN...

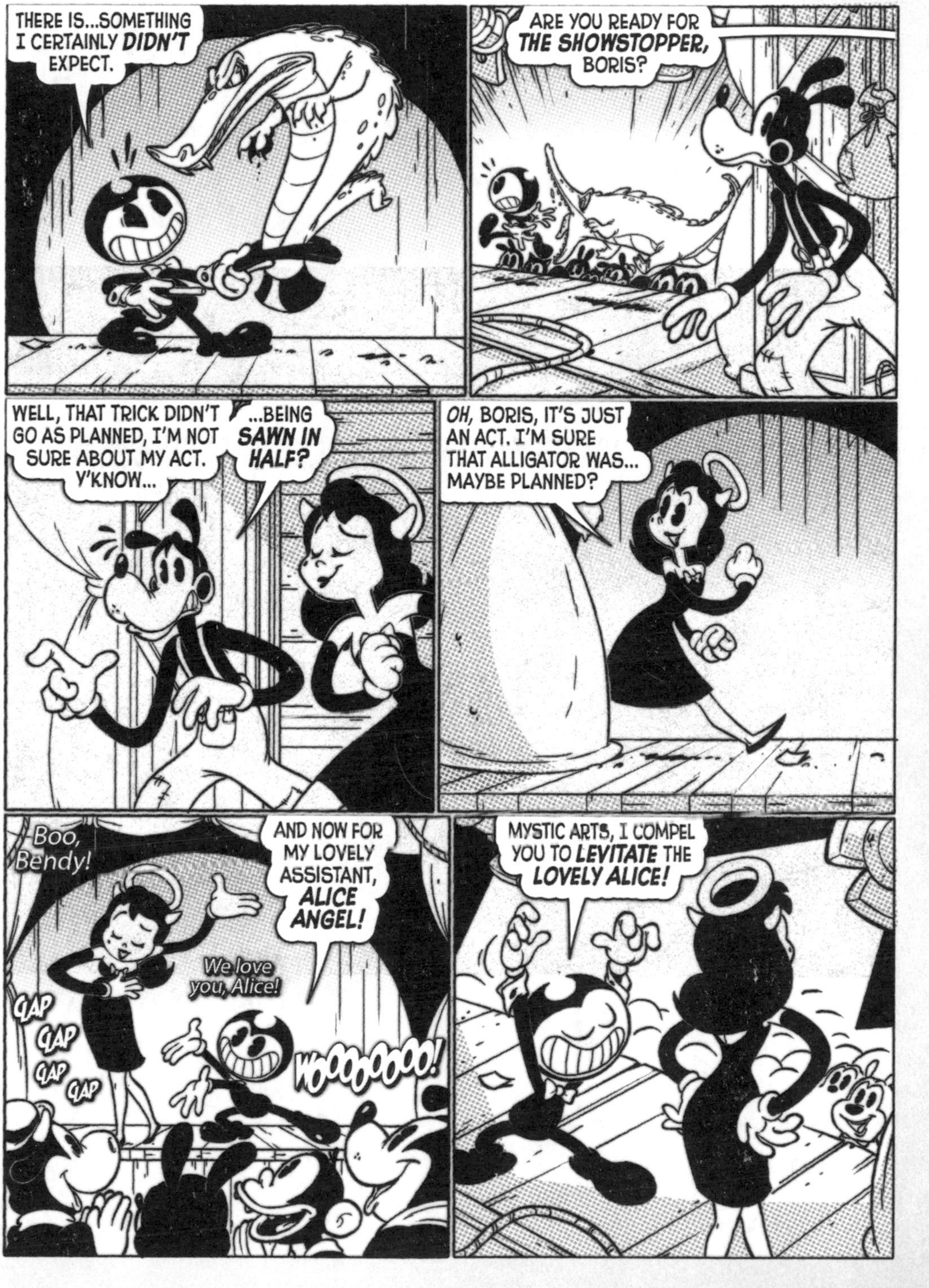
THERE IS...SOMETHING I CERTAINLY DIDN'T EXPECT.
ARE YOU READY FOR THE SHOWSTOPPER, BORIS?
WELL, THAT TRICK DIDN'T GO AS PLANNED, I'M NOT SURE ABOUT MY ACT. Y'KNOW...
...BEING SAWN IN HALF?
OH, BORIS, IT'S JUST AN ACT. I'M SURE THAT ALLIGATOR WAS... MAYBE PLANNED?
Boo, Bendy!
AND NOW FOR MY LOVELY ASSISTANT, ALICE ANGEL!
We love you, Alice!
CLAP CLAP CLAP CLAP
WOOOOOOOO!
MYSTIC ARTS, I COMPEL YOU TO LEVITATE THE LOVELY ALICE!

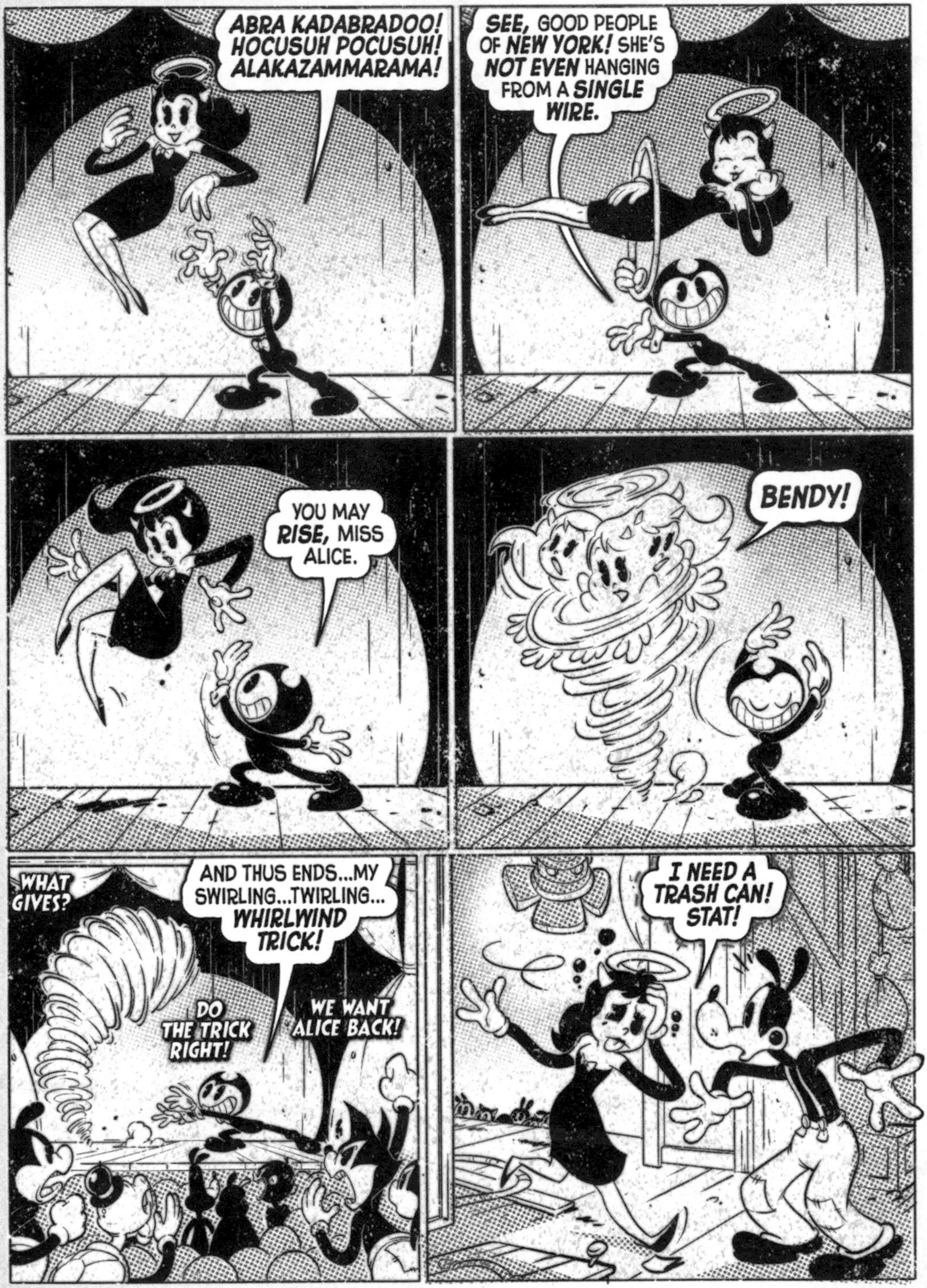
ABRA KADABRADOO! HOCUSUH POCUSUH! ALAKAZAMMARAMA!
SEE, GOOD PEOPLE OF NEW YORK! SHE'S NOT EVEN HANGING FROM A SINGLE WIRE.
YOU MAY RISE, MISS ALICE.
BENDY!
WHAT GIVES?
AND THUS ENDS...MY SWIRLING...TWIRLING... WHIRLWIND TRICK!
DO THE TRICK RIGHT!
WE WANT ALICE BACK!
I NEED A TRASH CAN! STAT!

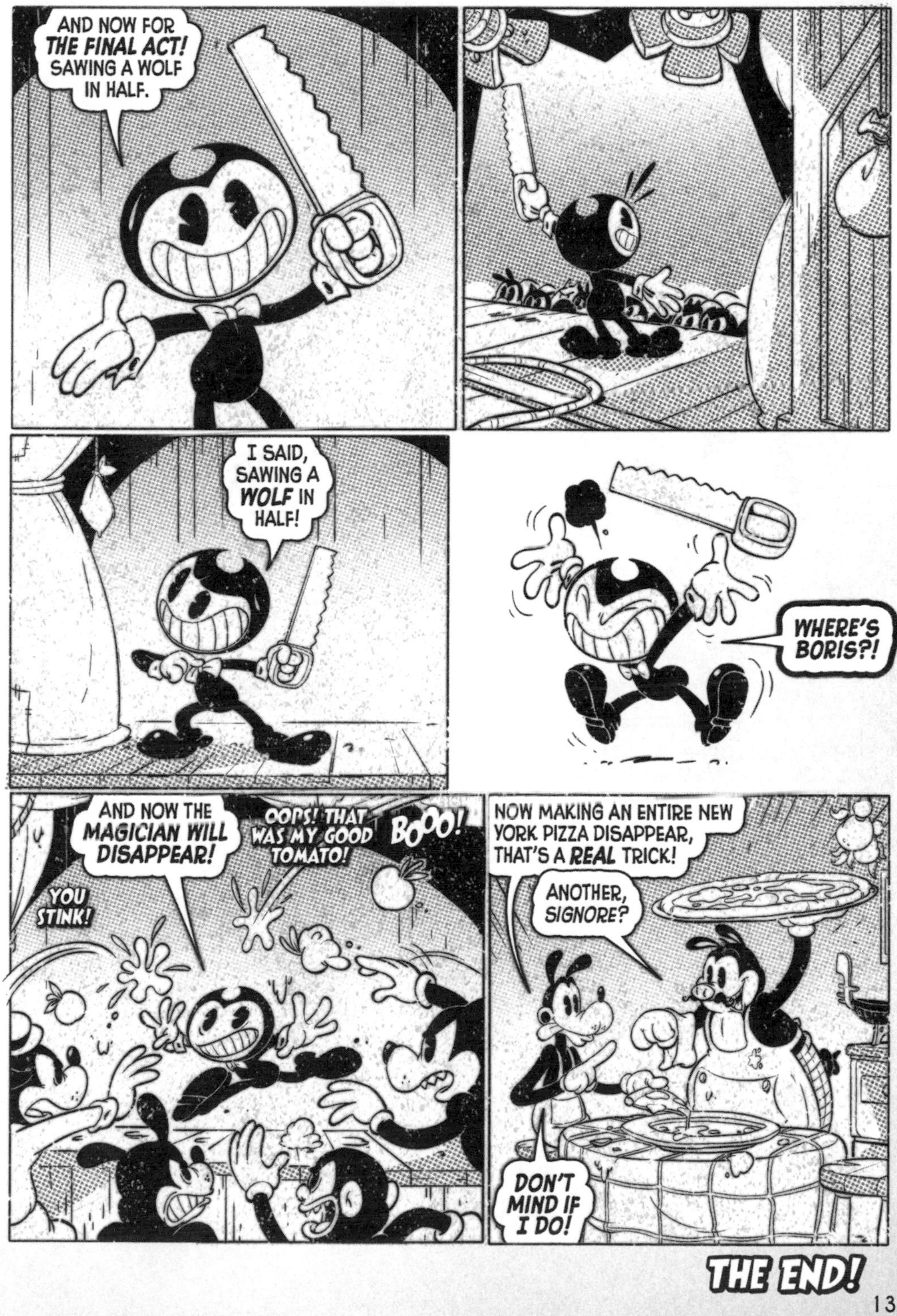
AND NOW FOR THE FINAL ACT! SAWING A WOLF IN HALF.
I SAID, SAWING A WOLF IN HALF!
WHERE'S BORIS?!
AND NOW THE MAGICIAN WILL DISAPPEAR!
OOPS! THAT WAS MY GOOD TOMATO!
BOOO!
YOU STINK!
NOW MAKING AN ENTIRE NEW YORK PIZZA DISAPPEAR, THAT'S A REAL TRICK!
ANOTHER, SIGNORE?
DON'T MIND IF I DO!
THE END!

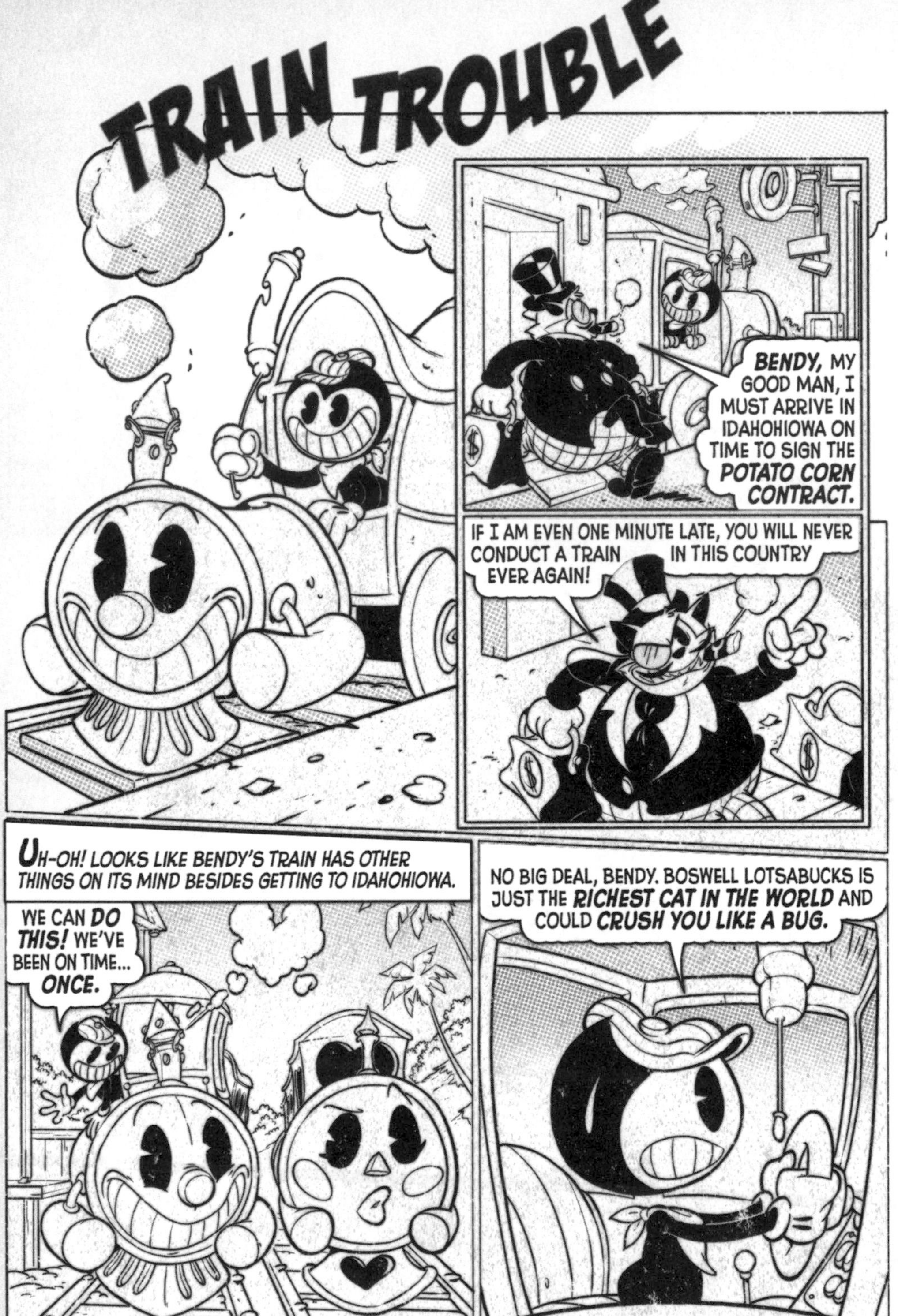
TRAIN TROUBLE
BENDY, MY GOOD MAN, I MUST ARRIVE IN IDAHOHIOWA ON TIME TO SIGN THE POTATO CORN CONTRACT.
IF I AM EVEN ONE MINUTE LATE, YOU WILL NEVER CONDUCT A TRAIN IN THIS COUNTRY EVER AGAIN!
UH-OH! LOOKS LIKE BENDY'S TRAIN HAS OTHER THINGS ON ITS MIND BESIDES GETTING TO IDAHOHIOWA.
WE CAN DO THIS! WE'VE BEEN ON TIME... ONCE.
NO BIG DEAL, BENDY. BOSWELL LOTSABUCKS IS JUST THE RICHEST CAT IN THE WORLD AND COULD CRUSH YOU LIKE A BUG.

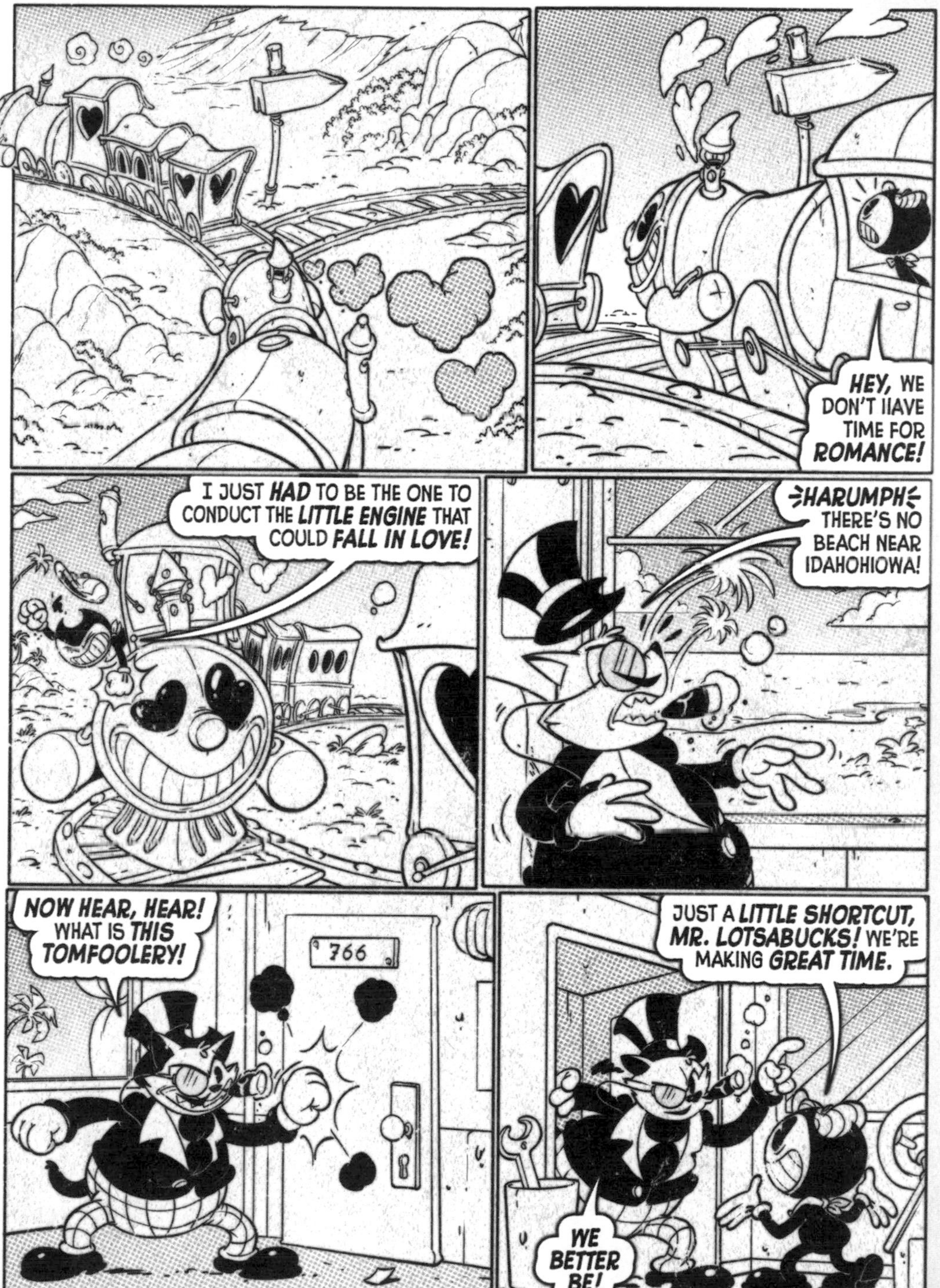
HEY, WE DON'T HAVE TIME FOR ROMANCE!
I JUST HAD TO BE THE ONE TO CONDUCT THE LITTLE ENGINE THAT COULD FALL IN LOVE!
HARUMPH THERE'S NO BEACH NEAR IDAHOHIOWA!
NOW HEAR, HEAR! WHAT IS THIS TOMFOOLERY!
766
JUST A LITTLE SHORTCUT, MR. LOTSABUCKS! WE'RE MAKING GREAT TIME.
WE BETTER BE!

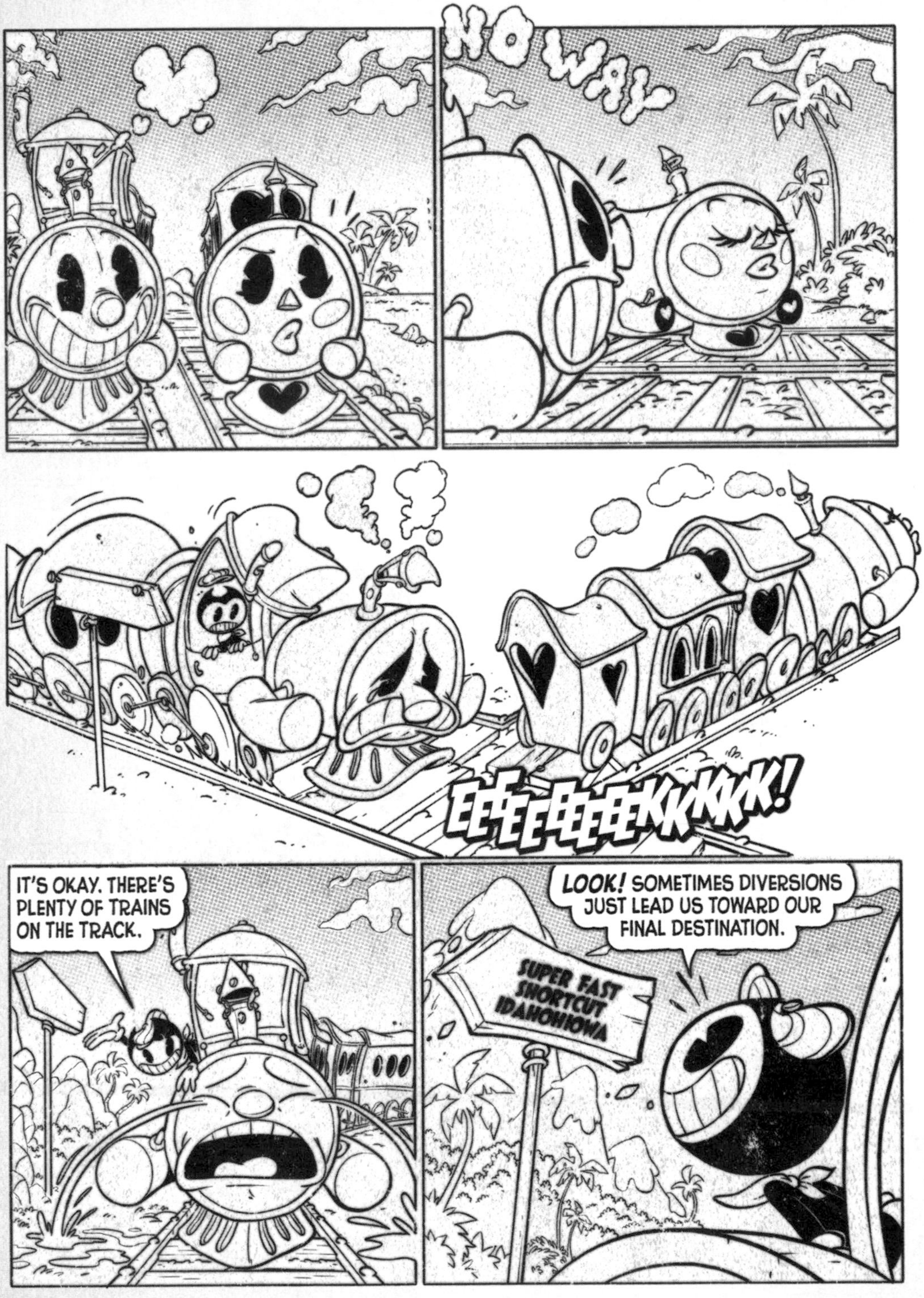
NO WAY
EEEEEEEEEEKKKKK!
IT'S OKAY. THERE'S PLENTY OF TRAINS ON THE TRACK.
LOOK! SOMETIMES DIVERSIONS JUST LEAD US TOWARD OUR FINAL DESTINATION.
SUPER FAST SHORTCUT IDAHOHIOWA

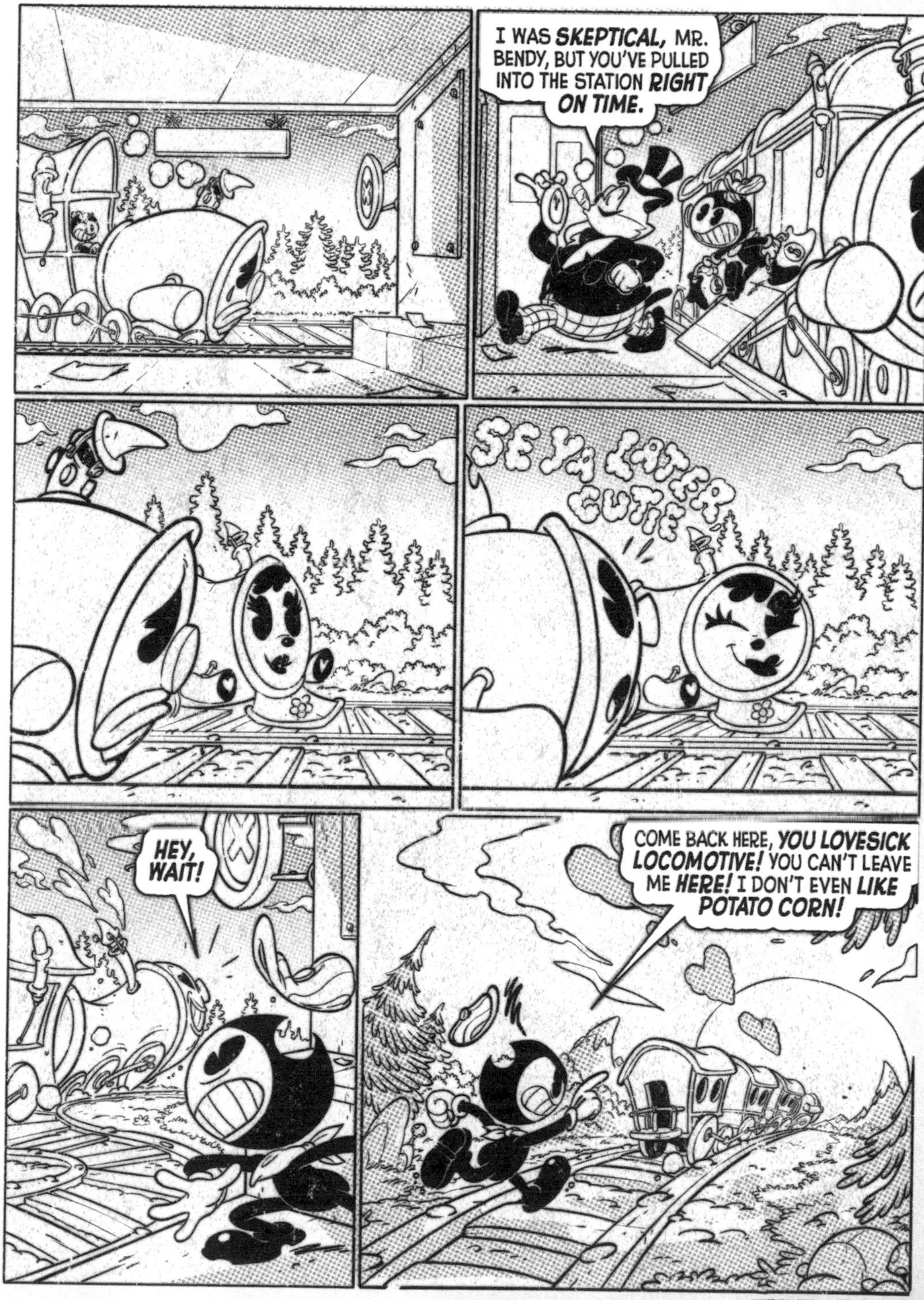
I WAS **SKEPTICAL,** MR. BENDY, BUT YOU'VE PULLED INTO THE STATION **RIGHT ON TIME.**
SEE YA LATER CUTIE
HEY, WAIT!
COME BACK HERE, **YOU LOVESICK LOCOMOTIVE!** YOU CAN'T LEAVE ME **HERE!** I DON'T EVEN **LIKE** POTATO CORN!

THE END!

THE DEVIL'S TREASURE

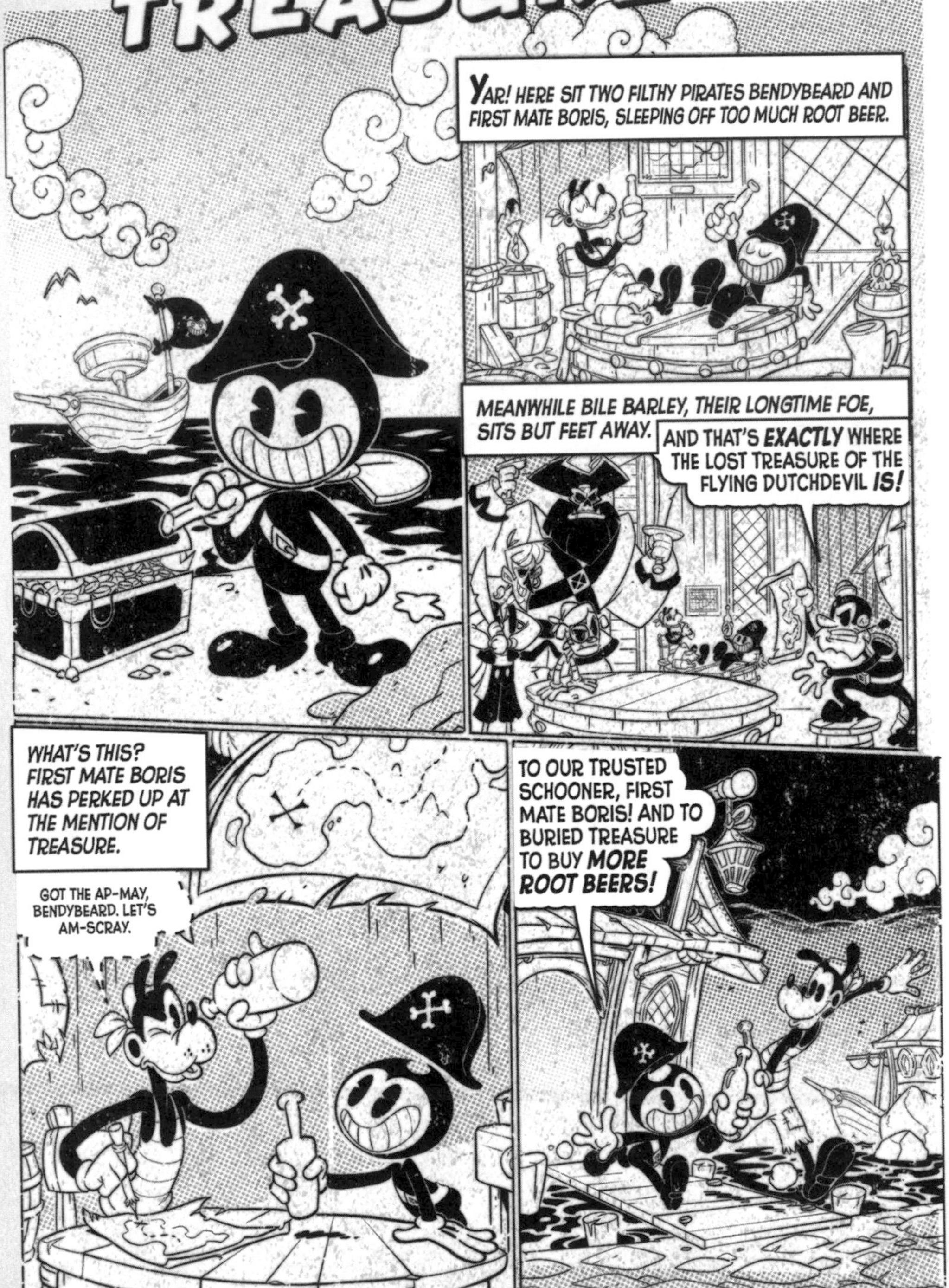
YAR! HERE SIT TWO FILTHY PIRATES BENDYBEARD AND FIRST MATE BORIS, SLEEPING OFF TOO MUCH ROOT BEER.
MEANWHILE BILE BARLEY, THEIR LONGTIME FOE, SITS BUT FEET AWAY.
AND THAT'S EXACTLY WHERE THE LOST TREASURE OF THE FLYING DUTCHDEVIL IS!
WHAT'S THIS? FIRST MATE BORIS HAS PERKED UP AT THE MENTION OF TREASURE.
GOT THE AP-MAY, BENDYBEARD. LET'S AM-SCRAY.
TO OUR TRUSTED SCHOONER, FIRST MATE BORIS! AND TO BURIED TREASURE TO BUY MORE ROOT BEERS!

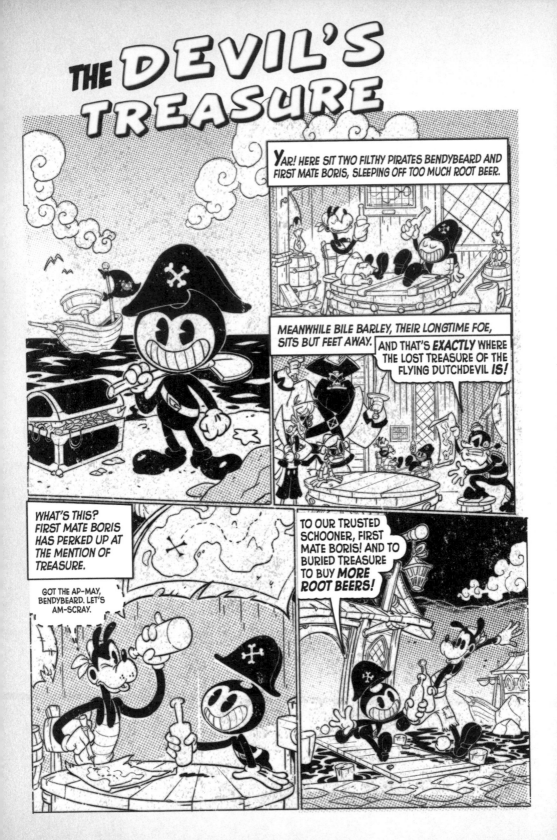

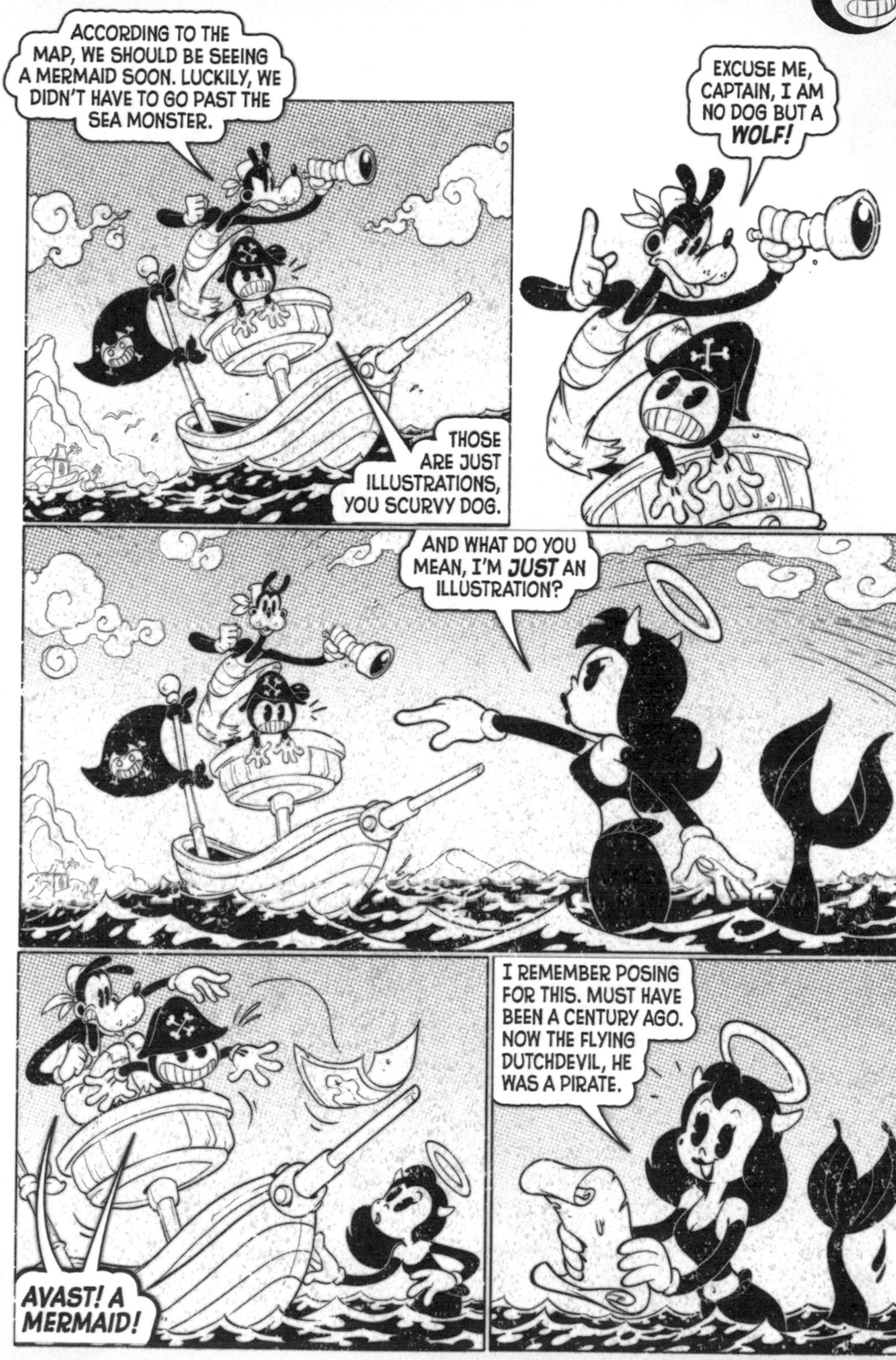
ACCORDING TO THE MAP, WE SHOULD BE SEEING A MERMAID SOON. LUCKILY, WE DIDN'T HAVE TO GO PAST THE SEA MONSTER.
THOSE ARE JUST ILLUSTRATIONS, YOU SCURVY DOG.
EXCUSE ME, CAPTAIN, I AM NO DOG BUT A *WOLF!*
AND WHAT DO YOU MEAN, I'M *JUST* AN ILLUSTRATION?
AVAST! A MERMAID!
I REMEMBER POSING FOR THIS. MUST HAVE BEEN A CENTURY AGO. NOW THE FLYING DUTCHDEVIL, HE WAS A PIRATE.

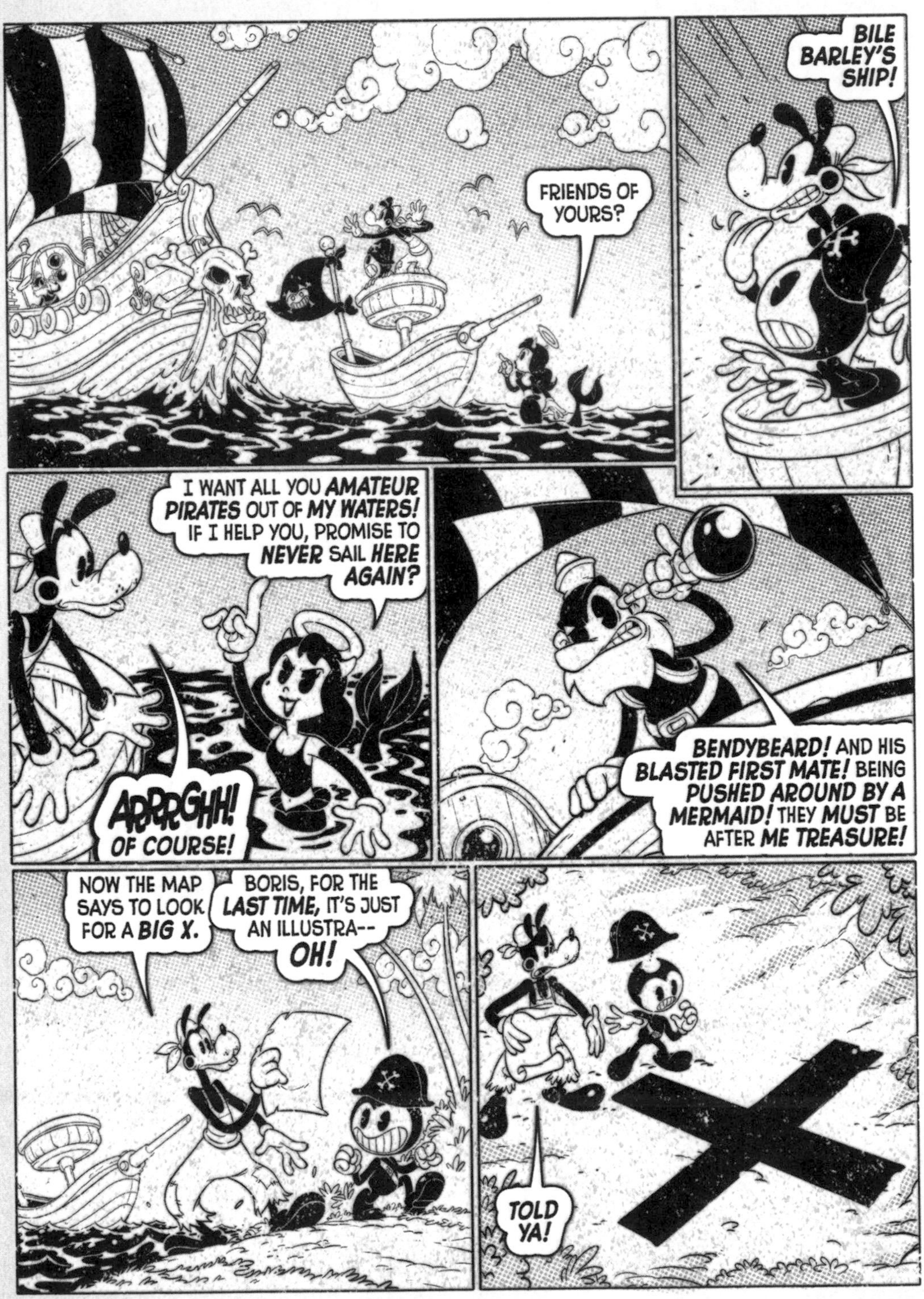
FRIENDS OF YOURS?
BILE BARLEY'S SHIP!
I WANT ALL YOU AMATEUR PIRATES OUT OF MY WATERS! IF I HELP YOU, PROMISE TO NEVER SAIL HERE AGAIN?
ARRRGHH! OF COURSE!
BENDYBEARD! AND HIS BLASTED FIRST MATE! BEING PUSHED AROUND BY A MERMAID! THEY MUST BE AFTER ME TREASURE!
NOW THE MAP SAYS TO LOOK FOR A BIG X.
BORIS, FOR THE LAST TIME, IT'S JUST AN ILLUSTRA-- OH!
TOLD YA!

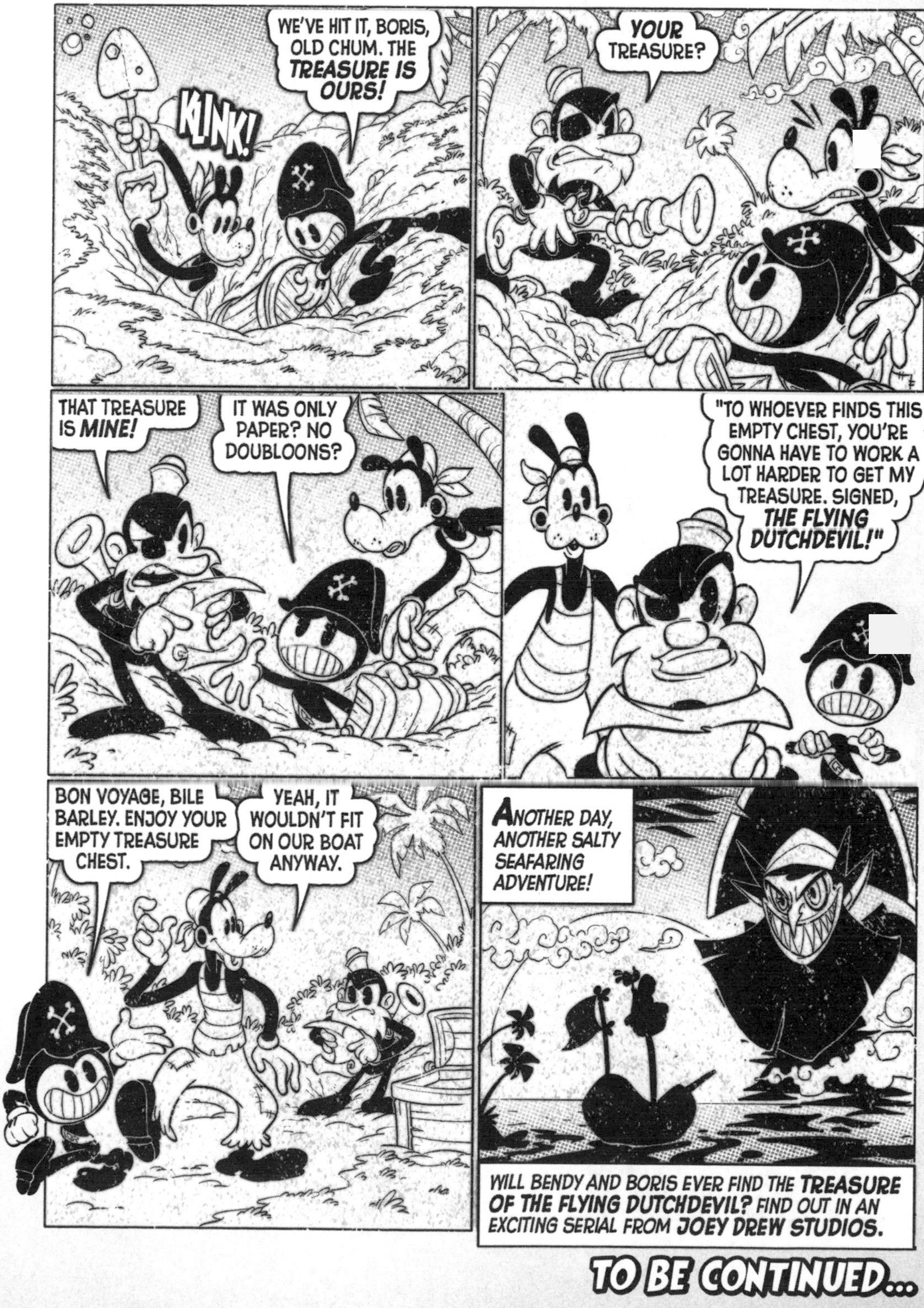
WE'VE HIT IT, BORIS, OLD CHUM. THE TREASURE IS OURS!
KLINK!
YOUR TREASURE?
THAT TREASURE IS MINE!
IT WAS ONLY PAPER? NO DOUBLOONS?
"TO WHOEVER FINDS THIS EMPTY CHEST, YOU'RE GONNA HAVE TO WORK A LOT HARDER TO GET MY TREASURE. SIGNED, THE FLYING DUTCHDEVIL!"
BON VOYAGE, BILE BARLEY. ENJOY YOUR EMPTY TREASURE CHEST.
YEAH, IT WOULDN'T FIT ON OUR BOAT ANYWAY.
ANOTHER DAY, ANOTHER SALTY SEAFARING ADVENTURE!
WILL BENDY AND BORIS EVER FIND THE TREASURE OF THE FLYING DUTCHDEVIL? FIND OUT IN AN EXCITING SERIAL FROM JOEY DREW STUDIOS.
TO BE CONTINUED...

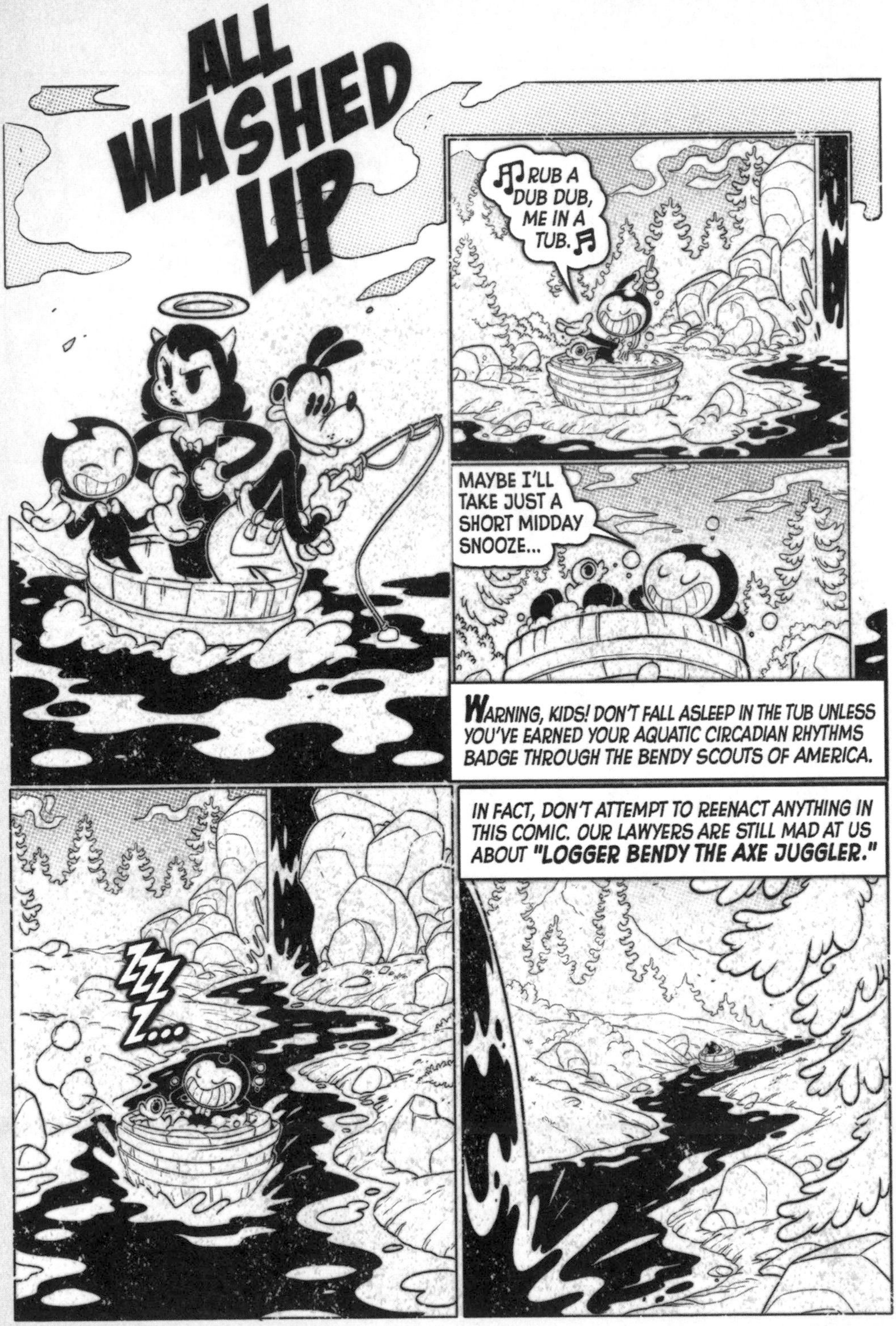
ALL WASHED UP
RUB A DUB DUB, ME IN A TUB.
MAYBE I'LL TAKE JUST A SHORT MIDDAY SNOOZE...
WARNING, KIDS! DON'T FALL ASLEEP IN THE TUB UNLESS YOU'VE EARNED YOUR AQUATIC CIRCADIAN RHYTHMS BADGE THROUGH THE BENDY SCOUTS OF AMERICA.
ZZZZ...
IN FACT, DON'T ATTEMPT TO REENACT ANYTHING IN THIS COMIC. OUR LAWYERS ARE STILL MAD AT US ABOUT "LOGGER BENDY THE AXE JUGGLER."

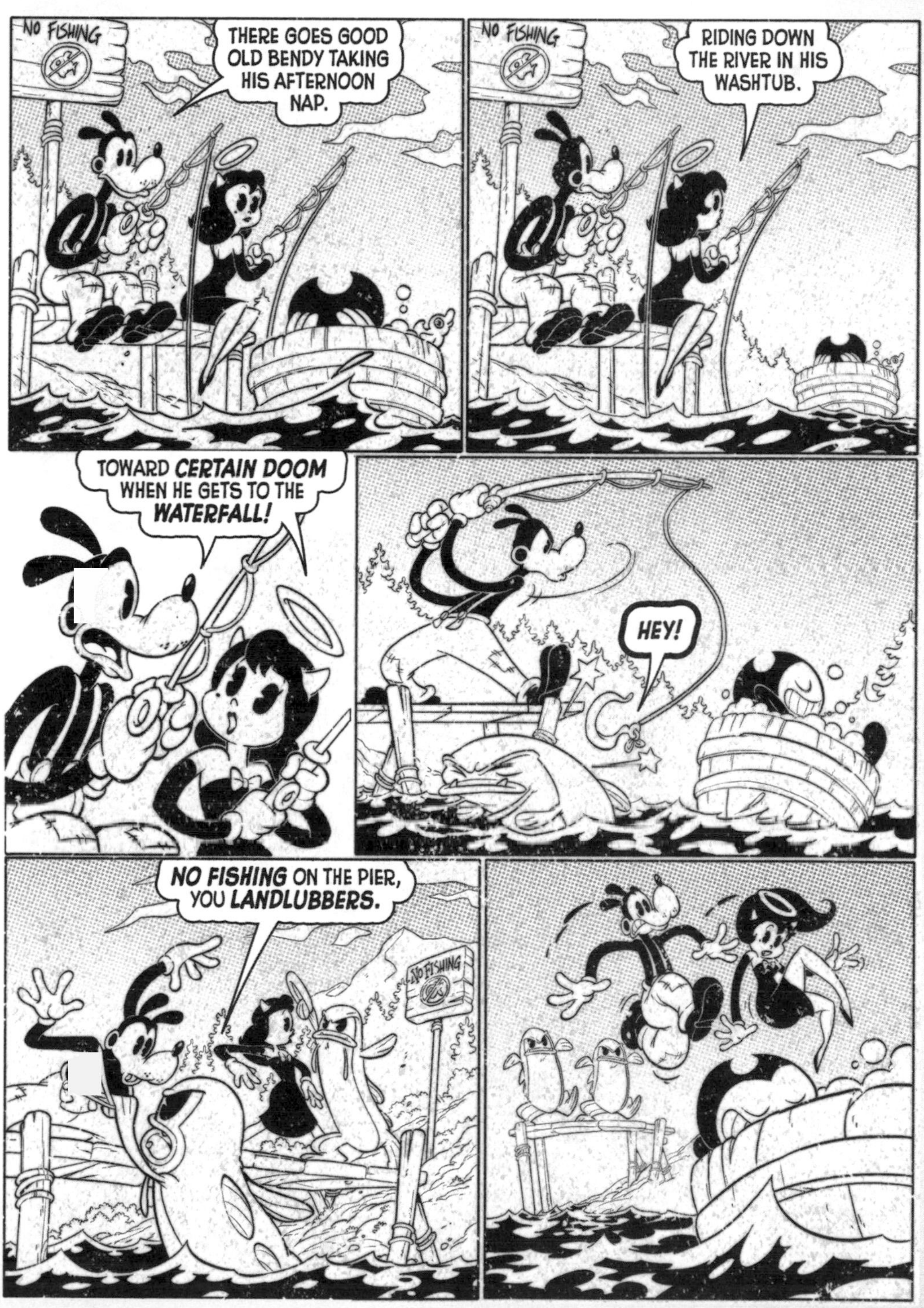
NO FISHING
THERE GOES GOOD OLD BENDY TAKING HIS AFTERNOON NAP.
NO FISHING
RIDING DOWN THE RIVER IN HIS WASHTUB.
TOWARD CERTAIN DOOM WHEN HE GETS TO THE WATERFALL!
HEY!
NO FISHING ON THE PIER, YOU LANDLUBBERS.
NO FISHING

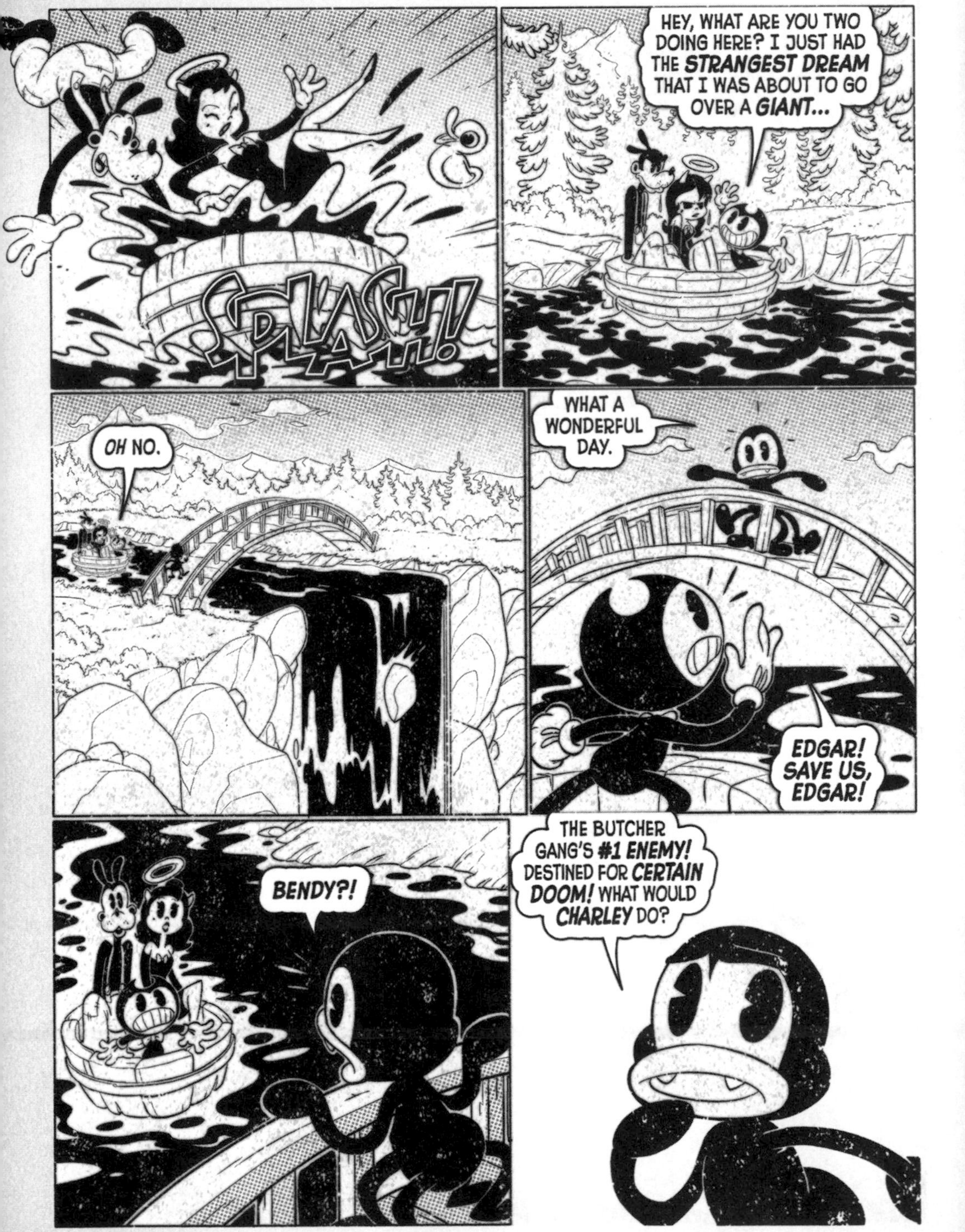
SPLASH!
HEY, WHAT ARE YOU TWO DOING HERE? I JUST HAD THE STRANGEST DREAM THAT I WAS ABOUT TO GO OVER A GIANT...
OH NO.
WHAT A WONDERFUL DAY.
EDGAR! SAVE US, EDGAR!
BENDY?!
THE BUTCHER GANG'S #1 ENEMY! DESTINED FOR CERTAIN DOOM! WHAT WOULD CHARLEY DO?

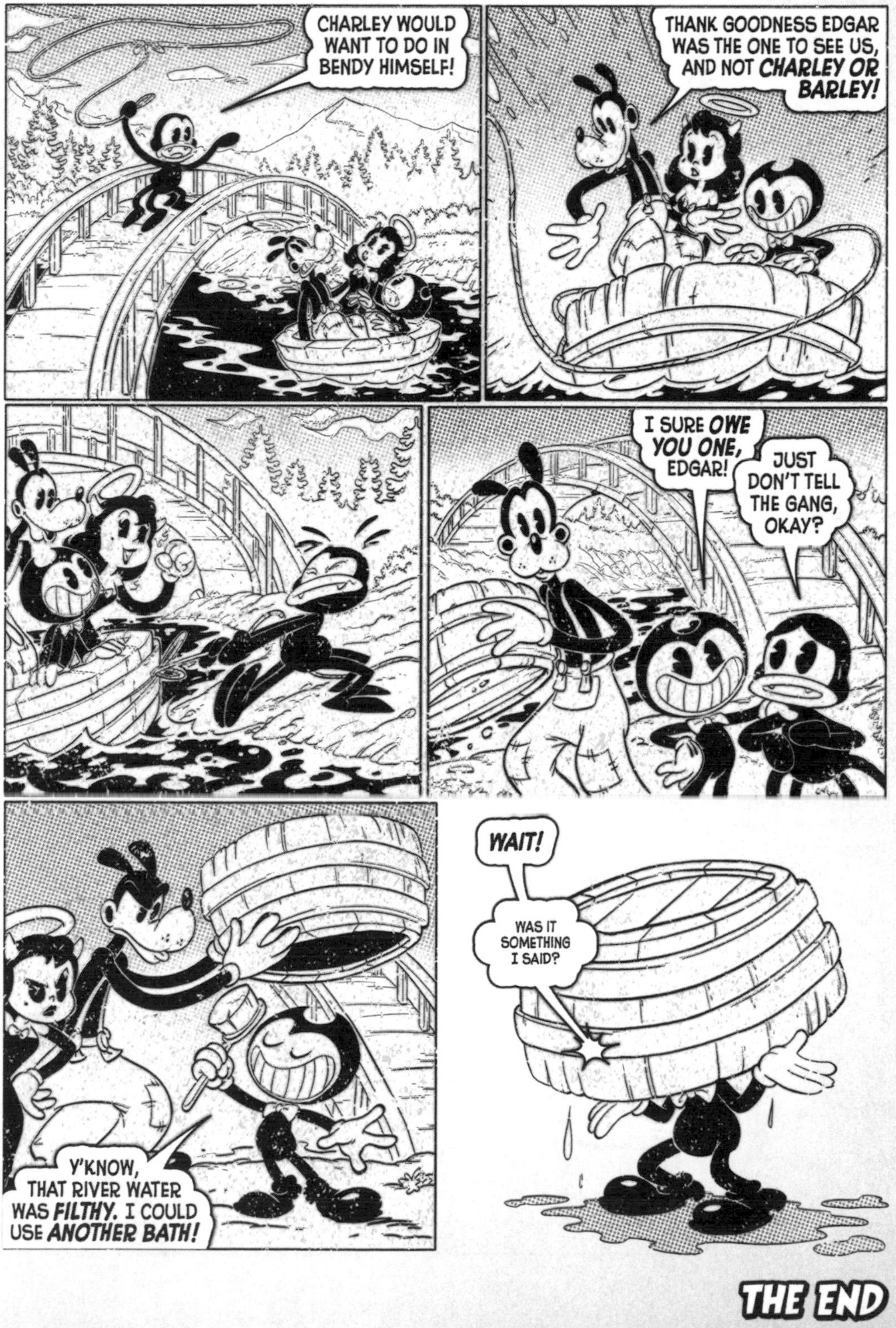
CHARLEY WOULD WANT TO DO IN BENDY HIMSELF!
THANK GOODNESS EDGAR WAS THE ONE TO SEE US, AND NOT CHARLEY OR BARLEY!
I SURE OWE YOU ONE, EDGAR!
JUST DON'T TELL THE GANG, OKAY?
Y'KNOW, THAT RIVER WATER WAS FILTHY. I COULD USE ANOTHER BATH!
WAIT!
WAS IT SOMETHING I SAID?
THE END

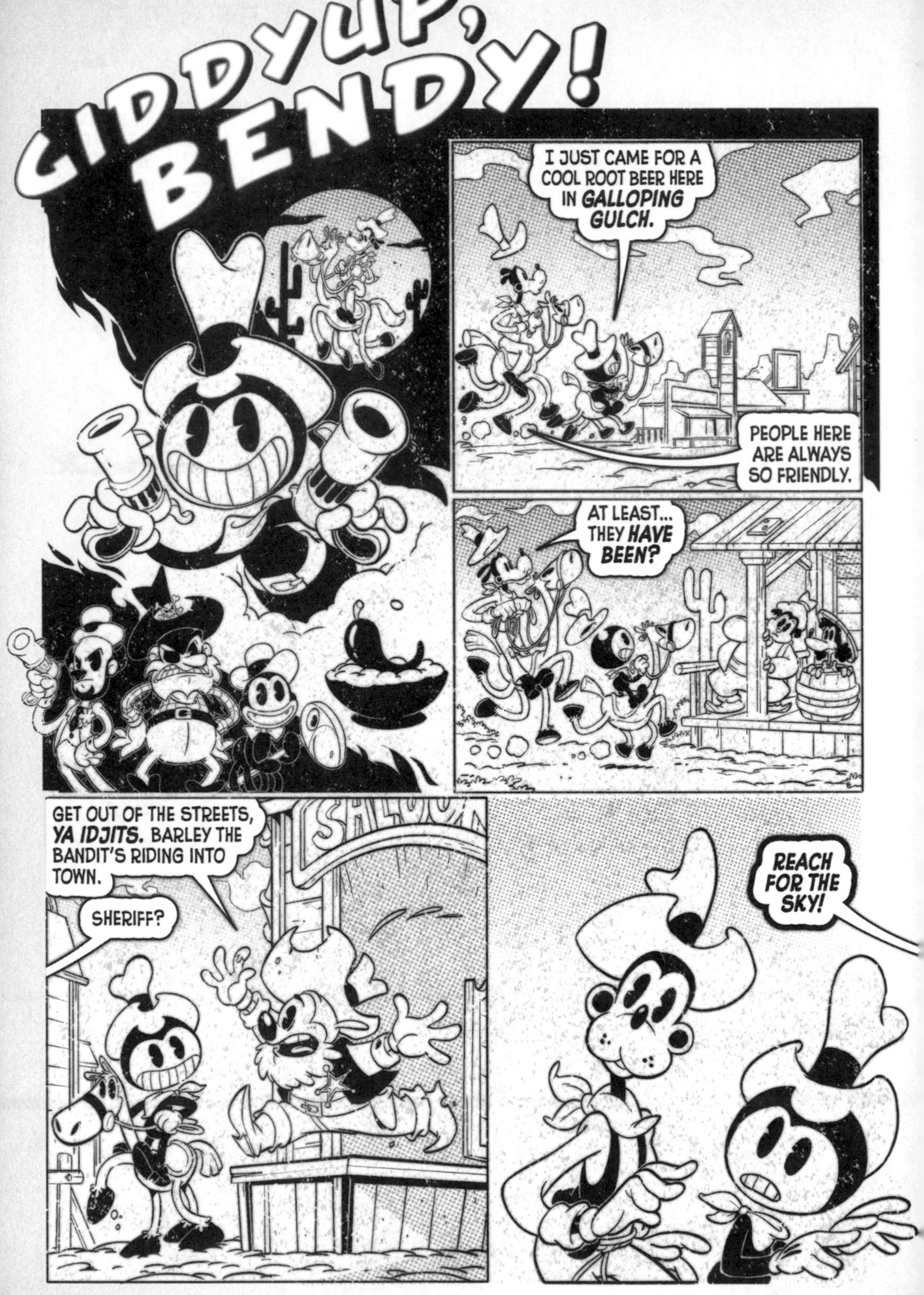
GIDDYUP, BENDY!
I JUST CAME FOR A COOL ROOT BEER HERE IN GALLOPING GULCH.
PEOPLE HERE ARE ALWAYS SO FRIENDLY.
AT LEAST... THEY HAVE BEEN?
GET OUT OF THE STREETS, YA IDJITS. BARLEY THE BANDIT'S RIDING INTO TOWN.
SHERIFF?
REACH FOR THE SKY!

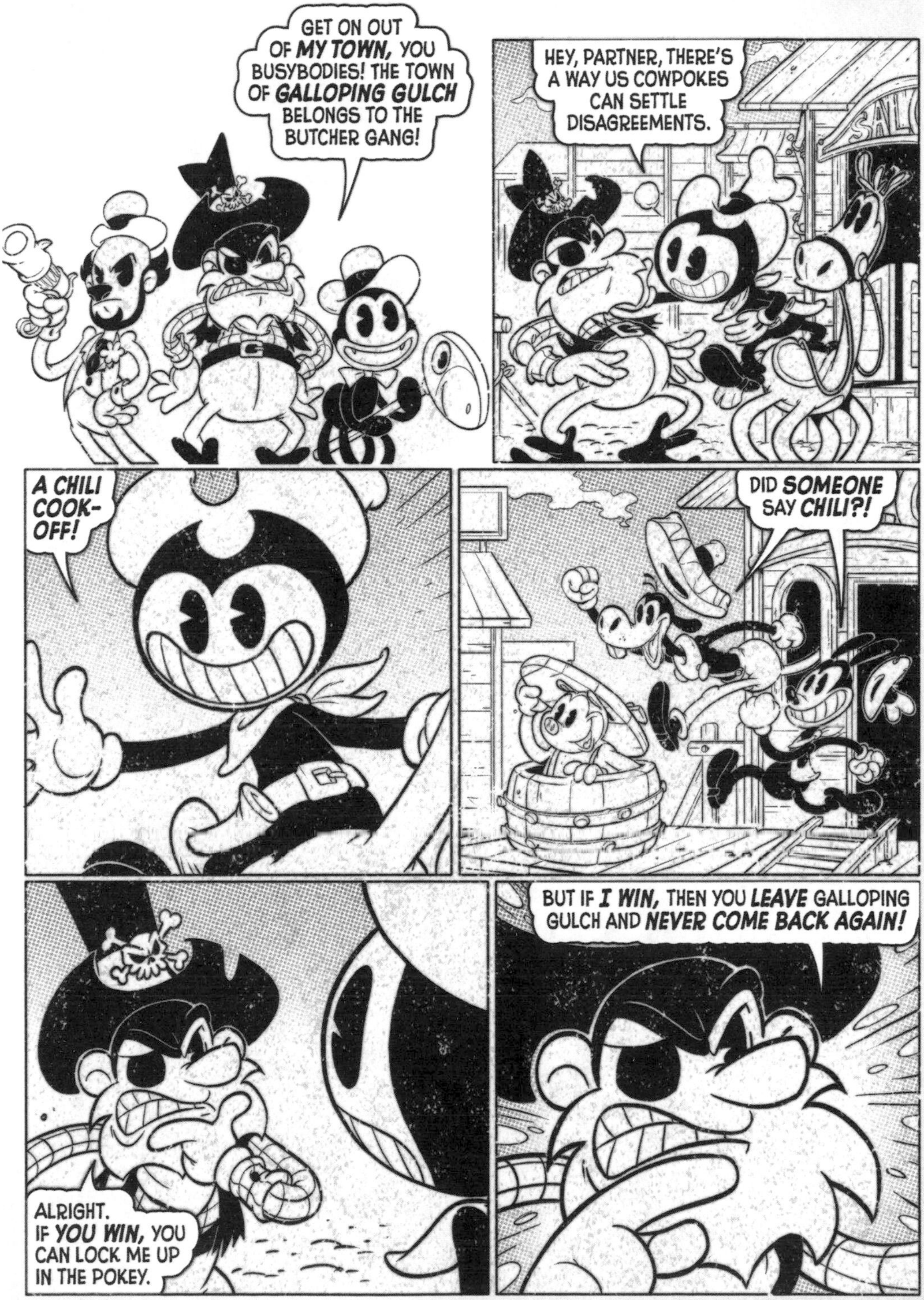
GET ON OUT OF MY TOWN, YOU BUSYBODIES! THE TOWN OF GALLOPING GULCH BELONGS TO THE BUTCHER GANG!
HEY, PARTNER, THERE'S A WAY US COWPOKES CAN SETTLE DISAGREEMENTS.
A CHILI COOK-OFF!
DID SOMEONE SAY CHILI?!
ALRIGHT. IF YOU WIN, YOU CAN LOCK ME UP IN THE POKEY.
BUT IF I WIN, THEN YOU LEAVE GALLOPING GULCH AND NEVER COME BACK AGAIN!

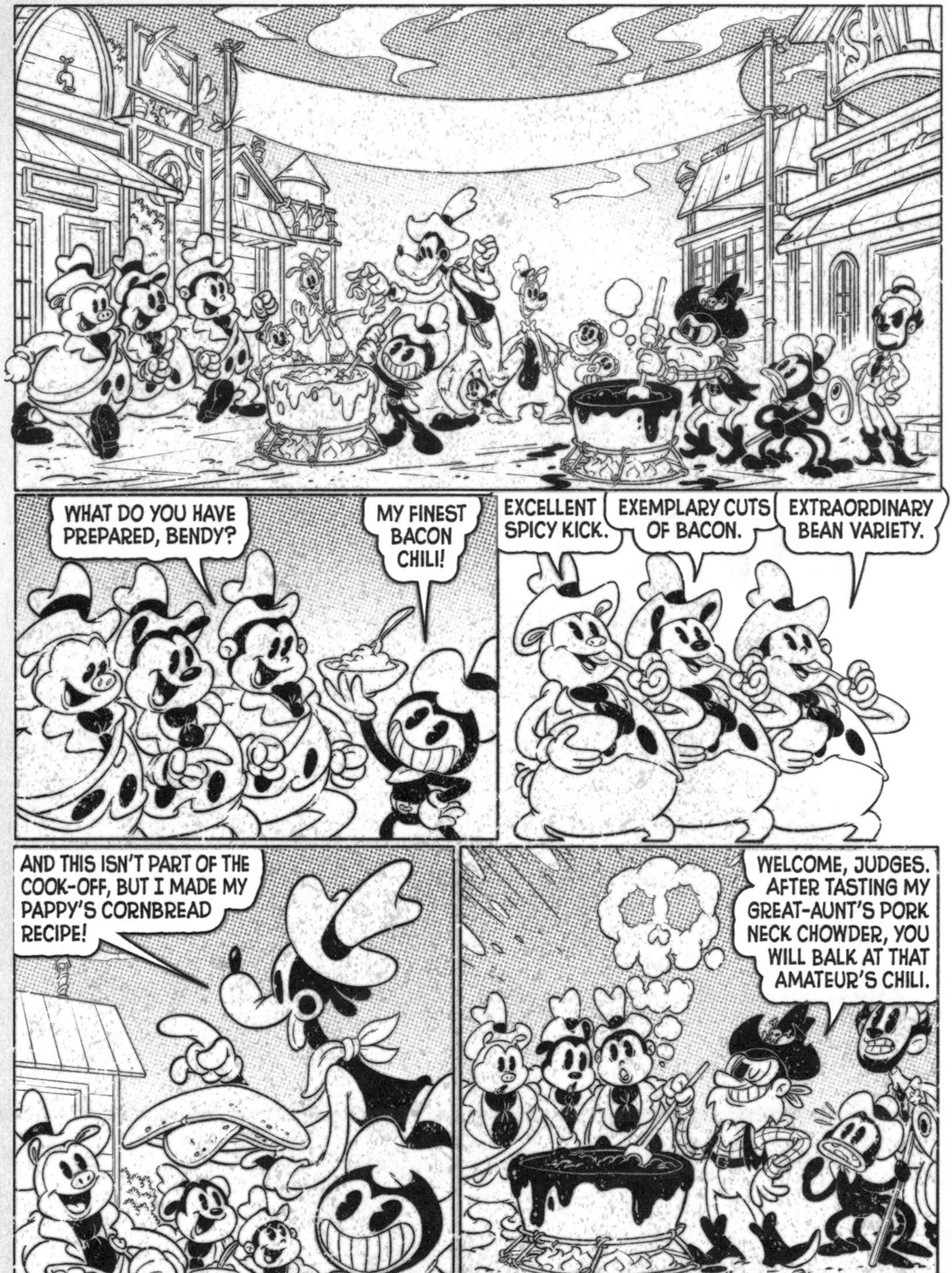
WHAT DO YOU HAVE PREPARED, BENDY?
MY FINEST BACON CHILI!
EXCELLENT SPICY KICK.
EXEMPLARY CUTS OF BACON.
EXTRAORDINARY BEAN VARIETY.
AND THIS ISN'T PART OF THE COOK-OFF, BUT I MADE MY PAPPY'S CORNBREAD RECIPE!
WELCOME, JUDGES. AFTER TASTING MY GREAT-AUNT'S PORK NECK CHOWDER, YOU WILL BALK AT THAT AMATEUR'S CHILI.

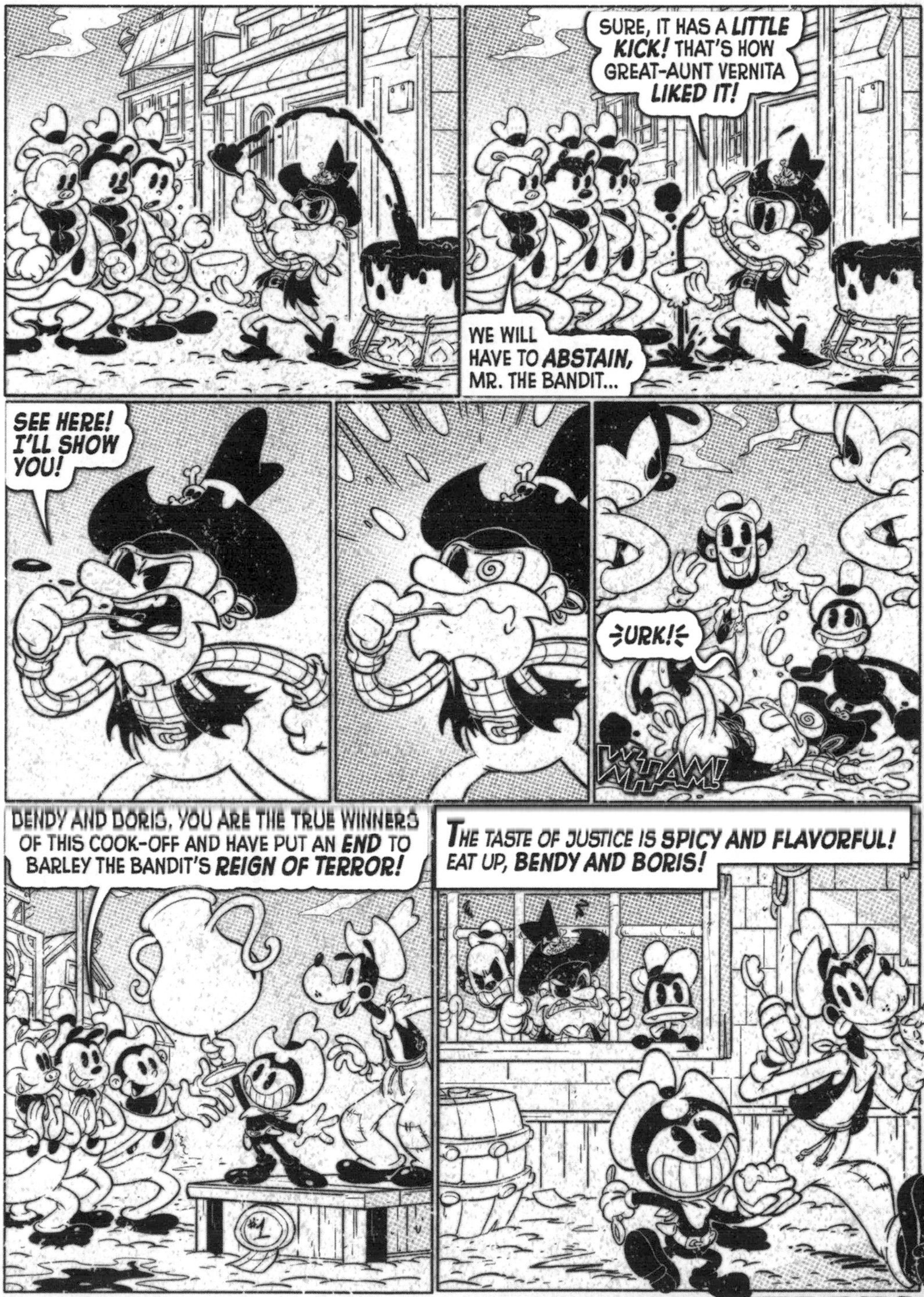
SURE, IT HAS A LITTLE KICK! THAT'S HOW GREAT-AUNT VERNITA LIKED IT!
WE WILL HAVE TO ABSTAIN, MR. THE BANDIT...
SEE HERE! I'LL SHOW YOU!
URK!
WHAM!
BENDY AND BORIS, YOU ARE THE TRUE WINNERS OF THIS COOK-OFF AND HAVE PUT AN END TO BARLEY THE BANDIT'S REIGN OF TERROR!
THE TASTE OF JUSTICE IS SPICY AND FLAVORFUL! EAT UP, BENDY AND BORIS!
THE END!

THE LEGACY

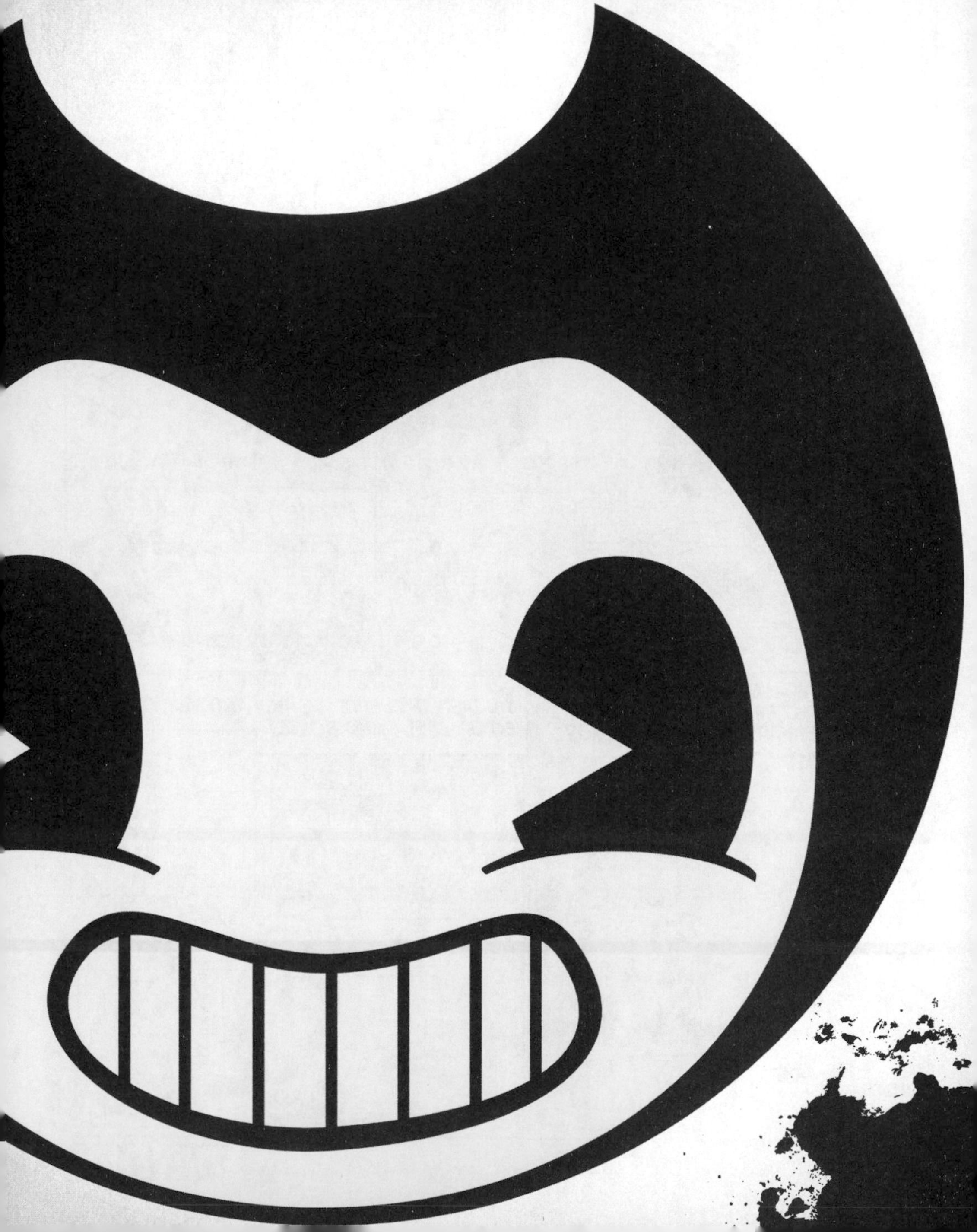

The Legacy of Bendy

I sincerely hope these Bendy comics have delighted you as much as they have me and my staff. The deeper we dig into the treasure trove of the Joey Drew Studios archives, the more surprises we find. And we've barely scratched the surface at this point.

Bendy was a media juggernaut back in the '30s and remained popular for decades before fading from public consciousness completely. Most children today have never even heard of Bendy! I know that Joey struggled with his own demons for many years and because of this and other difficulties the company floundered, taking Bendy's popularity with it. It breaks my heart.

However, Bendy is not finished. Far from it! I aim to keep the legacy created by my good friend Joey Drew alive and well. Bendy, Alice, Boris, and all their friends will be returning to the mainstream in a big way as we have GIGANTIC plans for them here at Archgate Films. We're proud and honored to be the new guardians of the franchise. Joey Drew Studios will live on with NEW Bendy cartoons, comics, and so much more. We have a talented staff creating new Bendy masterpieces, even as I write this. The sky's the limit! As Joey used to tell me, "Just keep dreaming, dreaming, dreaming!"

Thank you Joey. Here's to a great Bendy-filled future for all of us!

Nathan Arch
CEO of Archgate Films, 1972

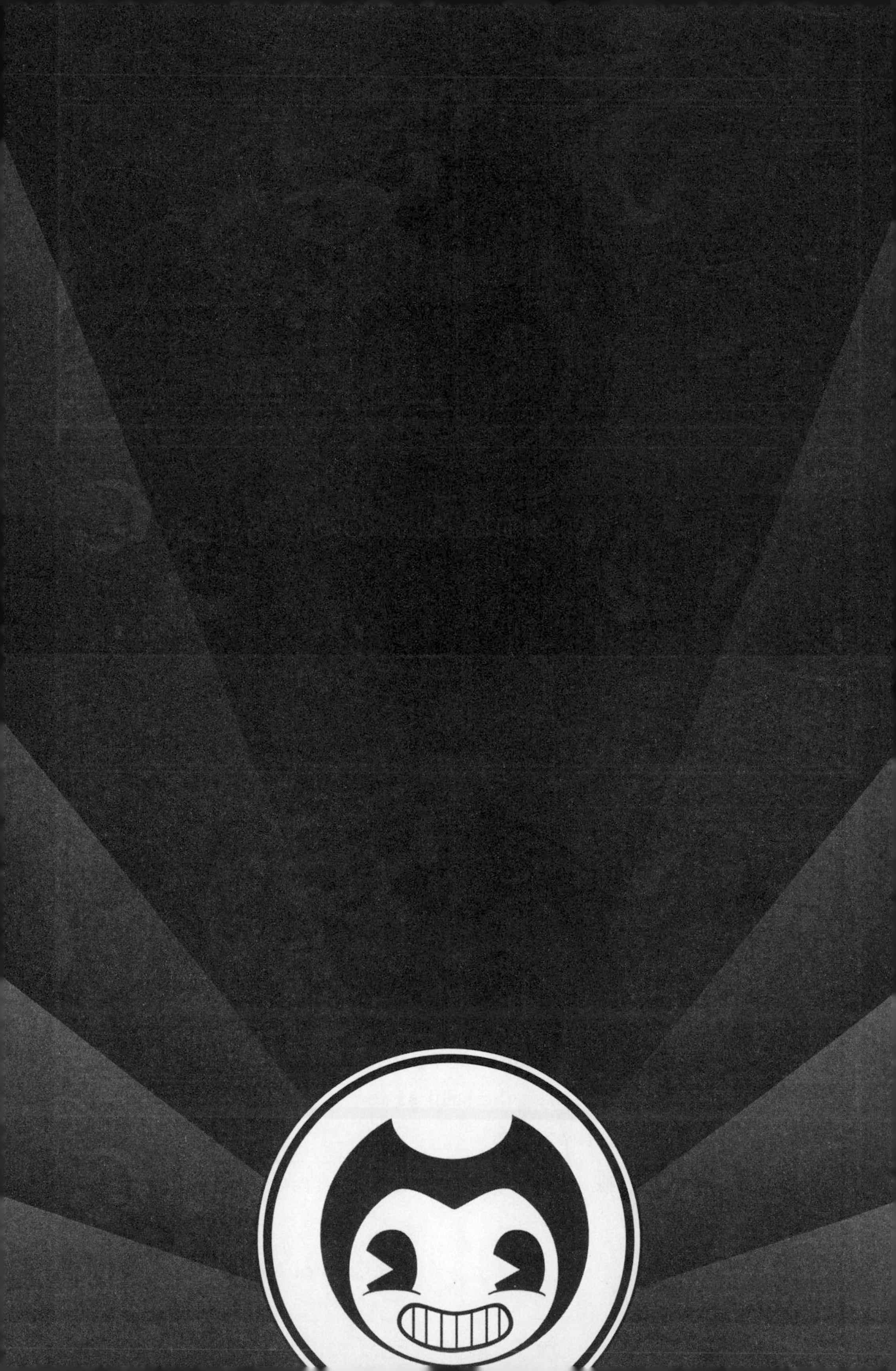